OUTSTANDING PRAISE FOR SHERRILYN KENYON AND HER NOVELS

"Kenyon gives readers scrumptious heroes—still with a dark edge and dangerous powers . . . she creates a world full of depth and intelligent details . . . and gives her stories an underpinning and a foundation in authenticity without sacrificing the breathless pace of her plots—no small feat!"

—*Romantic Times*

DARK SIDE OF THE MOON

"Boundless imagination . . . [Kenyon] is one of the defining authors of the new wave of paranormal romance."

—*Booklist*

"Taut action and jaunty humor. . . . it contains a delicious balance of suspense and sensuality."

—*Publishers Weekly*

UNLEASH THE NIGHT

"Kenyon defies expectations again . . . This depth and vulnerability of character have not been seen before in her heroes and prove a challenge for Kenyon, but the result is a thrill ride filled with magic, action, and scintillating passion."

—*Booklist*

SEIZE THE NIGHT

"[A] taut, rollicking romance . . . [Kenyon] succeeds in offering a lively read containing her signature blend of brisk action, sensual thrills, and light humor."

—*Publishers Weekly*

"Breathtaking . . . Kenyon really shakes up the storyline in this latest chapter in her amazing Dark-Hunter series."

—*Romantic Times* (4 1/2 starred review)

KISS OF THE NIGHT

"With its frenetic, *Matrix*-style fight scenes and feral, leather-clad heroes, this book makes it easy to see why Kenyon's fantasy world has caught on so quickly and even inspired some readers to role-play on her Web site . . . an entertaining thrill ride."

—*Publishers Weekly*

DANCE WITH THE DEVIL

"Move over, Anne Rice. Kenyon's Dark-Hunter books are changing the face of the vampire novel, making it hip, darker, and all the more appealing."

—*Publishers Weekly*

"*Dance with the Devil* cinches Sherrilyn Kenyon's place as a master of the genre! Zarek is a hero to die for, and his story will pull you in and keep you flipping pages into the wee hours; I couldn't put it down."

—Julie Kenner, author of *Aphrodite's Secret*

"A sensual, fast-paced read with a hero who is definitely worth the risk."

—*Booklist*

"Using figures from mythology, Sherrilyn Kenyon provides a deep novel that a romantic fantasy lover will cherish. A powerful story that makes believers of skeptics that ancient Gods and Goddesses, Dark-Hunters, Dayslayers, and other mythological characters walk among us . . . another fine myth from a superb storyteller climbing to the top."

—*Baryon* magazine

NIGHT EMBRACE

"With her steamy, action-packed Dark-Hunter novels, Kenyon is ushering in a whole new class of night dwellers . . . an abundance of hot sex and snappy dialogue keep the plot both accessible and appealing. With its courageous, unconventional characters and wry humor, this fast-moving fantasy will fill the void left by the end of the *Buffy the Vampire Slayer* series."

—*Publishers Weekly*

"The second novel in Sherrilyn Kenyon's hot series is just as exciting, sexy, and thrilling as the first. Kenyon has hit on a fabulous premise that promises to be fodder for many more outstanding page-turners."

—*Romantic Times*

St. Martin's Paperbacks Titles by

Sherrilyn Kenyon

(LISTED IN THE CORRECT READING ORDER)

Fantasy Lover

Night Pleasures

Night Embrace

Dance with the Devil

Kiss of the Night

Night Play

Seize the Night

Sins of the Night

Unleash the Night

Dark Side of the Moon

ANTHOLOGIES

Midnight Pleasures

Stroke of Midnight

Love at First Bite

My Big Fat Supernatural Wedding

THE DREAM-HUNTER

Sherrilyn Kenyon

St. Martin's Paperbacks

This is a work of fiction. All of the characters, organizations, and events portrayed in this novel are either products of the author's imagination or are used fictitiously.

THE DREAM-HUNTER

ISBN: 0-312-93881-0
EAN: 978-0-312-93881-9

Printed in the United States of America

St. Martin's Paperbacks edition / February 2007

St. Martin's Paperbacks are published by St. Martin's Press, 175 Fifth Avenue, New York, NY 10010.

10 9 8 7 6 5 4 3 2 1

THE
DREAM-HUNTER

Utter misery, and she would rather have fishhooks pounded into her body than ever step foot on this land again.

Her long blond hair, which she had swept back in a ponytail, slapped against her skin as she sought some peace for her troubled thoughts. But there was none to be had.

Only bottled-up rage met her.

Her estranged father was dead. He'd died as he'd lived . . . in pursuit of a stupid, reckless dream that had taken not only his life but also that of her mother, her brother, her aunt, and her uncle.

"Atlantis is real, Geary. I can feel it radiating out to me even as I speak. It sits in the Aegean just below us, like a lost, glittering gem, waiting for us to find it and show the world what beauty it once held." Even now she could hear her father's hypnotic voice as he held her hand on top of the water for her to feel the softness of the waves as they whispered against her tiny palm. She could still see his handsome, enthusiastic face as he first told her why they spent so much time in Greece.

"We're going to find Atlantis and show the wonder of it to everyone else. Mark my words, babe. It's there and our family is the one that's been chosen to uncover its magic."

That had been his lunatic dream. One he'd spent a lifetime trying to give to her, but unlike the rest of her kookie family, she wasn't stupid enough to buy into it.

Atlantis was a bogus myth made up by Plato as a metaphor for what happened when man turned against the gods. Like Lovecraft's *Necronomicon*, it was only a fictional invention that people wanted to believe in so badly they were willing to sacrifice everything to find it.

Now her father lay in his grave on the island he'd loved so much. He'd died broken and bitter, a shell of a man who'd buried his beloved brother, his son, his wife . . .

And for what? Everyone had laughed at him. Ridiculed him. He'd lost his job, along with his respectability, as a professor years ago, and the only way he'd been able to have his research published was in vanity presses.

Hell, even the vanity publishers had laughed at him and several had turned him down, refusing to even take his money to publish his ridiculous work. Still he'd carried on in his feverish desire to give people even more reason to laugh at him, which they'd done with relish.

But even with that, at least she'd seen him one more time before he passed and he hadn't died alone as he'd feared. Somehow, against the doctor's prognosis, her father had managed to hold on until she caught a plane from the U.S. and made it to his hospital room to see him. Though their meeting was brief, it had been enough to make peace with him so that he could die without guilt over abandoning her for his search.

If only she could have found a bit of that peace for herself. There still was no such forgiveness inside her where he was concerned. No matter how much her grandfather had tried to explain her father to her, she knew the truth. The only thing that man had ever loved had been his dream, and he had sacrificed his entire family . . . *her* entire family for it.

Now at twenty-four, because of him, she had no brother and no parents.

She was utterly alone in the world.

And her deathbed promise to her father to carry on his work burned inside her like a rampaging fire. It was one of the few times in her life that she'd been weak. But the sight of him as a frail, troubled man lying on a cold hospital bed while he desperately clung to life had torn her apart, and even though they'd barely spoken these last eight years, she hadn't had the heart to hurt him when all he wanted was to die forgiven.

She curled her lip as she watched the waves roll against the white shore. "Find Atlantis, my ass. I won't ruin myself like you did, Dad. I'm not that stupid."

"Dr. Kafieri?"

She turned at the sound of a heavily accented Greek voice to find a short, rotund man in his mid-fifties staring at her. A cousin to her father, Cosmo Tsiaris had been their family attorney here in Greece. A pseudo-partner in her father's salvage company, Cosmo had been instrumental in helping her father gain permits and investors for his antediluvian quest.

Although she'd known Cosmo all her life, she cringed at his greeting. Kafieri had been her father's name—one she'd cast off years ago after her applications to college had been rejected even though she more than met the requirements for admission. No self-respecting classics, history, or anthropology department would ever accept a Kafieri into its ranks for fear of the taint. So she'd learned to use her mother's maiden name to save her credibility and reputation.

Like the rest of her immediate family, Geary Kafieri had died on these shores.

"I'm Dr. Megeara Saatsakis."

A bright smile curved his lips. "You married!"

"No," she said simply, which made him literally deflate before her eyes. "I legally changed my name from Kafieri eight years ago when I went back to the States and sued for emancipation from my father."

She could tell by Cosmo's face that he didn't understand her reasoning, and that was fine by her. With his patriarchal mind-set, he'd never comprehend it.

Frowning, he didn't comment on her words as he held

a small box toward her. "I told Eneas that in the event of his death, I would make sure this was given to his daughter. That would still be you, yes?"

"Yes," she said, ignoring his sarcasm. Who else would be dumb enough to claim a laughingstock as her progenitor?

Megeara flinched at that thought. In all honesty, she loved her father. Even when his grief and quest had robbed him of everything, even his sanity and health, she'd still loved him. How could she not? He'd been a kind, caring father to her when she'd been a girl. It'd only been after she'd hit her teens and started questioning his research and fervor that they'd grown apart.

"*Atlantis is bullshit, Dad. All this research is. I don't want to be on this stupid boat anymore. I'm young and I want friends. I want to go to school and be normal. You're wasting your time and my life!*" He'd slapped her so hard on her fifteenth birthday that she swore she could still feel the sting of it.

"*Don't you dare spit on your mother's memory. On my brother's memory. They gave their lives for this.*"

Six months later, so had Megeara's brother when his diving line had tangled and his tank had run out of oxygen. That had been the final straw between her and her father. She wasn't going to be Jason. She wasn't going to give up her life for someone else's dreams . . . ever.

So what if she'd promised her father? He was dead now. He'd never know she reneged. He'd died happy and she could finally put the past to rest and carry on with her life in America.

Like her grandfather, she intended to leave this country and never step foot on it again.

Cosmo handed her the plain white box, then left her alone to open it.

Megeara stared at it for several minutes, afraid of what she might find. Would it be some personal memento that would reduce her back to tears? She honestly didn't want to cry anymore for a man who'd broken her heart so many times that she couldn't even begin to count them all.

But in the end, her curiosity got the better of her and she opened the box. At first, there appeared to be nothing but crinkled acid-free tissue paper. She had to dig to the bottom of it all to find what it contained.

And what she found there floored her. She stared at her palm in the bright sunlight, unable to even fathom it.

There were two items. One appeared to be a *komboloi*—a string of worry beads similar in style to a small rosary that some Greeks used when stressed, only she'd never seen anything like this before. The age and design of it appeared to predate any form of *komboloi* she'd ever heard of. It had fifteen iridescent green beads made of some unknown stone that had been carved with tiny intricate family scenes of people wearing clothes unlike any she'd seen before in her research. The carvings were interspersed with five gold beads that were engraved with three lightning bolts piercing a sun. Where a *komboloi* might hold a small Greek piece such as a dime-sized medal, this one held a circle with writing that was similar to ancient Greek and yet very different. So much so that not even she who had been bred on ancient Greek could decipher it.

Like most artifacts fresh from a dig, the *komboloi* had a small white tag attached to it by a red thread where her father had written finding notes:

9/1/87
sixty inches down from datum (see pg. 42)
absolute dating: 9529 B.C.

green stone unknown/unverified
writing unknown/unverified

The anthropologist in her leapt to the forefront of what this could mean historically. If this date was truly absolute . . .

It showed a sophistication and metallurgy previously unknown. At that time, the Greeks shouldn't have had this level of skill. In fact, the precision of the carvings and engraving looked as if they were done by machine and not by hand. Eleven thousand years ago, mankind simply did not possess the tools it would take to create something this intricate.

How could this be?

Intrigued, she turned her attention to the small leather pouch that lay in the bottom of the box. It, too, was tagged.

7/10/85
absolute dating: 9581 B.C.
metal unknown/unverified

Frowning, she opened the pouch to find five coins of varying sizes. They were old . . . *very* old and heavily coated with patina. Again, there weren't coins this old. They just hadn't existed at that period in time and especially not in Greece. Like the *komboloi*, the coins held that same peculiar writing, but beneath said writing was something she could understand. It was the ancient Greek words for "Atlantean Province of Kirebar."

Dear God!

Again, the coins didn't appear to be handmade, nor was their metal composite typical of anything she'd ever seen before. They were an orangish color, not silver, not gold, not bronze, copper, or iron—maybe a weird combination of those metals and yet that didn't seem right, either.

What the hell was it?

Even with the patina coating them, the images and writing were as crisp, clear, and precise as those on a modern coin.

Her heart pounding, she turned the largest coin over to look at the back. There was the same foreign symbol that marked the *komboloi*. A sun pierced by three lightning bolts. And with it were the unknown words on top of the Greek: *May Apollymi protect us.*

Megeara stared at it in disbelief. Apollymi? Who was that?

She'd never heard that name before.

"It's a forgery." It had to be, and yet as she looked at it, she knew the truth. These weren't forged. Her father must have excavated them from one of his many digs in the Aegean.

This was what had kept her father going even while the rest of the world had laughed at him. He had known a truth she'd denied.

Atlantis *was* real.

And if it was, then her father had been doubted by everyone . . . even her. Grief and pain tore through her as she recalled all the arguments they'd had over the years. She'd been no better than any of the others.

God, the fights the two of them had had over this. Why had he never told her? Why would he keep a discovery of this magnitude from her?

Unfortunately, she knew the answer. *Because I wouldn't have believed it. Even if he'd shown it to me right in the ground where he'd found it. I would have laughed at him, too, then thrown it in his face.*

No doubt he'd wanted to save himself the pain of facing *her* ridicule.

Closing the box, Megeara held it next to her heart as she regretted every nasty word and criticism she'd ever even thought about him. How much had those words hurt? She who should have had faith in him had been as cruel as everyone else.

Now it was too late to make amends.

"I'm so sorry, Daddy," she breathed through her fresh tears. Like everyone else, she'd assumed he was crazy. Misguided. Stupid.

But somehow he'd found these artifacts. Somehow they were real.

Atlantis is real. The words chased themselves through her mind. Staring out across the blue sea, she tightened her grip on the box as she remembered her final words to him. *"Yeah, yeah, I promise. I'll look for Atlantis, too. Don't worry about it, Dad. It's in good hands."* Those words had been rushed and passionless, and still they'd comforted him.

"It's there, Geary. I know you'll find it and you'll see. You. Will. See. You will know me for what I am, not for what you thought me to be." Then he'd slept for a time and he'd died only a few hours later while she'd held his hand.

In that moment of his quiet passing, she hadn't been a grown woman, she'd been a little girl all over again. One who only wanted her daddy back. One who craved someone to comfort her and tell her everything would be all right.

But there was no one in her life who could do that. And now that ludicrous, hasty promise meant something to her after all.

"I hear you, Daddy," she whispered to the olive-oil-laden breeze that she hoped would carry her voice to wherever he'd gone, "and I won't let you die in vain. I'm going to prove Atlantis exists. For you. For Mom and for Uncle Theron and Aunt Athena . . . for Jason. If it takes me the rest of my life, I'm going to fulfill my word to you. We *will* find Atlantis. I swear it."

But even as she spoke those words that were filled with her conviction, she couldn't help wondering if she'd be able to withstand the ridicule her father had borne all of his professional life. Just six weeks ago she'd been granted her doctorate from Yale and she was supposed to begin teaching in New York this fall. She was young to have attained so much, and great things were expected of her . . . by her and by the institutions and professors who'd bestowed that doctorate on her.

To walk this course would be nine kinds of stupid. She would lose everything. E-v-e-r-y-t-h-i-n-g. It was a massive step she was about to take. One from which she'd never recover.

My father believed it.

And her uncle and mother.

They had given their lives for this even while the entire world had laughed at them. Now a second generation of fools was about to follow the first down the road to ruin.

Megeara only hoped that in the end she would meet a better fate than that which had greeted the first.

Like father, like daughter.

She had no choice except to complete his quest because until she did, her name would be as worthless as his.

"Let the floggings begin. . . ."

CHAPTER 1

SANTORINI, GREECE, 1996

"MY KINGDOM FOR A GUN."

Shaking his head at Geary's hostile words, Brian calmly opened the car door for her as she approached their small taxi that waited in the heart of the crowded Greek thoroughfare. "You don't have a kingdom."

She paused on the sidewalk to glare at him. Given the fury in her system, she couldn't believe he'd dare point out the obvious to her. She'd been known to verbally let serious blood when only half this riled. Truly, the man had no sense of self-preservation. "And I don't have a gun—looks like I'm shit out of luck all the way around, huh?"

Still, he was his ever present calm self—which didn't really help her mood. For once, couldn't he get ticked off, too? "I take it you didn't get the permits . . . again."

She could have done without that "again" part. Really. "What was your first clue?"

"Oh, I don't know. That stomping stance as you

walked down the street, clenching and unclenching your fists like you're already choking someone, or maybe it's that way you're looking at me like you could claw out my eyes when I haven't done anything to piss you off."

"Yes, you have."

She could tell he was fighting a smile. Thank goodness he had the good sense to keep it hidden. "And that is?"

"You don't have a gun."

He snorted. "Come on now, you can't shoot every Greek official who gets in your way."

"Wanna bet?"

Brian stepped back to let her enter the taxi first. At six three, he was a good-looking man in his mid-forties. Very distinguished and intelligent. Best of all, he was independently wealthy and more than capable of financing their latest venture in futility without complaining too much.

Unfortunately, he wasn't into bribing public officials.

Was it too much to ask that she find a corrupt financier? Surely Brian should have some vice, and at the moment she couldn't think of a more self-serving one than that.

"So what do we do now?" he asked as he joined her in the car.

Geary sighed, wishing she had an answer. Her team was waiting on her boat at the docks, but without the permits that allowed them to excavate the mounds she and Tory believed to be a city wall, all they could do was dive over the surface of what they'd found and do nothing more than admire it.

Sad comfort that. It'd been the best lead they'd had in years. "I want another silt sample."

"You've already tested and retested those."

"I know, but maybe it will help to convince them to give us the permits." Yeah, right. She'd been given the run-around particularly good and the words from her latest visit still rang in her ears.

"This is Greece, Dr. Kafieri. There are ruins all around us and I will not allow you to begin tearing up the floor of the Aegean, which is a busy shipping area, when all you can give me is another this-is-Atlantis story. Really. I've enough treasure hunters trying to pilfer our national history for their own gain. I don't need any more. We here in Greece take our history most seriously and you're wasting my valuable time. Good day."

It was enough to make her want to bang her head on the man's desk until he either relented or had her committed. This wasn't about treasure, but trying to tell that to him had been as futile as trying to fly with wax wings.

"There has to be some way around this."

Brian stiffened. "I won't be a part of anything illegal."

And unfortunately, neither would she. "Don't worry, Brian. I don't want to go to jail for this, either."

But there had to be something else she could do. . . .

If only the pain in her head would let up enough so that she could think. But the throbbing pain, much like the official, seemed determined to ruin her day.

She leaned back in the seat and watched the beautiful buildings and landscape of the town drift by while people went about their business on the sidewalks. How she wished she could be carefree enough to roam in and out of the stores, shopping and laughing like the majority of them. Unfortunately, she'd never once been a tourist anywhere.

Geary Kafieri was always all work and no play.

Neither of them spoke as the taxi wended its way through the narrow streets to the dock where their research boat was waiting. While Brian paid the fare, Geary got out and made her way up the gangway to face their team with her gloriously redundant failure.

Tory met her first. At fifteen and very average in height, Geary's cousin had long drab brown hair and thick glasses. She was an awkward teen who had more interest in her books than much of anything else. Even though Tory didn't remember her father, Theron, she was just like him. Finding Atlantis was her only ambition.

"Well?" she asked, her young face expectant.

Geary shook her head.

Tory let out an expletive that made Geary gape. "How could they not let us excavate? What's wrong with those people?"

"They think it's a waste of time."

Tory screwed up her face in distaste. "That's stupid! They're stupid!"

"Yes," Geary said drily. "We're all stupid."

Tory scoffed at that. "I'm not stupid. I'm a certified genius. But the rest . . . Stupid."

"I told you not to bother."

Geary looked past Tory's shoulder to find her other cousin, Cynthia, joining them. Named for the Greek goddess of the hunt, Artemis, Thia hated everything to do with Greece. The only reason she was here was to get college credit and follow her latest fixation, Scott, who'd thought this would be a fun summer activity. Not to mention the small fact that had Thia stayed at home in New York, she'd have been forced to work in her mother's deli, which she hated even more than Greece.

At a cool six two, the titian-haired beauty was also one of the few women taller than Geary—something that was quite a feat given the fact that Thia was barely eighteen.

Geary frowned as she noted Thia's long blue skirt and white long-sleeved embroidered Grecian blouse. "I thought you were sunbathing," Geary said.

Tory leaned forward to whisper in her ear. "She was, and she took her top off earlier, hoping Scott would see her bare boobs and join her. He didn't, but the men on a passing boat almost fell overboard before Justina made her go belowdecks."

Thia curled her lip. "You little nark. While you're confessing things, you should tell Geary how you almost set fire to her reports because her cat scared you and you knocked over Teddy's Bunsen burner."

Tory blushed before she pushed her glasses up on her nose. "Genius, but not graceful. *C'est moi.*"

Geary smiled at the girl as Tory spoke the terrible truth. Grace had never been Tory's virtue, unlike Thia, who had more than her fair share. "It's okay, Tor. I'd have just made you redo them."

Thia gave a heavy sigh as she cast her gaze around the deck. "Is this not the most boring place on earth? I can't even get Scott to come up from below for more than a split second."

Obviously. If nudity didn't inspire the man to come up, nothing else would.

"He's down there with Teddy," Thia continued in an irritated tone, "draped over an excavation map—like that's ever going to happen. What is it about this godforsaken country that every time I bring a guy here he loses his mind?"

"Maybe it's from being around you too long," Tory said, tucking a stray piece of hair behind her ear. She leaned forward to whisper to Geary in their own unique language of ancient Greek and Latin. "I think she sucks the testosterone right out of them and then digests it for her own."

Geary laughed.

Thia went instantly stiff. "What did she say about me?"

Geary shook her head at Tory before she responded. "Why does it always have to be about you, Thia?"

"Because it is." And with that, she flounced off.

Tory let out a tired breath. "One day I hope she finds someone who can put her in her place. I'm tired of watching her emasculate poor Scott. I swear she has to be part succubus."

"Oh, don't go there. I wouldn't wish her on anyone."

"Good point." Tory paused before she turned a probing stare on Geary. "So tell me what happened."

As if she wanted to relive that misery. "Not much to say. They refused to give us permits . . . again."

Tory actually stomped her foot. "Ah, man. That's so not fair."

"I know," she said, patting Tory's arm. "We just have to be patient."

"To heck with patience. At the rate they're going, I'll be in retirement and will have to dig with a cane." She let out a sound of supreme disgust. "This is the closest we've ever been to finding the city. I know Atlantis is right there. I can feel it!"

A chill went down Geary's spine. Tory was just a little too close to their fathers in personality for her tastes. The same insanity that had possessed them drove Tory, too. It was like a madness in her blood that kept her working late into the night after everyone else had retired.

There were times when it truly scared Geary. All of the people in their family who'd ever shared Tory's level of dedication had met with an early death. It would destroy not only Geary but also their grandfather should anything ever happen to their youngest family member.

She was what they lived for.

Then again, Geary had often suspected that Tory used it as a way to distract herself from the pain she felt at being an orphan. The poor thing had no memory of either of her parents. Their work was the only way Tory could feel close to them. It was all they'd left their daughter.

"It'll be all right, *Triantafyllo*." Geary used the nickname their grandfather had given Tory. "Now I'm going to lie down for a bit and see if I can stop some of this headache that's brewing."

"Okay. I'll be below with Scott and Teddy reviewing the data that will be absolutely useless if we can't excavate. But what the heck? I'm young and have plenty of time to waste. You on the other hand . . ."

Geary blew her a raspberry. "I'm not *that* much older than you."

As she sashayed off, Tory tossed back, "Yeah, uh-huh. Get a cane, Grandma."

Geary shook her head at Tory's play, then cringed as pain sliced through her brow and throbbed behind her eyes.

Brian frowned as he joined her on deck. "Are you okay?"

"Another headache." She'd been getting a lot of those lately. Of course with her luck, it was an inoperable brain tumor and she'd probably end up at Thia's mercy so that her cousin could finally torture her without end . . . perish that thought. "I'll be fine. I just need to lie down for a few minutes."

"If you need anything, call."

I need a permit. Hello?

If only she could say that out loud and not lose her much-needed funding.

"I will. Thanks." And with that, Geary headed belowdecks to the small room she shared with Tory. There wasn't a lot of privacy on a research boat, but honestly it didn't bother Geary. Not like it had when she'd been Tory's age. The difference between them was striking.

While Geary had hated the lack of personal space, Tory was ambivalent to it. All the girl cared about was their quest.

But even with their differences, Geary adored her cousin. Tory was the closest thing she'd ever had to a sister, and since Tory's parents had died before the girl reached six, their entire family had embraced her and raised her as their own.

Geary smiled as she entered their room and found Tory's nightgown and matted old brown teddy bear tossed onto her bed. Tory wasn't known for her neatness.

"Okay, Mr. Cuddles, you have to stay on your side. Don't keep sneaking to my bed. I have a tendency to kick in my sleep." Geary set the bear on Tory's unmade bed, then folded the pink flannel gown before she placed it under Mr. Cuddles.

A light smile toyed on the edges of her lips. She could hear muffled voices overhead as the boat rocked softly under her, lulling her into a bit of a stupor. She really did need some rest. Her sleep had been fitful lately. Probably a result of having too much on her mind.

Toeing off her shoes, she pulled back her spread and tucked herself into the narrow bed.

She fell asleep almost immediately.

The noises of the boat faded as she drifted through her dream darkness that was laced with white mist and a cooling breeze. Ever since she'd been a child, Geary had been able to rapidly fall into REM sleep . . . usually within five minutes, which was virtually unheard of. It was a strange sleeping disorder that no doctor had ever been able to explain.

Her dreams flowing, she found herself standing on a dark beach where the snowcapped waves crashed against a foreign shore. The sound echoed in her ears as she curled her bare toes into the wet, black sand.

"Megeara." The deeply masculine voice was warm and erotic as it rolled with an accent so exotic and strange that it whispered through Geary like brandy-laced hot chocolate. Rich. Smooth.

Intoxicating.

She groaned in her dreams as her mysterious lover appeared behind her. As always, he was breathtakingly handsome, with long black hair that tangled in the wind and with eyes so clear and blue, they seemed to glow. Every angle of his face was perfectly sculpted, and those mesmerizing eyes were set off by a pair of black brows that slashed above them. He wrapped his tanned arms around her and pulled her back against his wickedly bare chest that dipped and curved with perfect muscles.

He was divinity.

Absolute seduction.

And for the moment, he was all hers. . . .

Closing her eyes, she allowed the scent of his raw, earthy maleness to seep into her until it made her completely drunk with pleasure. She leaned her head to the left as his hot lips brushed against her neck so that he could tenderly lick and caress her skin until her entire body burned.

She didn't know why she kept having these wildly erotic dreams. Why this incredibly sexy man haunted her. After all, Geary Kafieri wasn't known for her sensuality or femininity. Geary was as tough as nails. She'd spent her entire life fighting for her own beliefs, fighting to be her own person, and those battles hadn't left her time to cultivate the more girlie pastimes of makeup, hair, and feminine wiles.

From the moment she'd started down this path of restoring her father's reputation, she'd been trying to prove to herself and to her colleagues and investors that she could not only compete in a male-dominated field but also rule it.

And she'd succeeded admirably. So what if she wasn't the most ladylike of women? She had her accolades and had taken her father's failing company and turned it around in less than three years after his death. Kafieri Salvage was now one of the top companies in Greece, and while she'd rebuilt her father's company, she'd managed to carry on his private research.

That had always been enough for her.

Or so she'd thought until that sultry night two months ago when Arikos had first appeared in her dreams.

From the moment she'd laid her unconscious eyes on him, she'd been captivated.

He turned her around in his arms to face him. Biting her lip, Geary looked up into his searing blue eyes. He wore a pair of black leather pants and boots with nothing else. His wavy hair flowed around his face as the gentle breeze teased it, and strands of it became caught in the whiskers of his cheeks.

"What has you upset today, *agamenapee*?" he asked in that tone that never failed to send a shiver over her.

Geary leaned her head against the hollow of his muscular shoulder so that she could just breathe in his scent and let it soothe her.

If only he could be real . . .

"They won't give us our permits," she whispered, tracing the outline of his nipple and watching while it drew taut. "And I could kill them for it. I know we've found Atlantis. I know it. I'm so close I can taste it and now . . . Now it's hopeless."

She ground her teeth in frustration, grateful that she

had someone she could trust without having to put on her "game" face. Her staff expected her to be calm and collected at all times when what she really wanted to do was shake the official until he gave her what she needed.

Damn them for it.

"I'm going to fail," she said, her voice catching. "At the rate we're going, Tory's right. We'll be too old to even remember what it was we were looking for."

Arikos cupped her face in his large hands and stared at her with a frown. "I don't understand why this is important to you."

"Because my father died a broken alcoholic. I want everyone who ever laughed at him to have to eat their words. I want to prove to the world that my father wasn't a fool racing against windmills. I want to keep my promise to him. I owe it to him."

Arikos tilted his head and stared into her eyes as if he could see straight into her soul. "Finding it would make you happy?"

"More than anything."

"Then it is done. I will take you to Atlantis."

She laughed at the absurdity. Boy, when her subconscious went off into outer space, it really went off into outer space.

Even so, it meant a lot to her to have at least one person's faith. It didn't matter that he wasn't real. She needed his hypothetical support and she was grateful for it.

Arikos dipped his head down then and captured her lips with his. Geary moaned at the sweet taste of him. There was no one on this earth who tasted the way he did. No one who felt better in her arms, which was probably why he was relegated to her dreams.

But she was so glad to have him here. To feel the heat of his skin sliding against hers.

Oh, she could eat this man alive.

His hands deftly slid the white, flowing dress off her shoulders until she was naked before him while he nibbled and teased her mouth with his lips and tongue. It amazed her that she was so at ease with him, even in her dreams. In real life, Geary had never been the kind of woman to let any man whisk her off her feet. To let her passions rule her.

She was a woman of cold, hard logic and restricted emotions.

It was why she loved her dreams so much. Here she was free to have her way with Arikos without worry. There was no risk of pregnancy or disease. No worry about having to face him in the morning.

No risk of disappointment or cruel laughter. She was in control of her dreams and him. Her times with him were safe and warm and the best moments of her day.

He laid her down carefully on the sandy ground and covered her body with his. Oh, the feel of him like this was incredible. The leather of his pants caressed her legs as he separated her thighs with his knee.

He moved his mouth from hers, down toward her swollen breast that ached for his kiss.

Breathless and weak, she cupped his head to her as he flicked his tongue back and forth over her taut nipple. His breath was scorching against her flushed skin.

"That's it," he breathed as he dipped his hand down to ease the ache that wanted him inside her. His warm fingers stroked and teased her until she was cresting an orgasm. "Give me all of your passion, Megeara. Let me feel your pleasure. Let me taste it."

Kissing him wildly, she thrust her hips against his hand, seeking even more pleasure from him. "I want more," she demanded, reaching for his zipper.

He laughed wickedly. "And you will have it."

"Geary!"

The loud shout jolted her from her dream and left her heart racing even faster than Arikos had. Geary opened her eyes to find herself lying facedown on her bed.

Tory burst into the room. "You better come quick. Thia is about to drown Teddy. And I'm not kidding."

ARIK PULLED OUT OF THE DREAM WITH A CURSE AS HE hovered in the *strobilos* that gave him no form or substance while he spied on the human realm. Whenever a person awoke from their dream, it left a dream god in a vast nothingness. There was no sound, no color, nothing but blackness.

All he could feel was her fleeting emotions, and he was desperate to keep those.

"Megeara . . ." Arik called, wanting to return to what they'd been sharing. But he knew it was too late. His little fixation was stronger than the average human and didn't always come to him when he called for her.

Not even the Lotus serum could induce her to sleep until she was ready and agreeable. All it did was give her a headache as she fought against it.

Damn it. He wanted her back!

His body was aching with unsated need, but more than that he felt something strange in his chest.

Grief.

He craved her and he was angry at her loss. Never once in all the history of the human world had he felt anything like this. Dream gods were supposed to be devoid of emotions . . . at least all except for pain. That emotion alone had been left for them so that the other gods could control and punish them.

Only he didn't feel pain in his chest. He could still feel Megeara's emotions as his own, which told just how powerful her repressed passion and anger were.

She'd started out as a passing curiosity for him. Her dreams had been vivid and colorful—two things most people's were not. The average person dreamed in black-and-white with a lot of mist.

Most dream gods avoided those, especially the erotic Skoti like him who were ever questing for the more daring humans. Why dance in the dreams of an unimaginative person when the point was to experience feelings and senses through the sleeper?

So his kind skipped through dreams, seeking those who could create beauty and give to the Skoti what they needed.

Megeara's dreams had been awash in clever sensations. He'd first come upon her while she was bathing in a river of chocolate.

Rolling over on the misty ground that made up one of the dream chambers, Arik closed his eyes to summon the memory. There were still the remnants of Megeara's passion inside him even though their dream connection was severed, and that allowed him to remember the pleasure of finding her that first night.

Even now he could taste the dream chocolate on his tongue as he'd licked it from her naked body. Feel the warm sensation of it sliding over his skin as they made love in it. He wondered now as he'd wondered then what that chocolate would really taste like on the mortal plane.

Why had it given Megeara so much pleasure?

Most of all, he burned to know what *she* would really taste like. How she would smell.

His cock twitched in sweet expectation.

"Arikos?"

He turned his head away as a bright light burst into his darkness. "Fuck off, M'Ordant," he snarled, recognizing the voice of his older half brother.

"Is that anger?"

Arik pushed himself up and moved to stand beside the god who was equal to his height. Like him, M'Ordant had black hair and translucent blue eyes. All of their race were marked by those colorings, along with an unearthly beauty.

This time when Arik spoke his tone was flat and level, as was befitting one of his cursed species. "How would I know? I have no emotions."

M'Ordant narrowed his gaze and if Arik didn't know better, he'd swear his brother was puzzled. Even though they couldn't truly feel, they'd learned to mock expressions. It made the other gods less nervous around them. "You've been spending too much time with the human. You need to move on to another."

That was the way of it. A Skotos such as Arik was only tolerated to help drain humans of excess emotions. If Skoti spent too long with one person, they could, in theory, make the person go mad or even kill them.

The Skoti were normally given a single warning and if they failed to heed it, an Oneroi would be selected to either punish or eliminate them from existence. M'Ordant was one of many who monitored human sleep and who kept the Skoti in line.

"And if I don't want to leave her?"

"Are you being argumentative?"

Arik gave him an arch stare. "How could I be?"

"Then you are done with her." M'Ordant vanished.

The wisest course of action would be to heed his warning. But Arik was too drawn to his human to pay attention to M'Ordant's words. After all, that would require fear . . . something Arik knew nothing about.

Closing his eyes, Arik could still smell the scent of Megeara's flesh. Still taste the salty sweetness of her body on his hungry tongue. Feel her touch on his skin.

No, he wasn't done with her. He was only beginning.

CHAPTER 2

LEANING AGAINST THE SIDE OF THE BOAT SO THAT SHE could watch the nearby sailboats gliding over the clear blue water, Geary didn't know what was wrong with her. She was so sleepy she could barely keep her eyes open, and that wasn't like her.

"I think I have narcolepsy."

Tory paused by Geary's side before looking her up and down. "Possibly. Did you know that seventy percent of people with narcolepsy also suffer cataleptic attacks?" Before Geary could open her mouth to comment, Tory refuted her own theory. "That's not you, though. I've seen you angry enough times to know that that lovely symptom doesn't affect you. Of course, narcoleptics also have vivid hallucinations either while asleep or even while awake. And, of course, sleepwalking. I know you don't sleepwalk. Have you become delusional lately?"

Yes, but discussing vivid sexual fantasies with a

fifteen-year-old bookworm wasn't something Geary intended to do.

Geary scowled at her. "How do you know all this? Jeez, Tory, you're a kid. Act like it." Before she could even blink, Tory reached out and punched her on the arm. Hard. "Ow!" She rubbed her biceps where Tory had hit her. "What was that for?"

"Unexpected and irrational emotional outbursts. Isn't that what teenagers are supposed to do? Oh, and sulk. A lot."

Geary held her hands up in surrender. "Fine. Have it your way, *Dr.* Kafieri."

In an expression more akin to her age, Tory gave her a gleeful grin before she went to help the boat's captain with some line he was securing.

Shaking her head, Geary headed back belowdecks to find Teddy and Scott, who were grumbling about Thia's presence on their team while they worked . . . something Geary couldn't help since she'd promised Thia's mother to watch after her this summer. Apparently, the little shrew had attacked Teddy for taking up too much of Scott's time.

Geary hoped they'd get over their ire soon. She had banished her cousin to the city for a short round of shopping while they prepared to sail back to the area where Geary believed Atlantis was hiding. The last thing they needed was to have Thia gaggling about, complaining over everything.

Besides, Thia lived for shopping. The shinier the object, the more she adored it. So much so, the girl had actually worn red horns last Halloween that were decorated with dangling diamond hoops. As was fitting for her, Thia had dressed up as a shopping demon.

Brian had volunteered to accompany her and keep her out of trouble—which, knowing Thia, was a necessary assignment. Their luck, she'd end up being either abducted into white slavery or stolen by green aliens.

Meanwhile, Geary was so tired, she couldn't stand it. It was all she could do to stay awake.

"Megeara. Return to me. . . ."

A chill went down her body as she heard the deeply erotic voice in her head again.

From the corner of her eye she saw something move. She turned and there in the doorway, on the stairs that led to the top deck, was Arikos. Dressed completely in black, he stood to the side with wicked eyes that promised her an endless night of orgasm, and a seductive smile that froze her to the spot.

"Come, Megeara." His voice whispered like a phantom wind, caressing her. Lulling her.

He held his hand out . . .

Never had she seen a more compelling pose. All she wanted was to take his hand and have him sweep her up in his arms like he did in her dreams. She wanted to strip him bare and taste the perfection of his body.

To taste those inviting lips.

Without thinking, she held her hand out toward his. So close that they were almost touching. Only a breadth of a hair more . . .

But he wasn't real and she knew it.

"Geary? Can you hand me my ruler?"

She started at Teddy's voice. Dropping her hand, she glanced to her left and saw the ruler on the cluttered desktop. She barely blinked before she looked back toward the stairs.

They were empty, with no sign of Arikos waiting there

for her to return, and that filled her with extreme disappointment.

I am losing my mind.

Yeah, but what a way to go. Everyone should be stalked by such a sexy hallucination.

Not wanting to think about that, she picked up the ruler and handed it to Teddy, who was watching her with a concerned frown. Even though he was only a few years older than her, he acted more like a father to her than a friend or colleague. His short brown hair was always impeccably combed, and he had jolly brown eyes and a sweet set of kind dimples. "Are you okay?"

"Tired."

He scratched his head as if baffled by her response. "You slept fourteen hours last night."

She patted his arm. "I know, but I'm still tired."

"Maybe you need a physical."

More likely my head examined. She pushed that thought aside to smile at him. "I'll be fine. Really."

At least she would be if she could stop having these bizarre delusions. Even now she felt as if someone was watching her . . .

ARIK WANTED TO CURSE IN FRUSTRATION AS HE WATCHED Megeara smiling at another man. Why wouldn't she succumb to his serum? To his pleas?

How could a mere mortal woman be so strong?

"Arikos?"

As light intruded into his dark chamber once more he let out a tired sigh at the sound of his uncle Wink's voice. Arik was getting seriously tired of these interruptions when all he wanted was to be with his human target. "What?"

"I've been told to retrieve my sleeping serum from you. You seem to be abusing it and making your human ill."

Arik rolled over to face the older sleep god. Wink's long brown hair was braided down his back as his light gray eyes danced with mischief. Even though Wink was one of the oldest gods, he held the personality of a thirteen-year-old boy. There was nothing he loved more than to play pranks and tease—two of the very things that had gotten Arik and his brethren cursed.

At one time, they'd been too easily seduced and manipulated by the other gods and had allowed themselves to be used by Wink, Hades, and the others in private jests and wars.

Until the day Zeus had put a stop to it once and for all. Funny how he'd only punished the tools and not the ones who'd wielded them.

But then, Zeus wasn't known as a god of justice.

"And if I want to keep the serum?"

Wink arched a brow at that, then tsked. "Come now, Arikos, you know the rules." His face sobered. "You also know what happens to those who don't cooperate."

Of course he did. All of his kind knew. His back bore more scars than the sky held stars. There were times when he suspected his grandfather Hypnos, who oversaw their physical punishments, was nothing more than a sadist who could only feel pleasure when he was doling out pain to others.

How cruel was it to send the Skoti in to drain humans of excess or pent-up emotions, then punish them when they didn't want to leave because they finally experienced something other than pain?

But that was the way of it.

After his "chat" with M'Ordant, Arik had known it

would come to this. There was no use in arguing. Wink had been sent to retrieve the Lotus serum they used on humans, and all the bribery on Olympus wouldn't sway him. Wink was only a pawn who served the sleep gods.

Arik pulled out the small vial and handed it to Wink, who took it with a stoic smile.

"Cheer up, old boy. There are plenty of other dreamers out there for you to play with. Mankind is generous to you that way. They live for their dreams and are possessed of them constantly."

Yes, but none of those humans held the type of uninhibited, vivid dreams of Megeara. It made Arik long to know what she'd be like outside the dream realm. What she would be like as a human . . .

Arik watched as Wink withdrew, then left him in the dream chamber to face the darkness alone.

Perhaps this was just punishment after all. A son of the god Morpheus, Arik had originally been one of the Oneroi. As was customary for such, he'd been assigned humans to watch over and protect against the Skoti who sometimes preyed on them. In those days, he'd spent his life monitoring his subjects, making sure the ones under his protection had normal dreams that would either help them work through their problems or inspire them.

Until that one fateful night.

He'd gone to help one of his assignments who was ill. Because of her sickness, her dreams had become extremely vivid and emotional—so much so that one of the Skoti had latched onto her. Such a thing was common and even tolerated. Skoti fed from human emotions, but so long as they kept it under control and didn't lead the dreams or interrupt the human's life, they were allowed to drain humans. It was only when the Skoti began to return repeatedly and took control of the host that they were punished.

Humans held fragile psyches. A returning Skotos could easily turn human minds and either drive them insane or make them homicidal. In the worst case, a Skotos could even kill the human, which was why the Oneroi monitored them. If a Skotos spent too long with their host, then it was the Oneroi's place to step in and drive them out.

If all else failed, the Oneroi would kill the Skotos.

At one time, Arik's life had been dedicated to protecting his humans. To feel nothing and to only follow the orders of the elite Oneroi. In his day, he'd vanquished numerous Skoti without understanding or caring why they sought humans the way they did. Why they felt a burning need to risk their lives for their quest.

And then one night . . . no, one *encounter* had changed that and brought with it a clarification that still resonated within him.

Born of a human mother and the dream god Phobetor, Solin lived on earth, but at night he ran amok in the dreams of other humans. Completely amoral, he didn't care what he did to others so long as *he* enjoyed himself.

For centuries, the Oneroi had been trying to stop and trap Solin. He was one of the few Skoti who'd warranted a death sentence. His voracious appetites and fighting skills were legendary among the Oneroi who'd been unfortunate enough to confront him.

And Arik had been one of them. Still young by their years, Arik had thought to take Solin on his own.

Most of the Skoti fled at the approach of an Oneroi. The Oneroi had full backing of the other gods to do whatever they had to do to control the Skoti. Since a Skotos could drain emotions from any human, they normally left without issue and didn't waste time fighting when they could simply move on to someone else.

But Solin was stronger than most. Bolder. Instead of fleeing as Arik had expected, Solin had turned the human loose on him. By their laws, Arik had been forbidden to hurt the human, and Solin had known it. Arik had tried to pry her away without harm, but the moment her lips had touched his and he'd tasted her lust, something inside him had shattered.

He'd felt pleasure and arousal for the first time in his life.

And when the human had dropped to her knees and taken him into her mouth, he'd known his war in this was lost and his conviction shattered. In one heartbeat, he'd gone Skoti.

He'd been Skoti ever since.

Drifting from one dream to the next, he'd been searching all these centuries for someone who could raise his emotions to the level of that first night. But no one had come close.

Not until Megeara.

Only she was able to reach through the emptiness inside him and make him see vivid colors again. To make him feel her emotions. After all these centuries, he finally understood why certain Skoti refused to leave their partners.

Why they were willing to risk death.

Because of Megeara, he wanted to know what the world looked like through her eyes. What it tasted like. Felt like. And her ability to pull herself away from him was starting to seriously piss him off.

But what could he do? Even if he went to earth to be near her, he couldn't really experience her or her environment.

He wanted her passion. Her life force.

There might be a way to touch her . . .

Arik paused at the thought. It was true that both the

Oneroi and Skoti could take human form in the mortal realm, but because of their curse, they still lacked emotions. So what was the point? They were just as cold and sterile and unable to feel in human form as they were in their own god form.

That wasn't what he wanted.

No, he wanted to be human. He wanted feelings and emotions so that he could experience her to the fullest extent possible.

It's impossible.

Or was it? They were gods, with god powers. Why should such a thing be unattainable?

Your powers aren't capable of such. Zeus had made sure of that when he punished them for tampering with his dreams.

Then again, *Arik's* weren't. But there were others whose powers made a mockery of his. Gods who could make him human if they willed it.

Zeus would never concede such a thing—he hated the dream gods too much. His children would be too afraid of him to try. But his brothers . . .

They were a different matter entirely.

And Arik knew which one to barter with.

Hades. The god of the Underworld held no fear of anyone or anything. His powers were more than equal to any of the others', and best of all, he hated the other gods as much as they hated him. Because of that, Hades was always open to a good bargain, especially if such a bargain would irritate Zeus.

It was at least worth a shot.

With Megeara's niggling emotions retreating from him, Arik flew from the Vanishing Isle where most of the dream gods resided and descended down, straight into the heart of Hades' domain. It was dark as night here. Dismal. There were no ivory or gold halls like the ones found on Olympus. At least not until one visited the Elysian Fields, where good souls were sent to live out their eternity in paradise. Those lucky enough to attain residence there had any- and everything their hearts conceived of. They could even be reincarnated should they choose it.

But the Elysian Fields were only part of a much vaster realm. One that held nothing but misery for those who were damned to it. Especially this time of year. Three months ago the god's beloved wife, Persephone, had been sent to live with her mother in the upper realm. Until Persephone's return, Hades would be literally hell to deal with. From the moment she left until her return, he would spend his time torturing all those around him.

A saner god would wait to try to deal with Hades after Persephone's return, when he was more reasonable, but Arik was desperate. The last thing he wanted was to take a chance on another Skotos finding Megeara.

No, it was now or never.

Besides, Arik had never been a coward. He'd never once retreated from battle or conflict. It was what had made him one of the best of the Oneroi and what had made him one of the deadliest Skoti.

He always took what he wanted. Damned be the consequences. He had eternity to deal with those. What mattered most was the present, and that was what he focused on. Always.

As he flew past Cerberus, the three-headed dog rose up to bark at him. Ignoring it, he dove down into the catacombs made of the skulls and bones of Hades' enemies. Many of whom had been Titans and ancients who'd had the misfortune of irritating the somber god—they didn't even warrant Hades torturing them for eternity. He'd relegated them to nothing more than decoration.

That alone should be a warning to Arik . . .

But the brave and the desperate never heeded such.

Arik slowed his flight as he entered the main chamber of Hades' domain. This was the only room in Hades' opulent palace that was open to outsiders. . . . But there was a lot more to his home than this one room.

Arik knew that because no one was immune to the powers of a Dream-Hunter. No one. All gods were vulnerable whenever they rested, which was why they feared the Dream-Hunters so, and it was times such as those that Arik had ventured here to see what Hades kept so secret.

Now Arik faded to invisibility and rose up toward the black ceiling that glittered eerily in the dim light. Hades sat below, alone, on his throne. Made of Titan bones, his black throne had been polished until it gleamed like steel. Hard and intimidating as the god had intended, it dominated the dais where it sat. Beside it was a much smaller chair. One made of gold and cushioned with pillows the color of blood. It was where Persephone sat whenever she was home with her husband.

Hades stared at her throne with a look of such longing that Arik could almost feel his grief. And it wasn't until Hades moved that Arik realized the god held a small, delicate fan in his hand. One made of lace and ivory.

Closing his eyes, Hades held it to his nose and gently inhaled the scent.

Then he cursed and tossed the fan back to the throne by his side.

A heartbeat later, he got up to retrieve it and place it more carefully in a small holder on the right arm. Obviously that was where Persephone kept it.

Hades froze and cocked his head as if he was listening for something. "Who dares to enter my hall without summons?"

Arik lowered himself to the floor and materialized. "I do."

The god turned about slowly and narrowed his amber eyes on Arik. "What brings you here, son of Morpheus?"

There was no need to hide what he wanted. "I would like to bargain with you."

"For what?"

"I wish to be human."

Hades' evil laughter rang out in the hollow hall, echoing around them. "You know how to be human, Skotos. Stop eating ambrosia and drinking nectar."

"That would only make me mortal and I don't want to die. I want to feel, and for that I need to be a human and not a god."

Hades approached him slowly until he stood just before Arik. "Feel? Why would anyone in their right mind wish for that? Feelings are for fools."

Arik glanced to the fan. "Even you?"

Hades bellowed in rage as he flung out his hand and pinned Arik against the wall with his powers. The jagged bones bit into Arik's back, tearing the fabric of his clothes.

Arik fought the hold, but there was nothing he could do at the moment except bleed.

"For a god who doesn't wish to die, you speak of things you'd best not address."

The force holding him receded so fast that he barely had time to recover himself before he fell. He hovered over the floor for a heartbeat until he placed his feet on the ground.

Hades raised his brows in surprise. "You're faster than most."

"And in my realm, I'm capable of even more feats."

"What are you saying?"

Arik shrugged. "Only that a god of such power should be careful. Even the great Hades has to sleep sometime."

"Are you threatening me?"

"I'm only stating a fact." Arik looked pointedly at Persephone's throne. "And reminding you, my lord, that there's nothing worse than allowing a Skotos to know of a weakness."

Hades narrowed his eyes before he again broke out into laughter. "It's been a long time since anyone dared such boldness in my presence. Look around you, Skotos. Do you not see the remains of the people who have pissed me off?"

"My name is Arik and I see everything, including the beauty and comfort of the palace you hide behind this facade of death. But in turn, I would ask you what good does it do to threaten someone who can't feel fear?"

Hades inclined his head. "Point well taken. So tell me . . . Arik, what bargain do you wish to propose?"

"I want to live in the realm of the humans as one of them."

Hades tsked at his request. "That's not so easy to attain, dear boy. No Olympus-born god can live on earth for very long."

"But we can live there for a time. I would go there now, but there would be no point, since I could only witness what's around me and not experience it. It's the experience I want."

"What good is this experience when you'll only forget it once you return?"

What the god didn't know was that Arik wouldn't forget. He'd remember and he wanted that memory. Unlike M'Ordant and many of the others, Arik had no knowledge of true emotions or sensations—they'd been beaten out of him so long ago that he'd completely forgotten what it was like to feel. He wanted to know how much more intense feelings could be when not blocked by the curse.

"Does the why really matter?"

Hades considered that for a moment. Folding his arms over his chest, he frowned at Arik. "For what you want, there would have to be a steep price."

"I expected nothing less. Just tell me your fee."

"A soul. A *human* soul."

That was easy enough. Taking a human life wouldn't bother him. They lived finitely anyway and very few of them even bothered to appreciate the beauty that was the human existence. He, however, would savor his brief time as one of them. "Done."

Hades clucked his tongue at Arik. "Child, how naive of you. You agreed too soon. It's not just any soul I want."

"Whose then?"

"I want the soul of the woman who has compelled you to make a deal with the devil. Surely she must have a magnificent soul for you to come here and barter with me, the most despised of all gods."

Arik hesitated. Not out of feelings for Megeara but rather because he wasn't sure he would be through with her by the time he was forced to return. "And if I fail to complete this bargain?"

"It will be you who suffers here in her stead. If you fail to deliver her to me, I will kill you as a man and keep your soul in Tartarus. The pain you've felt to date will be nothing when compared to what you'll suffer then. And before you reconsider, remember that you've already agreed to this. There is no going back now. Our bargain is set."

"How long will you give me?"

"Two weeks and not a day more."

Arik had no time to even twitch before a strange thick blackness covered him. One moment he was standing in the middle of Hades' throne room, and in the next he was encircled by wetness.

It was water . . .

And unlike in dreams, his body was heavy. Leaden. Water poured in through his mouth and nose, causing him to choke as it invaded lungs that weren't used to really breathing. He tried to swim, but the water was too thick. It seemed to be sucking him down deeper into the sea.

Panic consumed him. There was nothing he could do.

He was going to drown.

CHAPTER 3

"GEARY, QUICK! THERE'S A BODY OVERBOARD!"

Oh good God, who had Thia attacked now?

Aggravated, Geary looked up from Tory's notes at Justina's call. Geary's second in command was pointing over the side of the boat. As Geary rushed to the side to peer over, she handed the notebook back to Tory. Sure enough, there was someone struggling in the waves. And by the looks of it, he was quickly losing his battle.

"Christof!" Geary shouted for the boat's captain. "We need . . ." She paused as the body sank down below the hungry waves.

There wasn't time.

Her heart pounding from the rush of adrenaline, Geary kicked her shoes off and dove over the side. The coldness of the water stunned her as it covered her completely. Kicking her legs, she swam upward until she broke the surface so that she could look about for him.

Even though the water was clear, Geary had a hard time finding the guy below the surface. She had to keep diving down, then returning for fresh air before she dove back to search for him. Thank God she was a strong swimmer who was trained as a lifeguard and a certified diving instructor. But then, it was expected of her as an underwater recovery expert. She had to be as nimble in water as a fish.

She just wished she'd had time to get her gear before she'd come in after him. If she didn't find the guy soon, he'd be dead, especially since he hadn't resurfaced.

Her lungs burned from holding her breath as she dove under the water again. Her ears were buzzing and popping from the pressure as images of him drowning consumed her.

Geary had been twelve years old when Tory's father had drowned only a few miles from this very spot. Images of her father trying to save Theron's life tore through her now as she remembered her father diving for him. Her father pulling Theron out of the water and doing everything he could to resuscitate him.

It'd been awful and the last thing she wanted to do was relive it.

C'mon. Don't you dare die on me. Where are you? She slowed her speed and turned about as she floated weightlessly in the sea. The light refracted and danced in the blue and green water, highlighting various fish and foliage, but there was no sight of the man she sought.

"Look down."

She frowned at the foreign voice in her head, not understanding the source of it, but she couldn't help obeying it. Looking down, she spotted him just below her. Even though he was trying to swim, he was sinking fast. . . .

His long black hair danced in the water as bubbles

floated around him and he waved his arms and legs to no avail.

Relieved she'd found him but scared it might be too late, she headed for him as fast as she could. She came up behind him, then pulled his large body against hers and kicked them toward the surface.

Good grief! The man was huge and made of solid muscle. With next to no fat on him, he was like an anchor in the water. It took a great deal of effort to get them to the surface.

By the time they broke through, both of them were sputtering and coughing.

"Hold on," she said to him. "I've got you." Even so, she half-expected him to fight against her. Most drowning victims did.

But not him. He went limp against her as if he trusted her completely.

Justina and Teddy were in the water already with a life preserver. Together, they got the man into the harness and had him hauled on board, then they followed suit.

By the time Geary was on board the *Simi* again, she saw the unknown man lying on the deck, covered with a blanket, while Thia was giving him mouth-to-mouth. Geary couldn't see the man's face for Thia.

"Is he dead?" Geary asked, rushing over to them as worry tore at her.

Just as she reached his side, the man coughed up a gallon of seawater. Gasping, he turned quickly to his side and started hacking and wheezing while Thia pounded him on the back to help him clear his lungs. His slick wet skin was completely bronzed and perfect, except for the deep welts that marred his back. The scars were old, but even so they were prominent enough to let Geary know how much they must have hurt when he received them. It reminded her of the way sailors were beaten for punishment back in the old days.

Why would a modern man have such scarring? Who would have beaten him like that and why?

And he wore nothing except a thin pair of long white pants that were plastered against his perfect body . . . and they showed absolutely *everything,* right down to his religion and the fact that this man had been rather gifted in a certain department.

He might as well be naked.

"Now there's a man who doesn't believe in underwear, huh?" Justina said in a low tone for only Geary's hearing as she wrung out her hair. "Not that I'm not grateful for it. He has the nicest ass on the planet. No wonder Thia grabbed him for resuscitation. I wouldn't mind a little mouth-to-mouth action with that body, either."

While Geary pretty much agreed with those sentiments, she didn't comment as Tory draped a blanket around her shoulders.

"Hell of a fish you found there," Christof said as he brought more blankets for them. He gave one to Justina and Teddy.

Ignoring him, Geary knelt down beside her catch. The man held himself up with one muscular arm as he continued to breathe in short, sharp gasps. His tangled wet black hair fell over his face, completely obscuring it from her and the others. The tendons of his hands were well defined and beautiful, which made her curious as to what his face would look like.

Would it be as scarred as his back or as pristine and beautiful as the rest of him?

"Are you okay?" she asked in Greek, assuming since they were in the Aegean that he would understand her better in Greek than any other language.

He nodded as he continued to struggle to expel the water from his body. It was almost as if he wasn't used to his own lungs.

His breathing ragged, he lifted his head to look at her through the strands of his wet black hair. And as soon as their eyes met, Geary gasped and fought the urge to cross herself and spit as she came face-to-face with the intense blue eyes of her dreams.

It couldn't be. . . .

It wasn't possible and yet there he was before her in all his almost naked glory. She knew those perfect, sardonic lips. The slash of his dark brows over eyes that were so pale a blue they radiated. She knew that strong jaw, dusted with whiskers. It was one she'd teased with her teeth and tongue for hours on end.

Against all reason, it was *him.*

Something hot and needful went through her like a sharp needle as she fought the urge to reach out and touch him to make sure he was really here.

Arik couldn't do anything more than stare at Megeara. She was even more beautiful in reality than she'd been in her dreams. Her deep blue eyes captivated him as tendrils of her wet blond hair hung down over them. Her pale skin begged for his touch just as her partially opened mouth needed his kiss.

He started toward those lips, then coughed more as he tried to breathe through the stinging pain in his chest. His body shook uncontrollably as he was assaulted by horrifyingly intense sensations and emotions. Even the cries of the birds above him were piercing to his ears—the droning of the ocean. And the heat of the sun on his skin . . . it was blistering. Never had he felt so out of control. Why wouldn't his body obey him?

Why the hell couldn't he stop coughing and shaking?

He half-expected Megeara to pound on his back as her accomplice had done. Instead, Megeara's touch was gentle as she lightly hit him to help dispel the water from his now human body.

Then she started to gently rub his back in a circle. Chills spread over him as he felt a heat the likes of which were unimaginable. Forget the heat of the sun, this was even more scorching.

No one had ever touched him so gently and he'd never really felt a touch before, especially not against his flesh. All he wanted was to pull her into his arms and taste the taut nipples that were so apparent through her wet white shirt.

If only his body would obey him.

"I think he's going into shock," Megeara said to the others. "Grab more blankets."

Another woman pulled Megeara away. "Let me look at—"

"No!" he snarled, reaching for Megeara's hand to keep her by his side. He hadn't come this far to lose sight of her now.

Megeara covered his hand with hers in a soothing caress. "It's all right. Stay calm." She took a blanket from a young woman with glasses, then wrapped it around him.

Arik closed his eyes and savored the fleeting sensation of her hands on his shoulders. The feel of her skin on his . . . it was electrifying. Hot.

If only he could stop shaking.

Geary wasn't sure what to do. She exchanged a frown with Althea, who was on board as their physician.

"I need to check him out and make sure he's okay," Althea said in English.

Geary agreed. "I know."

"I'll be fine in a few minutes," the unknown man said

in perfect, accented English. His voice was so deep and resonant that it literally echoed around them. Those intense, predatorial eyes pierced her. "Just don't leave me."

Geary found herself nodding even though the possessive command of that tone made her want to run. It wasn't in her nature to let anyone tell her what to do, but in his case, there was something unnaturally compelling about him. Alluring.

Honestly, she didn't want to leave him. And that really did scare her.

Her heart hammering, she used a corner of his blanket to towel dry his hair, then brushed it back from a face that was truly flawless.

"Do you prefer English or Greek?" she asked him.

"It doesn't matter."

Wow. He was extremely bilingual. He was also extremely exposed, and the sight of him with those pants clinging to his every asset brought the most wicked images to her mind. In her dreams, she'd twisted that body of his like a pretzel and licked every inch of it.

Okay, so it wasn't quite *that* body. In her dreams, there had been no scars. But his body was close enough to the one she was used to to evoke a fervent heat inside her.

Geary brushed a drop of water off his cheek with the blanket. "What happened to you?"

He looked away. "I don't know."

Thia gave her a wicked grin. "Well, it isn't every day we fish a nearly naked god out of the sea, now is it? Glad I came back early from my shopping trip. This was definitely worth it."

The man snapped his head toward her and gave her a fierce scowl. It was obvious her words touched a nerve with him.

"Thia?" Geary said in a steady tone. "Do you mind?"

She rolled her eyes. "Whatever. See if *I* save his life next time he's drowning." Turning around, she headed belowdecks.

Christof stepped forward. "We should report this to the authorities."

Even more fury snapped in those pale blue eyes. "No!" His tone was firm and commanding. "No authorities."

Teddy exchanged a frown with her. "Why? You running from them?"

"No. I just don't want to be interrogated when I can't remember anything."

Christof narrowed his eyes on him. "Do you know your name?"

He hesitated. "Arik."

"Arik what?"

He looked up at Geary with a confusion that tugged at her heart. "I don't remember."

Geary tilted her head, not sure what to think. Something deep inside told her he was lying, but she wasn't sure about what. "Did you hit your head?"

He nodded.

"He could have amnesia," Tory said. "If he fell from a boat he might have been run over by it. Or maybe he was beaten and then thrown overboard. Could be pirates."

"He's not bruised," Christof pointed out. "And there hasn't been a lot of pirate activity here for several hundred years."

"Yes, but I said *could.* Weird and unusual things happen all the time. Did you know that there were seventy-five pirate attacks on civilian boats last year alone? Six more were against the U.S. Coast Guard. One group even tried to take over a cruise ship."

Ignoring Tory's statistics, Geary dropped the blanket to Arik's shoulders. "What was the last thing you remember?"

"I . . . I don't know."

A strange, warm feeling came over her as she watched him. The whole moment was so surreal. She couldn't believe she was looking at . . . Arikos.

That had been a dream and yet the man before her was an exact copy. A copy named Arik.

Could they possibly . . .

Don't be stupid.

It was just some strange coincidence. Maybe some sort of premonition.

Her face flamed red at the thought. Well, not *that* kind of premonition. She wasn't about to jump naked into a pool of chocolate with this guy.

"Okay," she said quietly. "Teddy, take Arik below and find some clothes for him."

Arik started to protest leaving her, then stopped himself. She was skittish of him. He could sense it. If he pressed her too much, she might bolt and push him away.

That was the last thing he wanted.

No, he must tread carefully in order to gain her trust. He was here, in her realm. And he'd have plenty of time to seduce her shortly. For now it was best to humor her.

He stood up slowly, his eyes never wavering from her gaze. As a wave crashed into the boat, he staggered slightly and almost lost his balance.

Megeara reached out, her hands steadying him.

Arik closed his eyes as heat from her touch seared his every nerve. There was nothing to compare to the sensation of human contact—to the feeling of those delicate hands touching his flesh—and he couldn't wait to feel them stroking the part of him that was hard for her.

He bent his head low so that he could inhale her sweet,

feminine scent of open air and woman misted with a light touch of perfume. It was even more intoxicating than it had been in her dreams, and he wanted to bask in it.

Even more he wanted to smell it on his sheets and flesh. To drink her in for hours on end until he was fully sated and content.

Geary tensed at the feel of Arik's hot breath against her damp skin. What was it about this stranger that set her entire body on fire?

She forced herself to step away from him even though what she really wanted to do was walk closer to that magnificently muscled body.

His eyes showed his longing as he met her gaze again and he noted her actions. "Don't be afraid of me, Megeara." He all but purred in her ear. "I would never hurt you."

It wasn't until he'd left that she realized he'd called her by a name no one used.

CHAPTER 4

ARIK CRINGED AT THE HARSH SENSATION OF DENIM SLIDing against his bare legs. The roughness of it was hard to take. How did humans stand it?

The man, Teddy, had loaned him a white shirt and jeans. But the texture of each was itchy and heavy. The clothing Arik was used to had no weight or texture. At least none that he could feel, and in dreams . . . well, since he was considered an Erotikos Skotos, clothing was seldom ever worn since all it did was get in the way of other, more pleasurable sensations.

After fastening the jeans, he reached for the stiff white shirt at the same time the door burst open. He paused at the sight of Megeara standing in the low, narrow entranceway, looking much like a puppy caught in a deluge. Her damp khaki shorts fell to her knees. She wore a baggy white shirt untucked that made her appear to be a blob of material. Or at least it would if it weren't wet. As it was, it left very little of her lush body to his imagination.

In this realm, she hid every indication of the full curves he knew she possessed. Even her thick, blond hair was pulled back severely from her face into a tight bun.

But her face was the same. Those intelligent, sharp and clear, almond-shaped eyes that took in the world around her. The light smattering of freckles across the bridge of her nose. And her lips . . .

He had spent entire nights kissing those luscious lips. Watching them dance over his skin as she nibbled and teased him until they were both blind with ecstasy.

The memory of it, along with the sight of her tight, puckered nipples straining against her shirt, made his entire body burn with hunger.

"How do you know my name?" she demanded in an angry tone that was undercut by a note of apprehension.

He hesitated as he sensed her fear. He would have to play this carefully if he were to get what he wanted from her. He didn't know much about the human world, but he knew from dreams that scared hosts wouldn't let him touch them. So it only stood to reason that they'd be skittish in this realm, too. If he wanted her in his bed, he'd have to gain her trust.

"You told me." It wasn't a lie. On the night they'd met while they bathed in chocolate, she'd given it to him.

"No. I didn't. No one calls me Megeara. No one."

"What do they call you then?"

"Geary."

"Then Geary you are."

"Yes, but that doesn't explain how you knew my name when I hadn't said it."

"Maybe I'm psychic." He'd meant that as a joke, but by the look on her face, he could tell she didn't find it amusing.

"I don't believe in psychics."

"Then how do you explain it?"

Geary narrowed her eyes at him. He was playing with her, and she didn't appreciate it in the least. "Do I know you? Have we met?"

He hesitated before he answered. "There's no need to be afraid of me, Megeara. We did meet. Years ago when you were giving a paper at Vanderbilt."

Geary frowned as she remembered the event clearly. That had been her first paper in public . . . ever. She'd been incredibly nervous. So much so that she'd stumbled on her way to the podium, dropped her pages and notes in front of everyone, and then spent ten minutes, red-faced, as she struggled to put them together again. She'd been halfway through the paper before she realized that one page had fallen underneath the heavy wooden stand and they had to stop everything again to retrieve it.

The event had left her humiliated as people laughed at her. After that fiasco, she'd been lucky anyone had ever invited her to speak on anything.

"I don't remember you."

"I was in the audience at the time. Dr. Chandler introduced us afterward, but we didn't really converse. You seemed a bit harried before you were pulled away by Dr. Chandler to meet her old college professor."

She vaguely remembered that part. The fact that he did lent credibility to his claim. It was true that she'd been preoccupied with saving some dignity at the mixer . . . still, a man this hot should have been branded in her memory.

A teasing smile quirked one corner of his mouth up. "You left quite an impression on me."

She had to bite back a laugh. Yeah, right. A guy like this would actually remember an overweight frump who'd embarrassed herself? "I find that hard to believe."

But there was no laughter in his intense gaze. Only sincerity. "You shouldn't. It's true."

Geary frowned as she struggled to recall him from her past, but honestly, she'd been in such a fog that day that it was entirely possible they had met and she'd forgotten it. "Why were you there?"

"I was a student of anthropology. I asked you about Atlantis then and you were rather rude about it." The smile spread across his face as he teased her with his eyes.

She was still skeptical, but it did make sense. She would have taken his head off over Atlantis back then. It would also explain her blocking him out of her memory.

Maybe that was why she'd been dreaming about him lately. Maybe her subconscious had remembered him and his desire to find Atlantis.

"Anyway, it's why I'm here now. Like you, I want to find Atlantis."

She stiffened at those words. "Who says I'm after Atlantis?"

"You're an American in the Aegean with a scientific team, on a boat that's outfitted for probing and excavation. What else would you be after?"

"Any ancient artifact."

"Then why is it you wear an Atlantean coin around your neck?"

Her hand went straight to it. She'd had the coin mounted a month after her father's death to remind her of her promise to him. But what confused her most was the fact that the part with the writing was on the back. The part that showed to Arik was the image of the sunburst with three lightning bolts. "How do you know that?"

"That coin bears the symbol of Apollymi Magosa Fonia Kataastreifa."

…ymi who?"

…e Atlantean goddess of wisdom, death, and destruc-…. But she was mostly referred to in Atlantean as Apol-…ymi Akrakataastreifa. Apollymi the Great Destroyer."

There was no way he could know that. Not unless he'd seen the mysterious symbol somewhere else. "Where have you seen the symbol? How do you know what it stands for?"

"I'm from an *old* Greek family. There is nothing about this area that I don't know. Nothing. I also know that even if you have found Atlantis, you'll never get a permit to excavate it."

It was true. She'd been trying for years to gain one. But she was persona non grata here.

Arik's eyes narrowed on her. "You allow me to stay on this boat as a member of your team, and I can guarantee you a permit for anything you need."

"You're lying."

He shook his head. "I have more connections here than you can dream of. Literally."

"And how can I trust you?"

"How can you not? I'm the only hope you have of obtaining what you want most."

She sensed a strange double entendre there. "I don't trust you. How can you get my permits when you can't even remember your own name?"

"I've already told you my name."

"Arik and nothing else."

Arik smiled at her before he took a major risk. "Arik Catranides," he said, using Solin's human surname. It was a bold move given Solin's unpredictability, but his brother owed him this favor, and if he failed to cooperate, Arik would kill him.

Geary stared at Arik suspiciously. For over five years

she'd been bogged down in red tape as the Greek government ran her around so badly she felt like a small plastic car trapped on a racetrack in an endless loop of frustration. She'd gotten nowhere and she was quite certain she'd slammed off the track a few times and landed in a tree . . . face first.

Was it possible for him to get her the permits she needed?

No. Hell no at that. *Nothing is ever going to get them to budge and you know it.* All she had to do was call his bluff and he'd retreat.

"Fine, you want to prove yourself to me, get the permits. But the only way you get to stay on this expedition is if I meet the man who signs them and I watch him put pen to paper. I don't want a forgery that lands me in jail."

"No forgeries. You can trust me, Geary. I promise."

Still not sure she could, or even should, she nodded grimly, then turned to leave. Before she could make a clean exit, he gently pulled her to a stop. She expected him to say something. Instead he merely stared at her with a breathtaking expression that was part incredulous and part devouring. No man had ever looked at her like that.

Face it, at six feet tall, she dwarfed most men, and though she wasn't hideous, she wasn't skinny or beautiful. She was just average and men who looked like Arik weren't interested in women who looked like her.

Except in their dreams . . .

Could this whole day be nothing more than a delusion? Was she dreaming even now?

Arik wanted to tell her that he was here for her and her alone. He wanted her to know what he'd gone through to get here, but from what he knew of humans, she wouldn't react well to that knowledge. Especially not about the part where he'd bartered her soul for it.

But from the moment he'd touched her, words escaped him. He wanted to taste her, to hold her.

"I . . ."

She cocked a brow in expectation.

I want you with me, Megeara. Those words were on the tip of his tongue. They burned there, needing to be spoken. But to say them would cost him the very thing he was trying so hard to get.

"I need to contact my brother."

"Fine," she said softly. "You can see him once we dock."

"But I don't know where he is or how to find him. I'll need your help."

Her eyes turned suspicious once again.

"Please, Megeara."

"Geary," she said from between clenched teeth.

"Please, Geary. I have to find him."

She folded her arms over her chest. "What's his name?"

"Solin Catranides."

Her entire demeanor was one of doubt. "This better not be a trick, do you understand?"

"It's not a trick."

Still her eyes accused him. "Fine. You stay here and I'll let you know when we're back at the marina."

"I shall wait most anxiously."

She just bet he would. Giving him a warning glare, Geary backed out of the door and shut it tight. It was only then that she could breathe again.

Just what was she supposed to do now? Was there any validity to his claims? Or was he completely full of crap?

Unsure of what to believe, she headed topside where Brian and Teddy were chatting.

"Are you all right?" Brian asked as she joined them.

"I guess . . . oh hell, I don't know. Our newest passenger claims he can get us our permits."

Teddy laughed in disbelief. "What? Is he Zeus? Does he know the gods personally? 'Cause no offense, I think that's what it's going to take to get us any kind of permit."

Brian nodded. "I have to side with Teddy. It's beginning to look hopeless. I'm afraid I'm going to have to pull my funding."

Geary was sick to her stomach at the news. Even though she was the co-owner of her father's salvage company, her money was so tied up that she couldn't touch the kind of cash she needed to fund these summer trips.

"C'mon, Brian—"

"I'm sorry, Geary. It's too costly and now we have no permits."

They'd never had permits. At least not legal ones.

"Can you give it a day? Arik swears his brother is good for it."

Teddy snorted in contempt. "Who is his brother? King Constantine?"

"Some guy named Solin Catranides."

Brian's jaw went slack.

A twinge of hope went through her. "You know him?"

"The multi-billionaire playboy? Uh, yeah, I know *of* him. But I've never been able to get close enough to meet him. He's always surrounded by a harem of women trying to become his next pampered mistress."

Geary frowned. That didn't sound like a guy who would have a brother floating in the Aegean.

Then again . . .

"Do you know where we can find him?"

"I can make a few calls and see if my people can locate his people."

That worked for her. "Please do so. I want to know if Arik is lying."

Teddy scratched his cheek. "You know, it could be a different Solin Catranides."

She shook her head at Teddy. How many men could there possibly be with a name like that?

"Hey, you never know," he said defensively.

"Yeah, but what are the odds?"

Teddy laughed. "About as good as fishing a half-naked guy of the sea." He looked at Brian. "You've got to wonder about a guy like that. He wasn't drunk. What? Did he decide to take a swim twenty miles from shore? With no boat?"

"Oh, shut up, Teddy," Geary said playfully.

Brian left them to make his call on the satellite phone with Teddy following one step behind. But as she listened to Teddy's questions, she realized he wasn't being his usual puckish self. For once the man was making sense.

Why was Arik out here alone? How had he come to be in the sea when it was obvious the man couldn't swim?

"Are you okay?"

She turned to find Tory behind her. "I don't know. I'm wondering if maybe we should have left our mysterious swimmer in the water."

Tory frowned. "How not like you. Why would you say that?"

"There's something weird about him, don't you think?"

"You mean aside from the fact he was almost naked in the water?"

"Well, there is that."

Tory shrugged. "I don't know. I'm not the one who was really talking to him. What about him bothers you so?"

Geary smiled at her. "I don't know. Maybe I'm just tired."

"People only say that when they're not really willing to deal with the issue at hand. It's like when you ask a guy what he's thinking and he says 'nothing' but in reality you know he's checking out another woman and he doesn't want you to give him grief over it."

Geary gaped at her unexpected analogy.

"It's Thia's theory."

Geary shook her head. "I think you need to stay away from her before she corrupts you."

"Nah, it's too much fun. She has the most misguided views on everything. But I think what I just said is one of the few lucid thoughts she's ever managed."

Geary had to agree with that, too. "All right, Doogie Howser, go back to the books."

"You know, that's what you always say to me when I've hit too close to home with an observation."

She was right, but Geary wasn't about to let her know that. "Take your little scrawny self off and bug someone else before I make you a human sacrifice, Tor. I'm trying to think, okay?"

" 'Kay. I'll be below deck irritating Scott next if you need me."

Laughing, Geary watched her cousin walk off. God, how she loved that little girl. There was something very infectious about her.

Tory passed Brian in the doorway. By the look on his face, Geary could tell he had bad news.

She met him halfway across the deck. "What's up?"

"Apparently Solin is an only child. He has no brothers, sisters. Hell, not even a guinea pig."

Anger and victory whipped through her. "I knew it! I knew he was lying." Geary took Brian's arm and hauled him back the way he'd come.

"What are you doing?"

"I'm going to confront our guest with this and you're my witness."

CHAPTER 5

ARIK WAS FASCINATED BY THE BRISTLED TEXTURE OF THE blanket on Teddy's bed. It was scratchy and irritating. Why would anyone want that next to their skin? Even the pillowcase wasn't what he'd thought it'd be. In dreams, these items were as soft as air and they slid against his skin like warm water.

But here . . . He shivered.

This was a strange world mankind lived in. No wonder they escaped into dreams.

And he was tired of being here without Megeara. She was proving to be even more elusive in person than she'd been in her dreams. He didn't know where she was, but it was time he found her.

He'd just reached for the door when it swung open so fast he felt the rush of air against his skin.

A warm, sweet emotion went through him as he saw Megeara. At least it started out that way until he noted the look of anger on her face.

"What?" he asked, wondering why she was so vexed now.

"Solin Catranides is an only child."

Arik laughed at the ludicrousness of that statement. As a Dream-Hunter, Solin had thousands of siblings. Literally. "I assure you, he is not."

She gestured to the man behind her. "Tell him, Brian."

"I called a friend who knows him. She assured me that Solin has never mentioned a family of any sort."

Arik gave them a sardonic smile. "I'm sure he wouldn't mention our family to a woman when it's none of her business. Get him on the phone for me."

Geary glared at him over the commanding tone of voice he used. One thing she knew about Brian. He didn't take that tone any better than she did.

Brian's eyes flickered with contempt. "I've already made my inquiries."

"And they were wrong."

Brian tossed the phone at him. "You make your own calls, buddy."

"I don't know the number."

"Then you're screwed."

"Brian," Geary said in a gentle tone, trying to diffuse their prickliness. She took the phone from Arik and returned it to Brian. "Can you get Solin's number for me? I want to speak to him myself."

He curled his lip at Arik. "It's *his* brother. Shouldn't he know the number?"

"Brian, please. He could call any number in Greece and the person who answers it could be anyone pretending to be Solin. I want to make sure that I'm speaking to the right person."

Brian's features softened as he saw the sanity of her

request. "Fine." He took the phone and dialed it. After a few minutes, he pulled a pen and paper from his pocket to jot down the number. He hung up and handed it to her.

Geary frowned at the number. "You're sure this is right?"

"It's the only Solin Catranides I know of. Whether or not it's his brother remains to be seen."

"Okay." She dialed the number and waited while Arik passed a smug look at both of them.

After the sixth ring, a man with a deep British voice answered in Greek.

Geary kept her eyes on Arik, who was watching her back with a blank expression on his handsome face. "Is this Solin Catranides?"

"No. *Kyrios* Catranides isn't available at the moment. If you would like to leave your name and number, I will add your message to the others."

Could he have possibly said that in a snottier tone? Really, the man should teach haughty-butler school—advanced studies. "This is a bit of an emergency—"

"They always say that, *thespeneice*. No offense. The master has no desire to be disturbed this afternoon by anyone."

She narrowed her eyes on Arik, waiting for him to slip and show her if he was lying or not. "Not even for his brother?"

"I beg your pardon?" The snottiness was vacant now, replaced by incredulity.

"I have a man standing in front of me who claims to be his brother."

Now the man's tone was completely flat. "The master has no brother, *thespeneice*."

Before she could respond, Arik pulled the phone from

her hand and spoke something in a language she didn't know. It sounded as if it was Greek-based, but it was something else entirely.

Arik passed another smug look to Brian, then to Megeara. He was getting tired of her mistrust—not that he didn't deserve it. It was merely causing him aggravation—an interesting emotion that. He didn't like it. It was too . . . aggravating. "He's coming to the phone now."

Two seconds later, Solin answered in a peeved tone of voice. "Is this a joke?" he asked in the language that only the gods knew.

Arik answered in kind. "No, Solin, it's not. I need your help."

"If you are what you claim, and since you're using my native tongue, I have no doubt that you are a relative, you don't need my help."

"Yes, I do. I'm trapped on the human plane for two weeks without my powers and I need your assistance until I can go home again."

"I—"

"Don't you dare deny me," he said, clenching his teeth. "Because of you I turned Skoti. You fail to help me now and I can promise you that you'll never again sleep in peace. I'll spend the rest of eternity synched only to you. Every time you close your eyes, I'll be there . . . beating the shit out of you."

"My, that's some threat you've got going."

"No threats. Only promises."

Solin paused before he spoke again. "For the record, I don't take such *promises* lightly."

"And I don't give them lightly. If you doubt me or my skills, ask M'Ordant who I am and what I'm capable of. I've come a long way from the numbed Oneroi you turned centuries ago. I want your help, Solin. I know helping someone goes against your grain, but suck it up and assist me."

There was a few seconds of silence as if Solin was thinking. "If you're here as a human as you claim, I assume you have the backing of a god. Who is it?"

There was no need to hide that from him. If he really wanted to know, it wouldn't take him long to find out. "Hades."

Solin snorted. "You bargained with Hades? Are you insane?"

"I was definitely sane and in control while I was Oneroi. Then someone changed that. What I am now is anyone's guess, even my own."

More silence greeted him.

"All right," Solin said at last. "I don't make this a habit, but you've made me curious. What do you need from me?"

"I need permits for an American archaeologist to excavate Atlantis."

Solin burst out laughing. "I know you're insane now. Have they really found the site?"

"Does it matter?"

"On this plane of existence, yes. You start poking there and you'll piss off people best left alone."

"Since the human's days are numbered, I don't think that's going to be a problem. Let her have a bit of a thrill before she dies. What's the harm?"

Solin sucked his breath in sharply between his teeth. "No, you didn't."

"Didn't what?" Arik asked.

"Promise a soul exchange with Hades. You do have nerve, I'll grant you that."

He wasn't sure if impressing his brother was a good thing or not, but at least Solin sounded a little more agreeable.

"Aside from the permits, what else?"

"That's it. She wants to meet the official who grants them to make sure they're not forgeries."

"How soon do you need this?"

Arik glanced to the other two, who were watching him expectantly. "How soon can you do it?"

Another brief pause. "Give me an hour to arrange it. I have a few government friends who owe me. I just have to decide who I want to intimidate or blackmail."

Arik looked at Megeara and spoke in English. "He needs an hour to set the permits up. Can you meet him then?"

Her jaw slackened before she nodded.

"She can be there," Arik told Solin.

"Good. I'll pick you up."

"Why?"

"Because I have to meet the god who's this arrogant and stupid face-to-face."

Arik wasn't sure if he should be flattered or insulted. Perhaps he should be a little of both. "Then I'll allow the good doctor to give you your directions." He handed the phone to Megeara, who was still gaping.

Geary couldn't believe what she was hearing. Was it really that simple? Could nothing more than a phone call gain her the elusive papers she needed? "Hello? *Kyrios* Catranides?"

"Yes, and you are?"

"Dr. Geary Kafieri."

"Nice meeting you, Doctor. As my brother said, I'll be needing directions on where to pick the two of you up so that we can procure your permits."

Geary still was a bit reserved. It wasn't in her nature to trust people, and especially not after all the years she'd been trying to accomplish what the two of them seemed to be able to do in one hour. "I thought you were an only child."

Solin didn't hesitate with his answer. "Yes and no. I have a number of half siblings. One of whom happens to be Arik. Now if you'll be so kind as to give me your address."

She did, even though she kept expecting this to be a joke.

"Very good," Solin said once she finished giving him the address and directions for the marina. "I shall see the two of you in about an hour."

"Thank you."

He hung up.

Geary ended the call, then handed the phone to Brian. "He's getting us the permits. Do you think he can really do that?"

Brian shrugged. "If anyone can, he can. Solin travels in the highest of circles. Even those I can't ascend to . . . which tells you exactly how much money he has."

She looked to Arik, whose face was completely stoic. "And he's your brother?"

"Yes."

Brian cleared his throat. "Well, if you get those permits, I'll reconsider my backing."

That meant a lot to her. Without his backing, they wouldn't have any choice except to pack up and go home. "Thank you, Brian."

He inclined his head to her before he left them alone.

Arik offered her a seductive smile. "Are you happy now?"

"I don't know if *happy* is the right word. I'm still suspicious of you and your motives."

He clucked his tongue at her. "After all this, how can you continue to mistrust me?"

Was he serious? "Can you blame me? I still don't know you and here you are making grand gestures for no reason. Why would you be willing to help me?"

"Because I find you fascinating. You were so passionate in grad school, and now you're on an impossible quest, just as I am. One has to admire that. Not to mention the small fact that you saved my life. Helping you with the permits is the least I can do." There was something in his eyes as he spoke that glinted and glowed. She felt like a snake with its master charmer who was luring it from its basket to the highway for it to be run over by a Mack truck.

"What do you want from me? Really?" she asked.

"Just a simple smile. Nothing more."

"I find it hard to believe something so small would satisfy you."

His grin turned wickedly warm. "It would at least tide me over for a bit."

Geary wasn't sure what to make of him. On the one hand, he was helping her out in a way no one else could. He didn't owe her anything at all, and yet . . .

Could it be as simple as he was repaying her for saving him? He was Greek and it made sense when put in that context. The Greek people had a strict code of ethics about what was right and wrong. Repayment would be something they would do without hesitation. Perhaps she was being too harsh with him.

"Okay, Arik. I'm sorry I've been so irritable to you. I just don't trust people as a rule, especially those I don't know."

"I understand and we did meet under extremely odd circumstances."

A tiny smile spread across her face as she remembered hauling him on board. "True."

His features softened to the most seductive look she'd

ever seen from any man. "Shall we start over?" He held his hand out toward her. "I'm Arik Catranides."

She shook his hand. "Geary Kafieri, and I still want to know how you ended up in the sea."

He lifted her hand to his lips so that he could place a whisper of a kiss to her knuckles. "And I promise you that one day you will learn the answer to that mystery."

She wasn't sure why, but the hairs on the back of her neck lifted as an eerie chill went down her spine. It was followed by the memory of her dreams where Arikos had bathed her in chocolate whipped cream that he'd licked off her body slowly and easily. But this wasn't that man who'd seduced her.

Was it? Could it be that somehow her subconscious had held on to his memory all these years and it was only now that she needed him that she'd remembered him?

It didn't seem feasible. Yet how else could she explain his presence here on the boat and the fact that he'd been in her dreams these past weeks? She must have remembered him.

And now that she was more relaxed, there was something about him very calm and peaceful. Something that soothed her.

Except for his eyes. They spooked her. They seemed somehow omniscient and powerful. Probing and deadly.

"So where exactly do you live?"

He didn't answer. Instead, he moved behind her and wrapped his arms around her. It was what her dream lover had done a thousand times.

She stiffened in his embrace. "Who are you, Arik? Why are you really here?"

He rubbed his cheek against hers so that his whiskers sent chills over her. "You want Atlantis, yes?" He all but purred that into her ear as desire burned through her.

"Yes."

"Then what else matters?"

The heat in her body for one thing. It was unlike any she'd ever experienced before. All her life, she'd been forced to prove herself to others. And since her father's reputation had so impugned her own, she'd gone out of her way to not allow the fact that she was a woman make the more elitist scholars disregard her. She'd focused her entire life on being a serious scientist, to the exclusion of all else.

But with Arik, it was different. He treated her as a woman and he wasn't repelled by her protective barbs. He saw her as desirable. The novelty of that alone was titillating.

She wanted to close her eyes and lean back into him. To reach up and lay her palm against his whiskers so that she could feel the muscles of his jaw work. It was what she'd do in her dreams.

But this was reality and Dr. Geary Kafieri didn't have time for such play. Even though all she wanted to do was stay where she was, she pulled away. "I need to work."

Arik ground his teeth in frustration. But then, it was the power of her that had lured him to her in the first place. *I want you to stay . . .*

The thought had no sooner gone through his head than she turned on him with a vicious glare. "And I told you I have things to do."

He frowned at the anger in her tone. "Excuse me?"

"You said you wanted me to stay and I can't do that."

He cocked his head. "No, I didn't." He'd only thought it.

"I heard you loud and clear."

"But I didn't speak." How could she have heard him when he didn't have his powers?

Geary didn't know what to think. Something wasn't right about this. She could sense it. She needed to get away from him until she could sort through this.

Without so much as a good-bye, she left him and headed topside so that she could get a breath of fresh air and clear her thoughts.

Thia met her on deck. "Where's Mr. Cutie?"

"Down below."

A wicked smile curved her lips. "Now that's where I'd like to have him . . . *down below*."

Geary rolled her eyes at the bad entendre as a breeze brushed against her and gave her a shiver. She was still in wet clothes, and if they were truly going to meet with any Greek official she needed to change her clothes lest she offend him.

"Have at him, Thee. I'm sure he'd welcome that."

Kat laughed as she passed by them. "I really doubt that."

Geary frowned at the odd note in Kat's voice. At almost six and a half feet tall, she, like Thia, towered over the rest of the crew, women and men alike. Kat was also extremely Greek, with blond hair and sharp green eyes. She'd joined their team only a few weeks ago—right after they'd found the wall they were trying so desperately to excavate. "Do you know something about our guest?"

Kat shrugged nonchalantly. "Nope. Why would I?"

"Hmmm . . ." Geary wasn't so sure if she believed that or not. There was something in Kat's demeanor that said she might be withholding information.

"Kat, you're from Greece, right?"

She laughed again. "Born and raised. I seriously doubt anyone comes more Greek than me, why?"

"Do you really think this guy can help us get our permits?"

Kat sobered. "I guess we'll know soon."

But not soon enough in Geary's book. "All right. I need to change before we dock. I'll see you two shortly."

Kat waited until Geary had vanished belowdecks before she looked at Thia, who at eighteen bore a frightening resemblance to the goddess Artemis. "By the way, I heard Scott was looking for you."

Her face lit up. "Really?"

"Yeah. You better run before he changes his mind."

Thia couldn't have bounded off faster if she'd been wearing Hermes' enchanted sneakers. Which was definitely a good thing.

That should occupy the redhead for at least a few minutes so that Kat could go visit their latest acquisition and not be disturbed or, more to the point, overheard.

As soon as she was sure Thia was out of the way, Kat headed to Teddy's cabin, where Arik had been taken. She knocked once on the door before she pushed it open.

Arik stood by the window with his arms crossed over his chest as he gave her a very cool once-over. "You're not Megeara."

"No, I'm not. But what I'd like to know is how a person like you made it onto this boat."

"A person like me?"

She nodded as she took a step closer to him. "Tall, dark-haired. Sexy beyond belief with eyes so blue they glow? I suppose the question of the day is who's your daddy?"

"I beg your pardon?"

"Who's your daddy?" she repeated before she expanded the question. "Morpheus or Phobetor?"

He gave her a suspicious look. "Who are you?"

"Katra Agrotera. But most people in this realm call me Kat."

She saw the recognition in his eyes. "Agrotera?"

"Yes," she answered his unasked question. Agrotera was one of the names often attached to the Greek goddess Artemis—a name often used by her servants. The very same goddess who'd sent Kat here to watch over the progress of this team. "I'm one of her *koris*."

"What are you doing here?"

"I used to work with Geary's father from time to time, back in the day when the two of them weren't speaking. Since she's getting a little close to the matter at hand, Artemis thought I should put a few roadblocks in front of her."

"And why is that?"

"Simple. Atlantis can't be found."

He scoffed at her. "You're the second person to tell me that in less than an hour. Why is it so important to Artemis that it stay hidden?"

"The why isn't that important. Just believe me when I say you don't want to go there . . . in more ways than one."

He didn't flinch or show any emotion, which given his birth made sense to her. Still, it was time he learned to fear.

When he spoke, his tone was level and deadly. "Megeara wants to find it."

"And people in hell want ice water. The entire history of mankind is written by people wanting something they can't have. She'll get over her disappointment, trust me." She approached him slowly and lowered her tone to make damn sure that no one passing by in the hallway outside could overhear her next words. "But that still doesn't explain how it is a Dream-Hunter is here, in the flesh, on this boat. I'm sure you didn't come to this plane just to help the good doctor on her quest."

He was more guarded than a priceless treasure. "I wanted to know what it was like to be human. Is that a crime?"

"On Olympus, it can be."

"Are you threatening me?"

"I'm warning you to forget you ever even heard the name of Atlantis."

"And if I don't heed your warning?"

"Oh, it'll get ugly. *Real* ugly."

He gave her a cocky grin. "My flesh is used to being stripped from the bone, little girl. Is yours?" He didn't give her time to answer before he continued. "You can't threaten or intimidate someone who won't be able to feel any emotions in a few weeks. Pain doesn't scare me since it's all I know."

"You're a masochistic bastard, aren't you?"

"Isn't that the very nature of a Skotos? After all, it's what your kind damned us to."

Kat paused at his words. It was true. What had been done to the Oneroi was deplorable and unfortunate. But it still didn't change the fact that he couldn't be allowed to uncover Atlantis. Artemis wasn't the only god who would be furious to have it exposed. This little Skotos was playing with a fire he couldn't even begin to understand.

"So you're just here to be human and experience the world? Nothing else?"

"Nothing else."

Kat could almost accept that except for one thing. "And how does Geary fit into this?"

"Who says she does?"

Kat laughed as she noted the speculation in his crystal eyes—he was hiding something. "Don't mistake me for an idiot. You have no god powers, I can feel it. While your kind does come to this plane from time to time to scope out victims, you don't lose your powers when you do it. You've bargained yours to be here and to be human, and you're helping Geary. Why?"

"First you tell me why Artemis is interested in this and then I might answer you."

He was quick and clever. She'd give him that. "All righty then. It appears we've come to an understanding. I stay out of your business and you stay out of mine."

"Fair enough."

Kat looked past him, out the porthole, to see the docks coming into sight. It wouldn't be long before he took Geary for the permits.

Kat stifled a shudder at that. "Just remember one thing, Dream-Hunter. You get in my way and I will sacrifice you for my mission."

He laughed low in his throat. "And to that all I can say is a resounding 'ditto.' I won't let you interfere with why I came here."

She arched a brow at that. "You would dare to threaten me? Have you any idea what happened to the last man who harmed a *kori*?"

He shrugged nonchalantly. "I'm not afraid of Artemis. Even though I'm human now, I won't be for long. My powers will be returned to me in full. Both you and your mistress would do well to remember that."

She tsked at his arrogance. "Oh, Arik, Artemis is the least of your problems if you succeed in finding Atlantis. There are powers so deep and dark buried with that continent that they make a mockery of Zeus. I'm only a minion in the grand scheme of things. You have much more to fear than either me or my lady-goddess. And on that pleasant note, I will leave you with only one more piece of advice."

"Which is?"

"Things are very seldom what they seem. Atlantis and what happened there was a blight on the nose of many a god and many a pantheon. As you know, the gods seldom agree on anything, but they are all united when it comes to this. You would do well to leave here as soon as we dock, and find a new playmate for your dreams."

"So you're lying to Megeara about your presence here. Pretending to help while hindering. How noble of you."

"And you're here to seduce her and do what? Kill her? Is that your plan?"

He looked away and she didn't miss the fleeting grief that darkened his eyes before he hid it. "Does my intent matter since you've already made up your mind to kill her?"

Anger whipped through her at his words. "I've never killed any human. I'm not that cold. Hell, I even tried to save her father and it's for him that I'm watching over Geary now, instead of allowing another *kori* to be here. I don't want to see her die. She's too decent a woman for that. So again, I say to you, move on."

"And if I can't?"

"Then you and I are at war."

"Unfortunate, but I can accept that." He moved to stand before her and she hated the fact she had to look up at him. It was what he'd intended by the action, but it would take more than that to intimidate her. "Stay out of my way, Katra. For your own sake."

Fine then. At least she knew the stakes. Now she just had to visit her friend and do everything she could to get Geary to throw Arik overboard as soon as possible. He was human at the moment and couldn't play with Geary's thoughts or emotions. That was a blessing.

"Oh, don't worry. I intend to be the thorn in your side until I drive you mad with fury. You *may* succeed in seducing Geary, but you're not going to hurt her. Not on my watch."

Arik had opened his mouth to return her comment when he heard the door behind them opening. He turned his head to see the woman Thia standing there, gawking at them.

"Am I interrupting?" Thia asked in a snide tone.

Kat shook her head. "I was just leaving." She gave him a stony look. "Remember what I said."

"Ditto to you."

Fury blazed in her eyes before she pushed past Thia and left them alone. Arik didn't move as he considered this latest turn. So Megeara had one of Artemis's *koris* as a protector. . . .

That did put a bit of a crimp in things, but it by no means deterred him. He wanted to fully experience Megeara as a man. And nothing, not even Zeus himself, was going to stop him.

Now he just had to get Megeara to cooperate.

CHAPTER 6

GEARY HADN'T GONE NEAR ARIK SINCE SHE'D LAST LEFT him. She had no idea whether or not she should believe him, and until she had more facts, she wanted to be as reserved as possible where he was concerned.

They'd just docked and she was in the process of putting her things away for her trip back to town.

She looked up from the table as Tory burst into the room. "Holy Shinola, Gear, you've got to come see this!"

Frowning, she set her pad aside and followed Tory to the deck. Geary looked around but couldn't find anything that should have excited Tory. Nothing looked out of place. Christof and Althea were going over inventory while a couple of the other sailors were checking the lines. Thia was on the deck in a bikini, sunning herself.

"What's up?"

Tory pointed toward the shore.

Geary followed the line of Tory's finger. And as soon as she saw what Tory was pointing to, her jaw dropped.

Holy Shinola nothing. Holy shit and then some.

Just at the edge of the dock was a white Rolls-Royce that had a driver in full chauffeur regalia standing by the door with his gloved hands folded in front of him.

But that wasn't the impressive part. Not by a long shot.

What made her gape was the hot piece of cheese who was on the dock, striding straight for them.

With shoulder-length black hair, the man had a gait that was just plain sexy. It was one of raw determination and extreme confidence. He wore a white linen suit with a pale blue shirt that had been left undone to show the promise of a very well-defined body. On any other man that suit might have brought his sexual preferences into question, but on this one there was no doubt. He was all male and all deadly.

A dark pair of Versace sunglasses covered his eyes, which she had a sneaking suspicion were trained on her.

Tory cleared her throat. "I'm going to go out on a limb here and say that he's Arik's brother. What do *you* think?"

Yeah, that would be her guess. They both held an identical arrogant swagger—as if the world were their stage and they were the only actor in town capable of playing on it.

Without a word to Tory, Geary moved forward to meet the man on the gangplank.

He paused in front of her with a hint of a grin an instant before he deftly removed the sunglasses. Her breath caught as she saw the same exact killer eyes that Arik possessed. It was followed by a dimpled smile so choice that it actually made her heart race.

"*Kyrios* Catranides?"

He offered his hand to her. "You must be Megeara. Pleased to make your acquaintance."

She shook his hand, but before she could let go, he brought it to his lips and laid a very romantic kiss on her knuckles. Her hand actually tingled from the sensation of his lips on her skin. "It's a pleasure to meet you as well."

He released her at the same time the smile faded from his lips. His gaze slid past her.

She turned her head to find Arik standing there. He was silent and cool as he regarded his brother. So cool, in fact, she was about to get frostbite. There was definitely no love lost between them. They looked like two opposing soldiers sizing each other up before battle.

"Arik," Solin drawled in a velvet baritone. "*Long* time no see."

Arik inclined his head to Solin. "Yes, indeed. I hope you've been well."

Solin laughed. "It depends on whom you ask. *Well* has a variety of meanings. But I'm fit enough to cause problems. That really is all one can expect in life, no?"

"It's all I expect out of your life anyway."

Solin tsked at him. "And yet here you are, asking for my help. Call me crazy, but one would expect a little less belligerency."

"Would they?"

Solin seemed to take his brother's challenge in stride as he turned to Geary. "So tell me, lovely lady, where on earth did you happen to find my wayward brother?"

She glanced at Arik over her shoulder to see him watching her before she answered. "Floating in the sea, but he won't tell me how it is he came to be there."

"Knowing Arik, I'm sure he angered someone who threw him in, hoping he'd drown."

"Actually they threw me in hoping I'd land on someone else and drown *them*. Unfortunately, you swam away too fast."

Geary had to stifle a laugh at Arik's unexpected comeback. He had a very dry sense of humor.

"Well, score one for you." Solin returned his sunglasses to his face. "I have the permits waiting, but as a favor to Stefan we should not keep him late in the office or he might change his mind."

Geary practically leapt forward. "Most definitely not."

As they headed for the dock, Thia came running up behind them . . . still in her bikini. The top of which barely held the woman's assets in. "May I join you?"

Solin gave her a speculative once-over that Geary was sure took in her cousin's mussed appearance that somehow managed to seen both seductive and naive.

"I think you should stay here, Thia."

Folding her arms over her chest, which only emphasized the size of said chest, Thia pouted. But it did nothing to change Geary's mind. If anything, it only cemented her decision more. The last thing any of them needed was for Thia to hook up with a billionaire playboy.

Before Geary could wrangle the men to the car, Solin approached Thia with that deadly swagger. He gave her a proper bow before taking her hand and placing a light kiss on it. "Don't fret, love. We'll be back."

Thia preened under his attention. At least until Arik cleared his throat. "Isn't she a bit young for you?"

Solin answered with a deep, evil laugh. His gaze went to Geary for an instant before he released Thia and headed for his car.

"What was that?" Geary asked Arik as they followed along after him.

"His idea of a joke. I'm afraid my brother is a bit of a head case most days. You'll have to forgive him. I'm told he has the intellect of a ten-year-old."

Solin snorted. "And still you aspire to my level. Wow,

Arik. Does this mean you function on the intellect of an infant?"

Instead of being angry, Arik merely stared at his brother. "Perhaps. After all, infants and I do have at least one thing in common."

"And that is?"

Arik's gaze dropped to her breasts. "I think you can figure it out. Then again, maybe not. You are, after all, only functioning on the level of a ten-year-old."

Geary had never been aroused, amused, and highly offended all at the same time before. It was a strange combination. "Could we please change this topic?"

Solin paused at the car as his chauffeur opened the door for him. "Yes, let's."

They allowed her to enter first. Arik followed her in and then Solin. He sat across from them, and even though she couldn't see his eyes, she could tell his gaze was fastened on her.

When he spoke there was no mistaking the note of humor in his tone. "So you seek Atlantis. What an odd quest for such a beautiful lady."

Unlike Thia, Geary wasn't buying into his act. "You charm me, sir. I'm hardly beautiful."

"Not true. All women are beautiful and a woman such as you . . . I'm willing to bet there are some men who are willing to barter their souls just to be close to you."

She laughed out loud. "You should sell snake oil. I'm told it's highly profitable."

"Yes, but I've already made my fortune in other things."

"Such as?"

"Viagra," Arik said drily. "My brother learned to take a personal problem and profit by it."

"It's true," Solin agreed with a heavy sigh. "It pained me to see a man as young as Arik stricken with impotency. Therefore I had to do something to help the poor soul. But alas, there's nothing to be done for it. He's as flaccid as a wet noodle."

Geary had to cover her mouth to keep from laughing out loud.

Arik didn't miss a beat on his comeback. "How creative of you to project your problem onto me. But then, they say that celibacy is enough to make a man lose all reason. Guess you're living proof, huh?"

"Are you two going to battle like this for the rest of the trip?" Geary asked. "Perhaps I should sit up front with the driver and give you two enough space to beat the crap out of each other and settle this like grown adolescents."

Solin gave her a half-amused grin. "No need for that. I think we can manage a bit of a truce . . . for your benefit anyway."

"Hmm . . . makes me wonder why you're being so kind to Arik and me when it's obvious you two aren't exactly friendly."

Solin shrugged. "We're Greek. Family is family no matter what, and we always take care of our own. Right, Arik?"

"Yes . . . in more ways than one."

At that point, Geary gave up. There was something very odd about both men. Maybe she was crazy for even being here with them.

A tremor of fear went through her at that thought. Was she crazy? She'd jumped into the car so fast . . .

Oh God.

She really didn't know anything about these guys. She'd been so excited she hadn't even paused to be her usual suspicious self.

"Are you all right?" Solin asked.

"Fine," she said, trying to calm herself. But it was hard

as her imagination took off with images of them raping and murdering her.

Solin removed his sunglasses. "You're looking a bit pale. You're not thinking that we've kidnapped you so that we can have our way with you, are you, Doctor?"

"No," she said, hating the slight tremor in her voice. Her only consolation was that Brian knew Solin and the crew had seen his car. And all of them knew they were heading to the permits' office. "Why would I ever think such a thing? I mean, I've known you both, what? All of fifteen minutes. Maybe Arik makes it a habit of diving into the sea to catch unsuspecting women so he can lure them into your limo."

Solin passed an amused look to Arik. "Is that how you work, Brother?"

"No. Unlike some people I know, I don't like to frighten women. I find it tiresome." Arik turned in the seat to give her a sincere look. "I'm not here to rape you, Megeara. I told you you were safe, and you are."

She didn't know why, but she believed him. "I'm sorry. It's just been a really bad week for me. Everything has literally turned against me and I've had one disappointment too many."

Solin arched a brow.

Arik glanced at his brother as he heard Solin's voice in his head. *"Disappointed her, have you? And you call yourself an Erotikos Skotos."*

He narrowed his eyes. *"Not me, Solin. She's been harassed by your officials who won't allow her to excavate."*

"Um-hmmm . . . funny, whenever I'm preoccupied with a human, she's too busy trying to get back to me in her dreams to bother with such innocuous quests."

"Megeara is different."

By Solin's face Arik could tell his brother found that hard to believe. *"So tell me, how do you find the human world? Have you ever been here before?"*

"No."

Solin arched a surprised brow. *"Are you overwhelmed by it?"*

"Hardly. But I find parts of it confusing. It's very different from being in dreams."

Solin grinned. *"You've no idea."*

Megeara turned to Arik. "So why is Atlantis so important to you? I mean, if you could get permits this easily, why haven't you?"

Arik hated having to lie to her, but if he didn't give her some plausible answers, as skittish as she was, she'd flee and never let him near her again. "I didn't know where to dig for it. All of my research turned up nothing. It wasn't until I was speaking with Spiro the other day and he mentioned you that I had a clue."

"Spiro?"

"Gavrilopoulos. He turned you down two weeks ago." And luckily she'd mentioned the event and the man's name to Arik in her dreams. "I've been looking for you ever since to ask you about your findings. He said you were most emphatic about the site you wanted to excavate."

She sat back in the seat with a peeved expression. "So you know the little weasel."

"Weasel?" Solin asked curiously.

"Hmm . . . he laughed so hard over my request I thought he was going to choke and die from it."

Arik tried to placate her. "He can be a little callous."

"Callous, nothing. He was downright rude."

"Well," Solin drawled, "your luck is about to change."

Geary wanted to believe that. She could use a bit of

good luck in her life. And if not good, then at least mediocre.

Needing to distract herself from that line of thought, she looked at Arik. He didn't seem like the kind of guy who would be interested in anthropology. Both he and Solin seemed too self-absorbed to think about the past or the future. They appeared more the "me, me, me, now, now, now" kind.

"So what got you so interested in Atlantis?" she asked Arik. "How did you know what my necklace was?"

His eyes gleamed with amusement. "Do you ever ask a single question?"

"Sorry. It's the professor in me. One question invariably leads to another, and so as not to waste time, I generally ask both and then seek the answer. And speaking of, you still haven't answered my last two."

"Yes, Arik," Solin said with a hint of laughter in his voice. "Why are you so fascinated by Atlantis?"

Arik cut a nasty glare at his brother that she couldn't even begin to fathom. Why would that question upset him?

"I'm always intrigued by the unknown," Arik said, glancing back at her. "They say Atlantis is a myth, but I know better. I believe in it." He met Solin's gaze. "In fact, I think the gods still walk among us, even here and now."

Solin made a rude noise at Arik's conjecture.

Geary frowned at him. After the way her father had been treated while being right, she wasn't about to laugh at anyone else's beliefs. It pained her to see Solin so cruel. "You still haven't explained how you knew what my necklace was."

"I know a man who wears a similar medallion. He was the one who first told me stories of Atlantis."

Her jaw went slack at Arik's revelation. Someone else had found one? "Really?"

He nodded.

She was intrigued by the possibility. "Is he Greek? How did you meet? Could *I* meet him? I'd love to know where he got his necklace."

Arik shook his head. "Again with the multiple questions."

"Time is fleeting and I need answers."

He took pity on her. "Yes, he's Greek, and I met him back when I was very young. Sadly, he no longer mentions Atlantis. I think there's something about it that grieves him."

"You have *no* idea," Solin said with a laugh. "Acheron would kill you to hear you speak of him in such a manner."

Arik kicked at his brother's foot before he turned his attention back to Geary. "But enough about me. What changed your mind about finding it?"

"My father. I promised him when he died that I'd find it for him."

"That was kind of you."

Geary looked away as her emotions choked her. She only wished she'd been kinder to him when he'd been alive.

Solin let out a long breath as if her emotions upset him, too. "Well, let's all get maudlin, shall we?" He reached up and pressed a button for the intercom to buzz his driver.

"Yes, sir?"

"George, stop on the way and get us some red-hot pokers to put out our eyes. Oh, and while you're at it, I think we should see about adding salt for our wounds, too."

"Quite good, sir," the driver said in a dry tone. Then without missing a beat, he continued, "Is there any particular place you'd care for me to stop? I've heard the market is a good place for pokers. That is, if you're agreeable to a short detour."

Solin appeared to consider it. "What do you two think? Run-of-the-mill pokers, or a better quality? Oh hell, why not use rusty spoons? They'd hurt more."

Geary shook her head. "You are a sick man."

Solin arched a brow at her. "So are you telling me you're going to pass on my offer?"

"Call me crazy, but yeah. I think I'll pass."

"Okay. Thanks, George. It appears we'll go without the pokers after all."

"Very good, sir. Should I still stop for that salt?"

Again Solin appeared to seriously consider it before he answered. "No, I think we're fine for now."

"Very good, sir."

Geary let out a nervous laugh as she glanced back and forth between Solin and Arik. The two of them were so odd. And they had the most offbeat humor she'd ever encountered. "You two must have been a lot of fun growing up. I'll bet your poor parents are still having nightmares."

Solin burst out laughing. "Oh, you have *no* idea."

"You know I feel like I'm on the outside of this inside joke you two keep passing around."

"Ignore Solin," Arik said quietly. "I told you he's demented."

"Yes, but I taught Arik well. Didn't I, Brother?"

Geary didn't miss the fleeting glimmer of rage in Arik's eyes. It was subtle but unmistakable.

The car slowed down and turned a corner that Geary knew better than the street where her flat was. She'd walked this way so many times over the last five years that she could do it blindfolded.

They were almost there.

Frustrated doom settled like a lump in her chest as the driver parked on the street in the same exact location the taxi had used earlier that day.

It's just getting better and better.

The driver opened the door to let her out on the sidewalk. Arik came out behind her and then Solin, who left the car with a masculine flourish. Several women on the street practically swooned.

"Greetings, my lovelies," Solin said flirtatiously as he gave them a seductive grin.

They whispered among themselves as they continued on their way while glancing back to look at him.

Arik passed a droll look to Geary. "Strange how women can't help staring at a train wreck, eh?"

Solin rolled his eyes at Arik's remark. "Like you would know."

"True. I'm never a train wreck myself. I merely admire the way you skid from the tracks and burn."

As they approached the government building, a uniformed guardsman opened the door to admit them.

Geary started for the stairs only to have Solin divert her. "We don't go up there with the average people. Our man is this way."

She frowned at Arik before she followed Solin into an elegant office that was filled with Greek antiquities. The anthropologist in her was instantly fascinated by the perfectly preserved black figure vase in a glass trophy case. She'd never seen a more preserved piece. It was absolutely exquisite.

She splayed her hand against the glass as she stared in awe of the piece. "It's from the first century."

She sensed Arik standing behind her. "The battle of Troy. You can see Achilles dragging Hector around the walls."

Geary nodded as she saw them. "There's not a chip on it."

"Which is why it's in the case."

She turned at the perturbed voice to find a portly gentleman in his early sixties. She'd seen him here a time or two when she'd come in the past, but she had no idea of his name or job title.

He rocked back and forth on his heels as he sized her up. "Dr. Kafieri, I presume?"

"Yes."

He narrowed a look on her that said he didn't think much of her before he let out a suffering sigh. He turned toward Solin. "I hope you won't forget this favor."

"Believe me, I won't."

The portly man gave a curt nod before he took them into a small office with a black desk that was scattered with papers.

Geary's heart stopped as she saw the very things she'd been craving.

The permits.

She wanted to run to them, snatch them up, and cradle them to her chest. But without a signature and seal, they were worthless. Still, this was the closest she'd been to one. Her breath caught anxiously in her throat.

Without a word, he picked up the permits as if they didn't mean the world to her and sat behind his desk before he signed them and stamped them.

She reached for the permits without thinking, only to have him pull them away.

Again he narrowed those penetrating eyes on her. "You do understand that any artifact you find is Greek property? I expect full records to be delivered to me on a weekly basis, along with any findings you uncover."

"I understand."

He held the papers a moment longer before he finally extended them to her.

Her hand actually shook as she finally touched the permits. Honestly, she felt like crying. This was the closest she'd been to fulfilling her promise since Cosmo had given her her father's belongings. "Thank you," she said, her voice cracking from the raw emotions inside her.

"Don't thank me, Dr. Kafieri. Just respect your word to me and the favor I've done today. If I regret this moment, I assure you what I feel will be a trifle to what I'll put you through."

"I understand, sir. Believe me, you won't regret this at all."

"Then see to it that I don't."

Nodding, she held the permits to her chest and turned to offer Arik a tenuous smile.

Arik couldn't breathe as foreign emotions seized him. Her eyes were filled with unshed tears, but it was the gratitude in them that touched him most. He'd never felt anything like this. Her pleasure was so great that he could feel it himself.

"Thank you," she breathed.

All he could do was nod his head at her as he struggled to understand these strange emotions in him that made no sense. His throat was tight. His heart pounding. He wanted to laugh and to cry and he didn't know why. He'd never known such confusion. No wonder Hades had profaned emotions.

They were baffling.

Solin inclined his head toward the door. "Why don't the two of you go on to the car? I'll be out momentarily."

Arik opened the door for Megeara.

He'd barely closed it when she turned on him with a giddy laugh. She threw her arms around him and kissed him on the cheek as she jumped up and down against him.

Heat scorched him as her breasts pressed against his

chest and her soft lips brushed his skin before she pulled away. "I can't thank you enough for this." She let out a strange noise before she twirled around. "Oh my God, I can't believe this. I can't believe I'm finally holding my permits! Legal ones, too, and I didn't have to kill anyone to get them!" She made a strange "yee"-like noise before she hugged him again.

Unable to stand the onslaught to his body, he pulled her to him and kissed her.

Geary melted at that taste of Arik's lips. She was so excited and happy, she'd have done anything for him at the moment. Anything!

Or so she thought.

The moment he started lifting the hem of her dress up, she jerked back with an indignant squeak. Her jubilation snapped straight to anger. "What do you think you're doing?"

He looked completely baffled by her anger. "I thought . . ."

"What? That you could lift my dress and screw me in an open hallway? Are you insane?"

Solin froze in the doorway as he heard her words. "What did I just miss?"

She turned on him. "Your brother is an absolute jerk. He just lifted my dress up. Here. In public." And still Arik looked confused by her anger.

Disgusted with them both, Geary turned and stalked back toward the car.

Solin gaped at Arik. "What did you do?"

Arik held his hands up in frustration. "She kissed me. It turned me on, so I—"

"No, you didn't," Solin snapped, interrupting him. "Arik, are you an idiot? You could have exposed us all."

Rage flamed inside him at the insult. "It's what we've done before when she's gotten the permits in her dreams. She likes the way I touch her."

"Yes. *In dreams*. This isn't a dream. You're in the human world and people don't behave like that here. Now, Brother, you understand why I venture into the dream realm. There are certain behaviors and rituals you have to practice in this world. You don't just eye a woman here and then jump her. Damn. You're lucky she didn't slap you or have you arrested."

Arik raked his hand through his hair as he understood her anger, but it didn't do anything to sate the fire in his groin. "I came here to be with her."

"And you keep that up and you'll spend your time here behind bars. Damn, Arik, damn."

"I told you I needed your help."

Solin ground his teeth at those words. It wasn't in his nature to help anyone. Unlike Arik, he wasn't a full god. He'd been tossed out into the world of man and left here to suffer while the rest of his kind lived on Olympus or the Vanishing Isle, far away from the prejudice and fear of humans. And if that wasn't enough, the gods themselves had come after him to punish him over a birth defect he'd never wanted. He'd barely survived their relentless attacks.

Now one of them expected him to offer a help that had never been extended to him. It was almost enough to make him laugh.

He wasn't even sure why he'd come here today. Arik's threat of invading his sleep meant nothing to a man who'd had assassins after him in that realm. He'd earned his reputation for ruthlessness and he was proud of it.

Yet in all these centuries he'd never heard of a god trading his sanctity to be human. The only gods on this plane had been cursed or stripped. No one lived in this realm voluntarily.

No one.

Except Arik. "Why are you here? Really?"

Arik looked away without comment.

"Answer my question or I walk." He saw the anguish in Arik's eyes before he spoke in a low tone.

"You've always been human. You've always had feelings. You don't know what it's like to have them and then feel them leave you. The numbness is tolerable most of the time. But with Megeara . . ."

"You love her?"

Arik gave him a peeved glare. "How could I ever love anyone?"

He had a point. Self-sacrifice and such were alien concepts to Dream-Hunters.

Arik let out a deep breath. "I just want to understand where her passion comes from. Why something as simple as a drink of lemonade can make her laugh. Why her eyes light up when she dances in the waves. And why the thought of her father makes her cry, even in dreams."

Solin shook his head. Unlike his brother, Solin understood all of that. Emotions weren't a gift. They were the ultimate curse of the gods. What Arik didn't realize was that Zeus had done them a favor by demanding they be stripped of all their feelings.

It was why Solin had unleashed the human on Arik all those centuries ago. He'd been jealous of the emptiness the Oneroi lived in and he'd wanted them to suffer the way he had. He wanted them to crave things they couldn't touch.

To know what they were missing.

What he'd done had been cruel and he knew it. But the sad thing was he felt no regret over it. How could he?

Even now the Oneroi sought him in his sleep. He never had rest. No respite. They were evil bastards, all of them.

And yet as he stood here with a brother he didn't want to claim, something foreign tickled in Solin's chest. It was pity. Compassion. Two things he'd sworn he'd never feel again for anyone.

He hated Arik for that.

"Will you help me?" Arik asked.

Solin nodded. He'd help Arik all right, but not for the reasons he thought. Solin was going to do everything in his power to let Arik be human. To know Megeara to the fullest extent that was possible, so that when she died because of him, Arik would truly understand exactly what it meant to be human.

He was going to suffer as no god had ever suffered.

CHAPTER 7

GEARY SAT IN THE CAR, STARING AT HER PERMITS AS IF they were the mythical Holy Grail that had miraculously dropped into her lap while George politely ignored her. She didn't know what was keeping the men. Maybe Arik had found some other woman to molest. . . .

That bizarre thought triggered an odd jealous twinge—which really made no sense. At the moment, she'd gladly pay someone to take Arik off her hands.

"George?"

He met her gaze in the rearview mirror. "Yes, miss?"

"How long have you worked for Solin?"

"Long enough, miss. Long enough."

Boy, wasn't he the font of all information?

Before she could continue her questioning, the guys finally left the building.

They were much more subdued as they joined her in the car.

Solin offered her a tight-lipped smile. "Are you happy now, Dr. Kafieri?"

"Thrilled beyond belief."

"Good." He cleared his throat. "By the way, I would like to apologize for my brother's unconscionable behavior."

"I don't need you to apologize for me, Solin. I'm quite capable of doing it myself."

If George hadn't picked that exact second to pull into traffic, she'd have swung the door open and left. "And just out of curiosity, what made you think that that behavior was appropriate?"

Arik sighed. "I wasn't thinking at all. The truth is you surprised me and I reacted poorly. For that I'm truly sorry. I would never have insulted you in any way."

Okay, so the guy could be charming when he put forth the effort . . .

But she still wasn't quite ready to let him off the hook. "Do you always make it a habit of groping a woman's private places in public?"

Arik narrowed his gaze as he returned her question with one of his own. "Do you make it a habit of throwing yourself against men and kissing them in public?"

Her face flushed as a feeling of dread consumed him. He'd offended her. Again. Damn, being human was hard.

"No, I don't," she snapped, her eyes blazing. "And I can assure you that I will never do such a thing again. Especially not to you and not in public, private, or anywhere else."

"Good going, Arik," Solin said snidely in his head. *"Any more brilliant apologies and you'll be able to sell icicles on the equator."*

He glared at Solin. *"Have you a better one?"*

"Tell her that you couldn't help yourself, you were

overwhelmed by her beauty. That she is the most desirable woman you've ever kissed and because of that your emotions ran away with you."

"I don't think that's going to work."

"Trust me, it always works."

Arik wasn't so sure, but since Solin had more experience on this plane, he decided to listen to him. "I couldn't help myself, Geary. I was overwhelmed by your desire and I've never kissed a woman more beautiful than you."

Instead of placating her, that only seemed to anger her more.

"That's not what I said, Arik. Jeez."

"You were overwhelmed by my desire?" she said, enunciating each word slowly so that they conveyed the full weight of her anger. "What planet are you from?"

"Moronia," Solin said out loud. "Every full moon they teleport the Morons to earth and let them loose. Consider this your first encounter."

"Shut up, Solin," Arik said from between clenched teeth. Then he projected, *"I told you it wouldn't work."*

"It would have had you said it the way I told you to."

Before he spoke to Megeara, Solin glared at him. "I hope you can forgive my brother, Doctor. He was raised in the mountains where there wasn't any real civilization of any sort. He's basically a goat farmer and he isn't used to interacting with people. He lacks many social skills."

"Oh, thank you. Why not tell her that I wet the bed in my sleep while you're at it?"

"If it'll work, I will."

Megeara, gave him a gimlet stare. "Is that the truth?"

"Yes," Arik said. "I haven't had much interaction with human people."

She gave a light laugh. "Human people, huh? Are there any other kind?"

As a matter of fact there were, but now didn't seem like the time or place to educate her on that.

Grateful that her mood was lighter, he offered her a small smile. "Can you forgive me for my behavior? Please."

She looked down at the permits in her lap, then smiled. "I think I can, but only if you promise to never do something like that again."

"I swear it on Solin's life."

Solin sputtered. "Uh, excuse me?"

"I would, but there's truly no excuse for you."

He folded his arms over his chest. "Ha, ha."

Geary rolled her eyes at them, but deep inside, their bantering play made her ache. She and Jason used to bait each other like that. It would drive her father to distraction, and the weird thing was neither she nor Jason knew why they did it.

It must have been innate sibling behavior that made them constantly pick at each other. Jason had been a smart, good-looking teenager who would have followed her father to the ends of the earth without complaint.

God, how she missed Jason.

"Are you all right, Megeara?"

She met Arik's concerned gaze before she nodded. "Sorry, I was just thinking about something."

"Something?"

"Personal," she finished.

He nodded and she was grateful that he didn't pursue his line of questioning. Any time she thought about Jason, it made her cry.

"So what do we do now in preparation for the excavation?" Arik asked, changing the subject.

When she didn't respond quickly enough, Arik pointed toward her permits. "Remember our bargain?"

"I remember."

Solin sat forward on the seat. "What bargain is this?"

"That I would allow Arik to participate on the team if he came through with the permits."

Solin arched a brow. "Really? Well, in that case I want to join you."

Geary was aghast at his request. The boat was crowded enough with their team, they really didn't need anyone else. And especially not someone who would only get in the way. "I don't think that's a good idea. You don't strike me as the academic type."

A seductive smile curled his lips. "Oh, I assure you, I'm extremely knowledgeable about this subject. So much so that some swear I actually lived in ancient Greece."

Yeah, right. Mr. Rolls and Armani in a library—why did that image just not jibe with her? Oh wait, because he might get dust on his Ferragamos.

"Uh-huh. *You* study ancient history?"

"All the time."

She narrowed her gaze on him. "Fine. Give me the date of the Peloponnesian War."

"Which one?"

Geary was amazed that he knew even that much. "The first one."

"It began 431 B.C. between the Peloponnesian League led by Sparta and the Delian League led by Athens. Archidamus II, who was leading the Spartans, believed that he could keep them in a land war, which Sparta was unrivaled at, that would weaken Athens. Their commander Pericles believed he could use the Athenian navy, which was the backbone of Athenian power, to weaken Sparta. Needless to say, the war lasted much longer than either side intended. And while I find the writings of Thucydides a little on the dry side, I have to admire the way Aristophanes was able to poke fun at the leaders and events of the time." He paused for effect. "Of course this is all an extremely cursory overview that trivializes the entire event into an absurd CliffsNote."

Geary had to force herself not to gape at his unexpected dissertation and commentary. "Okay, so you're not faking. I have to say that I am impressed. It's not often I find anyone who has even the most modest understanding of what I'm talking about."

"Don't be. You'll find both Arik and myself quite useful when it comes to understanding antiquities."

She looked at Arik. "And what was your favorite event of the war?"

"I prefer the Peace of Nicias. Time's too precious to waste it with war and conflict."

His words made her smile. "But the peace was fraught with skirmishes and ultimately broken."

"Yes, and doesn't it piss you off that there are always assholes who just can't let other people live in peace? Really, some people should get a life."

He had a point with that. In more ways than one.

George pulled to a stop at the marina.

Geary glanced out at her boat where she could see Tory and Teddy sitting together while they compared notes. "Well, it looks like I'm home."

Arik reached out and gently took her hand. "What about our bargain?"

She really hated that bargain. When they'd made it, she'd thought he was kidding, but then again, she owed him much for what he'd given her today. "Fine. You guys can come. We're not going to do anything tonight except prepare for tomorrow's dig. Be here at dawn, *sharp*. I won't wait for you."

"We'll be here."

Solin groaned. "What is it with you morning people?"

Geary tsked at him. "You don't have to join us, you know."

Arik met her gaze without humor. "We'll be here."

"Then I'll see you tomorrow."

George opened her door and she left the men to themselves.

Arik didn't speak until after George had shut the car door. Then he turned back to Solin. *"What do you think you're doing?"* he projected the thought to his brother to keep the driver from overhearing them.

"Nothing," Solin said out loud.

Still, Arik wasn't placated. He knew Solin was up to something. Why else would he come on Megeara's expedition when he had no reason to? "Megeara belongs to me."

Solin scoffed at Arik's anger. "I have no interest in her, believe me. She's all yours."

"Then why are you coming?"

His face sobered. "To make sure *you* don't screw up. Have you any idea how bad it would be if they learned what you are?"

Relieved that was Solin's only reason, Arik sat back in the seat. "They won't."

"No, they won't, which is why I'm going with you. I'll be there to help cover any blunders you make. Now can you at least say, 'Thank you, Solin'?"

He said it from between clenched teeth and with no real sincerity. "Thank you, Solin."

"You're welcome." He pressed the button for his intercom. "George, it appears my brother is in desperate need of clothing."

"Very good, sir. I'll head to the store right now."

TORY MET GEARY ON THE GANGWAY. HER FACE WAS SO hopeful that it brought tears to Geary's eyes. "Well?"

Geary forced herself not to smile as she shook her head no.

Tory cursed until Geary handed her the permits. It took a full ten seconds before Tory realized what they were.

She literally jumped up and down. "Oh my God!"

"Yes."

"Oh my God!"

"Yes, Tory."

Screaming, she ran up the gangway, then stopped at the top and ran back to Geary. "They're not forgeries, are they?"

"No."

She screamed again and ran to tell Teddy.

Geary laughed at Tory's exuberance. For once she was acting her age.

By the time Geary reached the deck, the entire team was there.

"You really got them?" Teddy asked.

"I got them. We're starting at dawn."

You would have thought she'd brought home the winning lottery ticket—but then, maybe she had. All of them had been aching for this for years and now their patience had paid off.

They were going excavating.

Geary paused as she noted the reservation on Kat's face. "Is something wrong, Kat?"

"Oh no. I'm just stunned. I have to say that I never expected this."

"Yeah, I know. It's unbelievable."

"Yes," Kat said coldly, "it is."

"Aren't you excited?" Tory asked.

"Thrilled." But Kat's tone belied the word.

Geary frowned, wondering what had Kat so upset. But the rest of the team's happiness and her own quickly had her forgetting all about it as they planned what they were going to do once they'd found Atlantis.

Kat stood back as the group headed below the deck and a chill went down her spine. Geary had found the location and Arik had just handed her the key to the door.

"You can't let them snoop around the remains, Katra. . . ." Artemis's words rang in her ears. *"If you do, they will find the seal and release the Destroyer back into this world. Should Apollymi ever be freed, I know I don't have to tell you what she would do to us.* To me. *You can't let her be free. Ever."*

That was easier said than done, especially since Kat could hear Apollymi calling out to her from her prison in Kalosis. Apollymi wanted her freedom as badly as the rest of the gods wanted her trapped.

And Kat was caught in the middle.

But at the end of the day, she knew the real reason she had to keep Atlantis hidden. If anyone ever learned the truth of what had happened to the island, the one person who would be destroyed was the one person she loved more than anyone else.

Acheron Parthenopaeus.

Eleven thousand years ago he'd been enslaved to Artemis, and he had been mankind's champion ever since. He was the leader of the goddess's army of Dark-Hunters who protected humanity from the demons who preyed on them. And while he protected the Dark-Hunters and humans, no one had ever watched his back.

Except for Kat.

For him alone, she would do whatever she had to to keep this place sacred and buried. And if that meant sacrificing every person on this boat, including Geary, so be it.

No one would ever hurt Acheron. Not if Kat could help it.

CHAPTER 8

GEARY WAS LAUGHING WITH TEDDY AND SCOTT WHEN she caught a shadow out of the corner of her eye. Thinking it was Kat come to join them, Geary turned her head to welcome her in. Until she saw Arik standing in the doorway—just as she'd imagined him earlier that day. A chill of déjà vu washed over her as her humor fled. There was no denying the hunger in his light eyes as he watched her. The predatory gleam. All he had to do was extend his hand toward her and it would be her dream all over again.

Was all of this a premonition?

Tory caught Geary's distraction and turned to look. Like Geary, she went mute, and as the rest of the crew noted the women's behavior, they followed suit. Suddenly their laughter and good cheer turned into a rigid and questioning silence.

Geary cleared her throat as she approached Arik, who

didn't seem to be the least bit concerned or disturbed by their silence. "What are you doing here?" she asked in an emotionless tone.

Oblivious to the tenseness of the others, he shrugged. "I know how much this means to all of you, so I wanted to join in your celebration . . . that is, if you don't mind."

That seemed to soothe everyone in the room but her.

"Come on in," Teddy said, handing Arik a plastic cup of Cristal—yeah, it was a cheap way to serve the best, but they'd been saving the champagne for this particular event. Geary had two more bottles stashed for when they found hard-core proof of Atlantis's location. Then the real celebration would begin.

This was, Geary hoped, just the warm-up, with everyone drinking except the divers and Tory.

The team returned to their party.

Moving closer to her, Tory touched her gently on the arm. "Are you okay?"

"I'm fine," she said with a fake smile before she made her way from Tory to Arik.

Scott clanked his cup with Arik's. "Man, we can't thank you enough for getting those permits. You really have no idea what this means to all of us."

Arik inclined his head before he took a drink of champagne. As soon as it touched his tongue, he gasped and sputtered, then immediately started choking.

Scott pounded Arik on the back as Geary took the cup from his hand.

"Are you all right?" Teddy asked.

Coughing, Arik nodded. "I wasn't expecting it to be so . . . ,"—he curled his lips—"so strange tasting."

"Strange?" Teddy asked, gulping his. "This is the best shit to be had."

Geary remembered what Solin had said about Arik's sequestered upbringing. "Have you ever had champagne before?"

He shook his head.

Scott gaped. "Get out. Where you been living, under a rock?"

Arik cleared his throat. "Not exactly. But close."

Geary set his cup aside. "Arik was raised in the Greek countryside, away from civilization."

Scott shuddered. "Man, that sucks. I went up there once a couple of years ago and it was enough to convince me that I like American plumbing, if you know what I mean. And since you're from up there, I know you do."

Teddy and Scott exchanged a horrified look before Geary pulled Arik out of the room so that she could speak to him alone. Not that they had much privacy in the hallway, but at least they weren't in direct line of sight and hearing of the others.

She crossed her arms over her chest as she narrowed an agitated glare on him. "I thought you were going with Solin."

Arik looked less than apologetic. In fact, he was actually charming as he offered her a lopsided grin. "I don't want to be with Solin. I want to be with you, especially while you're happy."

On the one hand that was flattering, but on the other it made her nervous. She didn't like the feeling of being stalked by him . . . granted, most of her discomfort was caused by the fact that she'd seen him in her dreams these last few months. That wasn't his fault, but still . . . "Thank you, and while I can appreciate that, I don't like clingy men. I've always needed my personal space, okay? I mean, really, I barely know you."

Arik nodded as a fierce pain settled in his chest from her words. It constricted his breathing and made him literally ache. What was this sensation? He'd never felt anything like it before. Strange emotions seemed to be gathering in his throat to choke him. It was a physical pain and yet there was no physical reason for it. He didn't understand.

"Please, Megeara. Don't be angry at me. I don't have a lot of time left and I don't want—"

Geary cocked her head at his offhand comment. "What do you mean you don't have a lot of time left?"

He tensed as if he'd let something slip he hadn't meant to. "I meant . . . It's nothing. Forget I said anything." He started past her.

Geary gently pulled at his arm to stop his retreat. "Wait a sec. Go back to the 'lot of time' comment. What did you mean by that? Are you leaving to go back to the mountains?"

He was sheepish now. Not the man in charge who was on comfortable ground. Something about his demeanor reminded her of a little boy. "No."

"Are you going back to Solin's or your house?"

He shook his head.

"Then what exactly did you mean?"

He met her gaze and the anguish there actually made her heart ache for him. "I don't have a lot of time left here in this world. I'm going to have to leave it soon . . . *very* soon."

In the back of her mind that was what she'd suspected he meant, but having him say it out loud cut through her a lot more than it should. She'd lost so many people who were close to her that the thought of his dying so young tore her apart. "Are you telling me that you're dying?"

Arik hesitated. He didn't want to lie to her, but in a way it wasn't a lie. He would cease to exist as a human in two weeks and he would never again be here.

Ultimately, he settled on being completely honest. "My body was given an expiration date."

Geary covered her mouth with her hand as a wave of pity washed over her. He looked so healthy and prime. How could a man like this be dying? It didn't make sense. "Are you sure?"

He gave a light, nervous laugh. "Yeah. I couldn't be more positive."

"Oh, Arik, I'm so sorry."

"Don't be. I'm just glad I have any time here at all."

Those words touched her deeply. That he could look at the positive at a time like this and not be angry or bitter over the injustice spoke volumes about his character. She couldn't imagine being told that she only had a finite time to live. How awful it would have to be.

"I don't understand why you'd help me get my permits when I'm sure you had a lot better things to do with your life."

His handsome features softened. "I wanted you to have your dream before I left."

She couldn't understand his altruism. People just weren't that kind. "Why?"

He reached out and cupped her face in his warm hand. "You live your life like it's a rare treasure to be savored. You take pleasure from the simplest of things and you never take them for granted. I saw the joy on your face and the life in your eyes when you cradled the permits to your chest. I've never seen anything lovelier. I actually thought you would cry just from the joy of touching them. I've been numb all my life, Megeara, but you . . . you feel on a level that I can't even imagine, and for a little while I wanted to feel that, too."

And she felt like crying now at the thought of this gentle, considerate man dying. "How long do you have?"

Grief tainted the luster of his eyes. "Two weeks."

"Two weeks?" she repeated, her chest tightening even more. "Are you kidding?"

"No."

There was no mistaking the sincerity in his gaze. The man was really dying, or at least he believed it. "Well, maybe your doctor's wrong. Have you gotten a second opinion?"

"I don't need one," he said with a bitter laugh. "You can trust me on this. In two weeks, I won't be here, at least not with a human body."

And he had come to help her in his last days. . . .

"Oh, Arik," she breathed before pulling him close and hugging him. "I'm so sorry."

Arik couldn't breathe as her breasts pressed fully against his chest. Heat coiled through him, making his entire body burn. His groin tightened and swelled as he thought of how many times they'd touched like this and yet he'd never really felt it.

"Is there anything I can do?"

"Just be with me for a little while."

Why was that so important to him? "Don't you have a girlfriend or family you'd rather be with?"

"Only Solin, and honestly, he's not this soft. Even if he was, it'd be gross."

Stifling a laugh, she tightened her hold on him.

Arik leaned his cheek against her head and inhaled the sweet scent of sea and woman. There was a faint trace of peaches on her skin as her hair tickled his lips. He closed his eyes and savored the feeling of her against him. It was miraculous and wonderful, and it left him cold that he'd have to leave this behind and return to his sterile world again.

And she would be dead because of him. . . .

He winced with the thought. Regret had been something he'd never experienced as a Skotos, but he felt it now and it stung deep.

What have I done?

The only consolation he had was that when he returned to the Vanishing Isle, he wouldn't have human emotions to haunt him. No regret or sorrow.

Nor would he have Megeara's dreams. . . .

An aching pressure tore through him. It was raw and open and made him want to shout from the weight of it.

How did humans live with these feelings all the time? Honestly, they were enough to wear him out. To make him afraid to even move for fear of tweaking them to full capacity.

Basically, emotions sucked. Hades had been right. The gods had done the dream gods a favor by making them numb. And even knowing that, he still savored his emotions.

Megeara stepped away from him and took his hand in hers. The softness of her skin radiated through his body. "C'mon. Let's go back to the party and celebrate what you've given us."

AS SHE STOOD AT THE PROW, KAT FELT A BITTER CHILL THAT had nothing to do with the weather. It whispered against her skin like a light kiss, and it was the last sensation she wanted to experience tonight.

Unfortunately, she'd known this was coming.

"What the hell is going on here?"

She turned slowly toward the deep baritone voice to find an exceptionally tall and handsome man whose violet eyes were cutting even in the darkness. His dark blond hair was windswept and streaked with lighter tones that only emphasized the masculine beauty of his face. Zebulon, or ZT as he preferred to be called, was a creature of extreme power and nastiness.

Like the others of his kind, no one knew when or where he'd been born. All they knew was that he held enough power to kill a god with a single act. God killers, or Chthonians as they preferred to call themselves, were a rare breed and ZT was one with an unholy attitude.

He stood before her now, dressed in jeans and a long-sleeved maroon T-shirt that had the Greek phrase Σας προσέχω, είμαι φοβισμένος—"I am watching you, be afraid"—stenciled in gray on it. How apropos, since that was what he did. Aeons ago, he and his brethren had banded together as policemen for the gods. They were the check-and-balance system for the universe.

Until they'd turned on one another for reasons known only to themselves.

Now the handful who survived watched over mankind with a bitter eye and with no real leader. Rather, they were the epitome of a cold war where they were only kept in check by one another and rarely got along—unless it was to go after a god who'd stepped over whatever line they'd drawn.

Because of their hostility toward one another, the earth had been divided between them for safekeeping and they were highly territorial.

Greece and her surrounding areas belonged to ZT, and he tolerated very few treading on his turf, which meant that anytime Kat ventured here she got a nice visit from the crank.

The first time they'd met, she'd been a curious child who'd only wanted to see a chariot race. Her mother had sent her out with a chaperone. The sun had been bright when all of a sudden ZT had appeared out of nowhere and quickly scared her by telling her that if she ever broke Chthonian law, he would gleefully kill her.

She'd "loved" him ever since.

"Long time no see, ZT." Total sarcasm, since he kept a permanent watch on her anytime she was on earth. They'd crossed paths only two weeks ago when she'd been in the market and had sneezed, which caused her powers to shatter a nearby window. ZT had been pissed that she'd almost betrayed herself and, true to his badass form, had let her know it.

"Don't be coy with me, Katra. I know about the permits. How did that happen?"

She shrugged. "It was an unforeseen event, but I have it under control. There's no need for you to bother yourself."

His eyes flared in the darkness as he closed the distance between them. Raw esoteric power emanated from him, raising the hairs on her body. He tilted his head as if he was sensing the ether around them.

"A human god?" he whispered.

"His time here is short and he has no powers. Again, it's nothing to worry over."

ZT curled his lip at her. "I will decide what I worry over. Not you." He let out a vicious hiss. "He's meddling with human affairs."

Even though she knew it was foolish, she scoffed at him. "So do I."

"Which is why you're on my radar. I don't like the

games that Artemis plays and I like your part in them even less."

"Then why don't you stop her?"

He gave a bitter laugh before he gave Kat a cutting glare. "You're so naive."

Perhaps she was, but it didn't change the fact that he was overreacting. "You don't have to concern yourself with this, ZT. Really."

A muscle worked in his taut jaw as he looked out over the dark water. When he spoke, his tone was flat and emotionless. "I have you—a god of mixed heritage—on an expedition that could unleash the Destroyer from her hole. Arikos, another god, on the same team who is masquerading as a human. The demigod Solin, who I have to ride herd on constantly anyway, who gave them their permits. Megeara, a human who is sensitive and subjective to the voices of the gods. And the pissed-off goddess, Apollymi, who will do anything to be free, and once free wouldn't hesitate to destroy every one of us." He turned that deadly stare to Kat. "I can't imagine why I'm concerned over this, can you?"

"Granted it looks a little bad when you put it that way, but I can assure you that I won't let them near Apollymi's seal."

His doubting look was really beginning to piss Kat off. "And does the name Pandora hold any meaning for you? Anytime you allow a human near a box they shouldn't open, what do they invariably do?"

"It'll be different this time."

He made a rude noise in the back of his throat. "Don't be arrogant, Katra. I'm tired of cleaning up the messes left by gods who thought they could do better." He turned toward her and there in the moonlight she saw something she'd never seen on him before. A vicious scar that ran from his hairline to his neck. It looked as if someone had once sliced open his face.

But as soon as she saw it, it faded and left him handsome and unscarred. "Keep the seal hidden, Katra. Apollymi cannot go free."

Before Kat could respond, Tory came up on deck.

Both Kat and ZT froze as the girl innocently approached them.

She gave Kat a curious frown before she pushed her glasses up on her nose. "Are you all right, Kat?"

"Fine, Tory. I just have an old friend visiting, but he was about to leave."

"Oh, okay. Geary wanted me to check on you. She said you weren't feeling well." And before Kat could say anything, Tory held her hand out to ZT. "Hi, friend of Kat. I'm Tory Kafieri."

Kat expected the god-killer to tear Tory's hand off or make a nasty remark. Instead he took her hand in his and shook it gently. "ZT."

"ZT. What a cool name." She smiled up at him. "Well, I won't bug you two anymore. It's obvious you want to be alone. I'll tell Geary that you're fine, Kat. Nice meeting you, ZT."

"You, too, Tory."

Kat actually gaped as Tory left them and ZT didn't blast her. She waited until Tory was gone before she spoke again. "So you can be nice. Who knew?"

"My niceness has a very low threshold and that little girl just sucked it dry, so don't push me, Olympian. I don't want so much as a single Atlantean stone overturned. Guard it with your life because the next time I come here, that's the price I'm going to demand for your incompetence."

And before she could even flinch, he vanished.

"Nice talking to you, ZT," she called out after him. "I so look forward to your visits. Next time we'll do pastries, 'kay?"

Sighing, Kat rubbed her temple. This was turning into a beautiful day for her. She couldn't wait to see what was going to happen next.

CHAPTER 9

M'ORDANT WALKED SLOWLY THROUGH THE HALL THAT led to the Onethalamos . . . just in case someone was watching. It was in the Onethalamos that the three leaders of the Dream-Hunters, M'Ordant, D'Alerian, and M'Adoc, gathered to make policy, keep peace, and . . .

Issue death warrants.

Protected from the other gods and zealously guarded, this room contained all the secrets that the three of them would kill and, more important, *had* killed to maintain.

One of them being the fact that the three of them were no longer bound by Zeus's curse. Their feelings had come back, and with every year that passed, those emotions grew stronger, as did these Dream-Hunters' need to protect them. But outside the doors of the Onethalamos no one could ever know.

Inside the room, however, anything went.

The moment M'Ordant walked through the oversized gold doors, he slammed them shut with his thoughts.

M'Adoc looked up from his book with an arched brow. "Careful, *adelphos*. The last thing we want is for someone to know you have a temper."

"Yeah, and in about three seconds so will you."

Laying the paperback aside, M'Adoc sat back in his cushioned chair to eye M'Ordant suspiciously. "Meaning?"

"We have a renegade."

M'Adoc laughed. "And this is different how?"

"Oh, give me a second on this one," M'Ordant said, approaching M'Adoc's chair. "We're not talking one of our guys went Skoti. It should be so simple. No. One of our Skoti just went human."

It took several seconds for that shocking bit to fully penetrate M'Adoc's mind. "Excuse me?"

M'Ordant drew a ragged breath before he explained. "Arikos has cut a bargain with Hades. He wanted to be human for a few weeks. The price. One human soul."

The color faded from M'Adoc's face an instant before rage darkened his cheeks. "What is he doing?"

"Fucking things up for the rest of us." M'Ordant slammed his fist down on the table. "I swear, Zeus as my witness, I'm going to tear him limb from limb. How could he be so fucking stupid?"

M'Adoc shook his head. "Enough with the vulgarity. I know you love the word, but save it." He growled low in his throat, letting M'Ordant know he was equally willing to break eggs, heads, and bones in this as M'Ordant was. "Zeus and the others will question how Arik could have developed a desire so strong it would make him bargain with Hades to quell it."

"Yeah, and there will be hell to pay if they come knocking on our doors. If they ever find out that the curse is weakening . . ." He didn't finish the sentence. He didn't have to. Unlike Arikos, he, M'Adoc, and D'Alerian were the first ones they'd rounded up at Zeus's order and punished for the Oneroi's ability to manipulate dreams for their own personal gain.

To this day, the three of them, who had been innocent in the crime but held up as examples to the others, could still feel the pain and humiliation of that torture. When it came to absolute punishment, no one could match a Greek god bent on vengeance. It was what kept the three up at night and seeking the Skoti to make sure they didn't violate the laws Zeus had set for them. The three would do anything to not relive the merciless hell they'd gone through—and they were the three whom the gods would punish again if they ever learned the secrets M'Ordant, M'Adoc, and D'Alerian carried.

No one would show them mercy, and they knew it.

"Does anyone else know?" M'Adoc asked.

"Just Hades and us."

"How did you find out?"

Straightening up, M'Ordant folded his arms over his chest. "I make it my business to keep an eye on Hades and Hypnos." They had been the two most mischievous gods who'd gotten the rest of them cursed. "When they sleep, I'm there every minute of it. I just don't let *them* know I'm spying."

"Good man. We have to contain this. Call out the Dolophoni. We need that bastard dead, then if Zeus finds out, we can tell him that it was an aberration unique to Arikos that we handled."

"You think he'll buy it?"

"If not, we'll have to find some way to sell it to him." M'Adoc's phosphorescent blue eyes flickered with malice. "I don't know about you, but I have no intention of bleeding for another one of these assholes."

M'Ordant arched a brow at M'Adoc's word choice. He

generally profaned profanity—which told M'Ordant just how determined his brother was. M'Ordant held his hand out to M'Adoc. "I hear you, *adelphos,* and we're in definite accord."

M'Adoc wrapped his hand around M'Ordant's and shook it. "Arikos dies."

GEARY PAUSED IN HER CHAT WITH THIA TO WATCH ARIK bite into one of the Hostess cupcakes that Tory had broken out for the celebration. His eyes actually glowed with pleasure as he tasted it.

His smile was broad and enchanting. "This is incredible."

Tory laughed at him. "I can't believe you've never had one before. Man, that would stink, to grow up without Hostess. *This* was the staple of my elementary-school lunch box."

He practically inhaled it. "Do you have any more?"

"Hang on." She ran from the room.

Excusing herself from Thia, Geary made her way to Arik, who was frowning at the black cake that was stuck like glue on his fingers. Geary picked up a napkin as she approached him. "It must be bare in the mountains."

He licked the sugar from his lips before he responded. "I know what things are, but I haven't been able to experience them before. Like this cake. It's really very good."

"As the girth of my hips will attest."

By his face, she could tell he didn't understand she was calling herself fat. For some reason, she found that as endearing as his amazement that he couldn't easily get the cake off his fingers.

Smiling, she took his hand in hers so that she could help him out. She paused at the sensation of his flesh against hers as she wiped the pads of his fingers with the napkin. He had the most beautiful hands. Large and masculine, they made her want to lick them clean. In her dreams, she would have done that in a heartbeat.

He lifted his hand so that he could place a very sweet kiss on the back of her knuckles. "Thank you."

Geary swallowed as white-hot desire shot through her. What was it about this man that made her literally melt? "You're welcome."

Tory came running back in with her entire stash of junk food that she kept in a large shoe box that normally lived under her bed . . . protected by Mr. Cuddles of course. "Okay, Moon Pies."

Geary laughed in disbelief. "You're going to share a Moon Pie? Now? You know you can't get any more of those until you go back to the States, right?"

"It's for a good cause. We need more addicts. Besides, there's always Grandpa to bail me out with an emergency shipment if I get too desperate." Tory handed a chocolate-coated Moon Pie to Arik.

Geary shook her head. "Oh no, if you really want to be wicked to him, nuke it first."

Tory made a slight face of contradiction. "Yeah, but given his reaction to the cupcake, that might overload his taste buds with pleasure and kill him."

This was true. The mighty Moon Pie could be orgasmically deadly when nuked . . . it rated right up there with the infamous Australian Tim Tam Slam and the deep-fried Twinkie. "Good point. To be on the safe side, the first one should always be tasted at room temperature."

Arik frowned while Tory unwrapped the small, round cookielike object. And as soon as he tasted it, he was in obvious ecstasy. "Oh my God, that's good."

She exchanged a mischievous grin with Tory. "Reese's," they said in unison.

"Reese's?" Arik asked, puzzled.

"Oh yeah," Geary laughed. "You'll be dying the minute you bite into one." She started digging through Tory's shoe box until she found one. She made an evil noise in triumph as she pulled it out. "You know, Tor, I have no idea how you stay so skinny eating all this crap. I swear I gain ten pounds just rooting through it."

"I'm still growing."

Geary snorted. "So am I, but it's out instead of up. Remind me tomorrow to start my diet again."

Arik scowled at her. "I think you're beautiful as you are. Why would you want to change?"

Something warm tickled her at his words. "You're just trying to flatter me."

"No," he said seriously. "I'm only telling you the truth."

"Awww," Tory said dreamily. "He's such a sweetie. Can we keep him?"

Geary gave a nervous laugh. "He's not a puppy, Tory."

"Yeah, but we did fish him out of trouble. In some cultures that would make us responsible for him forever."

Arik gave her a hopeful grin. "And I wouldn't mind being kept for a while."

Geary shook her head at them. "You two are a terrible combination. Kind of like gasoline and fire." She looked past Arik's shoulder to see Kat entering the room finally. She had a very sour look on her face, as if something wasn't settling right with her. "Hey," Geary called out to Kat, catching her attention. "You okay?"

With an extremely fake smile, Kat walked over. "Yeah. Fine."

Tory set her shoe box to the side. "So where's the gorgeous ZT?"

Geary frowned at the name she didn't recognize. "Who?"

Tory made a clicking noise with her teeth like a woman calling a horse. "Kat was with this really cute guy on deck when you sent me up to check on her." She looked back at Kat. "Did he not stay?"

"No, he had to leave."

"ZT?" Arik asked with a speculative gleam in his eyes. "As in Zebulon?"

Kat gave a very curt nod.

Tory looked back and forth between them curiously. "You know him, too, Arik?"

"He knows him," Kat said in an odd tone. Her gaze was cutting as she met and held Arik's. "He sends you his best."

All emotion fled from Arik's features. "I'll bet he does. How is old ZT doing, anyway?"

"Charming as ever."

The sarcasm between them was so thick it could have been carved into an ice sculpture.

Arik put the unopened Reese's back inside the box as if he'd lost his appetite. "Nice to know some things never change."

Geary scowled even more. "How is it that you two have a mutual friend when you didn't know each other before today?"

"It's a small country," Kat said evasively. "The old families tend to stick together and Arik's has probably known ZT's for quite some time now."

"Yes," Arik said with a wry grin. "He's like a rash for which there's no cure. It only goes away for a bit before returning unexpectedly to ruin every pleasurable experience. He should have been named Herpes rather than ZT. Or maybe just Herpes Z, since he's a very special irritant."

Kat laughed. "Very aptly put, hell, it's even Greek and he is creepy—I'll give you that. But I wonder if he knows how you feel?"

"I'm sure he does. He's rather astute and I'm anything but subtle."

Okeydokey, this was getting a bit out of hand, and she wanted to avoid a herpes discussion in front of the walking/talking medical textbook who was only fifteen years old. So, trying to stave off the animosity and veer to safer territory, Geary stepped forward. "And on that happy note, children, I think we should all turn an eye to retiring. It's been a long day and we have a really big day tomorrow."

"Hear! Hear!" Teddy concurred from the other side of the room. "As long as we've been waiting for this excavation, I want to make sure that we all have one that's error free. We can't afford a single mistake, people."

There were a few grumbles, but overall everyone agreed. If they were to get cracking at dawn, then they needed their rest.

"So where's Arik bunking?" Tory asked.

Geary hesitated. There really wasn't any place to put him without inconveniencing one of the guys. Their rooms were cramped at best, and she was sure none of them wanted to bunk with a stranger.

Arik gave her a hopeful look that brought an unexpected smile to her face. "I already have a roommate."

There was no missing Arik's disappointment. "Who?"

Tory rocked back and forth on her feet. "Me and Mr. Cuddles."

"Yeah," Geary said, nodding, "and Mr. Cuddles is a jealous sort. He doesn't share us well."

Arik didn't miss a beat. "Does this mean I'll have to fight him?"

"You'd never win," Tory said sweetly. "Mr. Cuddles cheats. You think he's just a pushover teddy bear, but he's vicious, I tell you. Vicious."

Kat cast a speculative look at Arik. "You could throw him on a hammock on deck."

Geary considered it. It actually wasn't a bad thought. "We will be up at dawn, so it wouldn't really wake him once we hit the deck. . . ."

Tory leaned toward Arik. "Bet you're thinking you should have gone home, huh?"

"No," he said, his tone sincere. "I had a great time tonight." He looked at Tory and smiled. "And you're right. The mighty Moon Pie is the best. Thank you for sharing your treasure with me."

"Anytime." She rose up on her tiptoes to kiss his cheek. "Good night, Arik. I'll see you in the morning. Sweet dreams."

"You, too, Tory."

Kat gave him an odd look before she bid them good night and followed Tory to the hallway.

Thia came forward with a calculating gleam in her eyes. "Well, if no one else wants him . . . I could share my bunk with him."

"Go to bed, Cynthia," Geary said sharply, "before Justina kills you for pimping out your shared cabin."

Thia gave a weary sigh. "I was just trying to be friendly. They always say you shouldn't sleep alone in a strange bed."

"Yes, and they didn't have their cousin on board to watch over them, either. One who would report any sleazy behavior to their mother. Good night, Thia."

Tossing her hair over her shoulder in a huff, she left them alone.

Geary gave Arik a once-over as she realized he'd have to sleep in his borrowed jeans and shirt. "What are you going to do for clothes?"

"Solin said he'd return with something for me to wear in the morning."

"Ahh, okay. Well, I guess I'll grab a hammock and meet you topside."

Arik started to offer to go with her, but she was already feeling smothered by his presence. He would back off for a bit even though it was the last thing he wanted to do. "All right. I'll see you on deck."

He headed for the stairs to the upper deck while she went the other way, deeper into the boat. He paused at the handrail, amazed by the slick feel of it. Nothing here was what he'd expected. Especially not the food. He didn't know why the gods made such a fuss over ambrosia and nectar, given how wonderful human food tasted.

Perhaps the gods were in denial because they were only supposed to have the best and it bothered them to think that mankind had perfected some of their world even while they battled one another.

Or maybe the gods honestly didn't know better.

Dismissing the thought, he climbed up to stand on deck as a light breeze whispered against his skin. The sensation was exquisite, but it was nothing compared to the sight of the city that sparkled over a velvet black landscape. The water lapped quietly against the boat as a faint jingle of music and laughter reached him. No wonder humans didn't want to die. Their world was remarkable, and their lives were made even more precious by the fact that they had so little time to spend here.

How did they do it? How did they exist knowing that the specter of death constantly haunted them? It was enough to depress anyone, and yet for the most part they were happy with their lot. They ignored their impending doom and marched on toward their death with dignity and grace while finding shards of happiness to content them.

It was truly amazing.

But then, they didn't know how long their lives would be. Decades or weeks. So they prepared for the worst and expected the best. It was actually rather noble.

And how strange it must be for Solin and ZT and the others to live this close to walking corpses. No wonder they were closed off from everyone. Who would want to reach out and befriend someone when he or she could be torn away from you at any moment? When there was no chance of a lasting relationship. Everything here was doomed to finality.

It must be horrifying for them all.

Arik looked back the way he'd come and wondered what Megeara would think if she knew her life was about to end.

Because of him.

He went cold with the thought. Now there was something he couldn't dwell on. He'd been naive when he'd made his bargain with Hades. Now there was no way back from it. As M'Ordant and Wink had pointed out, there would be others to beckon Arik back to this realm once Megeara was gone.

And yet he knew better. She was unique in this place of overwhelming emotions. In all the centuries, he'd never met anyone like her.

Where he lived, the human world seemed vague and unreal. But here it was vivid and extreme. Too extreme perhaps . . .

"Here you go."

He turned to find Megeara heading toward the prow. Her face was silhouetted by the moonlight.

"You're lucky we have these. Otherwise it'd be a pallet on the deck for you."

Arik watched as she set about stringing the hammock out. "You like to sleep in the hammock on cool nights, don't you?"

She looked up with a panicked expression. "How do you know that?"

He knew it from her dreams, but he didn't tell her that, since his goal was to soothe and seduce her, not scare her more. "From the look on your face and the skill you're showing as you lay it out."

She blushed before she returned to her task. "Yeah, I like to look up at the stars at night."

He knelt down to help her as she untangled some of the lines. "And what do you find when you look up there?"

Her hands worked deftly to straighten out the canvas and lace the cord through the grommets. "When I was a little girl, my father used to lay on deck with me and my brother and point out the constellations. Then he'd tell us stories about how the Greek gods supposedly formed them."

He could hear the bittersweet agony of her memory. She'd both loved and hated her father. It was a dichotomy Arik barely understood. He held no feelings whatsoever for his parents. But then, he'd never really known either one of them. Morpheus had too many children to pay attention to any one, and Arik's mother, Myst, couldn't be bothered. She was a carefree goddess who held no real affinity for anyone or anything. At least nothing he knew of.

It wasn't that he was angry over it. He was truly ambivalent. It was how things were in his world, so there was no feeling there for his parents whatsoever, not even while he was human.

But it made him wonder what it would be like to love the way Megeara loved. To feel that pain of betrayal when the person was no longer there. To have that surge of joy when the person was. . . .

He helped her anchor a corner. "So which story was your favorite?"

She tugged the line to make sure it was taut. "Orion. I always thought it was cruel and tragic that Artemis loved him, and that her own brother tricked her into killing him because Apollo was jealous and hated the fact that she was in love with a mere mortal."

"That's only one version of the story. The other is that Artemis killed him because he raped one of her handmaidens."

"I've heard that one, too, but I believe the first one."

"And why is that?"

"I don't know. It just seems right."

She was astute and part of him wanted to confirm it for her, but he didn't dare. She'd spent her whole life studying the gods and ancient civilizations, looking for corroboration that they'd all existed, and here he was, living proof, right beside her. He wondered what she'd do if she ever learned that he was one of the gods, along with her friend "Kat."

It might be a little too much to expect Geary to take it in stride.

Geary was a bit nervous as she finished securing the hammock to the hooks. It hung about a foot above the deck. Not too high, but not so low it wouldn't be comfortable. Her only concern was that he might catch a chill even with blankets.

Would that worsen his condition? Not that she knew

what was wrong with him, but still the last thing she wanted to do was take even a moment of his life away with more illness.

Which begged the question of what was wrong with him? She wanted to know but didn't want to remind him of how short his life would be. It seemed somehow wrong.

Instead, she gestured toward the hammock. "All yours."

He tsked at her. "I really wish you were talking about you and not the hammock."

"Yeah, I'll bet you do."

As she started past him, he pulled her toward him, and before she realized what he intended, he kissed her. She moaned at the sweet taste of him, at the hunger of his embrace. For the first time in her life, she wished she were more like Thia. She wouldn't have a bit of trouble taking him to her bed. But Geary wasn't like that. She'd never been a one-night-stand woman. She preferred a relationship before she got naked with someone, which was why she seldom even dated. Her quest had left her very little time for anything else in her life.

But Arik was seriously starting to bring her ethics into question.

Pulling back, she picked the blanket up from the hammock and held it to his chest. "Good night, Arik."

He let out an exasperated breath as he took the blanket from her with a grimace. "Good night, Megeara. May the dream gods be good to you."

A tingle went over her at the way he purred those words. It was as if he knew she'd been dreaming of him.

Putting that thought out of her mind, she left him and headed below, but as she reached the stairs she couldn't help looking back at him. He was already lying in the hammock, watching her.

In the darkness, his eyes seemed to glow.

She swore she could hear his unspoken request for her to return to him. It reminded her of the same disembodied voice that kept beckoning her to the dig site—only that voice was definitely female. And it called out to her even now to find Atlantis and set her free.

I am losing my mind. Maybe she should see someone about schizophrenia. . . .

But she knew better than that. This wasn't schizophrenia. It was merely her quest calling to her to fulfill her promise. She understood that. What she didn't understand was this odd connection to Arik. Why she heard and saw him even when he wasn't around.

Go to bed, Geary, and forget it.

Waving good night to him, she went to her room to find Tory already in her nightshirt and bed with Mr. Cuddles tucked under her arm. Since Tory's glasses were on the nightstand by her head, she was squinting at Geary. "I wasn't expecting you to come back."

"What do you mean?"

"C'mon, Geary, I may be half-blind, but that man is the finest thing I've ever seen . . . blurry or not. If I were you, *I* wouldn't have come back here tonight."

Geary scoffed at her. "You're only fifteen, Tory. It's not like you've got a lot of experience under your belt to judge hot men by."

"Point taken, but it doesn't change the fact that he's gorgeous and he likes you. A lot. So why are you back here?"

"Because we have a four A.M. wake-up call."

Tory sighed and shook her head. "You're the only person I know who's more pathetic than I am. I'm an orphaned kid, Geary. You shouldn't have to be alone all the time."

"Oh, hush, and go to sleep before I kidnap Cuddles. And speaking of furry things, where's Kichka?"

"I don't know. I haven't seen her. Maybe she's stuck in the hold again."

As if on cue, Geary's cat came running in the open door to rub against her leg. A Bengal cat, Kichka had been Tory's Christmas present a year ago, but the cat had taken such a liking to Geary that all of them had finally given up and just let Kichka own her.

"There you are." Geary picked Kichka up from the floor and set her on the bed while she undressed.

Before Kichka curled up on her pillow to clean one paw, she meowed loudly at Geary.

Tory turned over and gave Geary her back.

Her thoughts on Arik, Geary turned off the lights, tucked herself into the bed, and closed her eyes while Kichka moved from the pillow to sleep on the small of Geary's back. Within seconds, the cat was purring, Tory was snoring, and the gentle roll of the boat was lulling Geary away from all her problems.

And before Geary knew it, she was drifting to sleep.

ARIK HAD NEVER SLEPT AS A HUMAN BEFORE. THE WEIGHT of his body was odd, especially combined with the swinging motion of the boat and hammock. But it didn't take him long to lose himself in the realm of dreams.

It was strange to be back where he lived. His dreams were misty and cold. At least in the beginning, but after a time they began to clear and he realized something.

His powers were back.

Arik paused, unsure if what he felt was real. Floating above the ground, he held his hands out before him and conjured a swirling ball of flames. The heat was warm but not painful as he built the ball with his mind to a dangerous height.

Invigorated, he threw it into the darkness, where it exploded even brighter than the sun. Harmless pieces of ember rained down around him as he threw his head back and laughed.

Oh yeah, it was good to be a sleeping dream god. He had emotions *and* his powers.

Which left him with one goal.

Megeara.

It was time to find her. But that proved to be easier thought than done. True, he had his powers again, but he didn't have the strobilos and finding her without it proved to be rather tricky. He was also lacking Wink's serum to keep Megeara asleep. If he found her, she could wake up and leave him all over again.

I'll kill her. But even as he thought it, he knew that was an empty threat. He'd never hurt the very woman he craved.

For several minutes he cruised through the subconscious realm, drifting through dreams of naked musicians writhing in money and Jell-O shots, a toy poodle attacking a Doberman, a woman who bore a strange resemblance to a lollipop who was singing with cows, and one curious incident of a hemorrhoid chasing one woman around a block of cheese until it exploded. . . .

Yeah, people were *very* odd beings.

No wonder he left these dreamers to the other Skoti. He much preferred sexually creative women.

Arik paused between dreams to take a deep breath. This was wasting time, and since Megeara was planning an early morning, he needed to find her quickly.

Closing his eyes, he felt the ether around him . . . listened to it as it breathed and whispered through his being. She was out there.

And then he heard it. The faint sound of her laughter. Honing in on it, he willed himself to her dream.

She was on the beach again, dancing in the surf to music only she could hear.

Arik froze at the sight of her there with her damp hair flying around her face. Her white dress clung to her body, showing him every lush, delicious curve. Every inch of flesh that he wanted to taste.

Unable to stand it, he dropped to the beach and walked toward her with a predator's intent.

His breathing ragged, he came up behind her and touched her shoulder.

She turned on him then and what happened next absolutely blew his mind.

CHAPTER 10

GEARY WAS LAUGHING WITH TRIUMPH OVER HER DAY AS the water splashed against her body. She was just about to go diving into the sea without her equipment to find Atlantis when she felt someone touch her arm.

She turned to find Arik there.

Joy rushed through her with a heady excitement and she did what she'd been wanting to do all day—she pulled him against her and kissed him for everything she was worth. The surf splashed up and over them, but instead of being cold, it was warm and soothing.

She growled at the taste of his mouth on hers, at the sensation of his hard arms enveloping her as their tongues danced together. His corded muscles rippled under her hands while he pulled her so close to him that they were virtually one person.

Oh, it felt so good to be held by him. To have all those muscles pressing against her body. She buried her hand in his hair, pulling at it slightly so that she could feel even closer to him.

"You are the absolute best," she breathed against his lips before she nipped them with her teeth. "Thank you for the permits."

He nuzzled her neck, sending chills over her. "Anytime."

She pulled back from him and literally ripped the white shirt from his body before she threw him on the ground and straddled him.

The beach elongated so that the waves would no longer overrun them. Instead, the sea pulled back, leaving them the damp beach, which wasn't sandy. Rather, it was like lying on a bed of rose petals.

Arik was completely shocked by her behavior as she groped and fondled him as if she were overwhelmingly consumed by her hunger for his body. This was the Megeara he'd expected to meet in the human realm. But she'd been so reserved all day that he'd given up hope of her receiving him like this ever again.

Now she was ferocious in her lust. His head swam as she buried her lips against his neck and tongued him until he thought he'd die from the pleasure of it.

He laughed in the back of his throat. "You're certainly rowdy tonight."

She slid down his body as she continued to lick and please every part of him. "You've no idea. It's been killing me all day to be so close to you and to not touch this body. God, you're gorgeous and sexy."

He trembled as she worked her way from his neck to his nipples and then down his abdomen until she got to the waistband of his jeans. Normally, Arik would have melted them off, but he was curious what she'd do in this mood.

She virtually shredded his pants in an effort to get to him. She tore chunks of the denim and tossed them over her shoulder until he was completely naked. He lay there on his back, watching her as her hands explored him at length. She attacked him with fervor, and he loved every second of it. As good as it'd been before when he merely fed from her emotions, it was even better now that he had his own to draw from.

He hissed as she found his hip bone and went to work on it with her mouth while she cupped him in her hand and massaged him until he was rock hard for her. He literally shook from the ecstasy of it.

He traced the line of her back with his hand, dragging his nails gently over her flesh until chills erupted all over her body. Needing more of her, he dipped his hand down to brush through the soft tangle of curls at the juncture of her thighs. He licked his lips, already tasting her, before he sank his fingers inside her.

She was so wet and ready. He toyed with her, biding his time until he could fill her completely.

Geary couldn't wait to taste him. Her eyes hooded, she watched the pleasure on his face as she toyed with his cock and he stroked her where she ached most. She loved the sensation of his hard body against her curves. The way his small hairs tickled her skin.

But it was enough of playtime.

Drawing her breath in in sweet expectation, she moved to draw the tip of his cock into her mouth, where she gently tongued him. The salty-sweet taste went through her as she moved lower. She felt him shudder under her. Giddy with the sensation of it, she drew him in even deeper, wanting to taste and please him for the rest of the night.

Arik cupped her face as he watched her. He loved it whenever she did this. He didn't know what it was about this one act, but there was nothing more pleasing to him. With his hands on her cheeks, he felt her jaw working under his fingers while she consumed him. His body was on fire, and in the back of his mind he wondered how much better this would be while he was awake.

What would her mouth really feel like on him?

It was weird to think about it, but he was technically a virgin. He'd never taken a woman outside of the dream realm. Until Megeara, he'd never really cared about that.

But now he did. He wanted to know what it was like to really share his body with her. To have her touch him like this while they were conscious.

Geary looked up to see Arik watching her. There was a look of extreme pleasure and one of amazement in his eyes. How she wished she could see a look like that from a man in real life. She'd never really had a boyfriend for any length of time. It was why she kept men at arm's length. She didn't like being hurt. Didn't like being disappointed.

It was so much safer to be alone, and yet as she lay with Arik she wanted to know what it would be like to have someone with her. Someone who was a part of her.

Someone to trust.

In less than a day, the man Arik had given her more than anyone else ever had. He'd given her her dream. And now he was here in her dreams, loving her.

Wanting to feel even closer to him, she pulled away to lay her body down on his.

Arik closed his eyes at how good Megeara felt against him. Her flesh was warm and soft against his. He held her close, reveling in the feel of her as he cradled her with his body. She leaned back to kiss him before she slid herself onto him.

He sucked his breath in sharply as pleasure pierced every part of his being. She made love to him furiously as the surf crashed around them. The waves rolled up but didn't quite reach him.

He could focus on nothing but the slick feel of her body as she took him in all the way. He held her hips, urging her even faster.

Geary rocked her hips against his, seeking peace and closeness. He was so deep inside that it made her ache. She loved having sex with this man, and she couldn't help wondering if the real Arik would be as kind and tender as her dream lover.

You could find out.

Yes, but that would leave her vulnerable and that was the last thing she wanted. Geary Kafieri had no desire to be hurt by anyone. It wasn't worth it. Especially since she knew Arik would be dying soon. To let him in would be to invite agony on herself, and she'd had so much pain already. Everyone she loved died. Everyone.

Except for Tory. It was why Geary was so protective of her. God help Geary if anything ever happened to her cousin. She wouldn't be able to live and she knew it.

But as she felt Arik inside her now, she wanted a future she knew she could never have, and it broke her heart.

It was her lot in life to be alone. There was no use fighting it.

At least she had him in her dreams.

Smiling at him, she quickened her strokes until she finally felt that moment of absolute pleasure right before her body released and blinded her with ecstasy.

Arik leaned his head back as he felt her body clutching his. Lifting his hips, he buried himself deep inside her before his own orgasm claimed him and she collapsed on top of him.

Now this . . . this was what he'd wanted. Truly, there was nothing more spectacular in this world or any other than Megeara. He held her tight against him as his heart continued to race. He'd never been more content.

She leaned up on one arm to stare down at him as she tucked a piece of hair behind her ear. Never had he seen a more beautiful woman.

Arik cupped her cheek in his palm, looking up at her as he laughed from his exhaustion. Megeara's eyes glowed in the moonlight as she kissed the line of his jaw.

"Now if I could only get you to do this while we're awake . . ."

She laughed, which caused her breasts to brush against his chest. "Never. I can't afford to be like this awake. No one respects a woman of easy virtue."

"Oh, I assure you that's not true. I would always respect you."

"Yeah, right." She pulled back to sit up.

Arik couldn't breathe at the sight of her resting on his hips as the moonlight cast shadows over her bare body. He reached up to trace the outline of her nipple as she glanced off into the ocean.

He watched her face as she began to frown. "What's wrong?"

"The sea . . ."

He turned his head to look and went instantly cold. The surf was rolling against the shore, but what made him pay attention was the strange motion of it. The whitecaps began to slowly form faces, and those faces started rising out of the water in liquid forms that became solid.

The Dolophoni.

Children of the Furies, the Dolophoni were essentially

the assassins of the gods. And they'd been the ones who'd rounded up the Oneroi centuries ago for Zeus to punish.

Now someone had unleashed the Dolophoni against Arik. He knew it. There was no other reason for them to be here. They weren't something Megeara would have conjured, and he could feel inside that they weren't from her dreams.

They were here to kill him.

"You need to go, Megeara." He slid out from under her.

Geary was frozen to the spot as ten people emerged from the waves, completely dry. Two women and eight men. As tall as or taller than Arik, they left the sea like a pack of rabid dogs ready to attack.

Their heads were bent low as they headed straight for Arik with a deadly swagger. Not a word or sound could be heard. Not even the surf. The air no longer moved. It was static and charged with the coming conflict.

Arik stood his ground as skintight black leather armor appeared over his body, and his hair magically pulled itself back into a ponytail. Spikes grew out of his forearms and one out of his left knee.

One of the men, who was at least six inches taller than Arik, had a bald head with a phoenix tattoo on one side of his face, the tail of which coiled down and around his neck. He wore a sleeveless black T-shirt that accentuated the bulging muscles of his arms, black leather pants, and a studded neck collar. Metal vambraces covered his forearms, and he carried an ax over one shoulder.

Another man was two inches shorter and much leaner and had short bright green hair that he had spiked on top of his head and over his eyes. He wore a pair of black wraparound sunglasses and carried a black staff with silver spikes poking out of both ends. His bare arms were covered with colorful tattoos, and a row of nine hoops hung from his left ear. He had two more hoops on his bottom lip.

The next man had short-cropped dark auburn hair that framed a face of perfect masculine beauty. His brown eyes flashed red as he drew an AK-47 out of the folds of his long leather coat.

The man beside him had the entire right side of his torso bare. His long black hair was pulled back in a ponytail while his left shoulder and arm were covered by black plate armor. There were scars all over his cheeks, and his black eyes were deep set into his face.

Two more appeared to be twins. They were equal in height to Arik, with short brown hair, and where one had three hoops in his right ear the other wore them in his left. Unlike the others, they were each dressed in slacks and a button-down shirt, with black leather overcoats that flowed around their booted feet. They moved slow and easy, with a fluid grace, as if synched to each other. Their faces were perfectly sculpted.

Two steps behind them was a man who had to be a minimum of seven feet tall. His blond hair was short and he was built like the Terminator, with a demeanor that would make the cyborg look weak. This man's face was rugged and harsh, and it was obvious he lived to bathe in the blood of others.

The last man was lean and wiry. Steel spikes were wrapped around his arms and over his hands. He wore tall biker boots with flames rising up from the toes to meet at the skulls at the top of them. Shirtless, he had the body of a ripped gymnast.

All of them wore expressions that said they were here for war.

One of the two women was even taller than Geary,

with black hair streaked with bright green. Her hair was pulled back into a ponytail, and the green seemed to be snakes. They slithered around her shoulders, coiling about her neck as they hissed and snapped.

The other woman was much shorter but no less lethal. Trim and lean, she was corded with muscles and had bright red hair and sharp features.

Geary scrambled for her clothes, not that the others even seemed to know she was there. Their attention was only on Arik.

"Who sent you?" Arik asked defiantly.

The man with the gun answered by firing it straight at Arik. He recoiled before he backflipped to the left and threw his hand out. It functioned as a gun and returned the bullets to them. He "fired" more bullets with his other hand.

The group dodged them before the woman with red hair threw out a circle that exploded all over Arik. It knocked him flat on his back and sent shooting sparks into the air around them.

Arik hit the sand with a force so lethal it shook him to his bones. Damn them. His senses were rattled, but he'd battled enough in dreams to know that this was his domain. He might be mortal while awake, but in here he was still a god.

And they were fucking the wrong Skotos.

No one took him out in his realm.

Growling, he flipped himself back to his feet and manifested a whip. He slung it out for the woman who'd stunned him and caught her about the waist. The cord bit into her and would have cut her in half had she been anyone but a Dolophonos.

As it was, it only cut deep and sent her to the ground.

The green-haired man paused to look at her as she writhed.

"You're strong," he said, betraying a set of vicious fangs. "Not many people get a shot off on Alera."

Arik swung the whip again, causing them to dodge it. "First mistake. I'm not a person. I'm a god. You want to fight in this realm, you need reinforcements."

The bald one dove at him so fast all Arik could see was the vapor trail. He caught Arik about the waist and they went down hard. Arik rolled with him, slugging him before he kicked him away. Before Arik could regain his feet, the other woman was on his back. He flipped her over his head and punched her in the chest. Without missing a beat, she sliced at him with a dagger that narrowly missed him.

The one bad thing about the weapons the Dolophoni used was that they were made by Hephaestus and that was one god who knew how to forge a weapon that hurt.

More to the point, he forged weapons that killed other gods.

Arik caught her around the neck with his whip, but before he could hurt her, one of the men kicked him from behind.

Letting go of the whip, Arik twisted around to confront him. But first Arik had to dodge the bald man's ax. Arik caught it in both hands and kicked the giant back.

He didn't budge. All he did was laugh.

"Laugh at this, asshole," Arik snarled, head-butting the giant. He staggered back, releasing the ax to Arik.

Instantly the other man swung his staff at Arik's feet, then his head. Arik dodged, then countered with the ax, which the man deftly ducked. He brought the staff up and planted it in Arik's ribs.

Arik felt the bite but didn't react to it other than to swing the ax. The man dodged it again, but one of the twins came in with an invisible block of some kind that shattered the ax into shards.

Cursing, Arik barely rolled out of the way of the staff swing. The man lunged at Arik's feet.

Arik jumped up, then caught the staff with both hands. He snatched it right, unbalancing the man before he swept his feet out from under him. Wresting the staff from the man's hands, Arik sank one end of it into the man's chest.

Screaming, he disintegrated on the sand.

One down. Nine to go.

Arik twirled the staff around and tucked it under his arm as he turned to face the others, who treated him with more respect. They weren't as cocky now as they'd been on arrival.

Their faces were marred with disbelief as they appeared to be speaking to one another mentally. Let them. Arik didn't need to hear their thoughts to know they planned on mangling him.

Arik backed up as they circled around him. They were sizing him up and he knew it. Feinting at him only to back away to test his reflexes and assess his weaknesses.

He toyed with them. Giving them false impressions. False reactions. Be damned if he was that stupid. He hadn't lasted this long in dreams by allowing others to get the better of him.

One of the twins came at Arik's back. He twirled with the staff, into a crouch so that he could swipe the man's feet out from under him. Arik rose to his feet to finish the attack, but before he could the other twin knocked him back with a punch so raw it lifted him off his feet and sent him flat on his back in the sand.

Arik swung the staff at the same time he rolled back to his feet. He ducked the knee the bald man sent toward him and turned away from the sword the woman was trying to skewer him with.

Geary could barely think as she watched the deadly dance of Arik with the others. She'd never seen anything like it.

Arik used the staff to lift himself up from the ground and drove his feet into the man with auburn hair. Then Arik swung around to attack the bald man and the twins at the same time.

Go, Arik.

But she couldn't leave him to this on his own. Even for a dream, this was getting bloody, and honestly, this wasn't what she wanted in her subconscious.

Wanting control again, Geary walked over to them. "Excuse me?"

Arik paused at her call, which allowed the bald man to deliver him a staggering blow to his face. He twisted back before snarling at her. "Run, Megeara."

"Run from what? They're circus freaks, and while this is mildly entertaining, I'd like to go back to what we were doing before they interrupted us." She waved her hands at the others. "So you guys, go poof."

The twins approached her slowly. "This isn't a game, human. Listen to the Skotos and go. We're not bound by the laws of the Oneroi. Killing humans is nothing for us."

Was that supposed to scare her? Yeah. What had she eaten for dinner that it was manifesting like this?

Oh yeah. Crab cakes. Those never really agreed with her. She'd eaten two of them. Maybe that was why there were twins. Or she was just tired, which was the most likely explanation.

At any rate, she was tired of this part of the dream.

"Well, aren't you all scary in black? Oooo. What are you two masquerading as? Evil Man and his trusty sidekick Bad Boy?" She let out a tired sigh. "Look, this is really annoying me. I want my dream back and that means all of you have to go now."

One of the twins reached to grab her, but before he could, Arik was there. He pulled her by the arm, away from the others.

He paused to send a fiery blast back toward them as they ran forward. "You have to go, Megeara."

"Not without you."

Arik wanted to curse the fact that she couldn't distinguish reality from her dreams. If she died on this plane, she died in her world, too. Same as him.

She stopped and grimaced. "Why are you playing with them? Just snow them in."

He didn't understand what she meant until she snapped her fingers and blocks of ice encased the Dolophoni. His jaw went slack as it stopped them dead in their tracks.

A human shouldn't have that ability. "How did you do that?"

"It's a dream, silly. I've always had control in my dreams. As a kid I used to pretend I was watching TV and if I didn't like the dream, I just changed the channel. Like this."

Suddenly the beach was gone. They were in a summer meadow with no sign of the Dolophoni to be had.

Arik's jaw slackened even more as he felt the sharpness of solar heat and smelled heather and wheat. How was this possible? Humans couldn't control dreams like this. If he didn't know better, he'd swear she had Oneroi blood in her.

But she didn't. There was a scent and aura that all the gods had—even those who only held a bit of god blood. Megeara had none of that. She was fully human.

Before he could ask how she'd gained control away from the Dolophoni, she captured his lips with hers. For a heartbeat all he could sense was her. With every part of him.

Unfortunately, he had more to focus on than how good she tasted.

"Please, Megeara. I would love to stay with you, but I can't."

She frowned up at him. "What are you talking about?"

He kissed her on the forehead before he pulled away. She had gotten them away from the Dolophoni, but they were still out there, looking for him, and they wouldn't stop until he was dead. They wouldn't care who got in the way. All that mattered to them was completing their mission.

The last thing he wanted was to see Megeara hurt.

"I'll be with you soon."

And with that, he pulled out of her dream.

Arik awoke in the hammock to the taste of blood in his mouth. His entire body ached to the point he could barely draw breath.

What was going on? None of this should be happening.

He didn't know why the Dolophoni had been sent after him, but then, the why didn't matter. All that counted was the fact that they wouldn't stop until he was dead.

They'd found him in the dream realm.

It wouldn't take them long to find him in the human world, too.

Holding his breath, he rolled out of the hammock and fell to the deck. He groaned as pain assailed him. He tried to stand, but his body wouldn't cooperate. With no

CHAPTER 11

GEARY WOKE UP AT DAWN FEELING INVIGORATED. SHE'D had a restful, dream-free sleep the night before and now she was anxious to be about the excavation. It was time to get cracking and set fire to the world.

Tory was already up and dressed, sitting in the corner with a flashlight as she reviewed pictures of their site. She looked like an eerie specter in the darkness.

"What are you doing?" Geary asked.

Tory pushed her glasses up on her nose and gave Geary a wistful look. "Wishing I could dive with you. It would be so cool to be down there and be the first on site, touching everything."

Geary nodded. At two hundred feet down, it was far too deep for Tory, who was only a recreational diver. Not to mention, it was just too dangerous for her to chance. Both Jason and Tory's father had died during diving accidents. That was one family legacy Geary had no intention of bequeathing to anyone.

"Next time."

Tory sighed. "Yeah. Just keep the live feed going so that I can see it and pretend I'm there, too."

"Yes, my queen. Anything else you'd like?"

Tory grinned. "A million dollars and Brad Pitt."

As Geary threw back the covers and left her bed, she laughed at Tory's stock answer. "You forgot world peace."

"I'm feeling a bit selfish today. Teenage hormonal overdose, I think. Or just general excitement."

Geary rolled her eyes as she went to brush her teeth. It didn't take her long to get dressed. As eager to get started as Tory, she all but sprinted to the upper deck. The sky was just starting to lighten. Pink was laced with the blue as orange broke through in ribbons that spiraled above her, promising her good weather for the dive and excavation. Closing her eyes, she inhaled the fishy scent of the sea and smiled.

It was a good day to be alive.

And grateful to the man who'd given her this dream, she went to the hammock to wake him.

Only Arik wasn't there. He lay on the deck with his back to her. Afraid he was ill, she rushed over to him and knelt by his side.

"Arik?"

He groaned ever so slightly as she shook him. Rolling onto his back, he opened his eyes, and she saw a slight bruise on his forehead.

"What are you doing on the deck?"

Arik gestured to the hammock above him. "I fell out of the hammock while I was sleeping."

"On your head?"

"Apparently. Good thing it's hard, huh?"

She grimaced at his misplaced humor.

Arik's breath caught as she gently brushed the hair back from his brow to examine his cheek and forehead. The look of concern on her face was enough to make him want to bruise himself again to see if she'd duplicate it.

Luckily, he wasn't *that* masochistic.

Yet.

"You need to be more careful."

"I intend to," he said honestly. He wasn't about to let the Dolophoni get the drop on him again. While on the boat he was semiprotected, since they wouldn't cause a commotion in front of a group of humans.

At least that was the lie he was telling himself. The problem with the Dolophoni was that they didn't really have a set of rules to follow that anyone knew. You merely hoped they'd abide by the ones set down for everyone else.

In the end, they, like the Chthonians, were a law unto themselves. The only difference being that the Cthonians truly had no one holding their leash. At least with the Dolophoni, the Erinyes could call them off. Not that they did that often. The Furies had a tendency to revel in conflict, and there was nothing they loved more than a good bloodbath.

Megeara sat back on her heels to stare at him. The dawn's light highlighted her hair and made it glow. Her cheeks were pink, and all he could think of was the hours he'd spent kissing those lips.

And the hours more he'd like to spend making love to her.

He was already hard for her, wanting to taste her again. Why wouldn't she grab him in this realm the way she did in the other?

"You are so beautiful."

She gave him a doubting look. "Man, you hit your head hard, didn't you?"

He frowned. "Why can't you take a compliment?"

"Because I'm just not used to them. I come from a family that doesn't believe in randomly patting people on the back. The assumption is if no one's yelling at you, you're doing a great job. And no one ever complimented each other on appearances. Those are trivial. It's what's inside that matters."

His smile turned gentle and guileless. "And you're even more beautiful there."

Geary merely stared at him. What did a woman say to that? "Thank you." But that was extremely inadequate for what she felt. Everything about Arik touched her deep and made her want to stay with him.

"Hey, Gear?"

She turned at Teddy's call. "Yeah?"

"We got a kink in the dredge. Justina is working on it right now. I just wanted to let you know."

"Thanks."

Geary pulled back and smiled at Arik. "We've got a lot to do. You feeling up to it?"

"Absolutely. I'm here to help."

And over the next hour as they prepared the boat and equipment, he proved to be true to his word. No matter how hard or dirty the task, he lent himself to it without complaint.

They were just about to weigh anchor when Solin showed up on the docks looking perfectly groomed and highly offended.

His eyes heated, he boarded the boat and made his way straight to Geary. "You weren't about to leave me, were you, Doctor?"

Geary didn't know what to say. Honestly, she'd forgotten about him.

Luckily, Arik showed up at that moment and distracted Solin from chastising her. A stern frown creased Solin's brow as he noted the slight bruise on Arik's forehead. "What happened to you?"

"He fell out of his hammock last night," Geary explained. "And if you two will excuse me, I want to get under way immediately."

Arik didn't speak until he was alone with Solin.

"Hammock?" Solin said with a mocking laugh. "It looks more like you had a run-in with something hard."

"I did. The Dolophoni showed up last night in my dreams."

Solin went completely still. Anger radiated out of him with such ferocity that it actually singed Arik. One would think they'd attacked him instead. "How many?"

"Ten."

Solin arched a shocked brow. "And you lived? I have to say I'm surprised."

"I don't go down easily."

"Apparently. So how did you get away from them?"

"They pulled back after I killed one of them, then—"

Solin gaped. "You what?" he asked in disbelief.

"I killed one of them."

Solin gave him a look of supreme respect. "How did you manage that?"

"I'm real good at what I do." He didn't say that arrogantly, he was only stating fact.

"Yeah, and have you any idea of the firestorm you've just unleashed for yourself? The Dolophoni don't like people to get the better of them."

"I know and I'm sure we'll battle again."

Solin shook his head as he looked out over the water.

One corner of his mouth lifted into an evil grin. "So which bastard did you nail?"

Arik didn't know their names, but he had a feeling Solin must have had more than his fair share of run-ins with them to be this interested. "The one with a staff."

Solin laughed. "Erebos. Good man. Wish I could have seen it. Zeus knows I've been wanting to shove that staff up his ass for centuries." He indicated Arik's face. "Are you sore, too?"

"Yes."

"Amazing."

And it was. None of this made sense. There shouldn't be a single remnant of their battle on him. With the exception of death, things that happened in the dream realm shouldn't transfer to the human plane. It just didn't happen. "All I can figure is it has something to do with the fact that I'm Skoti and don't belong in this realm. Maybe that's why I can feel dream pain in this world."

"Maybe."

Suddenly the sound of a tin whistle rent the air as the boat engines started up. Arik cocked his head as someone started playing an Irish tune. A few seconds later, he heard a beautiful voice singing the folk song "I'm a Man You Don't Meet Every Day." The rest of the crew picked up the song as they pushed away from the dock and headed out of the harbor.

Every one of them was working together, and the sight of them like that warmed him.

Arik smiled at the camaraderie. "They're incredible, aren't they?"

"What? Humans?"

He nodded.

"They can be, I suppose."

Arik watched Solin as he kept himself apart from the

others, and he couldn't help wondering what it would be like to have the best of both worlds. To be able to feel and walk among humans both in this realm and in the sleep one. How could Solin be so lackadaisical about it all? Surely he had to appreciate the beauty of this world. "So what's it like?"

Solin frowned. "What's what like?"

"Being human."

He let out an angry scoff. "Basically sucks. I highly recommend returning to your godhood as soon as you can."

Arik didn't understand that. There was so much charm here. So much of everything. "Listen to their song . . . look at the landscape. How can you not love it here?"

Solin curled his lip. "Disease. Filth. Waste. Crime. Brutality. What's there to like?"

"There's brutality on Olympus."

"True. But I hate humanity as much as I hate the gods. Both groups are selfish bastards bent on destroying everything around them. They were given a perfect world and rather than enjoy it, they'd rather destroy it and each other. Excuse me if I don't look at them with love in my eyes but rather scorn in my heart."

Arik cocked his head at the heated rancor that bled from every part of Solin. "Yet you're helping me. Why?"

His features blank, Solin shrugged nonchalantly. "Nothing better to do. Eternity is boring. Really boring. I'm hoping that when you pop the seal on Atlantis, there will be a giant explosion to add some humor and interest to my life. If we're really lucky, Apollymi will come out and thoroughly entertain us with a massive fireworks display. Hell, if she does half of what she did last time, there will be belly rolls aplenty for those of us who hate the Olympians and humanity."

Arik didn't understand how anyone could get bored

with the sensations of the human existence. Never mind hate it to such an extent. But then, Solin had been here for centuries. Perhaps, given time, he'd become jaded, too.

As the song ended, the crew picked up with the Beatles' "Revolution 1."

"Hey, Arik?"

He turned as Tory came running up to him with a small foil package that she handed to him. "Frosted Pop-Tarts. Fudge. Trust me." Then she went bounding off again.

Laughing, he realized it must be more food. She seemed bent on corrupting him.

Solin wandered off while Arik broke into the package and realized that Tory had excellent taste. These things were delicious. While the Beatles melted into the Bee Gees, the boat picked up speed as it raced them to the spot where eleven thousand years ago a very pissed-off goddess had destroyed her family and sent an entire continent to the bottom of the sea.

Popular legend told that it'd been Apollo who had destroyed Atlantis because their queen had ordered the death of his child and mistress. It was good propaganda for the Greek pantheon, who wanted to be thought of as the most menacing. But the truth was very different.

They were neophytes compared to the Atlanteans. Their power nothing.

Apollymi the Destroyer would have swept over the entire earth until nothing was left standing had she not been imprisoned in the middle of her bloodthirsty tirade by a trick of fate. Now she sat trapped in her netherworld, Kalosis, watching this one, waiting for someone to free her.

Even though Arik lacked his god powers, he could hear

the Atlantean goddess calling out for release. She was like a beacon, summoning people to her. It was probably why so many quested for Atlantis.

The other gods were why those quests ultimately failed. No one other than Apollymi wanted her released.

He looked up to catch Kat's gaze from where she stood on the prow. They were at odds over this, but so long as Megeara didn't disturb the seal, what was the harm in her poking around the ruins? So she'd find a few shards of pottery and maybe some jewelry. None of that would interfere with Apollymi's prison.

They were safe.

At least that was the lie he wanted to believe.

SOLIN FROZE AS HE MOVED ALONG THE DECK AND SAW the exceptionally tall woman standing by the railing. Lithe and graceful, she was completely striking. But greater than her beauty was the power emanating from her. It was an aura he knew well. She was an Olympian.

And there was nothing he hated more than Olympians.

He approached her cautiously, sizing her up and wondering how much power she carried. "You have the presence of a god, but I don't know you."

Her green eyes narrowed suspiciously on him, and he knew she was feeling his powers to measure him just as he was her. "I'm a servant to Artemis."

He laughed at those words. "*You* a servant? You have much more power than that and we both know it."

"And you have a lot of juice for a demigod. Makes me wonder if you haven't made a deal with someone yourself."

Solin gave her a cocky smirk as he glanced about to make sure the humans couldn't overhear them. "I like to keep people guessing about me."

"I'll bet. So what brings *you* here? Isn't it unusual for two Dream-Hunters to work together?"

"Not really. There are a lot of tag-team Skoti out there who make it their habit to work together." He looked her up and down, taking in her delectable body. She was prime material for his kind to play with in dreams. "I'm surprised you haven't been visited."

"Oh, I'm not. Artemis fed the last person who made a pass at me to a wild boar. When it comes to my dreams, she's even worse. Only the most suicidal would tread there."

"Oooh." He sucked his breath in sharply at her warning that actually made him smile with anticipation. It also made him instantly hard. "You make it all the more tempting."

She returned his smile, only hers was beguiling, with a hint of malice and challenge. "And you still haven't answered the question of the day. Why are you here, Skotos?"

He shrugged nonchalantly. "Originally, I was just going to screw with Arik. But I'm rethinking that now. I mean honestly, this whole situation shouldn't be the least bit interesting, but with you here that means that Artemis is extremely interested. And anything she's interested in I'm interested in, which means things around here are about to get really interesting. Wouldn't you say?"

"Not really. Why not save yourself the headache and sod off?"

"Oh see now, that's no way to get me to leave. You're pushing me away. Why?"

"I find you irritating."

He laughed at that. "I haven't even begun to irritate you yet. Imagine what I could do if I applied myself?"

Her eyes narrowed dangerously. "I can imagine. I can

also imagine ripping your throat out and tying my shoes with your larynx."

"Really, *kori,* you have to stop. You're seriously turning me on."

She screwed her face up at him. "You're a sick bastard, aren't you?"

"Is that not the very definition of a Skotos?"

She stepped back from him before she looked around the boat to make sure no one was within earshot. Her gaze paused on Arik. "As you can see, we already have one of you on board. We don't need another."

"That's what everyone thinks, but they were running a special. Two Skoti for one, so here I am in all my glory just to get under your skin or skirt. I'm really not particular."

"Yes, but there is a law that says you can send back defective merchandise. I can't think of anything more defective than you."

"I can. An immortal possessing god powers who passes herself off as a servant and expects the rest of us not to notice. Definitely defective, don't you think?"

"I think it's none of your business."

"Hmm. . . ." He really was becoming intrigued by her, and that was highly unusual for him.

She cocked her head and looked at him. "Why do you hate Arik so anyway?"

The question was a non sequitur and surprised him. "Excuse me?"

"I have the powers of a god, remember? I can feel your emotions and they are ripe with malice. Why do you hate him?"

He gave her a patronizing smirk. "If you know that much, then you should know the answer."

"I can only feel emotions, I can't trace their roots. And

you are eaten alive by what I feel, which also begs the question of how a Skotos has emotions that strong."

Solin shrugged. "I'm only a halfling, remember? We're immune to the curse."

"Ah," she said as if she finally understood.

He was intrigued by her tone. "What?"

"I was wrong. It's not hatred, it's envy."

He laughed at the very idea. *Him* jealous of a Skotos? Pah-lease. "You don't know what you're talking about."

He could tell by her tone that she was amused by his denial. "Yes, I do. The smell of it is all over you. You're ripe with it. Envy is just gnawing away at you like a worm inside a juicy apple." She tsked at him. "Yep, there's not enough deodorant in the world to mask that odor."

She was being ridiculous and he was growing tired of dealing with her.

"This discussion is over." He started away from her.

"Wait."

He paused to look back. "Yes?"

"I've already told Arik and now I'm telling you I will not allow him, Geary, or anyone else to uncover Atlantis. Ever."

He sneered at her concern. "As if I give a shit about Atlantis. I have much more self-serving interests at heart."

"And what would those be?"

"As you so eloquently put it, it's none of your business. Good day, goddess. And good luck."

ARIK PAUSED AS THEY NEARED THEIR DESTINATION. APOLlymi's voice grew louder as the boat slowed. They were only a few feet away from where the main harbor of Atlantis had once stood. If Arik closed his eyes, he could still see it in his mind.

It'd been a bustling port, filled with merchants, pirates,

and fishermen. Prostitutes, sailors, and officials had blended in seamlessly on the docks that had always been crowded to overflowing. The smell of fish, spices, and perfumes had hung heavy here as the capital city had glistened on a mountain from behind stone walls.

Highly advanced, the Atlanteans had been a peaceful race who'd only wanted to help others. But Zeus and Apollo had refused to let them exist that way. The Greek gods had waged war on the Atlantean pantheon by manipulating their people.

In the end, it'd been those people who'd suffered most.

Pushing that thought aside, Arik glanced about the boat that was filled with people wanting to learn the truths he already knew. Humanity was better off with Atlantis at the bottom of the sea.

The crew rushed about as they set up for their doomed excavation. Arik crossed the deck to where Solin stood by the pump. "I need a favor."

"Haven't I done enough for you?"

Arik scoffed. "Considering what you did to me, no. Or more to the point, hell no."

"I would disagree, but curiosity has me by the throat. What is it that you want now?"

"Knowledge," Arik said simply.

"Of what?"

"How to dive."

Solin's eyes narrowed speculatively. "Why?"

Arik gave him a droll stare. "Why do you think? I want to make sure they don't venture into the wrong area and disturb a certain goddess. I can't do that two hundred feet above her, can I?"

Solin still looked less than convinced. "Megeara won't let you go."

"If I know what I'm doing, how can she stop me?"

Solin laughed. "You've got a lot to learn about women." He narrowed his eyes before he placed his hands on Arik's head.

Arik felt a sharp stinging pain an instant before he had all the knowledge he needed to dive like a pro. Unfortunately, he also had a nosebleed. "What the hell?"

Solin looked on him derisively. "You're human and I just rewired your brain. It doesn't like that. As gods, we can accept these things. As a human . . ." He pulled out a handkerchief and handed it to Arik.

Great. Just great. Arik wiped the blood away before he went over to Megeara, who was checking the air hoses. "Where's my suit?"

Geary actually gaped at the unexpected question. "Excuse me?"

He indicated the dry suits that were beside her. "I plan on going with you."

Her mouth worked for several seconds before sound would actually come out. "Uh . . . no. This isn't a game, Arik."

"And I'm not playing. I intend to go with you and help. Trust me. I know what I'm doing."

Geary was skeptical. The last thing she needed was an amateur on board.

"He's not lying," Solin said as he joined them. "I can assure you, he's part fish. Jacques Cousteau has nothing on him. Aquaman, either."

Still, she wasn't sure as she frowned at Solin. "You do know how dangerous this is?"

"I wouldn't send him down there if I didn't fully believe he'd be back to piss me off." Solin had a delivery so dry, she could rent him out as a dehumidifier.

Geary hesitated. She didn't want any of her team hurt.

Or Arik, either. "If you can swim like a fish, how is it you were drowning when we met?"

Arik tensed. He'd forgotten about their meeting. Luckily he was quick with a response. "I'd been swimming for a while when you found me and was tired. Normally, I don't have any problems. I was just lucky that day . . . in more ways than one."

There was no missing her skepticism.

Kat came up to her. "What's going on?"

"Arik wants to dive with us. I don't know."

Kat and Arik exchanged a look that was both hostile and respectful. "Do you know what you're doing?" Kat asked.

"Yes."

"Then let him go with us. What's the worst thing that could happen?"

Geary scoffed at Kat's nonchalance. "Death."

Kat shrugged. "You can die crossing the street, and there aren't many cars two hundred feet down."

She strangely had a point.

Kat wrinkled her nose at Geary. "Let him go. I'll keep an eye on him. Believe me."

Kat was the only person Geary knew who was an even stronger swimmer than she was. If Kat said it was okay, then it should be. Geary looked back at Arik. "All right. You can suit up."

Geary watched Arik closely to make sure that he wasn't lying about his expertise as he prepared for the dive. She had to give him credit. He wore the gear as if he'd been born to it and he did know how to dress in it. There was no hesitation in his movements at all.

But that confused her. "Tell me how someone who was raised in the mountains would have been diving."

Arik froze at the question as he tried to think up a

plausible tale. "I told you, I've been searching for Atlantis. It's hard to do that on the surface. I've spent a lot of time on research boats here in the Aegean."

"Hmm . . . you know, there's something about you that doesn't make sense. But I can't figure it out."

He offered her a soothing smile. "All you need to know is that I'm here to help you."

Instead of those words drawing her closer to him, she took a step back and her eyes flashed with suspicion. "Yeah."

Arik wanted to curse in frustration, but he didn't have time. They were getting ready to go down. There were four of them for the dive. Geary, Kat, him, and Scott.

Geary led them to the platform that would lower them, along with a dredge, to the water. None of them spoke until after they'd submerged. Arik could hear his own breathing as he followed them deeper, away from the surface light.

It was murky and dark. But it was the pressure of the water against his body that was the strangest part of it all. And the deeper he went, the worse it became. It was almost oppressive, and part of him wanted to panic. But that was ridiculous. It was only water, and he was with people who knew what they were doing.

For that matter, he knew what he was doing.

Geary paused at the first dive station to let her body adjust to the pressure and depth. "How's everyone doing?"

Scott grinned. "Great, boss lady."

Kat nodded. She looked at Arik.

He inclined his head to her. "Fine."

But something belied that. It was an instinct she had, and she didn't know why. "Are you sure?"

"Yeah. I'm just having a vision of what would happen if someone were to jerk one of our helmets off at two hundred feet down."

Geary screwed her face up in distaste.

"Ew," Kat snapped.

Geary concurred. That was the kind of thing that no one wanted to think about.

Scott cleared his throat. "Is it too late for me to go back? I'm not sure I want to be down here with Freddy Krueger having these kinds of visions. What's to keep him from having an experiment?"

Geary shook her head. "Arik was just kidding. Weren't you?"

"Absolutely. But—"

"No buts," the three of them said in unison.

Geary patted Arik on the shoulder. "Let's just think happy thoughts, shall we?"

"You know," Tory's voice filled their heads from the link. "Now that Arik mentioned it. At two hundred feet, given the pressure on the human body—"

"Tory!" Geary snapped. "Please don't give me odds or stats right now, 'kay?"

"You're such a spoilsport."

Ignoring the pout in Tory's tone, Geary started down to the next station. She'd factored in four stops to help them adjust. But honestly, she wanted to be able to dive straight to the site.

If only.

It took them a little bit of time to get to the area and then to stake it out. They had to be careful to anchor the grid but not accidentally damage something that might be hiding under the silt and sediment.

Geary's father had drilled into her head that much of the historical Troy had been lost because of Heinrich Schliemann's fervor to find proof of it. He'd damaged as much as he'd salvaged.

She didn't want to make the same mistake.

Once the datum was set and photographed, they regrouped.

"How's everyone doing?" she asked them.

They each gave her a thumbs-up.

"Everyone's air supply is steady?" she double-checked.

Scott nodded. "Doing great, boss."

"I'm good," Kat chimed in.

Arik grinned at Geary. "Let's dig."

Something hot pierced her at his eagerness. He really did seem to mirror her enthusiasm. Geary headed for the first section she wanted to explore. They carefully suctioned the area until they could find what appeared to be an encrusted wall.

Her hand actually shook as she touched it. She just wished she weren't wearing gloves, so that she could have the tactile sense of it. "This isn't a natural object," she said, looking at Scott for verification.

"No. It's too precise."

Geary took a picture of it while Scott scraped a sample of the sediment.

"I see you. . . ."

She froze at the sound of the low, seductive female voice in her head.

"You're so close, little rose. Playing with the wall. But that's not what you want, now is it?"

Geary looked at the others, but they didn't appear to hear the voice. *Who are you?* she asked in her head.

"I am what you seek, Megeara. I am Atlantis. Move closer to me, child. Three feet over. Dig down below the silt. There's a box waiting for you. . . ."

It was crazy to even entertain the idea of obeying the voice. What could it know?

And even as she told herself to ignore it, she found herself doing what the woman had said.

"Geary?"

She ignored Kat's voice as she dug into the silt. It swirled around her in a hazy blur. As she dug deeper, she found nothing.

I am insane.

"Geary!" Tory's voice was sharp through the intercom. "Stop moving."

She froze.

"Move the camera half an inch right."

Geary did as ordered. "Why?"

Before Tory could answer, Geary saw what her cousin had seen on the feed. It was the corner of something that appeared to be a box.

No . . .

Geary held her breath as she gently pulled it free. It was encrusted with funky deposits from the sea. But that wasn't what fascinated her.

The box was ancient, with a clear design of lions pulling a chariot where a tall god holding a staff stood, directing them. It, like her necklace, held that strange indecipherable writing.

Her hands shaking, she carefully pried the lid off to see what the box contained.

"What is it?" Tory asked, her voice filled with anticipation. "I can't see it, Geary. What's inside?"

Geary let out her breath in frustration as she realized the box was empty. "Nothing, Tory. But the box is old."

She handed it off to Scott so that he could preserve it for examination topside later.

Hoping to find something even better, Geary had bent down to continue her search when she heard what sounded like Tory dropping something. There were muffled voices in the background like someone was arguing, but Geary couldn't tell what was going on.

"You okay, bud?"

There was no answer.

"Tory? Christof?"

Two seconds later, something popped loud in her ears. It was followed by nothing but empty static.

CHAPTER 12

THERE WAS NO WORSE FEELING FOR GEARY THAN TO THINK that someone she loved was in danger and to not be able to get to them. Geary was hysterical as she forgot about her quest and swam as quickly as possible through the dark water.

"Geary!"

She ignored Kat's call. The only thing that mattered was getting topside to see what was going on.

Suddenly Arik was there, pulling Geary back. "You've got to calm down. You're breathing too rapidly."

She shook her head at him. "That sounded like an explosion. I have to get up there."

"All we heard was a pop." His tone was level and calm as those blue eyes haunted her. "It could have been anything. All we know is the intercom is malfunctioning. You don't want to die over that, do you?"

He was right and she hated him for it. Nodding, she

pressed her hand against her helmet to listen more carefully. "Tory? Are you there? What's happening?"

There was still no answer.

"Tory? Christof? Justina? Thia? Dammit. Someone answer me . . . please."

Arik held his breath, wishing he could ease her mind. But as the silence stretched on, he knew what she did. Something had to have—

His thoughts stopped as a piece of twisted metal shot past him on the right. It was followed by more pieces that rained down around them through the water.

And it was obvious what the metal was.

"Uh, folks," Scott said, his voice shaking. "I think that's our boat trying to kill us."

Yeah. Arik had a bad feeling the kid might be right. Shit.

Arik looked at Kat and could tell she had no more information than he did.

He closed his eyes and summoned his brother with his mind. "*Solin . . .*"

There was no answer from that end, either, which boded even more ominously than their exploded boat.

Arik let go of Megeara. "All right, let's head up. Safely."

"Okay." But he could hear the panic and fear in Megeara's voice.

He hesitated as Megeara and Scott went first so that he could swim beside Kat. "Any clue?"

She shook her head glumly. "You know if the boat's gone, so's our air supply."

He'd thought of that himself. So far their air was holding. Which was another reason they needed to get up immediately. They didn't have much reserve, and since he was human, he could die here, which was the last thing he wanted. Kat was the only one of them who didn't have that fear. Lucky bitch.

As they swam for the first decompression station, Arik tried his best to reach Solin repeatedly while Megeara continued to call through her intercom for the others.

And repeatedly there was nothing from above, except for a few pieces of metal that continued to float by as they headed for the floor of the sea. Yeah, nothing like watching your life pass you by, knowing you were even more sunk than it was if you didn't get to air soon.

They reached the first tank, which held two breathing hoses. The women went first, then he and Scott. They traded the lines back and forth as they waited for their bodies to adjust to the new depth before they swam any higher.

But each of them was rattled by what could have happened to the boat and the others.

"Arikos . . ."

He hesitated as he finally heard Solin's voice in his head. *"What's going on?"*

"The boat was blown up."

"No shit. We rather got that, as parts of it almost crushed us in the water. What happened and why didn't you stop it?"

"Yeah, right. Stop it, my ass. I'm not messing with this one."

Arik cursed at Solin's selfishness. *"Dammit, Solin. There's not enough air in the line for us. We might not make it back."*

"Is that supposed to mean something to me? You're all going to die anyway, right? What's the point? I still have to live here after you're all gone."

If Arik could lay hands on Solin, he'd kill him.

"This isn't a game, Solin."

"No, it isn't. And you're on your own. Good luck."

Arik ground his teeth as he took the hose from Megeara so that he could take a turn breathing. *"You better pray I don't make it up there to you."*

"Praying's for amateurs and you got much bigger problems than me."

Arik felt Solin drifting away from his thoughts. Megeara took the hose and breathed deeply before she swam upward again. Arik and the others followed her.

They were halfway to the second station when more debris started falling through the water. What the hell? Had another boat blown up?

Arik swam up to Megeara as she started moving even faster.

"Megeara. Stop. We have to breathe slowly. You know that. Stay calm and focused."

Geary wanted to shove him away from her, but she knew he was right. She couldn't afford to fight him in the water. Right now, they had reserve air at the stations. They could stay there until their bodies readjusted. Then they could hold their breath and move to the next. But this was taking too long for her tastes.

She had to know what was going on. What had happened to the others.

Her heart heavy, she looked at Scott, who had tears in his eyes. "We'll be okay, Scott."

The doubt he held burned through her. "Yeah, right."

"No more talking," Kat snapped at them. "We have to preserve what air we got."

Arik took Geary's hand and squeezed it before he urged her up through the water. Geary obeyed, but as she swam, a thousand thoughts went through her mind. Her brother had died over a malfunction in his tank.

She'd always wondered what had gone through Jason's mind in those last few minutes as he realized his life was about to end. She had to say it sucked. Memories and unfulfilled dreams poured through her with a burning intensity.

She didn't want to die. She was young and though she hadn't dated much, she still held on to the dream that one day she'd meet a great guy and have kids. That she would grow old with someone who treasured her as much as she treasured him. Was that too much to ask?

There was so much she wanted to do. And now she might never even see daylight again. It wasn't fair—to come so close to her goal and die before she could finish her quest.

But the worst thought was that Tory and Thia might be dead. Justina, Teddy, Christof, and all the others . . .

And it would be her fault. *All* her fault. God, how had her father lived with the guilt? No wonder he'd become an alcoholic. In that moment, she had an understanding of him that she'd never had before. She'd spent so much time blaming him that she hadn't even considered the blame he'd reserved for himself. The gnawing pain of knowing he'd endangered his family and the memory of them dying because of his actions.

I am so sorry, Dad.

If she got out of this and if the others were okay, it was over. She would never jeopardize other people again. This was just a stupid dream that wasn't worth another drop of blood. Another life. Atlantis didn't want to be found.

She was through.

Suddenly Geary realized that the water was getting lighter. Looking up, she could see the sunlight refracting in the waves over her head.

Not much farther . . . Her joy was tempered by the fear

of what she would find there waiting for her. Of what had happened to the rest of their crew. Horrific images haunted her. Thoughts of Tory and Thia lying facedown in the water. Or disfigured . . . of them calling out to her for help . . .

Please, please, please be okay.

Her throat was getting tighter as she neared the top. The pain of having no air in her lungs was oppressive and painful. Her lungs burned like fire as even more panic tore through her. How tragic to die this close to their destination. Just a few feet more and she'd reach the surface.

She began unfastening her helmet as she kicked up. Her limbs felt so heavy. Her heart was pounding from the strain. She wanted to take a breath so badly but knew that she couldn't.

Please. . . .

By the time she reached the top, she had the helmet off. Geary tossed it aside as she finally gulped air. She was shaking and cold as water rushed into her suit. But it was so good to be breathing freely again that she didn't even care.

She turned a circle in the water trying to get her bearings. The first thing she saw was the smoldering remains of their boat—not that there was much of it left.

Hysterical, she started swimming for it, only to have someone pull at her. She turned to find Arik there.

"They're dead," she sobbed, pulling away from him. "I have to go find them."

"They're not dead."

Anger tore through her and as she opened her mouth to tell him not to patronize her, he pointed in the opposite direction of the boat.

She looked to find the small life raft that held Tory,

Justina, Solin, Althea, Kat, Thia, Christof, and Brian. Relief tore through her with such ferocity that she sank back under the waves.

Arik caught her against him and helped her back to the surface. She was laughing and crying as she wrapped herself around him and kissed him. He'd never seen anything like this. It was like her emotions were completely beyond her control. She smiled at him before she left and headed for the others.

Baffled, he treaded water while Kat and Scott popped up beside him.

"Thank the gods," Kat said after she'd tossed her helmet aside.

"What the hell happened to the boat?" Scott asked.

Kat gave him a "duh" stare. "It appears to have blown up."

"Yeah, but why?"

She gave Arik a harsh stare. "That's an interesting question, isn't it?"

"Yes, it is."

Scott immediately swam after Megeara while Kat and Arik hung back.

"Do you think Zebulon had a hand in this?" he asked her.

Kat shook her head. "Not his style. He'd have simply crushed all of us and left nothing behind. No, this was a thoughtless act."

"Human then?"

"I don't know, but I will find out."

Arik frowned. There was an odd note in her voice and he had a sneaking suspicion that she knew exactly who was behind this and didn't want to betray them.

Arik would have blamed this on the Dolophoni, but it wasn't their style, either. Their fight was with him, which meant they'd have come to fight him in the water and not bothered threatening the ones on the surface. Not to mention, the Dolophoni wouldn't have been this sloppy. No, had they been here, he would have known it. For that matter, he'd be bleeding from it.

So then who?

Damn, enemies were falling out of the trees. Lucky them.

LAUGHING HYSTERICALLY, GEARY PULLED HERSELF ONTO the raft and grabbed both Tory and Thia in a giant hug.

"Hey! You're getting me wet!" Thia snapped, shoving at her.

Geary ignored Thia as she held her close. "Thank God you guys are all right."

Tory kissed her cheek. "And so's Kichka." She held up the material in her lap to show a very upset cat, who was hissing at them. "I scooped her up on the way out."

Geary kissed the top of her cat's furry head before she took Kichka from Tory and looked around at the others. Everyone was there and accounted for. "What happened?"

Tory indicated Solin with her thumb. "Solin said he smelled a gas leak. If not for him, we'd all be dead now."

Geary scowled at the explanation. "Gas leak? How? Christof and I are always meticulous about inspecting everything."

Tory shrugged. "I don't know."

They both looked at Solin, who seemed strangely imperious even though his hair was tousled and there were black stains on his immaculate suit. "I merely smelled it and had a bad feeling that something was about to, pardon the pun, blow."

"Uh-huh," Geary said, stroking her cat. "You have these psychic moments often?"

One corner of his mouth lifted into a mocking grin. "You have no idea."

There was such a strange note in his voice that it actually sent a chill down her spine.

Teddy passed a small flask toward her. "For you, Skipper. We're glad all of you made it back in one piece."

Geary thanked him as Arik, Kat, and Scott joined them on the raft. She didn't miss the hostile look Arik passed to Solin before he came to sit beside her.

"You better?" he asked.

She nodded.

"Good." Arik reached to pet Kichka on the head. Kichka hissed and spat at him before she reached out with one paw to pop his hand.

Arik jerked his hand away from her claws.

Geary was stunned. In all the time she'd had her cat, Kichka had never behaved in such a manner.

Arik scowled before he moved out of the cat's reach.

"Kichka," Tory admonished. "What's gotten into you, girl?"

It was Solin who answered. "She's probably just upset over what's happened. It's been a crazy, mad day."

Maybe. But there was something very strange going on here and Geary wanted to know what it was.

Geary turned her head to look at the remnants of the boat as help came. It'd been a close call. Too close. Today they had all been lucky.

But tomorrow . . .

She didn't want to think about that. God, what if Solin hadn't smelled the leak? What if the others hadn't listened to him? Instead of boat chunks flying by, it would have been her friends and family.

The thought sobered her.

"We have backups of all the data," Tory said, taking Kichka from Geary's hands. "We can redo everything."

"No," Geary said, her tone firm. "We're through with this."

Everyone on the raft with the exception of Solin and Kat gaped at her.

"What are you talking about?"

"How can we quit?"

"Are you insane?"

"We just got the permits! How can you even say that?"

The questions were fired at her in rapid succession. Geary held her hands up to quell their fury. "Look, guys, I'm not my father. I can't live knowing that I caused someone else to die. Least of all the people who are sitting here on this raft. We don't need this. I've been to one too many funerals in my life and I'm tired of it."

Tory glared at her.

"Yea!" Thia said happily. "Does this mean I get to shop more?"

"Shut up, Thia," Scott snapped. "Geary, think about what you're saying."

Tory held Kichka up to her chin. "Geary's had a bad shock today. Give her time to calm down and she'll change her mind. You'll see."

Geary started to correct her but didn't want to argue the point. Her mind was made up and there was no way she'd ever take another group this far out. Today had taught her a valuable lesson and she was going to heed it before it was too late.

Her resolve set, she stayed on the raft while the others boarded the small rescue boat.

Arik hung back with her. "Are you sure about this?"

"Completely."

She expected him to ride her, but instead he asked a

simple, flat-toned question. "Then what are you going to do with the rest of your life?"

She laughed. "I don't know. It's been years since I've thought past this interminable quest. What would you do?"

A devilish light glowed in his eyes. "Well, I personally would go back to shore. Shower and change into something nice, then go out to dinner with this guy who wants to spend a little time with me. Then I'd take him back to my place and rock his world."

His words warmed her and she couldn't resist teasing him. "Daydream about a lot of guys, do you?"

He laughed. "No, that's just what I'd do if I were *you*."

Smiling, she shook her head. "You're relentless."

He gave a weary sigh. "I'm never going to wear you down, am I?"

Geary had to admit he was gorgeous sitting there with his wet hair plastered around his sharp features, bruised though they were. And those eyes . . . they were the stuff of legends. What could one dinner with him really hurt? After all, he'd kept her calm today and watched after her. If not for him, she might very well have panicked and died today.

"All right. I'll take you up on it."

He actually gaped at her. Then his smile turned wicked. "Shall we get naked now? I definitely want to see you rock my world."

"The dinner, you loon. And *only* the dinner."

Arik pouted playfully. "Fine. If that's your best offer . . ."

"It is."

He stood up and helped her to her feet, then he assisted her in climbing up after Teddy. Geary tried not to notice the strength of Arik as he easily swung her up on board the rescue boat, then climbed up behind her. He was nimble and fast.

And he made her body melt.

Images of her dreams haunted her.

"Dr. Kafieri?"

She turned away from Arik as one of the officers came up to her. "Yes?"

"I need to ask you a few questions about your boat."

Nodding, she expected Arik to join the others. Instead, he stayed by her side, lending her his unspoken support while she was interrogated.

Kat moved to the back of the boat and remained silent as they headed for the docks. Solin joined her by the side with an intense look of displeasure etched into his features.

For a man who was completely amoral, his actions today surprised her. "Why did you save them from the explosion?"

He shrugged nonchalantly. "It was a momentary lapse in judgment, I assure you."

She wasn't buying that argument. "There's more human in you than you want, isn't there?"

"I have no idea what you mean. Whatever humanity ever existed has long since died."

Uh-huh. "Did you happen to see who was behind this?"

"I didn't see anything, but I felt . . ."

"Felt what?"

"A presence near and dear to your heart. It appears Artemis also has an interest in ending this expedition. Perhaps you should take this matter up with her."

Kat was frozen into place as he drifted away. It was as she thought. Her anger boiling, she stopped a passing sailor. "Where's the restroom?"

He gave her directions to it. Thanking him, she immediately headed for it and locked herself in. Then she closed her eyes and flashed herself to Olympus to speak with said goddess.

A warm breeze whispered against her skin as she opened the golden door to Artemis's temple. Dressed in a flowing white gown that set her pale features and vibrant red hair off to perfection, the goddess was lounging about on her throne while Satara, another of her handmaidens, played the harp for her entertainment.

Kat came to a stop before her goddess and crossed her arms over her chest. She looked to the other *koris* before she barked a single order, "Leave us."

Artemis sighed wearily. "You don't make that whisper, Katra."

"It's *call, matisera.* The phrase is 'you don't make that call.' But today I do."

The other *koris* lifted stunned eyebrows as they waited for Artemis to blast Kat. But she knew she was safe from death. Punishment she could handle.

Artemis pushed herself up. "Fine. *Koris,* leave."

They were immediately flashed from the room. Artemis narrowed her eyes as she rose from her throne to stand beside Kat, who was a good two inches taller than the goddess she served. "What is your breakage?"

"Damage, *matisera.* The phrase is 'What is my damage?' And I want to know why you blew up the boat."

Artemis rolled her eyes and made a disgusted sound in the back of her throat as if she couldn't believe Kat would ask such a trivial question. "Because I felt like it."

"You felt like it? Good grief, *matisera,* have you any idea how disconcerting it is to be underwater when the boat that's supplying you your air comes floating down past you?"

She scoffed. "Why are you so angry? It's not like you can die. Get a grab."

"Grip."

"Whatever." Artemis turned on her with green eyes

blazing. "I don't care what it takes or who has to die. Preserve that seal, Katra. I heard Apollymi calling to you and to that other bitch. I know she was guiding her toward the seal. Box, my elbow. Apollymi knew what she was doing. She won't rest until she's free and I'm dead."

"You can relax. I'm not going to allow Apollymi to be free."

"No? Then act like it. Remember at the end of the day which of us has protected you. Shielded you. Nurtured you. You're nothing but a tool to Apollymi."

"And what am I to you, *matisera*? Am I not your tool?"

Artemis's face flushed with color caused by her anger. "You know what you are to me. Now go and do as you're told. Keep that human from Atlantis."

Kat ground her teeth at the order. "When will you learn to trust me?"

"Trust you?" Artemis asked in an aghast tone. "You went behind my back to Kalosis and then bound yourself to my most mortal enemy. Why should I ever trust you again?"

That ignited Kat's own temper. Why did Artemis always bring up something that had happened thousands, and it was *thousands,* of years ago? "You know why I had to see Apollymi."

It didn't placate Artemis in the least. "After all I have done for you, sacrificed for you, you slapped me in my face. If it were anyone other than you, I'd have killed you for what you've done."

"Then kill me."

Artemis hissed at her, "Don't tempt me, Katra. Ever."

"And don't push *me, matisera*. I know the source of your powers and you know the depth of mine. If we ever go to war, who do you think would win?"

Artemis curled her lip. "You are your father's child. Impudent. Surly. Argumentative and spiteful."

Kat laughed at that. "Strange, I would have sworn it was my mother you're describing."

Artemis's hair flew around her as her face mottled with rage. Her incisors grew to fangs as she spat at Kat. The air around Artemis sizzled with power an instant before she raised her hands and shot a bolt at Kat.

But it didn't hit her.

Before it came near, Kat flashed herself back to the boat.

"Heed me, Katra," Artemis growled in Kat's mind. *"I am not one to be trifled with."*

Katra rolled her eyes at the angry voice. "My loyalty to you is above reproach, *matisera*. One day, I hope you will know that."

"I will know it only when you help me kill Apollymi. Until that day, I will always have my doubts."

"I can never hurt her."

"Then I can never fully trust you. So long as your loyalty is split between us, you are as great a threat to me as she is."

"Do you honestly believe that?"

"Believe it? I know it. And that is why your boat is lying on the seafloor. Next time you go near that seal, I will make sure that you pay for it with flesh and bone. And the humans will pay with their lives."

That was a beautiful thought. "Love you, too, *matisera*. Thanks."

"Kat?"

She jerked as she heard Tory's voice. "Um, yeah?"

"Are you okay in there? I heard you talking to someone."

Kat flushed the toilet before she opened the door. "Just thinking out loud."

By Tory's face Kat could tell the girl didn't believe her. "You were speaking in ancient Greek."

"Just practicing. You never know when it could come in handy."

"True. We might one day clone Aristophanes and need an interpreter."

"Yeah." Kat stepped past her and headed back to the topside. As she ascended the ladder, a whisper went through her.

"I will be free, Katra. Neither you nor Artemis can keep me bound here forever."

Kat could actually feel Apollymi's breath on her neck. Feel the touch of her hand. *"We both know why you can't leave Kalosis."*

"And we both know why I must. . . ."

Kat had no sooner stepped on the upper deck than she met Solin, who gave her an amused stare.

"I really hate voices in my head, don't you, Kat?"

She forced her features to remain blank. "I have no idea what you mean."

"Of course not."

As he moved away, she stopped him. "For the record, I'm not on their side."

He arched a brow at her. "Whose side?"

"Anyone's. My loyalty is to myself."

"Why are you telling me this?"

She smiled. "Because we are similar creatures. I have my own agenda here and I know you do, too."

"And what is your agenda?"

"To survive this expedition."

He laughed in the back of his throat. "That's something easier said than done, isn't it?"

"It's beginning to appear that way." Kat looked over to where Arik sat with Geary. They were leaning toward each other, and even though they weren't touching, there was no missing the electricity between them. How Kat wished to feel that way toward a man, but she wasn't that type of creature. Every woman she'd ever known had been ruined by a man.

She would never be so stupid.

"What about you, Solin? What do you want out of this?"

He gave her a harsh stare. "Mine is simple. I only want revenge."

"On who?"

"Everyone."

Before she could ask him to elaborate or at the very least to narrow his choice down from the few billion people on earth and in other realms, he drifted out of her reach. "Nice talking to you, too," she said under her breath. She was getting really tired of gods drifting away from her.

But that was no matter.

She was stressed enough walking the tightrope between Apollymi and Artemis.

Geary laughed at something Arik said. He was smiling as he looked up and caught Kat's gaze. She cocked her head at the way the two of them were acting as she felt the attraction between them. She understood the physical, but what surprised her was what she felt from Arik.

He thought he lusted for Geary, which he did. But there was more to his feelings than that. As a Skotos, he was used to taking his emotions from others. What he didn't realize was that his newfound emotions came from his feelings for Geary. They weren't Geary's feelings. They were his own. The giddiness and joy he experienced right now wouldn't be there if Geary were somewhere else.

And in that moment, Kat understood why Solin was helping him. Solin wanted Arik to know these feelings so that when they were gone and Geary was no longer here, Arik would mourn her. It was cruel beyond belief.

Be careful what you wish for, you just might get it.

Arik had wanted emotions and now he would experience the full array of them. May the gods have mercy on him.

Sympathetic pain sliced through her, but it was mitigated by the fact that none of this was her business. Arik had chosen this path.

And he would be doomed by it.

CHAPTER 13

GEARY STOOD IN FRONT OF THE FULL-LENGTH MIRROR, exhausted by her day and yet strangely thrilled at the prospect of being with Arik. She hadn't been on a date in over a year, and the last one had been particularly bad. She'd made the mistake of accepting an offer for dinner from a man she'd met at the local market. Since she'd spent a great deal of time in Europe, she was used to the differences in culture. But this guy . . .

He'd been commanding, controlling, and worst of all had monopolized the entire dinner conversation—which had mostly been about how great he was and how he'd make the world a better place if he were emperor. Of course, in her opinion, he'd be dragged through the streets and stoned fifteen minutes after he took that office.

She should have been so lucky—it was a pity the man hadn't been crowned emperor *before* their dinner.

It'd been the only time in her life she'd actually considered crawling out of the bathroom window to escape an obnoxious date.

If only she hadn't been in a low-cut dress and high heels. . . .

Tonight she had on pants and low-heeled Clarks—just in case.

"Geary, Mr. Arik is here for your date."

She smiled at Tory's loud voice, which was followed by a high-pitched meow from Kichka, and was again overwhelmed with gratitude that no one had been hurt today. Geary honestly wouldn't be able to survive knowing she'd killed someone in her quest.

Nothing was worth sacrificing a human life for.

Pushing that thought away before she became completely maudlin, Geary checked her makeup one more time, especially since she wasn't used to wearing it and hoped that she hadn't applied it too darkly. Or, more to the point, that she didn't look like a Kabuki actor.

"You can do this," she said to her reflection, trying to bolster her confidence. It was only dinner. She could survive that. There were no strings attached. Just two humans having food and good conversation . . .

Which she hoped wouldn't end with Arik thinking he was an all-powerful god of the known universe.

She pulled her light crocheted sweater out from under Kichka, who meowed in protest before swatting her hand with an indignant paw, then headed to the living room, where Tory was sitting with a copy of Plato's *Republic* in ancient Greek on her lap. Geary laughed. "Don't you ever get bored reading that?"

"Not really. There's always something in it that I missed the last time. The man is really, really deep."

Geary shook her head. "You're a sick girl, Tor. Sick, sick, sick."

"I know. I come by it honestly." She gave Geary a meaningful look over the top of her glasses.

"It's true," Geary agreed. "We come from a long line of people who live to read boring texts—I think it may be why we all die young. Complete boredom."

Tory stuck her tongue out at her.

Geary paused as she saw Arik waiting by the door. He was positively striking in a black suit with a white silk shirt that had the top two buttons undone to show a delectably tanned neck. His black hair curled becomingly around his face and shoulders while those crystal blue eyes radiated heat and intensity. For the first time since they'd met, he was clean shaven, which made him appear somewhat more tamed and cultured. But only a tiny bit. There was still that aura of raw power that emanated from him.

As she drew near, he handed her a bouquet of white roses. Geary smiled at the gesture as she took them and cupped them to her nose so that she could inhale their sweet scent. "Thank you."

"My pleasure." Then he crossed the room and handed a smaller bouquet off to Tory, who actually put her book down and beamed happily.

"For me, too?"

He nodded. "Least I could do for the woman who introduced me to fudge Pop-Tarts."

Tory squeaked as she took them and buried her face in their soft petals. "I love roses. Thank you."

"Anytime."

Geary kissed his cheek before she handed her roses to Tory to take care of. "Are you sure you're going to be all right by yourself?"

Tory scoffed. "You're the one wigging out over today, not me. I'm fine. You two go and have fun. I have plenty of stuff here to entertain me with. Plato rocks."

Geary glanced to the mountain of ancient Greek books on the coffee table and knew that Tory would be up all night reading. The girl really was insane. "Okay. But if you need anything, call Teddy. He said he was staying home tonight."

"Will do, Captain."

Arik opened the door for Geary to walk through. She paused as she saw Solin's limousine on the street, waiting for them. "Should I be afraid?"

He offered her his arm. "Not at all. Solin has already prepped me on how to behave tonight. No public gropings no matter how much you turn me on. He even showed me how to use cutlery so that I wouldn't embarrass you."

Geary frowned, wondering if he was joking. He didn't seem to be, but surely . . .

Her thoughts drifted as she entered the car with Arik behind her. A weird sense of déjà vu went through her, along with the scent of his aftershave and the strength of his body. He was a choice specimen who caused every part of her to sit up and beg for attention.

How she wished she had more of Thia in her. If she did, she and Arik would be getting naughty and naked in the back of the limo and poor George would be going blind from their raucous play. But she wasn't that type of woman. All she could do was dream. . . .

Arik sucked his breath in as Megeara slid over the seat to the opposite window. The way she moved, slow and easy, reminded him of her sliding over his body. If this were a dream he'd be able to pull her to him and kiss her until they were naked and blind with pleasure.

His swollen cock burned with need. But unfortunately, this wasn't a dream and she would probably have his head if he tried . . . and he didn't mean the one on his shoulders.

"You look incredible," he said as George shut the door.

Her cheeks pinkened. "Thank you. You look pretty good yourself."

He smiled. "Good. Solin can live another day."

"What do you mean?"

"He's the one who told me what to wear tonight. I didn't know if I should trust him or not, though. He's not the most reliable of people."

Her eyes softened as if she understood. "You two have an odd relationship, don't you?"

"You could say that. It often reminds me of a blowfish and a barracuda."

"Interesting analogy. So which one is you and which is Solin?"

He winked at her. "I'll leave that for you to decide."

Not sure what would least insult him, Geary didn't speak while they drove to a small seaside café. Her heart clenched as they left the car and she realized where they were.

Arik paused as he noticed her hesitancy. "Are you all right?"

She had to force herself to respond over the lump of sadness in her throat. "Yeah. Sorry. I was just thinking about something."

"What?"

She pointed to an old brick wall across the street that was beside a set of stone stairs that had been worn over time by intensive foot traffic and the elements. "My brother and I used to climb over that wall when we were kids. We'd pretend it was the wall of Troy." She gave him a sheepish look. "Yeah, I know, we were strange children. Jason would play Hector and I was always Achilles. We'd lob dirt clods and rocks at each other until either one of us was bleeding or my father would yell at us to stop. Then we'd sneak attack each other and plot our revenge."

She took a deep breath to stave off the pain. "God, how we'd play. Then when we were older, Jason used to come here to sit at this café and sketch what he thought this whole area would have looked like centuries ago." The corner table that he would always lay claim to because it had the best view was still there just as it had always been. The table looked as if it were waiting for the young man who would never again pass this way.

Her eyes misting, she looked up at Arik as all those memories ripped through her. Jason would spend hours telling her his concepts for his drawings. He'd been so precise and detailed in his descriptions that there were times when she would have sworn he had to have lived back then to know them all. How she wondered what he'd have been like now. What he'd think of her . . .

Shaking her head, she tried to dispel her bittersweet memories and the grief they caused.

"Can you imagine what the island must have looked like a thousand years ago? Two thousand?" she asked Arik.

Arik wished he had his powers. If he did, he would have granted her that wish. In one heartbeat, he could have shown her exactly what this place had looked like—firsthand.

Then again, he did have that power in another realm. "I'll bet when you dream tonight you'll see it."

He saw the doubt in her eyes before she answered. "Sure. Why not? I dream of enough other weird stuff."

"Such as?"

She blinked before she stepped away. "Nothing. Shall we eat?"

He hated whenever she closed herself off from him.

Especially when he knew how much more she was hiding. But then, he'd known her for a while now.

In her mind, they'd just met and they were all but strangers.

Regretting the necessity of that, Arik directed her toward the café. Solin had prepped him on how to greet the hostess and request a seat, but it was still very strange. It was odd how people left such trivial matters out of dreams. They simply cut to the chase and didn't waste valuable time with incidentals. If someone wanted to eat, they were in the restaurant, eating. There was none of this getting to it and requesting tables or waiting.

Dreams really were superior to reality.

After a bit of a wait, Arik and Megeara were seated at a table that overlooked the sea. Even though it was dark, they could still hear the surf and see the whitecaps as they rolled onto shore. Lights from boats and buildings in the distance twinkled like stars that had fallen to earth, while the smell of cooking food made his stomach grumble and cramp.

Arik was surprised by the sensation. He'd never been really hungry before. And the sights and sounds were overwhelming as they brought a peculiar ache to his chest. He didn't understand the source of it. He felt sad and happy for no apparent reason, and when he looked at Megeara, all he wanted to do was reach out and touch her. To ask her if the sight and sounds made her feel the same way.

"I've never eaten here before," Megeara said as she skimmed her menu. "What do you recommend?"

He frowned as he looked at his menu and wondered what he should suggest. "I don't know. I didn't think to ask that of Solin. Is that something a date normally knows?"

She gave him an arch stare. "Only if the date has eaten

at the restaurant before." Then she chided him, "Don't tell me you've never been on a date."

Arik realized he'd already made another mistake. She would never believe that he'd reached whatever age he appeared to be without having taken out a woman—it would be completely illogical for a human male to have kept to himself. "No, I have . . . just not like this."

She still wasn't buying it. "Not like this how?"

Think, Arik, think. "With a woman."

Her other brow raised as she gave him an amused smile. "So you've been on dates with men?"

Smooth move. Solin was right. He was a moron. "No, no. What I mean is that I've never asked a woman out on a formal date. I usually spend an evening or two with them and then leave." There, that sounded better and it was the truth.

"Then you what?" she asked, her voice tinged by anger. "You leave them waiting by the phone for a call that never comes? How wonderfully kind of you."

Why the sarcasm? What had he said that was so upsetting?

"No, that's not what I meant." How could one man get himself into so much trouble with just words? But he could tell from her body language and the fury in her eyes that he wasn't helping himself in this at all. "Why are you being so hostile to me, Megeara?"

"I'm not hostile. I'm merely trying to understand you and the things you keep telling me. I mean, how did you manage in Nashville with such a limited understanding of people and how things work?"

Nashville? What was she talking about now? He'd never heard of such a thing before. He was constantly baffled by her. "What is Nashville?"

She gave him a "duh" stare. "Where you claim to have met me. Remember?"

He shook his head. "No. That was Vanderbilt where we met."

"Yes, and Vanderbilt is located in Nashville, Tennessee."

Arik froze as he realized what he'd just done. In her dreams she'd never made mention of what town the school was in, and since he wasn't from this plane there was no way for him to know it.

He cleared his throat as he tried, yet again, to cover his blunder. "Oh, it's been a long time."

Instead of being comforted, she looked even more suspicious. "Six years isn't that long ago, especially not for a man who remembered me so well. And I don't see how a man raised in rural Greece could forget his trip to a bustling American city so easily, either. What's going on, Arik?" She narrowed her eyes on him. "You didn't meet me there, did you?"

"Of course I did," he said defensively. He had no choice except to try to brazen this out. "Why would I lie about that?"

Geary didn't know what to think. But something wasn't right with all of this. She could feel it in her gut and she could see it on his face. He was hiding something extremely important about their meeting. "How should I know why you'd lie? But you're not who you say you are, are you?"

"I am."

Yeah, right. "Be honest with me, Arik. Who the hell are you?"

"I've told you. I'm Contranides."

"Yeah, you keep saying that, but why don't I believe it?"

"I can't imagine. It's the truth."

Still, her gut warned her to put distance between them. Had they been alone, she would have. But they had plenty of people around them and she wanted some answers. "Tell me the truth, Arik. Why are you here with me?"

"I just want to spend time with you."

Wrong answer. "You keep saying that."

"Because it's true. I swear it."

She clenched her teeth as a wave of anger went over her. Why couldn't he tell her what was going on? Honestly, she was getting tired of his cryptic ways and things about him that just didn't add up. "I don't believe you."

"Then what do you believe?"

She didn't know, but the more the thought it over, the less any of it made sense. Something wasn't right with this. With him. She knew it. And his constant denials were making her feel as if she were losing her mind.

Glancing away, she caught sight of an incredibly intense man who was staring straight at them. At least six six and with an aura of "don't look at me or I'll kick your ass," he was wearing a long black leather coat and dark sunglasses even though it was nighttime. He had a small goatee and short black hair. There was something ominous about him. It was as if he was looking for someone to fight and kill.

She had to drag her gaze from him, back to Arik. "Do you know him?"

He followed her line of vision to see the man who was now making his way toward them. There was a knowing smile on the man's sardonic lips as he paused at the table next to them. The "killer" whisked his coat off with a flourish, and as he moved, a tattoo of a double bow and arrow on his biceps peeked out from beneath his sleeve.

"Evening, folks," he said to them in Greek as he took a seat.

"Good evening," she answered.

Arik merely inclined his head. But there was no missing his tenseness. He didn't like the newcomer and it was obvious.

"Is he a friend of yours?" she asked in a low tone.

Arik cursed silently at the presence of the Dark-Hunter. Immortal warriors in the service of Artemis, they protected mankind from the things that would prey on them. No doubt the Dark-Hunter could sense the essence of Arik's soul. Even though he was technically human at this time, he still had the soul of an immortal, and since Dark-Hunters were the protectors of human souls, the Dark-Hunter would know that Arik wasn't human.

Could the Dark-Hunter's timing have been any worse? Megeara was already suspicious enough. The last thing Arik needed was her asking questions about immortal vampire slayers.

And then he felt *it*. It was a whisper against his soul. A touch.

A threat.

The Dolophoni had found him. Their presence on this plane was unmistakable. They were here and they were looking for a fight. He glanced around the restaurant and street but couldn't find anything out of place. Everyone around him, except for the Dark-Hunter, was human.

"Is something wrong?" Megeara asked as she noticed Arik's fidgeting.

He knew the smile he offered her was extremely fake. "No. Nothing."

"You don't look like nothing's wrong. You look really nervous all of a sudden. What? You owe the guy next to us money or something?"

How he wished it were that simple. No, he owed one Greek god a human soul and a dozen more his life. Yeah . . . well, it was time to put a stop to at least one side of that statement. "I just need a moment. You wait here and I'll be right back."

Geary frowned as Arik got up and left her alone. She didn't know what concerned her more, the strange man at the table next to her who kept looking over as if he knew a secret she didn't, or Arik's peculiar behavior.

"You have an interesting friend there," the man said.

Geary cocked her head as she picked up a slight brogue in his Greek. "Are you Scottish?"

He laughed before he answered her in English. "I used to be something like that."

Geary frowned at his words. What? Something like a Scot? Was the man a Pict? He had the bearing of one of their ancient breed. . . . Yeah, right. That would only make him a couple of thousand years old.

She buried her sarcasm before she spoke again. "Do you know Arik?"

The man nodded before he looked off into the direction where Arik had vanished. "I met him a long time ago. He helped me out of a bad situation. He's helped a lot of people over the years."

There was an odd note in his voice. Dubious. And it made her wonder if Arik was a drug dealer or some other criminal. "Helped them how?"

"With this and that."

The vagueness was really starting to wear on her and it made her suspicions climb. Why wouldn't he tell her unless she was right and it was something highly illegal? Maybe they were arms dealers—Solin had never answered her question about what he did for a living. Ah jeez, that would be her luck. Hooking up with wanted fugitives.

Great.

She lifted her water glass up in a mocking toast. "Thanks for being ever so helpful."

He took her salute in stride. "My pleasure really. Have a good night."

Have a good night. Why did that not seem possible? *'Cause I'm having dinner with an arms dealer.* Or some other kind of criminal. She dismissed that thought in favor of another one. Where was Arik? He should have come back by now.

As if he heard her question, the man at the other table cocked his head as if listening to the air around them. His face turned to stone before he got up and jumped over the small chain that separated the café area from the street. He quickly made his way to the side of the building and vanished without even looking back at his coat.

What was that not so stealth action?

Geary knew that where he was going and what he intended was none of her business and yet she felt a deep compulsion to follow after him.

Don't be stupid. He could be an undercover cop of some sort. Hell, he could even be CIA. Interpol. Scotland Yard. Even an assassin or space alien. Her imagination went wild with possibilities.

But before she could stop herself, her curiosity won out and she got up and headed in the same direction where he'd disappeared.

Even as she went, she called herself every name she could think of. How stupid was this? What kind of idiot chased after a man who looked like a killer and was heading off into who knew what? *I'll stick to the shadows and if it gets bad, or looks scary, I'll run right back.*

You're an imbecile, Gear, a total flaming imby!

But the silent berating stopped the instant she entered

the alley to find Arik in the middle of a fight with the same twins she'd seen him fighting in her forgotten dreams. In one instant, the entire fight on the beach came rushing back to her.

Geary froze as she gaped at the impossibility of what she was seeing. This could not be happening.

The man she'd followed approached the twins slowly, with purpose. Arik was bleeding as he kicked one twin back and the other backed up to confront the newcomer.

"Stay out of this, Dark-Hunter," the twin warned the man she'd followed. "This doesn't concern you."

He shook his head. "Arikos and I go way back. You want to fight him . . . it involves me."

The twin started for him, but Arik ran at the twin and knocked him into the wall. Arik's gaze met hers and she saw his concern for her. "Get Megeara," he snarled at the one called Dark-Hunter. "Keep her safe."

The other twin literally ripped Arik away from his brother before he twisted open a butterfly knife and plunged it into Arik's side. Blood instantly soaked his shirt and poured over the man's hand.

Geary choked on a scream as she saw the pain on Arik's face. He gasped an instant before his eyes narrowed in anger.

"We're not in the dream realm now," the twin snarled into his ear, "and you're not so tough here, are you, Skotos?"

Arik hissed before he head-butted the twin and knocked him away. Then Arik jerked the knife from his side and held it in a bloodied fist. "Don't dismiss me, asshole. Here or there, I can still kick your ass." He moved to stab the twin, only to have the other twin lunge at him.

The Dark-Hunter caught Arik's attacker and kicked him back.

Geary turned to go for the police and instead ran into a huge man who had a demeanor so lethal and a body so solid that he should rent himself out as a wrecking ball. His face bore the wrath of hell as he pushed past her and threw his hand out.

All four men hit the ground hard, as if they'd been struck by something invisible. Including Arik, who lay on his back.

But the twins shot up immediately and when she said "shot up" she meant "shot" up. They literally cleared the ground by five feet as they arced from where they'd fallen to land just in front of the newcomer.

They stood before him united in strength and power. It was as if they existed in perfect symmetry.

"Stay out of this, Zebulon," the one on the right warned in a ragged voice full of venom. It was so raw and primal that it sent a shiver of fear over Geary.

Zebulon shook his head as if he couldn't believe them. "You guys come to my town, you don't call. You don't write. And you expect me to just let you run amok in front of the humans? Really, Deimos, don't tread here unless you want to bleed."

The other twin bared his teeth. "He belongs to us." He turned toward Arik, then froze.

"I'm not your bitch, Phobos. You didn't drag me out of the pound to put a collar on me. Don't expect me to heel because you say so. You are on my turf now. Think about it."

Deimos curled his lip. "We were sent here for him. How dare you interfere with the gods?"

Gods?

Geary took a step back as she again heard the female voice in her head telling her to take note. Note of what? Her fleeing intelligence? The fact that she was having a massive hallucination?

She was losing her mind . . . she knew it. But even so, she had to check on Arik. He was bleeding profusely and lay on the ground as if he was heading into shock.

Zebulon scoffed at the twins. "Did you miss my job description? Or were you just not paying attention the day I busted heads on Olympus? Fucking with you people is what I do. It's what I live for and I'm really tired of you now."

The twins vanished instantly.

Ignoring her, Zebulon inclined his head toward the Dark-Hunter. "You all right, Trieg?"

"I'm not the one bleeding, ZT. That's a question best asked of Arikos."

Geary was already at his side. Arik lay on the ground with his hand over the wound that was bleeding profusely. The blood coated his fingers and made her stomach wrench at the sight of it. The wound was so deep, she could actually see exposed bone. Sweat covered his face as he kept his jaw clenched to deal with the pain.

She brushed the hair back from his brow. "We need to get you an ambulance."

"Not really," Zebulon snapped from behind her. "You just need to move your butt and let me see him."

Before she could respond or move, Zebulon pushed her aside and ripped Arik's shirt open.

Geary cringed at the ragged wound the knife had left behind. "Don't hurt him."

Zebulon curled his lip at her. "Do you think I came all the way over here to hurt him? If I'd wanted him hurt, I'd have left him to Tweedle Dumb and Dumber." Turning back to Arik, Zebulon hovered his hand about an inch over the wound, and as he moved it back and forth the wound knitted itself closed.

Geary stared, dumbfounded, as shock poured through her.

Of course the wound healed itself. Sure. That made perfect sense, didn't it? Arik had left her alone at the café and a weird Scottishesque guy had led her to a battle with two men who'd been in her dreams, who could leap higher than the bionic kangaroo on steroids, and another scary dude who could heal gaping wounds with his hand.

It all made sense.

If you were on massive quantities of illegal drugs.

"Okay, I'm dreaming. Hallucinating. Brought on by stress. I had a hard day today and this is my mind trying to protect itself from . . . from stuff. Lots of stuff."

The three men were frowning at her, which only served to set off her temper.

"Oh, like I'm any less sane than the three of you just because I talk to myself."

Trieg cleared his throat. "I'm thinking you should wipe her memory, ZT. Do that Were-Hunter thing so that she goes back to normal and forgets all about us."

Zebulon scoffed. "I'm Chthonian, Trieg. We don't do that."

Grimacing at the response, Trieg rubbed the back of his neck. "I'm thinking you should start."

Geary took a step back and pointed with both index fingers over her right shoulder. "And I'm thinking I should take myself home." She pointed her finger at the men, winked, and made a small clicking noise by sucking her breath between her teeth. "You guys have a great night . . . with whatever it is you people do. See you later." She turned and took a step away, then swung back to face them. "On second thought, no offense, I never want to see any of you again. Good night."

With a quick word of thanks to ZT, Arik pushed himself up from the ground and ran after Megeara. Just as she left the alley he caught up with her and pulled her to a stop.

"Megeara—"

"Geary," she snapped.

"Geary," he said, hoping to placate her as he rubbed her arm in case he might have harmed her any by stopping her. "Please. I didn't want you to see any of that."

"See what?" she asked with a bit of hysteria in her voice, "I didn't see anything. There were no scary people there. Nothing freaky." She patted him on the biceps, then smiled as if nothing were wrong. "I'm going home now and tomorrow I'm going to have the doctors check for a brain tumor. Full battery of tests. Whole nine yards. Whatever's wrong with me, we'll find it and deal with it. At this point, my vote is either tumor or space alien testing. Either one works for me."

"You don't have a tumor and there aren't any aliens running around here. You're not insane."

"No?" Her face was aghast. "Then what am I?" She held her hands up before he could answer. "No, wait. The better question is, what are *you*?"

Arik wasn't sure how to answer. But then, there was no use keeping anything from her, since she'd already seen so much. It was time for complete honesty. "Do you know what an Oneroi is?"

The sarcasm in her voice was so deep it could drown a champion swimmer. "A Greek god of sleep. I did actually have to study this stuff before they allowed me a doctorate, you know?"

"I know," he said calmly. "Oneroi are gods of sleep." He spoke slowly, enunciating each word carefully. "You know me, Geary. You've known me for a long time. . . ."

She let out a nervous laugh and he could see the clarity

in her eyes as she looked up at him. "So what are you saying? You're an Oneroi?"

He nodded slowly.

Geary laughed. Hard. Until she realized that he wasn't joining her laughter.

She froze as a chill went over her. "You're a god, huh? Then tell me something only a god would know."

He didn't even hesitate with his answer. "The first night I met you in your dreams, you were bathing in a river of chocolate. Your entire body was coated with it and you were cupping your hands under the waterfall, then drinking the chocolate. I came up behind you and kissed your neck, then gave you a goblet that we both drank out of. You filled the cup, then poured the chocolate over me and licked—"

She placed her hand over his mouth to stop him from speaking. "You *were* there."

"I was there."

Disbelief poured through her. It couldn't be. It just wasn't logical. "What about Vanderbilt?"

"You dream about that at times. Reliving the horror of it. I snooped a bit."

Geary dropped her hand as memory after memory of her making love to the dream Arik played through her mind. Now to find out that it was real . . .

It pissed her off. "Snooped a bit? No, buddy, you've snooped a lot." Geary was mortified as various memories went through her mind. "I didn't know you were real. No. You can't be real. This is crap. It's all crap. You're lying to me."

"It's real, Geary." He took her hand into his and held it against his chest so that she could feel his beating heart. "*I'm* real."

She looked down at where he'd been stabbed. There

was no blood. No tear in his clothes where she'd seen his wound with her own eyes.

But there was still blood on *her* hands.

His blood.

He looked just as he had when he'd picked her up at her flat. Just as he'd looked when he had left her at the table and vanished.

Her gaze drifted over his shoulder to where Trieg was watching them from the shadows.

She pulled her hand away from Arik and gestured toward Trieg. "And he's just plain odd." She turned away from Arik and instantly walked into Zebulon again. Okay, it bothered her that he could just appear like that out of the blue, without warning, but she'd had enough. "And what is your problem that you keep putting yourself in my way?"

He answered with a sadistic laugh, "She's feisty, Skotos. I can see the appeal."

Arik snorted. "Oh, you've no idea."

When she tried to move past him, Zebulon stopped her. "Not to be rude, but what the hell? I live for it. You can't start running your mouth about what you've seen here tonight."

Oh, that was priceless. "Great threat you've got going there, big ZT. News flash, I didn't want to see anything. You people dragged me into this against my will, not the other way around, and who am I going to tell anyway? The last thing I want is to be dragged off and committed because I saw . . . something that no rational human being has ever seen before."

Zebulon gave her a cocky grin that conveyed both amusement and irritation. "I don't think you understand what's going on here, do you?"

"Not a clue and, no offense, I like it that way. Clueless rules."

Still the beast wouldn't let her pass. Zebulon inclined his head toward Arik. "The Skotos has risked his life to come here to be with you, Geary. Those two who attacked him. They're assassins and I'm sure they're going to be back. Probably with reinforcements. And now that you've seen them, they'll come for you, too, which is the only reason why I'm still talking to you. I feel morally obligated to at least warn you that they're gunning for you. Now in theory I can kill them and save you, but then that just opens up a whole can of worms and gets so messy that I really can't. I'm better off letting you die than taking them out. See my dilemma?"

She gave a bitter laugh. "Not really. The only dilemma I see is my imminent death that you appear ambivalent to. Hello? Did you hear any of what you just said to me?" How could this be happening?

"I heard, but when you get to my age, you understand that some things are just best left alone. Death is only natural."

"Oh yeah," she said, sweeping his body with a derogatory glare, "you're an old man. You're all of what? Twenty-five?"

He was definitely amused as he responded. "More like twenty-five *thousand* years old. Give or take a few hundred years. At my age we really don't count anymore."

Geary swallowed at that deep, dry tone. "You are joking, aren't you?"

He shook his head.

She looked at Arik, who duplicated the gesture. Nervous and suddenly uncertain, she looked back at Zebulon. "You're twenty-five thousand years old?"

"Well, if you're looking for precision, twenty-seven thousand, five hundred and forty-two, but really, does it matter?"

Geary felt her jaw drop. There was no way he could be that old. "That would put you at having been born during the Aurignacian Period."

"Not quite—that predates me by a few hundred years. But I'm close to it."

She could barely comprehend what he was saying as she ran through her ancient, ancient history. "And that would make you—"

"A Cro-Mag," he said with a smirk, "so yeah, when you call me a barbaric caveman, I am. Literally. Hell, I even knew a couple of Neanderthals who once kicked my ass all over what is now Toledo, Spain. But here's the fun part. Your boyfriend over there is even older than I am and he's considered a baby by his family."

And given the ludicrousness of those statements, the most screwed-up thought of all went through her head. "You were both around during the time of Atlantis."

That was how Arik had known about her necklace. How he'd known about the site.

Oh God, it was true.

They were . . .

She couldn't even complete the thought. She couldn't.

Trieg moved forward to touch her sympathetically on the shoulder. "It's a bit of a stunner when you first hear about it. You should have seen my face the night I met Artemis. A bit of advice to you, love. Go with it. And on that note I need to be patrolling. Good night to you all."

Yeah, sure, let the man with flashing fangs go back to his life. Why not? She had nothing better to do than be stalked by the deadly duo who wanted her dead.

And Mr. Freakzoid Neanderthal Cro-Mag man.

Speaking of the devil, Zebulon was watching her with an amused smirk that she dearly wanted to wipe off his face.

Arik was the only one who seemed to appreciate the seriousness of all this.

Zebulon turned his attention to Arik. "So, bud, how long do I have to watch for the Dolophoni?"

Arik let out a tired breath before he answered. "I'll be gone from this world in two weeks . . . if they don't kill me first."

Zebulon nodded. "You honestly think they're going to let you go home?"

Her anger was mirrored in Arik's eyes. "Not really. I figure I'm basically dead one way or another."

"Good," Zebulon said drily. "You're not as stupid as I thought you were. My only advice is for you to keep them off my streets and out of the public's eye. I don't like cleaning up these kinds of messes."

Arik looked even less amused than she felt. "I'm not exactly the Ty-D-Bol Man myself."

"Then we have an understanding. Keep the riffraff off my turf or I mop the floor with all of you."

"I'll do my best."

Zebulon inclined his head before he literally melted into nothing.

Geary was torn between outrage, hurt, and fear. Part of her wanted to slap Arik for dragging her into this, while another wanted to run as far away as she could. What won out was her sarcasm. "Thanks so much for the date. Had a blast. Really, we must do this again sometime. I really like these near-death experiences we have whenever we're together. They're very invigorating."

He reached to touch her again. "Geary—"

"Don't touch me," she snapped as she pulled away from him. "Don't you dare."

Arik withdrew his hand reluctantly. He understood her anger and she was fully entitled to it. Funny how he hadn't considered how all this would affect her before he'd come here. Honestly, he hadn't cared.

But now it was different. Now he cared in ways he hadn't been able to imagine before.

And he'd only been with her for a short time. What would it be like after they'd spent more time together?

What had he been thinking when he made his bargain with Hades? How could he have offered her up so easily?

It was such a selfish thing to do, and now that he could feel, he understood exactly how selfish it was. And he regretted it with every part of himself. She deserved so much better than what he'd done to her.

She deserved so much better than him. What he'd done was wrong. He knew that now, but he couldn't change it.

Geary shook her head. "I just don't understand this. You lied to me about who you were. Why?"

Arik swallowed as he heard the pain in her voice. It was so intense that he felt it himself. "Why? What would you have said had I come to you and told you that I was a god from your sleep who wanted to meet you in the flesh? Would you have welcomed me in or would you have called the authorities on me?"

"It is ludicrous," she admitted.

"Yes," he said, trying to make her understand why he needed to be near her. "You can't imagine the world I was born into, Geary. There's no laughter there, no joy or happiness, and then one night I accidentally found you. You who laugh at the warmth of the sun when it touches your skin. You who have . . . what was it you called it once? A chocogasm from eating a Hershey's Kiss—whatever that is. You feel things on a level most people never imagine. In all the centuries I've lived, I've never known anyone like you. And for two weeks I just wanted to be with you. To feel you, human to human, and to understand this world that is so vivid through your eyes."

Geary didn't know what to think. No one had ever spoken so passionately to her, never mind been so passionate about her. What should she say to that?

"I just wanted to know what it was like to be human, Megeara. Just for a little while. To touch you as a man and to hear the real sound of your voice as you said my name, and not the voice that was distorted by your dreams." He reached for her hesitantly and took her hand into his. "You can't imagine how good this feels when you've never known a gentle touch on your flesh."

Something inside her melted at the sincerity of his tone. The sincerity in those pale blue eyes. He meant every word he spoke. "So you're not dying?"

He shook his head. "Not in the sense that you use the word, no. But I will have to go back to my world and most likely die there. Apparently coming here pissed off some serious people who have no intention of letting me live after this."

"Then why did you come here if you knew they were going to kill you for it?"

"Honestly, I didn't know that at the time, but even if I had, I doubt it would have changed my mind. I would still have come for you."

How could he say that and mean it? How could seeing her be worth his life? "You're insane, aren't you?"

"Only when it comes to you."

Geary closed her eyes as she let everything that had happened over the last few minutes sink in. It was awful. She felt as if something had turned her inside out. She no longer knew what to believe in. She no longer knew what was real and what wasn't.

Instinctively she reached for the necklace—she needed to feel something solid to help ground her. But the instant she touched it, her heart stopped as their earlier discussion went through her mind. "You know where Atlantis is." It was a statement.

He nodded.

Disbelief washed through her as every part of his presence in her world hit her. "Then my father was right. It did exist. Right here. Right where he said it was."

Again Arik nodded to confirm her words. "You were swimming over its harbor this afternoon when you found the box. You were right there, Geary. You really touched it."

Tears actually came to her eyes at the thought of her completing her task. Of her holding in her hand one of the keys to her promise. "Was I really?"

"Yes. You were right, Megeara. And so was your father."

She covered her mouth with her hand as she took a step back. It was one thing to suspect but an entirely different one to know.

"Then we're there," she said with a giddy laugh. "We've found it."

But Arik didn't mirror her joy. He was tense and serious as he eyed her with warning. "That's the good news for you. The question is, do you want to know the bad?"

Not really. She'd rather savor the good stuff. At least for a second or two. But there was no use in delaying the inevitable. As the old nursery fable went, one could never outrun trouble. There was no place far enough to avoid it. "Oh sure, what could be worse than what happened here tonight?"

He shrugged. "I don't know. Does the fact that the goddess Artemis blew up your boat today top that or not?"

Geary blinked as those words sank in. Honestly, in all

her wild imaginings, that one had somehow eluded her. She much preferred the thought of Arik as an arms dealer or assassin.

"Excuse me?" she asked, hoping he might have been playing with her.

"You heard me correctly. Artemis is one of many who want you to stay away from Atlantis."

"And what did I do to earn this privilege?"

"Basically the same thing you did tonight," a deep male voice said from behind her. "You were meddling in a place you didn't belong."

Geary turned at the foreign voice, then stiffened at the sight of the rest of the people who'd attacked Arik in her dream.

Oh. Shit.

CHAPTER 14

DREAD FEAR WHIPPED THROUGH GEARY AS SHE SAW THE doom in the eyes of the ones confronting them. "I'm really getting tired of these guys."

Arik made a rude noise in the back of his throat. "Believe me, I share your sentiment entirely."

That didn't really comfort her. "So what do you suggest we do?"

Arik shrugged with a nonchalance she couldn't even begin to fathom. "There are nine of them and two of us. They have the powers of a god and we're human." He gave her a very Sean Connery/James Bond mysterious kind of smile. "Therefore, I suggest we run. Fast."

Before she could even think to respond, Arik shoved her in the opposite direction of the mean army of darkness that was out to shorten their lives. Geary's heart was pounding as he took her hand and led her through the alley and down the cobbled street at a pace that would make a sprinter proud.

She had a moment when she thought it might work, but that hope died quickly as one of the women appeared out of nowhere in front of them to block their way.

The goddess tsked at Arik. "What's the matter, Skotos? We bathed and everything. Surely you don't want to leave us without at least saying hi."

"Hi." Then without hesitating, Arik let go of Geary and kicked the goddess away.

Spinning about, the goddess countered with a staggering blow to his solar plexus. Arik grimaced, then backhanded her so hard, she stumbled back.

Geary grabbed at something on the woman's waist that looked like a billy club attached to her belt. She jerked it free before she struck the goddess with it across the back. A blinding light sparked on said contact and was followed by a vibrant burst of power so strong, it knocked them both apart.

"You okay?" Arik asked.

All Geary could do was nod.

He kissed her on the cheek before he took the club and turned to face the others.

Rattled by the surge that continued to burn through her body, Geary stumbled away while he moved to engage the twins again.

"Megeara . . ."

That deeply hypnotic female voice whispered through her mind. It was the same one that had been calling to her for weeks now. But she didn't have time for it. Geary shook her head to clear it.

"Listen to me, Megeara. Use the medallion you wear. Place it under your tongue and let me into you."

"What?" she breathed.

"Just do it, child, and I will take care of them for you. Trust me. I can protect you."

Yeah, she was gone, seriously gone, and yet even as the thought went through her, what harm would there be in trying it? She and Arik were already getting their butts kicked. What harm could it do?

After all, they were fighting a band of gods out to kill them and, given all she'd seen in the last few minutes, what were a few more leaps of faith?

"I can't believe I'm doing this." She pulled the small coin up and placed it in her mouth, under her tongue. She grimaced at the salty metallic taste. But that only lasted a nanosecond as something warm invaded her mouth. Whatever it was, it didn't stop there. It spread through her like lava, heating her body and making her heart race.

And as it went through her, images filled her mind. Images of an ancient world. Of a hall filled with gold. She saw the face of a beautiful blond woman who had mercurial eyes that swirled like a silver mist.

Words whispered through Geary in a language she'd never heard before.

Then something snapped. Geary felt as if she'd been pushed outside of her body so that she was nothing more than a ghost, looking down on the others—yet she was still in her body. Only someone else was in complete control of her. It was the strangest sensation. To be cognizant and not responsive. No matter what she tried, her body ignored her instructions.

One of the gods came up to attack her. She laughed at the warm power cascading through her before she headed toward the man to confront him. He swung at her. She ducked like a seasoned pro and elbowed him in the knee. Hissing painfully, he dipped as his knee gave way.

She rose quickly, then swung her arm so that she caught him under his chin with her fist. That blow sent him twisting, straight to the ground.

Deimos approached her next. She wasn't sure how she knew that it was him, but she did.

He backed up. "Aekyra Apollymi?"

Are you Apollymi?

Even though his question had been asked in Atlantean, she understood it and, better still, answered it even against her will. "Naiea."

He took another step away from her. As he did so, her hands heated up even more. She threw them out and a blast emanated from her fingertips that flooded the alley with light.

Two seconds later, the gods went flying as if she'd struck them all with lightning.

Arik raised his hand to shield his face as he felt the heat of an Atlantean god bolt. But what stunned him more than the fact that he felt the impact of something that hadn't existed for over eleven thousand years was that it had come from Megeara.

"Apollymi!" Deimos snarled in Atlantean. "This is not your fight. Back down."

"Naiea, Olygaia eta."—*Yes, it is, Olympian*. The voice was Megeara's and at the same time she spoke the Atlantean words like a native. "Anekico ler aracnia."

Victory to the spider. It was an old Atlantean saying that meant "patience wins the day."

"Ki mi ypomonitikosi teloson semerie."

And today my patience ends. Even though her teeth were clenched, her voice was loud, clear, and angry as she snarled the words in a tone he could tell reached all the way to the halls of Olympus.

More important, it was enough to convince the Dolophoni that they didn't want even a tiny piece of the Destroyer when she was in this mood. Deimos looked to the others before he called for a retreat.

They vanished instantly.

Arik wiped the blood from his lips as he made his way cautiously to Megeara's side. Even though he lacked his powers, he could feel Apollymi's essence as it filled Megeara's body. Her eyes were swirling in color and dotted with silver. Rage and vengeance bled from every part of her.

She started after the others, but he pulled her to a stop before she could pursue them and possibly hurt Megeara in the process.

"Ochia, Apollymi. Anekico ler aracnia epitrepedio. Efto ler kariti u topyra."

No, Apollymi. Let the victory go to the spider. This is not the time or place.

She hissed at him and would have attacked had he not pulled the necklace from Megeara's lips. The abruptness of it caused her to collapse against him. He lifted her in his arms and held her there while the goddess was forced to retreat out of Megeara's body. He held her close as she trembled.

Geary could barely breathe as a foreign weakness invaded every part of her. She'd been so strong before; now she was as weak as a newborn. Leaning her head against Arik's neck, she was grateful for his support, because at the moment she couldn't even lift her own arms.

"What was that?" she asked weakly.

"The Atlantean goddess Apollymi. Even though she's trapped in Kalosis, she can reach out and at times possess people and the elements. Her powers are a pittance on this plane to what they would be if she were free, but they're still impressive."

"Why did she do that? Why possess me?"

"Because she needs you to free her and if they kill you, she has no hope."

"I don't understand."

"You must have pure Atlantean blood in your ancestry. I think that's why you can hear her when most can't. It's the only thing that makes sense. . . . Before it was destroyed, there were two races who inhabited Atlantis. The natives who were born of the Atlantean pantheon and the Apollites who took refuge there after they were thrown out of Greece. Apollymi needs the blood of an Atlantean to break her seal and to summon her out. Because of that, she would protect you for all she's worth."

Geary had to struggle to raise her hand to her necklace so that she could see the writing on it. "I thought this was only a coin."

"No. That is the medallion that was worn by her priestesses. Whenever they were in danger, they would do as you did, place it in their mouths, and she would protect them."

Wow, hell of an insurance policy. There weren't many people who could have a goddess at their beck and call. Made Geary wonder what Apollymi would do for a false alarm.

Then again, given how easily Apollymi had fought the Dolophoni off, Geary didn't want to even think about it. With that kind of power, Apollymi could easily turn on the person who wrongfully summoned her.

"Why didn't our attackers just pull it out of my mouth once I started fighting them?"

"They're from the Greek pantheon. I doubt they knew that trick or I'm sure they would have." He slid her slowly down his body until she was on her feet.

It took Geary a full second before she was able to stand again. And even then, her legs were so unsteady that she held on to Arik's arm for support. The warm smell and strength of him steadied her even more, and she was grateful for his presence. "How is it you know the trick?"

He gave her a devilish grin. "The benefits of being an ex-Oneroi. Since we can trip through anyone's dreams, we know a lot of tricks the other gods don't."

"But not how to fight those guys in human form," she reminded him.

He looked a bit sheepish, which she found intriguing and endearing. "Well, not and win. But in my own body and in my realm . . . I'm lethal."

Geary could feel the muscles of his biceps working under her hand as she stared up into those clear eyes. In her dreams, she'd kissed that mouth a thousand times. Had run her tongue over the stubble of his chin and had licked every inch of him. It amazed her that he'd been as captivated by her as she was by him. But more than that, she found it almost impossible to believe.

"Did you really come here for me?"

He nodded, his eyes scorching her with their heat. "Yes."

"And are you disappointed?"

One corner of his mouth lifted into a seductive smile. "Only that you don't rip off my clothes and have your way with me . . . in chocolate."

Geary shook her head at him as she went over everything she'd discovered in the last twenty-four hours. She should be horrified, and on one level she was. But on another she was actually relieved that he was a god on the human plane. At least now she understood part of what had been happening to her.

Though it didn't make it better, the explanation went a long way in saving her sanity.

She took a step back from him as she tried to comprehend everything. "I don't really get all of this. How did you first find me in my dreams?"

He took her hand in his and held it while he explained. "We have rooms that are like chambers where I live. We don't have to use them, but they make connecting with humans a bit easier—they can amplify our powers, and it gives us someplace to rest undisturbed while we're doing it. The only drawback is that it allows the powers-that-be an easier way to monitor us while we're at it. Whenever we're in the *strobilos,* we hover about and drift in and out of dreams. Whenever we find someone who is having a vivid dream we're drawn to them."

"And you were drawn to mine."

He nodded.

Incredible. She couldn't imagine being able to do that. To spy on people and participate in their sleep. "So what's it like to be in someone else's dreams?"

"It's like bathing in Jell-O. It feels kind of thick and at times can be overwhelming. You never know what you're going to find. Many of the Skoti I know prefer nightmares, since they get such an adrenaline rush from it."

That didn't sound like what she'd read about the Oneroi. "From my research, it says that you guys channel and direct the dreams, that you cause them."

"At one time we did. The Oneroi were extremely active in granting dreams and using them to manipulate both the gods and humanity. Then one day one of my brethren made the mistake of making Zeus crave a goat . . . sexually. He did it as a joke, thinking it would be funny and that the head god needed to be brought down a peg or two after insulting him. Zeus, once he came to his senses, was so outraged that he had our insistent friends, the Dolophoni, round us up and bring us to him. A small group, including the one responsible, was killed. Another group was heavily punished, and the rest of us were cursed to have no emotions of any kind."

"Why?"

"Without ambition, envy, humor, and the rest of the emotional gamut, Zeus thought that it would keep us from messing with him or any of the other gods ever again."

Geary could understand his reasoning, but it seemed a bit cruel to punish everyone over the actions of one stupid being. "And it worked?"

"Not exactly. Without us there to direct dreams and inspire people, certain humans and other creatures began to lose their minds. Zeus learned that we were needed to help channel pent-up feelings and to help humans and other beings determine what they desired in a contained environment. Dreams provide a necessary outlet for everyone. So the Oneroi were charged with helping others in their dreams. It worked for a time, until we realized that in a dream state we had emotions again. Fear, love, passion . . . they were all there, and whenever we found a special class of person they were extremely amplified. But once we leave the dreamworld, the borrowed emotions evaporate and leave us vacant and cold again."

She could see where this was headed. "So some of you became addicted to emotions. Like a drug."

He nodded. "Those who crave it are called Skoti."

Geary remembered Zebulon calling Arik Skotos. "You say that like it's a bad thing."

"In my world it is. Skoti are deemed uncontrollable, and if they fail to heed the warnings of the Oneroi, they're hunted down and severely punished or killed."

She frowned. "Why?"

"The gods fear us and therefore they want to control us any way they can."

"But if you have no feelings, how can punishment matter?"

"Because that is the one emotion left to us."

"No," she corrected him. "Physical pain isn't an emotion. It's a biological response to negative stimulus. No wonder you still have it."

"You know, the rational explanation really doesn't help. Either way, it sucks to be one of us."

"Sorry." Geary reached up to brush a lock of hair from his forehead. It was inconceivable that he was here with her and real. That he was flesh and blood and for all intents and purposes human. How strange.

She didn't know if she should be angry or flattered or both that he'd come here just to meet her.

She tightened her grip on his hand. "And what about Solin? Is he really related to you?"

"Yes. He's my cousin, but we dream gods consider ourselves brothers and sisters whether or not we share parents. Solin's father was Phobetor and his mother was human. He didn't know he was a demigod until he hit puberty and his powers manifested. Then his mother cast him out and the Oneroi began to hunt for him. He's hated all of us ever since."

Now she was beginning to understand. "Which is why he said initially that he didn't have a brother."

"Exactly."

Geary fell silent as she digested that last bit. God, this was all so complicated. Unbelievable, really. How did a woman who only wanted to redeem her family name find herself in a situation like this? "So where does this leave us?"

"Confused?"

She laughed. "You have *no* idea."

"True, I didn't understand confusion until I found myself floating in deep water."

She let out a small laugh at his reminder of how they'd met. "Since you're being so honest now, how did you happen to get there?"

"Hades. After he made me human, he threw me out and put me in your path. I guess I should be grateful he didn't dump me on a busy street somewhere, under a truck."

Geary shook her head at his humor. "Hades." Bitter amusement filled her. "And to think I used to mock my father for his belief that the ancient gods were real. I thought he was insane and I told him that on many an occasion. But he was always insistent that they had to have lived." She sighed as she remembered the way he'd described them and the quirks he'd invented for the pantheon. "So what is old Hades like anyway?"

"He's a cranky bastard who hates everyone not Persephone."

Well, that made sense. She was his wife after all. "So what's she like?"

Arik's features softened. "She's kind and dainty. Petite and shy. Very unassuming. She actually reminds me a lot of your cousin Tory."

"Really?"

"Yes, and Thia is a dead ringer for Artemis, right

down to the red hair, height, selfishness, and bitchy attitude."

For some reason, that didn't really surprise Geary. "No kidding, huh? What about me? Am I like any of the gods?"

He narrowed his eyes as if considering it before he answered. "Athena, except she has black hair and is usually sporting her pet owl on her shoulder. But your mannerisms are very similar, and like you, she lives a life of celibacy."

"Oh gee, thank you for that one."

He lifted her hand up to kiss the back of her knuckles. In spite of her anger, the gesture warmed her. "It's true, but that's okay. I like that about you."

"I'm sure you don't."

He cupped her face in his hands and stared at her. "Megeara, there is absolutely nothing about you that I don't like."

"Can you honestly say that?"

He stroked her cheeks with his thumbs. "Okay, I don't like it when you walk away from me, but other than that . . ."

She laughed. "Yeah, I guess that makes sense. You transcend a dimension to come here and I brush you off. I can see where that might get annoying."

Arik smiled at her playful tone. All in all, she was taking this a lot better than he'd have thought. "You still want to find Atlantis?"

Her face sobered. "Not if it means anyone's life. I won't make that bargain. Believe me, there's nothing there worth my life and definitely nothing there worth someone else's."

A twinge of guilt went through him as he realized that he'd made that bargain without hesitation.

"Is something wrong?" she asked with a scowl.

"No," he lied. "I was only amazed by the woman in front of me. By your compassion and caring."

She gave him a doubting stare, but for once she didn't argue. Instead she changed the subject. "Tell me something, Arik. Was Atlantis beautiful?"

"Like a dream."

She closed her eyes as if she was trying to imagine it.

He leaned forward to whisper in her ear. When he spoke, his lips brushed the soft skin of her cheek, which only whetted his appetite for her. "Tonight while you sleep, I'll take you there and let you see it for yourself."

Joy glowed in her eyes. "Really?"

"Cross my heart."

Geary felt tears prick at the backs of her eyes at the thought of seeing it. But more than that was the fear of what else might be waiting for them in her dreams. "Will those assassins be in our dreams, too?"

He looked away before he answered. "Probably. But don't worry about them. I can handle it in that realm. And if I can't you can always change the channel again. I have to say that was the neatest trick I've ever seen." He winked at her.

She blushed at the memory. Shaking her head, she reached up to lay her hand against the whiskers of his cheek. It was so odd to be with him, knowing all the things they'd shared. "So how many women have you visited in their dreams?"

He hesitated. "Is this one of those questions that if I don't answer it correctly, you get angry at me?"

She laughed. "Probably."

Scowling, he hesitated before he answered. "If it

makes you feel any better, you're the only one I've ever wanted to be human for."

Ironically, that was just what she needed to hear. "You are a fool, Arikos."

"Only where you're concerned."

She still couldn't believe that he'd come here for her. Who would have made such a bargain? "So what do we do now?"

"Well, if I can't have you naked in my arms, then I vote we stay alive."

That sounded good to her . . . both parts, actually. "All right. But I want to make sure we don't endanger anyone else. Do you think Solin will help us?"

"That's a hard question to answer. Solin is a bit self-absorbed and highly unpredictable. Although I have to say that it surprised me he rescued the others earlier, so there might be a chance he'd help us, too."

"Okay, then. Let's try him and see what he thinks."

But an hour later, after they'd gone to Solin's villa and explained it all to him, Geary learned that Arik had been right. The egotistical bastard had no intention of helping them.

Dressed in a pair of slacks with an open light blue shirt that showed off his tanned six-pack, he scoffed at them before he took a drink of the brandy in his hand. "They'll come for me if I help you, and no offense, no one has ever bled for me, so I'm not about to bleed for anyone else. You can all go to hell for what I care." Then he slammed his empty glass down and glared at Arik. "I've done enough helping. You've already brought Zebulon down on my ass and now the Dolophoni. It took me centuries to reach an impasse with them and I like our cold war a little too much to jeopardize it for you."

"I understand."

"Good. Now if you'll excuse me, I have some things to take care of." He left them alone in his study.

Geary let out a sigh as she turned to face Arik, who sat beside her on the leather sofa. "He's a fuzzy-little-bunny guy, isn't he?"

To her surprise, Arik defended him. "Don't judge him too harshly. You have to remember that for centuries he was persecuted by humanity and hunted by us. His resentment and anger are more than understandable."

"Is that compassion you feel?"

Arik paused as he considered the tenderness inside him. "Yeah, I think it is."

"How does it feel?"

"Strange and comforting, but mostly disturbing." And it was. He wasn't sure if he liked having emotions or not. There were extreme advantages and disadvantages to both.

Megeara reached over to squeeze his hand. "So what's it like to live without them?"

He toyed with her fragile fingers, delighting in the sensation of her hand in his. "It's hard. Imagine a world without taste. A world where you can see the colors and all, but you can't feel it. A beautiful clear day can never choke you up. A child's laughter doesn't make you smile. You don't look at a bunny and think, *How cute*. You feel absolutely nothing. It's like being wrapped in thick cotton all the time."

"And when someone touches you?"

"I can feel the pressure, but not the sensations. There's no blood rushing through my veins, making my heart beat faster. No excitement or chills. But the weird part is that when I'm with you, I don't even have to touch you to feel that. I get hard for you just thinking about you."

Geary swallowed as she felt her own chills rise. No one had ever said a kinder thing to her. And as she contemplated that, she realized something else. . . . "You've never slept with anyone in the flesh, have you?"

"No."

Amazed, she remembered the expertise he possessed. In bed, he was highly creative.

His blue eyes were haunting in their need and sincerity as he brushed his lips against her cheek, then whispered in her ear, "There's nothing I want more than to touch you, Megeara. I want to taste your skin on my tongue. To know what it's like to slide into you while you hold me close."

Her breasts tightened as warm heat seared her. She should be offended by his frankness. She wasn't. It oddly turned her on. No one had ever been so blatant and open with her before.

And he had crossed worlds to be with her.

His breath scorched her neck as he nuzzled her cheek with his.

He would be gone in two weeks. There was no hope of anything with him more than a brief physical relationship. That was the last thing she wanted. "Arik? What are the odds of your surviving this?"

His expression turned dark as he pulled back to look at her. "Hard to say. As a human, pretty much nil, but once Hades returns my godhead, my chances go up exponentially."

"So you just came here to screw me and leave?"

Arik paused. Yeah, that had basically been his plan, which Hades had changed by demanding her life for it.

I am a rank bastard.

And in that moment he had a bad epiphany. "You're right—that was my intent. I'm no better than Solin. I was so fixated on the novelty of being human with you that I never thought past my blind obsession. You gave yourself so freely in your dreams that I made the assumption you lived your life that way, too. But you don't. I think that's why you're so uninhibited in dreams. You keep everything bottled up inside you."

"Yeah," she said in a low tone. "I'm so inhibited here that it's the only place I feel free to roam without someone trying to judge me."

He nodded and for the first time ever, he felt guilt. Real, true, and bitter. More than that, he cared for her. He didn't want her hurt in any way, and he didn't know how to stop the course he'd already set into motion.

When he'd seen her there in the middle of the fighting, it had made his heart ache. He'd actually been afraid for her.

Oh, this was getting way too complicated.

"I've made such a mistake by coming here, Megeara. I'm so sorry. I should have been content to stay in your dreams." If only he'd been able to. Had he stayed there, they would have driven him out of her life completely.

Now he just wanted to stay here with her forever.

If only he could. . . .

Geary pulled him into her arms and held him close. She didn't know what to think about any of this, but then, maybe she shouldn't be thinking at all. She'd cherished those dreams with him. He was both naive and experienced. Trusting and suspicious. She'd never known anyone like him.

No kidding. He was a god turned human who lived an existence she couldn't even begin to understand.

But she wanted to.

Today he'd given her her dream by taking her to Atlantis and letting her hold a piece of it in her hands. And if they were meant to die, then she wanted to make sure he had the one thing he'd wanted most.

Rising up from the sofa, she took his hand and pulled him to his feet.

He frowned at her. "Where are we going now?"

"Somewhere that we can be alone so that I can strip you naked and ride you into the ground."

CHAPTER 15

ARIK'S BREATH CAUGHT IN HIS THROAT AS SHE UTTERED the words he'd been dying to hear since the moment he'd made his deal with Hades. A slow smile spread across Arik's face before he slung his hand out to lock the door. Nothing happened.

He cursed as he remembered his human limitations. If he wanted the door locked, he'd have to do it manually, which seriously sucked.

Time's wasting. Arik raced to the door and locked it tight.

Megeara was frowning at him as he returned to her side. "What are you doing?"

"I'm not going to take a chance on your changing your mind. By the time we find someplace else, something could happen to ruin your mood, and I don't have any chocolate here to entice you with."

She laughed. "So we're just going to make out in here like horny teenagers?"

"Works for me."

She looked around the room rather sheepishly. Afraid she'd chicken out, he pulled her against him and slow-danced with her. "Come on, Megeara. Walk on the wild side with me. Let's get naked and ruin Solin's upholstery. It serves two purposes. We're happy and he's pissed."

Geary bit her lip in indecision. Arik was adorable when he was like this. Playful and charming. How could she resist him?

She cast her gaze around the room again. "There's no comfortable place in here."

"I'll be on bottom. I promise, I'll make you a good cushion."

He was incorrigible. "There's nothing I can say to dissuade you from this, is there?"

"Nope." He took her hand in his and pressed it against his fly so that she could feel his swollen cock in her palm. "I'm too desperate for you. You have to take pity on me."

Geary's heart pounded as she lifted her chin to receive his kiss. Oh, he tasted like divinity. She wrapped one arm around his neck as their tongues danced and she stroked him through his pants.

Arik drew a deep ragged breath as Megeara nibbled her way around his jaw, down his neck while her hand massaged him with an irritatingly slow rhythm that only added to his craving for her. The stroke of her tongue on his flesh was like being hit with electricity over and over again. Every part of him shook from the sensation. His nerve endings were alive and throbbing.

Growling, he jerked his shirt up over his head so that there would be no more barriers between her mouth and hands and his skin. He only wanted to feel her touch.

She gasped at the sight of his torso and splayed her palms against his bared chest.

Geary couldn't believe the scars Arik carried. They were everywhere. Mostly faint and faded by time, she'd failed to see them when he was fished out of the water. But up close, they were extremely prominent. "What have they done to you?"

He ran his hand gently through her hair. "They tried to control me."

It was obvious from the amount of damage that they'd failed repeatedly. Arik was truly a stubborn man.

He dipped his head to kiss her, but she pulled away. "What will they do to you over this latest action?"

"Don't know and right now I don't care."

"*I* care, Arik."

He scowled at her as if he couldn't understand her words. "Why?"

"Because no one should be tortured. It's wrong."

"It's the way of things. You break the rules and there are consequences. I'm willing to pay that price."

She trembled as he returned to nuzzle her neck. How could he be so nonchalant over this? But then, judging by the look of his body, it was such a common occurrence that he most likely didn't even blink over it.

As he said, to him it was normal. But to her it mattered. She didn't want him to be hurt, especially not for being with her. He was a decent man who deserved so much more than this. She couldn't stand the thought of his being punished any more—it ached like a physical pain.

Arik was fascinated by the true softness of her skin as he toyed with her neck. By the way her body smelled so fresh and sweet. She skimmed her hands over his back while he unbuttoned her shirt. He'd expected her to be bare beneath it. Instead she wore . . .

Bondage gear. Pulling back, he scowled at the white

thing that wrapped around her chest like an oversized bandage. "What is *that*?"

Geary laughed as she realized that in dreams she never wore a bra. And judging by his reaction, she deduced that no one else ever had, either. "It's a bra. Haven't you ever seen one before?"

He ran one finger under the strap and curled his lip as if it were the most repugnant thing he'd ever seen. "No. What's it for?"

"It keeps me in place."

"Yeah, but I don't want you in place. I want you in my hands."

On any other man, that line might have angered her to the point of nailing him in a certain part of his anatomy and walking away. But it was said with such growling sincerity that it only made her laugh again. She reached around and unsnapped her strap. The look on Arik's face as the bra fell to the floor was priceless. No man had ever looked at her with such satisfied hunger.

He lifted one hand, then hesitated as if afraid to touch her breasts. She took his hand and led it to her. The instant he touched her, she moaned and ached at the center of her body. And all she could think of was having him hard and deep inside her.

Arik's breath caught in his throat as he cupped her swollen breast in his palm. It was so soft. . . . He'd never felt anything like it.

He brushed his thumb over the taut nipple and was delighted as she literally squirmed. Grinning, he dipped his head down to draw that peak into his mouth so that he could taste her. She let out a moan as she cupped his head to her breast.

Oh yeah. This was what he wanted. He reveled at the

taste of her, at the way her puckered nipple rolled against his tongue. But all it did was make him burn for more of her. He wanted to see her completely naked.

With that thought in mind, he quickly unzipped her pants. She kicked her shoes off as he slid the pants down her body and then tossed them over his shoulder.

"More surprises, huh?" he asked as he studied the small pair of panties.

Geary couldn't speak as he reached up to brush his fingers between her legs. She felt on fire from his touch. And all she could think of was her dreams when he'd licked her until she'd screamed out in pleasure.

He massaged her with his thumb through this silk until she was wet and begging for him. She buried her hand in his hair, as he continued his relentless torture.

Arik pushed the silk material aside so that he could touch her intimately. She was so wet already and he was dying for a taste of her on his tongue. He hooked his finger in the bottom of her panties and pulled them off.

He was still in his slacks while she stood naked before him. Gods, but she was the most beautiful woman he'd ever seen. She wasn't skinny or lean but rather voluptuous and tight. He could see the outline of her bikini where her skin went from tan to a paler tawny color.

But that wasn't what held him captive. . . .

Geary licked her lips as their gazes met and locked. Arik took her hands into his and led them to the center of her body that ached for his touch. Using her thumbs, he spread the folds of her wide so that he could see the most private part of her body.

He ran one long finger down her cleft, drawing a shiver along her spine. "You're so much softer than I thought," he whispered. "Wetter."

And when he slid his finger deep inside her, she almost

came just from the sheer pleasure of it. Groaning low in her throat, she panted while he explored her at length. His fingers swirled and teased until she was weak from it.

Just when she was at her end, he lifted himself up and replaced his fingers with his mouth. The shock of pleasure was so great that she rose to her tiptoes. She gasped his name as he tongued her with an unrivaled skill. Widening her stance, she lowered herself on his mouth as his tongue flicked inside her over and over again.

Unable to stand it, she came with a small cry. But still he didn't stop. He continued to tease and torment her with his mouth and tongue until she was cresting another orgasm.

Wanting him inside her more than she wanted anything else, she buried her hand in his hair and pulled him away from her.

Arik was dazed by her taste and by the fire in his blood as she sank to the floor and captured his lips with her own. Her hands sought out his body with an unrivaled eagerness.

Now this was the Megeara he'd come to know. She was relentless with her exploration. Relentless with her kissing. Shoving him back on the floor, she quickly removed his clothes so that she could run her hands over his body.

He spread his legs for her as she ran the back of her hand over his sac. He actually whimpered from the pleasure of that sensation.

Taking no mercy on him, she dipped her head down and took him all the way into her mouth. Arik arched his back as unimaginable pleasure ripped through him. Everything was swirling. In all the times he'd had sex, he'd never known anything like this. Never felt any pleasure equal to it.

He tilted his head to watch her and met her hungry

gaze. The look of her there tore through him. He reached down to stroke her cheek as she again took him in all the way. Her throat tickled the tip of him before she pulled back to nibble the very tip of him. He was in ultimate heaven.

Megeara sucked him in hard before she pulled away again and kissed her way up his body until she was able to straddle him. Blind with ecstasy, he lifted his hips as she impaled herself on him.

Arik cried out from the warmth of her body surrounding his. It was all he could do not to come immediately, but he didn't want this to end so soon. He wanted to stay inside her forever.

Geary smiled at the unabashed pleasure on Arik's face as he held her hips in his hands and urged her on. And she did just as she'd promised. She rode him with everything she had.

Fast and hard, pulling him in as deep as she could and then rising up until he was about to fall out. There was nothing better than the feel of his hardness inside her.

And as she thrust against him, she knew they had no future together. But even so she felt closer to him than she'd ever felt to anyone.

It was like he was a vital part of her and for once she didn't feel self-conscious around him. She was completely at ease with her nudity and with her sexuality. Completely at ease with his knowing how much she craved him. There were no barriers between them now. No secrets.

And when she came again, she actually screamed out loud.

Arik groaned at the sight of Megeara's ecstasy. It was so intense that it set off his own. He drove himself deep inside her as his body shook out of his control. A thousand emotions and sensations tore through him, robbing him of all reason and thought.

All he could do was feel. Feel her and the moment of pure, uninterrupted bliss as his body spasmed inside hers.

She leaned over him to kiss his lips. Arik held her there, letting his senses swirl.

"Are you all right?" she asked, her brow creased by worry.

"I don't know," he answered honestly. "I think my body just turned inside out. And I can't understand why Solin would ever venture into dreams if this is what it's like in a human body. He must be out of his mind."

She laughed at Arik's indignation. "That was not what I was expecting to hear. But I'm glad you enjoyed yourself."

He cupped her face in his hands before he kissed her again. "I could drink you in all day, Megeara. What is this feeling that I have inside me? The one that hurts with the thought of not being with you? The one that wants to be inside you again even though I just had you?" He hesitated before he whispered his last question to her. "Is this love?"

"No," she answered quietly. She didn't believe in love at first sight. "Real love takes time to build. What you feel is just infatuation."

"But it doesn't feel temporary."

"It never does at its onset. It's only in hindsight that we realize the difference between infatuation and love."

He didn't seem to buy her argument. "And what if it's not?"

"What are you saying, Arik? That you love me?"

Arik fell silent as he considered it. There was no denying what he felt. But then, his feelings were very new and they would expire in only a few more days. It might be love now, but how could someone continue to love when they had no emotions?

Maybe she was right. Maybe it was only infatuation.

But even as he thought that, he knew better. The very idea of returning to his old existence burned through him with so much pain that he could barely stand it. It made a complete mockery of any punishment he'd ever known. He wanted to stay with her for all eternity.

Afraid of losing her, he held her close, naked body to naked body, and tried to forget how soon his departure would be.

Geary lay there quietly, listening to Arik's heart beating under her cheek. How strange to be with him now knowing how finite their time together would be. There was none of the optimism of most affairs, where you hoped they'd last forever. In some ways that made her lucky. She knew to the second how finite their time was.

But it was also a curse to know when she was going to lose him—because she suspected that she was already in love with him. How could she not be? He was the only man who'd ever seen the real her. In her dreams, she'd told him everything. Her hopes, her disappointments. She'd never been restrained with him. Never held back. He knew her in a way no one else did.

And that was why she couldn't let him go.

"There has to be some way to keep you here."

She hadn't realized she'd spoken out loud until he answered her. "I could stay, but I wouldn't be the man who's with you now."

"What do you mean?"

"I could give up my godhood, but it would change nothing other than I'd become mortal. When my time is up, I'll revert back to what I was. I won't have any emotions and I wouldn't be able to visit you in dreams. There would be no reason to be around you then."

"I don't believe that. You have emotions. You feel too deeply not to."

"In the dreams, I was syphoning off you. Everything I felt came from you. I promise you that if I were to become mortal, that would stop. I wouldn't even have the power to feel you anymore, either physically or emotionally."

"How do you know that?"

"It's the curse, Megeara. There's no cure for that. No god can alter the curse of another. I'm damned."

She still couldn't accept that. It wasn't in her nature to just accept things because someone said so. She was a scientist and she needed proof of his theory. "Has any Oneroi ever gone free?"

"No," he said emphatically. "There has never been a single case of freedom for any of us. The few who tried were hunted down and killed."

"That's not fair. You should be able to go free if you want to."

He let out a deep breath as he stroked a lock of hair from her forehead. "Who has ever said that life is fair?"

"Maybe, but I'm going to ask Tory about this."

"Tory's just a child."

"Yes, and she's obsessed with Greek mythology. If ever there was an escape for you, she'd know it."

Arik adored the fact that Megeara was willing to try, but he knew it was hopeless. No human knew more about Greek mythology than he did. Megeara was human and he was a cursed god. All he could hope for was to find some way to keep her safe once he was gone.

As long as they were at Solin's they had a haven. Solin had told them that he had a truce with the other gods. They didn't tread into his home uninvited and he wouldn't kill them for it. But Arik and Megeara couldn't stay here every minute of the day. And she wouldn't be content to live her life here within these walls. She'd never liked cages of any sort.

She's going to be dead, so just stay here and enjoy her company until it's time to return.

Return to what? Emptiness? Coldness?

That was bullshit. He didn't want to go back to the Vanishing Isle.

Then you die in her stead.

Arik leaned his cheek against the top of her head as she lay against him. She felt so good in his arms. So good with her naked skin resting against his. *I would rather be dead than live without her.*

It was true, and actually that was the only solution that made sense. He would spend his time with her and then surrender himself to Hades. Hades would torture and kill him, then everyone would be happy.

You won't be happy, dumb ass.

That was actually quite true, but even if he gave her up and went home, he'd still be tortured, not to mention the Dolophoni would kill him anyway.

So why not just let them have him and end this?

"Live your life with purpose."

Arik blinked as those words came out of the very distant past to haunt him. It'd been back in his days as an Oneroi when he'd ironically gone to help Trieg. Acheron, the leader of the Dark-Hunters, had summoned him so that they could discuss the problems Trieg was having over the death of his family and how best to help the man cope with them.

Tall and black-haired, the Atlantean had been even wiser than Athena. He'd been trying to make Arik understand the human psyche and essence. "Remember, Arikos, the key to humanity is simple. Live your life with purpose. They need goals to strive for. All of Trieg's have been taken from him by his enemies, so we need to replace them with new ones that matter to him. Without goals, humanity is lost and a single man can't function."

Acheron had been wrong about one thing. Without goals, everyone was lost. Even the gods.

Until now, Arik's goals had always been selfish in nature. As a Skotos, his goal had been to find the greatest pleasure to be had. As an Oneroi it had been to do just as he'd been told so as not to be punished. He'd never once considered anyone else's feelings or life.

But now he understood how to live with purpose. He understood sacrifice. There were things worth dying for. His was simple. Megeara. His only regret was that he wished he'd enjoyed their past more. He should have savored every second of their time together.

Still, he had a few days left. Those he would make count. And when the time came, he would put his neck in the noose with no regrets.

Yeah, right.

Okay, so there would be one single regret—he'd never see or touch Megeara again.

He could die with that.

And in the back of his mind was that same sarcastic voice laughing at him. *"Trust me, boy, you will."*

CHAPTER 16

"HOUSTON, WE HAVE A PROBLEM."

M'Adoc turned around from the bay window where he was looking out onto the waterfall behind their palace to see Deimos entering his private suite without invitation. He let out his breath slowly and silently, falling instantly into his emotionless appearance.

"How colloquial American of you, Demon." He raked the demigod with a practiced mocking brow that only M'Ordant or D'Alerian would know wasn't feigned, and forced his voice to remain steady and bland. "By your unbloodied presence here I take it that you failed to kill him . . . again."

Demon's eyes narrowed. "I can do without the patronizing undertone."

Clasping his hands behind his back, M'Adoc crossed the floor to meet Deimos halfway. "We both know I feel no such thing. But to be fair, I can deal without the incompetency. How hard is it to take out a restricted god on the mortal plane?"

"Pretty damn impossible when he has a Chthonian and an Atlantean god standing watch over him."

M'Adoc had to struggle to hide his confusion. "Why would Acheron care about any of this?"

"Not him, his mother. Remember her? Tall angry blond bitch who seriously spanked her whole family into oblivion over a hangnail?"

M'Adoc's lips itched to smile, but he was so used to catching himself that it was all too easy to keep it hidden. "It was more than a hangnail and she's locked in Kalosis, so how can she be a problem?"

"Not entirely, she isn't. Someone dug up one of her special little priestess medallions and it's now in the hands of the woman who has a vested interest in us not harming her boy toy . . . or her. Seems she has an issue with dying prematurely. Go figure."

M'Adoc was less than amused by Demon's summation. "Well, that sucks for you, doesn't it?"

"It sucks for all of us, Oneroi. If you want this handled, I suggest you do it yourself."

M'Adoc really did have to make an effort to keep his sarcastic tone at bay. "I never thought I'd live to see the day a mere mortal could scare the Dolophoni. You guys have really grown soft over the centuries, haven't you?"

Deimos curled his lip. "Calling me a coward is no way to goad me into suicide. As I said, we have extenuating circumstances. You're the one telling me how easy it is to kill him. Then why don't you try getting your hands bloodied for once?"

Little did he know, M'Adoc's hands had been coated in more blood than a seventy-five-year career surgeon's. He had no problem with executing his nuisances, he just had to be careful not to let the other gods know about it. The idea of an Oneroi taking a life without their implicit approval tended to make them jittery. "My job is to protect."

"Yeah, your own back. And mine is to watch over my team—one of whom is now dead." He took a step forward to make sure M'Adoc understood his rage. "You know I've never shirked at killing anyone or anything. But this . . . this is different. I'm not going to lose another brother needlessly. This is getting out of control." He hesitated before he added one final comment. "They're currently at Solin's house—under his protection. I'm sure you remember him, too."

Of course he did. He and Solin had battled it out on more than one occasion. Both of them were scarred by those fights.

But that was neither here nor there.

M'Adoc gripped his hands tightly behind his back, tempted to send a bolt straight at Demon's head, but he couldn't afford to let Demon know this was anything more than a routine hit or that his failure upset him in any way. He must remain perfectly calm at all times. Demon would love to have an excuse to turn the gods against M'Adoc, and he knew that. It was a dangerous line he toed.

He inclined his head. "Thank you for your services, Demon. I will make sure that the next time I need to consult with the Furies I summon one of the females, as they are much more vicious and competent."

That barb wasn't lost on Demon, who sneered at him. "One day, M'Adoc, you're going to learn why they nicknamed me Demon."

And one day Demon was going to learn why M'Ordant and D'Alerian referred to M'Adoc as Fonias—Slayer.

In the meantime, M'Adoc had a mess to clean up and

he would make sure that this time the job was done correctly. Let Arikos have a couple of days of peace so that he'd relax a bit. Then when his guard was down, M'Adoc would take full advantage of it.

ARIK SMILED AS MEGEARA BUTTONED HIS SHIRT. EVEN though they'd slept together, this one act seemed somehow more intimate. Her hands were graceful as she wove the buttons through their holes. Her fleeting touch made his nipples harden and his body warm. The scent of her was heavy in the air, and all he wanted to do was take her away someplace private where he could be with her alone for the rest of eternity.

She glanced up at him. "Are you all right?"

"Fine, why?"

"You have a strange look about you."

"I'm just thinking how delectably kissable your lips are." And before he even realized what he was doing, he was kissing her again.

Geary sighed as she melted into Arik's arms. The steely feel of his body was electrifying, and it made her want to rip his clothes off and have another round with him. If only she could. But right now they had a lot of things to think about.

She pulled back as a chilling thought went through her head. "You don't think they'll go after Tory to get to me, do you?"

Arik pulled back with a scowl. "Excuse me?"

"The Dolophoni. They won't go after her to get me or you to come for her. Will they?"

To her relief, he shook his head. "Not their style. They only kill who they're sent after. They don't worry about bystanders unless the bystanders attack them. They're actually rather ethical, which for gods and assassins is an amazing feat."

"Then why are they coming after me if not to get to you?"

"Someone wants you dead."

His emotionless tone sent a chill over her. "Remind me later that we need to work on your tact." Geary shook her head as she tried to understand. "Who could possibly want me dead? I haven't done anything."

"You were digging around Atlantis. It's why the boat was blown up. The gods do not, under any circumstance, want that place disturbed. And they're all willing to kill to keep its secret."

"What secret is that?"

"I assume why it was destroyed. Not even we really know what happened the day it vanished. Whatever went down there went down fast, and those who know the truth have kept it hidden ever since."

Geary cocked her head as she remembered her research. "Plato wrote that it was human hubris that caused the gods to destroy it as punishment."

Arik scoffed. "Plato wrote of a parable about a nation that was destroyed long before his ancestors had been born. He knew nothing of the truth. Anyone who'd ever gotten close to learning about Atlantis didn't live long enough to tell anyone else."

She stepped back as pain filled her. "That's why my family's dead, isn't it? We got too close."

He gave her a sympathetic nod. "I'm sorry, Megeara. But yeah. Your father was all over the real site."

A single tear fled down her face, but she quickly wiped it away.

"Come for me, Megeara, and I will grant you vengeance on those who've wronged you—those who've taken the ones you love most. Come here, child, and let us both deliver to them what they deserve. For petty vanity

they took from us both the very people we loved. Help me and I will help you." It was the same angry woman's voice Megeara had always heard here.

"Apollymi?" She whispered the name.

"It is I. And I will protect you, child, if you listen. I would have saved your father, but he denied my help and they killed him. I would spare you a young death."

"Is she talking to you?" Arik asked in a whisper.

If it'd been anyone else asking Megeara that question, she would have denied it emphatically. "She says the gods took from her someone she loved."

"Her son. At least that's what Zeus claims. Her husband, Archon, slew Apostolos, and in grief she destroyed her entire family."

But that didn't make sense. "Then why does she want revenge against the Greek gods and not her own?"

"Because Apollo has long asserted that he was the one who killed Apostolos. Back then, Greece and the Atlanteans were in a very strained truce. They'd warred against each other for centuries. The Atlanteans had tried to kill Apollo's son, but he'd managed to remove the baby from the queen's womb before she birthed him, and he substituted another child there that they killed instead. He then took his son Strykerius to Delphi, where he was raised by Apollo's priestesses."

That didn't make sense. "If Apollo saved his son, why would he kill Apollymi's child?"

"Because twenty-one years later Apollo had another son on the Greek island of Didymos. Atlantean assassins broke into the palace in the middle of the night and executed the baby and his mother, who was Apollo's sanctified mistress. To exact revenge on the Atlanteans for their crime, Apollo claims, he killed Apostolos, then cursed everyone of their bloodline to die horribly on their twenty-seventh birthday—the age of his mistress at death. That is what set Apollymi off. Like Apollo she wanted revenge for the death of her son, but Apollo was the greater god, so he trapped her in Kalosis, where she now sits, plotting her revenge against him and the rest of the Greek pantheon."

Megeara tilted her head as she caught a strange note in Arik's voice. "But you don't believe that."

He looked away. "I've met Apollymi and I know Apollo . . . he is not the greater god. I've never seen a god yet who would go up against the Destroyer. Even her own family was scared of her, and rightfully so. They say it took her less than ten minutes to blast all of them to oblivion while they were gathered together in their own hall. Knowing gods as I do, I'm quite sure they didn't go quietly to slaughter. But rather they put up one hell of a fight, and out of an entire pantheon there's only one of them still standing."

"Apollymi."

He nodded.

A vicious thought went through her. "Then she could deliver her promise to me? She could save you and restore my father's reputation without anyone being hurt?"

He cupped her face in his hands and stared at her intently. "Listen to me, Megeara. The gods don't act selflessly. None of them will help anyone without getting something out of the bargain. Ask yourself what it is Apollymi wants from you."

"Freedom."

He shook his head. "It's never that simple, love. Apollymi wants revenge and she doesn't care who suffers for it. If she is ever released, she will destroy the entire world. *All* of it. No one will be able to stop her. That's why she's imprisoned and why everyone is willing to keep her there." His look intensified. "She can't ever go free."

Geary understood that. It made sense. And yet she was so close now to her goal. Her father had been right and she could prove it beyond a shadow of a doubt. She could expunge his record . . .

But at what cost? Was it worth it?

And still Apollymi beckoned in her head with promises of revenge.

"Vengeance only destroys the one who seeks it." Geary paused as she remembered her grandfather in New York telling her that after she'd returned to the States to live. During World War II, his entire family had been slaughtered while celebrating his birthday by a raiding Nazi troop who happened upon them. Only nine years old, her grandfather had been wounded, blinded, and left for dead.

While he was unconscious, protected by the lifeless bodies of his family, a mysterious man had come and saved him. The man had bandaged her grandfather up and brought him safely to America to start his life over.

As an angry teenager, Geary had asked her grandfather if he'd ever thought about the ones who took everything from him.

Her grandfather had patted her lovingly on the hand. "Of course I do, Megeara. I've never had a birthday since that day that I don't hear the gunfire. That I don't see them kicking in the door of our cottage to murder us all. The last thing I saw before they blinded me was my mother dying while trying to protect me. My fourteen-year-old sister being dragged off to be raped and murdered. Do you honestly think, little one, that I don't remember that day constantly and wonder why I alone survived it? If I wouldn't have been better off dead, too? Yet here I am and I'm grateful for it. Because had I died that day, there would be no you."

Rage for him had burned inside her. "I would have gotten revenge on them. I wouldn't have been able to live until they paid for their crimes."

He'd nodded at her in that understanding way of his. "I thought about that, too, and even went so far as to book passage back to Europe after the war to find them."

"But you didn't go."

"No. My Saving Angel"—his name for the one who'd brought him to America—"came to me again as if he knew what I planned and he told me that it is by our actions we are destroyed or saved. The choice is ours. He said he didn't save me that day to see me die so foolishly. And he told me that vengeance only destroys the one who seeks it. If I chose to go, he wouldn't stop me. But he asked me if the lives I sought to take would be worth the one I could make here away from the hatred and sorrow. So I chose to stay here and let go of the past. Yes, it haunts me, but it doesn't rule me. And because I stayed here, I met your grandmother and had all of you to warm my heart and to ease my sorrows. My only regret is that I've never seen the beauty of your smile with my own eyes."

He'd smiled tearfully at her then and patted his heart. "But I feel its beauty here and I know there is not a lovelier, more precious child in this world than you and your cousins. I am glad that though someone did me grossly wrong, my final mark on this world is not one of countering hurt with more hurt but is one of love and friendship. We will always be known by our actions. Let them always be good ones."

Geary had to clear her throat as the memory surged

and made her eyes tear. She loved her grandfather Theo so much. He was a good man and she wouldn't hurt him ever if she could help it. He'd lost enough people in his life. She wouldn't let him bury another loved one.

"The quest has ended."

Arik's brow furrowed in disbelief. "Has it really?"

She nodded. "I think the boat explosion was an omen, huh? I think we should just leave it alone before someone gets hurt."

"Do you think Tory will let you do that?"

He had a point, but it didn't matter. "I'll ship her back home if she says anything."

"Will she go?"

"Kicking and screaming." Geary cringed at the thought of how irate the girl would be. But better alive and irate than dead and happy. "Sometimes we don't want what's best for us"—another thing her grandfather was always saying—"but we need it anyway."

Arik never ceased to be amazed by her. He was so used to people who could only think of themselves that her altruism was baffling. That she would give up a goal that meant so much to her to keep someone safe . . .

It was miraculous.

And because he knew how much it meant to her, he wanted her to have it. No one should get this close to their dream without attaining it. It seemed cruel to him.

That would be his final gift to her. Before he died he wanted to see the look of joy on her face for redeeming her father. "How about we make a compromise?"

She gave him a droll stare. "How would that be possible? You said it yourself that all the gods are against this."

"We can try. I'll take you back to the site and we can salvage a couple of incidental artifacts that won't hurt to have known—enough to prove your father wasn't insane—and then we can tell Tory that the site is too unstable for excavation. Tell her part of it caved in on us and we barely escaped. We can cut the live feed and make it seem real. Then we can say that Atlantis needs to remain at the bottom of the sea where the gods intended it rest."

Geary was stunned at the beauty of that argument. Until reality came crashing down on her. "I'd have to give up the location in my findings report."

"Lie. Who would know? You can give them a location somewhere else. Tell them the site was off the banks of Mykonos."

"But if someone else digs—"

"They find nothing and they don't die. People have been looking for Atlantis for eleven thousand years without finding it. It's just one more chapter in this chronicle. You will still have irrefutable proof that Atlantis existed. No one will be able to argue against it."

Would that work? It truly sounded too good to be true. "Are you sure the gods will be appeased?"

"I think so. I just need Kat's number from you."

"Why?"

Arik hesitated before he answered. He wouldn't out Kat and her relationship to the gods. If she wanted Megeara to know, it was Kat's place to tell her, not his. "We'll need another diver on the project. Just in case. She's more levelheaded than Teddy and I think she'd understand our reasons for keeping it hidden."

"Good point. You want me to call her?"

That would defeat the purpose of not outing her. He needed to explain this to Kat before they went back. The last thing he needed was for her to try to kill them, too. "I'd rather do it myself."

Stepping back, Geary eyed him warily. "Is there something about Kat that you're not telling me?" The suspicion in her gaze deepened. "Is she one of you?"

"No." That was the honest truth. She was in a class all by herself.

"Then I'll call her."

How did he keep getting himself into these messes? Kat would flip without his explanation. "Why don't we wait until tomorrow to talk to her then? Let her rest tonight."

"Okay."

He was grateful Geary didn't push this. By tomorrow he might have a better idea.

Suddenly someone was pounding on the study's door.

"Excuse me," Solin snapped angrily from the other side. "Last time I checked, this was *my* house. Why am I locked out of my own study?"

Arik moved to open the door. "Anything to piss you off, Brother. Why else?"

Solin scoffed as he entered the room. "Oh, that's easy enough to do. Basically the fact that you breathe does that."

Arik closed the door and turned to face him. "Love you, too."

"Of course you do, like a plague on your privates."

Well, at least Solin understood the nature of their relationship. "So what brings you back?"

"What part of *my* house did you miss?"

Arik countered with his own argument. "What about the part that we could stay here if we needed to?"

Solin opened his mouth to retort, then snapped it shut. He was silent for a few moments before he spoke again. "I did say that, didn't I?"

"You did."

"Fine," he said irritably, "stay. But whatever you do, put down a blanket or something next time you two want to get frisky on my hardwood floors. That's just . . . disgusting."

Geary sputtered at his indignation. "How do you—"

"He's a demigod," Arik answered in an unamused tone, cutting her off. "Never get too close to one if you want to maintain secrets."

Her cheeks pinkened to let him know she was quite embarrassed by it. "Well, that's not fair."

Solin gave her an arch stare. "You seem to have an issue with fairness, don't you?"

"I don't like things to be disorderly, if that's what you mean. There should be a degree of fairness in the world."

Solin snorted as he looked at Arik. "She's priceless." He returned his cold stare to her. "Sweetie, in our world, fair's got nothing to do with anything. He who has the greatest power wins. It's why we're all willing to kill each other off without flinching."

She cast a confused look at Arik before she responded. "But you helped me and Arik. Why would you do that if you really feel that way?"

Solin shrugged. "What can I say? It's so much more enjoyable to snatch victory from the hands of the gullible. You guys make the most delightful sound of agony when you're betrayed."

There was a part of her that wanted to think he was kidding, but another part wasn't so sure. He sounded pretty damn sincere. She glanced at Arik, who was every bit as skeptical as she was.

"Are you in with them then?" Arik asked.

Solin gave him an exasperated smirk. "If I was, do you think I'd let you stay here?"

Arik shrugged. "I don't know. It wouldn't hurt you. It's not like letting us stay here will make them hate you any more than they already do. If anything, our presence here would piss them off, which would be a bene for you. As you said, it would be a way to snatch victory from the gullible."

Solin turned completely stoic. His face, his demeanor,

even his voice. "I won't defend or explain my actions to you or anyone else. My motives are my own. Good, bad, indifferent."

Geary cocked her head as she noticed something about him while he spoke. A slight tenseness on his face. "What are you afraid of?"

Solin curled his lip at her. "I fear nothing."

"You fear intimacy, don't you?" she asked. "With anyone. That's why you say nothing about yourself. It's why you prefer to traipse through dreams rather than sleep with women in the flesh."

"Thank you, Dr. Ruth." You would need a chainsaw to cut through the venom and sarcasm in his voice. "But I honestly don't think you know even the most basic thing about me. So until you do, you should keep your opinions to yourself."

"You're right, I don't. But the question is, does anyone? Can you name me one single friend you have or have had in the past?"

"I don't need friends. All they do is eat your food, drink your beer, then spew your secrets the first time you do something that displeases them. No offense, but when you have as many enemies as I do, you keep your secrets under lock and key. Isn't that true, Arikos?"

Arik's gaze met hers and it softened in a way that made her heart speed up. "Sometimes it pays to trust the right people."

Solin curled his lip at them. "Such rotten sentimentality, and gullible until the end—both of which will ultimately get you killed. It is, after all, how I got you converted." He paused for effect before he stepped toward Geary to address her. "You should have seen him, Megeara. He was so sure he could take me in a fight. He was getting all ready for it when I did the unexpected."

"And that was?" she asked.

"I turned my human lover loose on him. She was in a dream state and had no idea what she was really doing. Arik, being the good Oneroi he was, wouldn't fight her. Protect the humans at all costs—that's their credo. Unless the human is a half-breed." He spat the words as if they were bitter tasting on his tongue. "Then we deserve to die for no other crime than the fact our father went slumming with a hard-on and knocked up some bitch who couldn't keep her legs crossed."

Solin invaded her personal space, making her take a step back as his blue eyes snapped fire at her. "So don't talk to me about fairness. I've no patience for it or you, and that, little human, is all you need to know about me."

Backing away, Solin raked them both with a sneer. "Stay or go. I really don't give a shit. But if you stay, I want you to continue your play upstairs in a bed, like civilized people." Then he turned and left them.

It took Geary a couple of minutes to recover her composure from his unwarranted rancor. "Well, isn't he Mr. Happy Sunshine?"

Arik didn't respond as he studied the floor.

Geary took a moment to consider everything Solin had told them, including the piece of history that explained another mystery in their relationship. "So he's the one who turned you. I'm surprised you would even speak to him."

He took a deep breath before he answered. "Honestly, I'd rather have my brains ripped out through my nostrils, but I wanted to stay with you, and without the permits you would never have allowed me near you. I had no choice except to call on him. Besides, you can't blame him really. He has every right to hate us."

Her chest tightened at the thought of Arik's seeking out a

bitter enemy for no other reason than to be with her. It was incredibly romantic, if not somewhat stupid. "Compassion looks good on you, Arik. You should wear it more often."

He took her hand into his and toyed with her fingers. "I'm trying to, but honestly, I'd rather be wearing you." He offered her a smile that warmed her heart.

"Ooo, that was a good one."

He lifted her hand to his lips to nibble her fingers. "It's the truth."

God, she was in love with this man . . . god . . . or whatever he was. They'd known each other such a short time and yet it seemed like forever. She'd confided everything to him, and here he was, trying to help her.

How could she let him go?

She already knew that answer. She couldn't. He'd come to mean too much to her. And as that thought went through her, it was followed by another. There was someone who knew more about this than Tory or even Arik.

"Apollymi?" she let her mind shout, hoping that the Atlantean goddess hadn't abandoned her.

"Yes, child?"

"Is there some way to free Arik from his bargain without killing him? Can he be made mortal?"

"A god can do anything. Free me and I will grant you any wish you have."

"Do you swear it?"

"On the lives of my Charontes. You free me and you will never want for anything so long as you live."

Geary pulled Arik into her arms and held him against her. She was grateful he couldn't hear her thoughts or her conversation with the goddess.

He felt so good in her arms. . . . She never wanted to let him go.

Don't make a pact with a god, her mind warned. In all

her ancient readings she couldn't recall a single time that such a bargain had worked in the favor of the person who made it.

Not once.

But that was fiction and this was real. Apollymi was real and so were Arik and Solin.

Geary would allow Arik to take her back to Atlantis and then she would let Apollymi guide her. After all these centuries, the goddess would be free again.

Geary's only hope was that Apollymi would keep her word. But even then, Geary's doubt was strong.

What choice do I have?

She couldn't allow him to die if she could stop it. And she was willing to make a deal with the devil to ensure Arik's life.

CHAPTER 17

THE NEXT FOUR DAYS WERE FILLED WITH ANSWERING OFficial inquests about the exploding boat, dealing with the insurance company, and trying to calm down Tory, who wanted to head right back to the site and excavate even though much of their data had gone up in flames. The only ones happy about the delay were Thia, who had more time to spend with Scott and Brian, and Kichka, who was able to hunt uninterrupted for stray mice in the alley behind their flat.

And deep inside, Geary was more than fine with the delay, too, since it meant more time with Arik. He proved himself to be a tremendous help to her. He kept her completely grounded even while her temper was snapping, and he had an unnatural ability to get the Greek officials to bend to his will. If she didn't know better, she'd swear he had his god powers back.

But he was definitely still human. He just knew how to influence people to get what he wanted.

She sighed as she lay naked in bed with him in the late afternoon. It'd been a particularly grueling day. Between dealing with her usual business with the salvage company and a couple of clients who didn't want to pay for having their cargoes retrieved or their boats towed, and the insurance company that was trying to prove she'd intentionally blown up her boat to get the money out of it, she was thoroughly exhausted.

The only good thing had been the mind-blowing sex, and now Arik was rubbing her back while she lay beside him.

"What are you thinking about?" she asked. He'd been unusually quiet all day.

"Nothing."

She turned her head to look up at him. He was completely naked except for the sheet that was pooled in his lap. His hair was mussed and his lips swollen, while he had a day's worth of whiskers on his cheeks. He was a little flushed from their play, which only made his eyes paler and bluer. "I don't believe that. You seem preoccupied. What's on your mind?"

He squeezed her shoulder with a touch so expert it wrung a moan from her before he answered. "You've had enough stress. I don't want to add to it."

"Oh, what the heck?" she said with a smile. "Add away. At this point, one more problem would be nothing to me."

Laughing, he kissed the shoulder he was working on before he moved down to massage her arm. "I was just thinking how strange it is that no one has attacked us these last few days. I keep waiting for the Dolophoni to return."

She propped herself up on one arm to watch him. "Maybe Apollymi scared them off."

He took her free hand into his and massaged it between his fingers. The small circles went up her arm and made her literally melt. "I don't know. They're not the type to scare all that easily."

He did have a point, but honestly, she preferred the thought that Apollymi had scared them off. That meant they wouldn't be back. "So what exactly are you thinking about their absence?"

"That they're waiting for me to get comfortable here so that they can strike while I'm not looking."

She liked that thought even less. "Maybe you're just being paranoid."

"Do you really think so?"

No. But she couldn't bear to say the word out loud. It was just too hard to think about. And the other thing she didn't want to think about bulldozed its way into her thoughts right behind it—Arik's time here was getting shorter by the second.

Which triggered her to glance at the clock. As soon as she realized the time, she jumped up, clutching the sheet to her breasts. "Hey, we need to get going if we're to meet Kat on time."

Arik nodded even though he was starting to dread this meeting and he didn't know why. He'd been the one to suggest they return to Atlantis, and yet he had a bad feeling that he couldn't place. Something was going to go wrong. He knew it.

Perhaps he'd been human long enough to develop a degree of intuition. Or maybe he'd been attacked enough to know that the most likely place for the Dolophoni to strike next time would be underwater, where he and Megeara wouldn't be able to escape or really fight. . . .

It was a chilling thought.

Because of that, he kept it to himself as they showered, dressed, and then headed for their rendezvous with Kat. He didn't want anything to taint Megeara's happiness after the last few days she'd had. Everyone had been chipping small pieces of her joy away, and he much preferred her smile.

This was what she'd dreamed of, and no matter what, he was going to give it to her.

Megeara was beautiful in a light summer top and jeans as she drove him out to the docks, which looked like they had a gaping hole where her old boat had been. In a weird way, he missed that boat and was sad to see it gone. He could only imagine how hard it must be for Megeara, since it was the same boat her father had used on his expeditions. She didn't say it, but Arik could tell by the longing on her face as she looked to the empty moorings that she missed the boat, too.

For this excursion, they were going to use one of her smaller company boats—just to make sure no one knew what their intent was. It was also small enough that they could man it with just the three of them.

"Is Tory going to be here?" he asked.

Megeara parked her car in the sandy lot that was off to the side of the marina. "No. I told her I needed her to reconstruct the excavation maps that'd been destroyed. She has no idea that we're even heading out today. She thinks we can't move until she finishes her project."

"That was evil of you."

She gave him a shy smile. "I think we're all a bit evil when it comes to protecting our families."

"Are we?"

Geary turned in the seat to look at him. "You have no idea what I'm talking about, do you?"

"No, not really. I mean, yes, I know the definition of family, but our families on Olympus don't work the same way yours does and we don't have the same attachment for each other."

"What about your mother?" Geary asked. "Surely she took care of you?"

He nodded. "True, she birthed me."

"And then?"

"I was handed off to attendants who tended my needs until I was old enough to be trained."

"Yeah, but didn't one of the attendants love you?"

He frowned at her. "They were servants, Megeara, not family. There was no love, and even if there were, I was too small to remember it."

"How small?"

Arik sat quietly, thinking, but nothing came to mind. He didn't have very many memories of childhood, and there was nothing there as he struggled to remember anyone taking care of him. "I don't remember. That's just the way it's always been done and I'm sure I was no exception. I honestly remember nothing of being a child, except for my training."

Geary was doing her best to understand his world, but it made no sense to her. "And what kind of training was this?"

He sighed as if the matter irritated him. "Even though we're cursed, we still have residual emotions when we're born. Those have to be stripped from us and we have to be shown how to enter dreams, as well as what is allowed for us to do there and what is forbidden. Then we have to learn how to fight the Skoti who will ultimately fight us for control of the human host. It takes years to fully master our powers, and it's all very complicated."

It sounded like it. But one part of that stuck out in her mind. "And how do they strip emotions from you?"

"Usually by beating," he said in an empty tone. "It's actually quite Pavlovian. You show an emotion and the punishment is such that you learn it's better to feel nothing than to suffer the consequences of having them."

"Does the training ever fail?"

"Sometimes."

"So what do they do then?"

"They execute us."

She wouldn't have been more stunned had he reached over and slapped her. "You have got to be kidding me!"

"No," he said in all earnestness. "At least I don't think I am."

Still, Geary was incredulous over his blasé tone and that they would simply kill the Oneroi for no other reason than they continued to have emotions. How cruel was that? "And all of you accept this?"

He appeared to be equally baffled by her standpoint as she was by his. "Have we a choice? Unless we mount a revolution against Zeus, this is what we have."

"Maybe it's time you did revolt."

He scoffed at her indignation. "It's not that simple. The pantheons have a balance of power and you have to be extremely careful adjusting it. One wrong move and you can destroy the entire world. What good would overthrowing them be then, when we'd all be dead?"

As much as she hated to admit it, she'd lost this argument. "You make an awesome point."

"Yeah."

Geary opened the door and got out while his words haunted her. Her poor Arik. She had to save him from this nightmare he was caught up in. She couldn't bear the thought of returning him to that life where there was no one to care for him. To hold him or love him. It just wasn't right.

"Why are the gods so callous to our suffering?" she asked as he joined her in front of the car.

He took her hand in his before he answered. "The

world is filled with suffering. If you open yourself up to it, it will consume even a god. But not all of them are callous. ZT is one who cares."

"I thought you said he wasn't a god."

"True. He is *technically* human, but he does have the powers of a god and immortality, and he does care about humanity in spite of what he says. And in spite of what they've done to him, he's never lost his compassion for others. There are several more like him who feel the same way. Who protect humanity."

"Yes, but is there a true god who does so?"

He thought about it a few seconds before he answered. "Apostolos."

Geary was surprised by his choice. "Apollymi's son?"

"Yes."

"I thought he was dead."

"That's what the rumor says."

"But you don't believe it?"

Arik shrugged. "You hang out in dreams and you hear all kinds of fascinating things. Apostolos is alive and I've heard his mother speaking with him. I know that he often tries to calm her down when she's extremely irate and threatening to destroy the world."

Geary took a second to let that soak in. "How ironic that the Great Destroyer's child would be the one who cares about the very people she wants to destroy."

"It is, but he does. He understands the grand scheme of things and consequences better than anyone else, and unlike the other gods, he won't punish people for their mistakes."

"Why not?"

"Let's just say that if I had to choose between my life and his, I'd much rather live mine."

Geary frowned. Jeez, how horrible had Apostolos's life

been that Arik would make that declaration? It was a scary thought. "Wow. You seem to know a lot about him even given the fact you hang out in dreams."

"Yeah, well, I've been in his a time or two, too. I just hope he never remembers it or I'm really screwed."

"Hi, guys."

She looked up as she heard Kat's voice. The tall blonde stood on the docks in a pair of shorts and a loose T-shirt.

"Hey, babe. Glad you made it."

Kat shrugged. "Well, if you really intend to go poking around Atlantis again, I want to be there for it."

"I'll bet you do," Arik said under his breath.

Geary scowled at Arik's odd tone but chose to ignore it as they neared Kat on the docks. "Do you have all the gear ready?"

"I do."

Geary was grateful.

"Did you tell anyone what we're doing?" Arik asked Kat as they joined her by the boat.

"Not at all. I know how to keep a secret."

"Good." Geary rubbed Arik's arm before she headed to the boat. "Come on, kids, let's get this under way. We have a date with destiny."

Arik paused as Kat narrowed her gaze on him with such intensity, he could actually feel his skin burn. *"How many times do you have to be warned? I can't believe you're this stupid."*

"I'm not. She and I have an agreement. We give her a couple of innocuous trinkets to prove that Atlantis is real and save her father's reputation, and then she will doctor her findings to help send others off on a wild-goose chase. She will help us safeguard the location of Atlantis."

Kat looked stunned by his declaration. "Are you serious?" she asked in a low tone that only he could hear.

"Yes. She understands why it can't be found and is in full accord."

"I don't believe you."

"Ask her."

Kat led him on board the small boat where Geary was already making preparations to sail. "So, Gear . . . where's the rest of the team?"

Megeara looked a bit sheepish. "I'm thinking we only need the three of us."

"Why?"

She met Arik's gaze before she answered. "Look, Kat, I know how much finding Atlantis means to everyone, especially you, but I've done a lot of thinking and I don't want it really found. I know it doesn't make sense to you right now, but I think this is for the best and I want you to trust me."

Kat still looked unconvinced by Geary's reasoning. "So why are we going back?"

"A couple of reasons. One, I want inarguable proof that it's there, to silence everyone who laughed at my dad, and two, we need to destroy the datum so that no one will see it and get curious about it. The last thing we need is someone digging down there on a site we helped set up."

Kat folded her arms over her chest as she gave Geary a doubting stare. "Are you sure about this?"

"Positive." Geary reached out to pat Kat's shoulder comfortingly. "I'm sorry, Kat. I know you wanted to be there when we unveiled the discovery, but we can't tell anyone where Atlantis really is."

Kat shrugged. "Don't apologize to me, Doctor. It's your excavation."

Geary couldn't believe that Kat wasn't angry or hurt. But she was grateful for her friend's levelheadedness.

Of course, there was a third reason Geary wanted to go. Apollymi. If Geary unleashed Apollymi, she would save Arik. But since Kat didn't know that and Arik would kill Geary if she mentioned it to him, she kept that to herself. No matter what, she had to save him. She couldn't stand by and let him die because he'd wanted to be with her. It was wrong and she loved him too much for that.

In less than an hour, they had the boat prepped and were under way. Kat was at the helm while Geary stayed on deck, looking out at the passing boats around them. The island was breathtaking in the background, rising up out of the water with a grand majesty unparalleled. Her father had been right. Greece was one of the most beautiful places in the world.

And this was the first time in years she'd headed toward the site without feeling anxious and elated.

There was definitely nothing but dread in her stomach now. She glanced over to where Arik stood, checking their diving gear. For once there was no guessing about Atlantis. There was no doubt. It was there. Waiting. Just as her father had said.

She was about to show it to the world.

And release a goddess. . . .

Geary gripped the rail as she again heard Apollymi's voice in her mind, calling out to her. She could save Arik. Keep him safe forever.

The promises sounded so good to her, especially as she watched him laying out their gear.

There's no other way. She'd done her own research and checked it with Tory. Neither of them had been able to think of or find any example of a god becoming human. At least not unless the god was cursed or there was some other extenuating circumstance that didn't apply to this case.

It was hopeless. To keep Arik, Geary would need Apollymi.

"What am I doing?" Geary whispered. "Don't meddle in the affairs of the gods unless you want to get eaten." It was a lesson that resonated through ancient literature.

Who was she to tamper with fate? But as she watched Arik, she couldn't stand the thought of losing him. The thought of sending him back to die.

"It's an interesting moral dilemma, isn't it?"

Geary tensed as she heard a voice to her right. She turned her head to find a handsome man standing in the shadows, barely a silhouette. His black hair was short and the glowing blue eyes marked him as another of Arik's brethren.

"Who are you?"

"M'Adoc," he said in a low tone. "I'm one of the three leaders of the Oneroi."

A wave of fear went through her. "Are you here for Arik?"

He glanced over to where Arik worked, unable to see him in the glare of the afternoon sun. "Ultimately, yes. But I know from my dealings with humans that you're going to fight me if I try to take him, and that I don't want."

"You're right about that. I won't give him up. Not now. Not ever."

"I know. You love him. It's why I heard Apollymi laughing a few minutes ago." He glanced back to Arik, who was checking their small dredge. "I give my brother kudos . . . to gain the love of a human is no small feat. The ability of the human heart to sacrifice for the one it loves . . . there is nothing on Olympus that can even begin to compete with that."

A weird chill went over her body at his words and the way he said them. It gave her insight to this stranger. "You've known love." It was a statement.

His jaw flexed as if he was gritting his teeth, and a flash of pain darkened his eyes, confirming it. "The Oneroi know nothing of love and the Skoti know even less."

Still, she didn't believe him. He'd known it and, by the looks of it, he'd lost it. "Then why are you here?"

"To warn you not to be foolish."

Well, that was nice of him. But she didn't need his warning. She'd never been a stupid woman. "And how am I foolish?"

"You've given your heart to someone who has sold you out completely." He cast his gaze meaningfully at Arik.

Geary scoffed at him. "You're wrong. Arik loves me."

He shook his head. "Arik has no conviction. If he had, he'd have never been turned by Solin."

"You don't know that."

"Oh yes, I do. Arik is weak. He's always been weak."

"You—"

"Sh," he said, cutting her off. "Before you defend him, ask yourself this. How does a Skotos become human?"

"He already told me that. He made a pact with Hades."

"Yes, and you're a woman who has spent her entire life steeped in ancient Greece. Have you learned nothing of our ways? Has a god ever given such a gift without receiving something extremely valuable in return?" There was an ominous note in his voice.

"What are you saying?"

"You mean so much to Arik that he bartered your life to be here. He isn't the one who will die when his time ends, sweet child." His blue eyes were searing with heat. "*You* will."

Geary shook her head in denial. That was total crap and she knew it. "You're lying."

"I can't lie. I'm Oneroi."

"What the hell are you doing here?" Arik came out of nowhere to rush M'Adoc. She expected them to fight. Instead, M'Adoc allowed Arik to grab him by his shirtfront, shove him up against the wall, and hold him there.

Like a true Oneroi, there was no anger or any emotion evident as M'Adoc stared unblinkingly at him. "I told her the truth."

"You what?" Arik asked from between gritted teeth.

"I told her of your deal with Hades. That you swapped her life for your mortality."

Arik's face went pale as his eyes filled with absolute horror. He didn't deny it. Rather, he looked guilty.

Geary knew then that M'Adoc wasn't lying. "Is this true, Arik?"

He cursed before he shoved M'Adoc again. "I have no intention of fulfilling that bargain."

M'Adoc looked at her. "As I said, he has no conviction. We don't understand human emotion and we can't handle it. When he returns to his true god state, he will come back here for you and kill you. As promised."

"Bullshit!" Arik roared.

Geary wanted to believe in Arik's rage. She needed to. But part of her was drawn toward M'Adoc. He made a convincing argument.

He looked at his brother with those cold, unfeeling eyes and it made her wonder if that's what Arik would look like once his time had expired. "You know it's true, Arik. When you are no longer corrupted by human emotion and Hades tells you to kill her, you will do it. You won't have a choice and you won't have any feelings left for her."

"Never!"

"Not even when you're chained in Tartarus, under Hades' constant abuse?"

Arik flinched. He couldn't help himself. Too many centuries of torture hit him at once, and those had been doled out by Hypnos. No one was better at making a god suffer than Hades. Everyone knew that. Arik met Megeara's worried gaze.

"He's telling the truth, isn't he, Arik?"

Arik watched as she backed away from them. He released M'Adoc and turned to face her. "Megeara, please . . ."

She shook her head back and forth as she looked at him as if he were scum. That look cut him straight to the marrow of his bones. "Why didn't you tell me about this?"

"Because I was stupid, okay? I didn't want to hurt you." He reached for her, but she stepped away.

"You intended to kill me?"

He tried to explain, but his tongue seemed to thicken in his mouth as fear seized him. How could he even begin to make her understand? "It wasn't like that."

"Then explain it to me."

"I'd already made the deal when Hades set down the terms. I had no choice. He sent me here before I could even try to renegotiate."

"And so you intended to kill me," she repeated.

"In the beginning, yes, but—"

"But what?" she asked, her tone ragged with pain and rage. "There's no *but* here, Arik. You *fully* intended to kill me. How could you?"

"He's Skoti."

"Shut up!" he snarled at M'Adoc. Arik turned back toward Megeara. "Please, baby." He reached for her again.

She stepped back. "Don't touch me."

Arik couldn't breathe as he saw the tears in her eyes. The betrayal. She was hurting, he knew it. He could feel it like his own pain. It cut through him, lacerating his heart. "I would never hurt you. You have to believe that."

"Great words for a man who'd planned my death from the beginning, huh?"

She was right. How could he ever convince her that he'd changed? He was Skoti and Skoti were nothing.

He turned on his brother, hating him for telling her. "Damn you, M'Adoc."

"There's nothing to damn me over, Arik. I'm not the one in the wrong here. You are. You should never have made that bargain."

He wanted to kill M'Adoc for this. But he was right. It'd been wrong of Arik to come here. He should have been content to stay with her in her dreams.

M'Adoc spoke calmly. "Skoti are forever selfish, Megeara. It's why we must police them. They become mad with their hunger to the point they don't care who they harm or how they harm them so long as they get what they want. Arik wanted you and so he was willing to kill you for it." He met Arik's gaze. "If you truly mean what you say now, then for once, do the decent thing. Surrender yourself to me."

Every instinct inside Arik rebelled at the very idea of it. Every one. They would kill him and he knew it.

But then, he would die anyway. Hades would never allow him to renege on their bargain. No one backed out of a deal with the devil.

And perhaps this was the kindest end. Megeara hated him now. She thought him the lowest of forms. If he left with M'Adoc, she wouldn't grieve for him or ask herself if maybe there was something she could have done to save him.

She would be at peace.

That would be the best gift he could give her.

"He's right, Megeara," Arik said, forcing all emotions out of his tone. "I would have killed you once I returned to my natural state. I'm sorry."

Geary couldn't breathe as he spoke those words. Part of her had still believed in him over M'Adoc. She didn't want to think that her Arik could ever harm her.

But if what they said was true . . .

It stung her so deep in her heart that she felt as if she'd die from the pain.

Arik turned to M'Adoc and whispered something to him. She couldn't hear it, but M'Adoc inclined his head before Arik sighed. "Then I'm ready to go."

His crystal gaze met hers and the love she saw there singed her to the spot. "Good-bye, Megeara."

She noted the satisfaction in M'Adoc's eyes.

Satisfaction . . .

"Even in human form we feel nothing." M'Adoc should have no emotions at all. None.

But he was satisfied.

Realizing that if M'Adoc could feel, he could lie, she opened her mouth to stop them. But before she could make a single sound, M'Adoc placed his hand on Arik's shoulder and the two of them vanished from the boat.

"No!" Geary shouted, her heart pounding as reality crashed through her.

Arik was gone.

He was going to kill you, her mind tried to rationalize. But the scariest bit was that part of her didn't even care. It wanted him back no matter what.

She felt the boat slowing down.

Kat came out on deck and approached her slowly. "Where's Arik?"

Unable to even begin to explain Arik's disappearance, Geary burst out laughing hysterically until she started crying and gesturing hopelessly toward the prow. She honestly felt like she was having a nervous breakdown. How could she tell Kat everything? The woman would think her crazy and who could blame her?

Gods in the real world? None of this would be believed. Ever.

Kat scowled. "Hon, are you okay?"

"No," she said, trying to gain a handle on herself. "No, I'm not."

Kat cocked her head in a gesture that reminded Geary of Solin whenever he was "listening" for something preternatural.

"What are you doing?" Geary asked.

Kat let out an uncharacteristic curse. "M'Adoc was here? How could you let him take Arik?"

That snapped Geary out of her hysteria.

Surely, not . . .

"If you tell me that you're one of them, then I'm absolutely going to freak out."

Kat's face was deadly earnest. "Then you better freak."

"Good God, is no one what they seem? Is Kichka the Egyptian goddess Bast in disguise?"

"No, Kichka is a cat."

Uh-huh. She was supposed to believe that after the bomb Kat had just dropped on her? "And let me guess. You're a god, too, right? Which one? Athena? Hera? Oh, what the heck? Aphrodite?"

Kat gave her a droll stare. "No. I'm not a god. I'm a servant to Artemis."

"Artemis?" Yeah. That just sounded so much better . . . not. "The goddess of the hunt, huh?" Geary looked down at the wood deck. "There must be some kind of vapors coming up off the floor of the sea—like the oracle of Delphi. That's why I'm seeing and hearing all this insanity." She nodded, liking the sound of that argument. "I'm hallucinating, aren't I?"

"Oh, get a grip," Kat said irritably. "If you can accept Solin, Arik, and M'Adoc, you can certainly accept me, too."

"One would think that, wouldn't they? But I've known you too long to think that all this time you've been hiding a secret like this from me."

"And now you know why I wasn't thrilled when you found Atlantis and wanted to start digging around the city."

Well, since she put it that way, it did make sense. "And were you in on my death plan with Arik, too? Are you the one who killed my father?"

Kat's eyes blazed in anger. "Excuse me? You don't need to be tossing around ludicrous accusations like that. I had nothing to do with your father's death. I loved that man. He was weird and strange, but I loved him and I would have done anything to keep him safe. While you were off in America, I was here with him, doing the best I could to help him and keep him alive even though he was bent on killing himself."

Tears filled Geary's eyes at the truth. "I'm sorry, Kat. I'm just upset and I don't mean to be taking it out on you."

Kat nodded. "No offense, but you *should* be sorry. How could you let M'Adoc take Arik?"

"Arik was going to kill me."

"Hardly."

"It's true," Geary said past the lump in her throat. "Arik admitted it."

Still, Kat scoffed. "Arik loves you, Geary. It's so obvious it's painful. No man, god or otherwise, watches over a woman the way he does you and then lets her die, never mind kills her. That's just stupid."

"Yeah, he loves me now, but when he loses his emotions next week, what then? M'Adoc said that he'd kill me without question. He said that Arik would have no emotions or choice but to do as they said." There, it sounded rational. Kind of.

"Arik?" Kat asked incredulously. "Do what he was told? Please. He hasn't followed the directions of any god in thousands of years. That's why he's Skoti."

All of Geary's fears that M'Adoc was lying came rushing back. "What are you saying, Kat?"

"No offense to you, kid, but what I'm saying is that you just ordered a man who loves you to his death."

CHAPTER 18

WITH HIS HANDS CUFFED BEHIND HIS BACK, ARIK DIDN'T flinch or struggle as M'Adoc hauled him into the sanctity of the triumvirate's hall. He'd never been inside this place before, not even in dreams. It was the sacred domain of the triumvirate who zealously guarded it from all the rest of their kin.

No one knew why, but Arik had to give the guys credit. It was an opulent palace made of glass and gold that they'd constructed here. It was fit for a dream god and even Zeus would be at home . . . The council room where they were was decadently comfortable with padded chairs and even a laptop computer that was so out of place as to be funny . . . if Arik wasn't about to die.

M'Ordant was seated before it, and as they came in he looked up with an unguarded expression that showed both confusion and shock—two emotions he shouldn't have. "Damn, M'Adoc, how did you manage this one?"

M'Adoc shoved Arik against the solid glass table, the

corner of which bit into his hip bone and bruised him. He had to grind his teeth to keep from lashing out at M'Adoc. But Arik had given his word, and so long as the god kept his and didn't harm Megeara, Arik would submit, even though it went against every part of his genetic makeup to do so.

M'Adoc shrugged as he moved to stand beside Arik. "He surrendered willingly. In exchange for our keeping his human safe."

There was no missing the stunned look on M'Ordant's face.

"Was there no fight?"

Arik turned his head slightly as he heard D'Alerian's deep voice from behind him. He couldn't see him, but he could feel D'Alerian's presence. Of the three of them, his had an unmistakable aura. He wasn't the most powerful, but his presence could be felt all the way to the marrow of someone's bones.

"He knew better than to fight me," M'Adoc said in a sinister tone.

"Get over yourself, M'Adoc," Arik snarled. "You had nothing to do with this. There was no need in my staying in the human realm any longer since all you did was hurt Megeara by telling her of my bargain with Hades." She would never forgive him, and that hurt even more than a thousand beatings. Strange how originally the thought of her death had meant nothing to him. Now he grieved over every tear and doubly over the ones he'd caused her. "Just take me to Hades and end it."

M'Adoc took him by the arm. His lips were twisted as he raked Arik with a sneer. "Oh no, Arikos. I don't think so. See, I hand you over to Hades and he's going to start questioning how it is you have so many emotions that you're willing to surrender yourself to save a simple human's soul."

"Because Hades made him human," D'Alerian answered in a dry, stoic tone. "There won't be any questions over it. It would only stand to reason."

M'Adoc turned on him with a hiss. "Are you willing to take that chance?"

D'Alerian's jaw flexed. "There's no chance involved, Adarian. He is human, by Hades' command, and he acted as a human. The god would expect no less."

Arik frowned as D'Alerian used M'Adoc's real name, Adarian. As part of their punishment, and to push them away from the idea that they were individuals of any merit, many of the original Oneroi had been stripped of their names and given new ones to designate their roles. *D'* meant that D'Alerian was normally assigned to watch over immortals such as the Dark-Hunters. *V'* designated a human helper—as an Oneroi, Arik's name had been V'Arik or V'Arikos, which he now hated, since it sounded like a vein condition. And the *M'* was reserved for those who policed them all. There were many who called D'Alerian M'Alerian. But for reasons no one understood, D'Alerian continued to use the name they'd given him before he'd risen to the ruling ranks.

M'Ordant closed his laptop as he faced them. "He's right. We should hand him over to Hades. We don't want to cross the god of the dead. He's a nasty bugger."

M'Adoc scoffed at them. "And when Hades kills Arik and his immortal soul is stripped bare while Hades tortures him in Tartarus, don't you think King Badass is going to discover the fact that little Arikos can feel something other than pain without having a human host to sponsor those emotions?"

A rivulet of shock went through him. What was M'Adoc saying? Arik froze as he began to suspect that the emotions he'd thought were residuals left from Megeara's might have been his own after all. "What's going on?"

"Shut up, Arik," M'Ordant snapped angrily.

M'Adoc glared at his brothers. "We can't take a chance of them learning the truth. Ever." His gaze bored into D'Alerian. "Of everyone in this room, Neco, you have the most to lose. Don't let your compassion for him stop you from doing what needs to be done."

Pain flickered across D'Alerian's face before he gave a subtle nod.

There wouldn't be any mercy given to Arik, not that he had expected any. Honestly, his welfare didn't matter. "I don't care what happens to me," Arik said to M'Adoc. "Just remember you promised to take care of Megeara."

One corner of M'Adoc's lips twisted up into a mocking smile. "Oh, don't worry. I fully intend to take care of her. Immediately."

D'Alerian scowled. "I don't like that tone, *adelphos*."

M'Adoc cast a belittling smirk at him. "No one gives a damn what you like, Neco. She's a liability to us. She knows the location of Atlantis and she knows we exist. Would you have me leave a threat like that out there?"

He was going back to kill her. Arik knew it with every ounce of his being.

"You swore to me, you lying bastard." Arik turned on M'Adoc, intending to fight, but as soon as he neared him, he felt something hot and solid pierce his stomach. Pain tore through him.

Arik staggered back and looked down to see a long, bloodied dagger in M'Adoc's hand. He couldn't believe it as his knees weakened from the agony of his wound.

M'Adoc moved toward Arik with a merciless glint in

his eyes. He buried a fist in his hair as his empty, cold gaze burned into Arik's. "Sweet dreams, Arik," M'Adoc said an instant before he stabbed him again and everything went dark.

GEARY WAS NUMB AS THEY RETURNED TO THE DOCKS. Over and over she kept going through everything with Arik. But deep inside, she knew Kat was right. Arik had loved her. In spite of everything or maybe because of everything, they'd fallen in love with each other, and she'd just thrown him to the wolves.

She should have trusted in him. Arik wouldn't hurt her, she knew that. He might have had bad intentions in the beginning, but he wasn't like that now. Why hadn't she given him the benefit of the doubt?

"What am I going to do, Kat?" she asked as they tied the lines.

Kat sighed. "There's nothing to do. He's gone."

Geary straightened up to stare at the taller woman. "I can't accept that. I can't."

But Kat was immune to her pleading look. "You're going to have to."

"Why?" Geary asked.

"Because sometimes life just basically sucks, and this is one of those times."

"And if I don't want it to?"

Kat shook her head. "When has it ever listened to you?"

She did have a point. But it didn't stop the pain inside Geary from hurting. How could she have let M'Adoc take Arik? She should have fought. Should have told him she loved him.

Instead, she'd just stood there as he was taken and done absolutely nothing.

Damn me, I'm such a fool. She'd waited her entire lifetime for love, and then when she'd finally found it she'd cast it aside in one moment of hurt anger. How could she have been so stupid?

"This can't be how it ends."

Kat's features softened as she neared her. "Geary, look. Arik sacrificed himself to keep you safe. Don't ruin it by putting yourself into danger and dying. Let him go."

She stared at Kat. "If someone you loved were suffering because of you, could you let him go?"

Kat screwed her face up as if she was in pain. "This isn't about me," she said in an anguished tone that answered Geary. "Oh, okay, so I wouldn't stand by and let the man I love suffer when I was the one who caused it. . . . Damn."

"Yeah. Damn. We have to find some way to help him."

Kat raked her hand through her hair as if irritated beyond her tolerance. "I don't even know how to begin to fix this."

"I do."

Geary put her hand to her temple as she heard Apollymi's voice in her head. *"Not now, please."*

"Don't dismiss her," Kat said out loud. "Apollymi's probably our best hope right now."

"You know about . . ." Of course she did. "You hear her, too?"

"All the time. She has a bad habit of nosing her way into pretty much everything I do. She's terribly nosy that way, but she's always a friend to me." She smiled before she addressed Apollymi. "*Mibreiara,* have you any suggestions that don't involve one of us letting you out?"

"That is the suggestion I *prefer."*

"Yes, but neither Geary nor I will do that. You got anything else?"

"Yes, but it's tricky. Listen to me, my girls. You're about to have an important lesson in men and god politics."

• • •

"SOLIN?"

Solin cursed as he heard Arik's voice in his head. *"I have nothing to say to you."*

"Fine. I don't want to hear it anyway. What I need is for you to listen."

"Listen, my ass."

"I need your ears, Solin," he said wryly, *"not your ass."*

"Go to hell."

"I'm already there."

Solin paused as he felt something odd brush against his collar. It was the touch of the dead and he knew it, even though it'd been centuries since he'd last felt one. "What?"

A Shade of Arik appeared before Solin. His features were ghastly white, his eyes dark and pain-filled. He wore nothing but a pair of tattered pants. "M'Adoc killed me."

Solin couldn't have been more shocked had he been the one who'd died. "How?"

"I surrendered myself to him to protect Megeara. Now he's reneged on our bargain and is heading for her. I need you to protect her from him."

Of course he did, and Solin was through being the dupe in this. Why should he put his life on the line for anyone? Who would he go to for help once he was a Shade? No one. "Do you think I even care?"

"I know you do, Solin. In spite of your protestations, I can see the real man inside that you try so desperately to ignore and hide." He paused before he spoke again. "Please, Brother. She's not a fighter and he won't stop until she's dead. Don't let an innocent die over nothing."

Still Solin didn't want to get involved in this. He'd made a similar mistake before and paid dearly for it. "Do

I look like an Oneroi to you? I'm not here to protect humans. Why don't you go warn her yourself?"

"She won't speak to me or listen. M'Adoc told her of my bargain with Hades. She hates me now."

Solin didn't miss the tremor of pain in Arik's voice. Nor the look of absolute misery on his face. The fact that she was hurting tore Arik apart. "You love her?"

"Obviously more than my life," he said, his voice trembling from his emotions.

Solin narrowed his eyes on Arik. "It hurts, doesn't it? To have that one person you love learn the truth of what you are and hate you for it?"

"You have no idea."

"Yeah, I do." And instead of feeling the satisfaction he'd anticipated when Arik tasted his own misery, Solin felt nothing but more pain. There was no joy in hurting someone else. At least not for him. "Where are you?"

"I'm on the banks of Styx. M'Adoc won't allow Charon to ferry me over for fear of Hades finding me and learning the truth. I'm sure that when Hades learns I'm dead, he'll go for Megeara to fulfill my bargain, and that I can't allow. She's innocent in this and shouldn't have to pay for my stupidity. I have nothing to give you, Solin, but please, if there's any decency left in you, don't let her die because of me. I'm begging you."

Solin knew that kind of love. He'd tasted it once and it'd been burning on his tongue like a bitter pill for countless centuries. "Just so you know, I've never had a drop of decency in me." Arik literally deflated before Solin's eyes. "But I won't let them hurt her. Rest easy."

Even as he spoke, he knew that would never happen. Hades wouldn't allow Arik peace once he learned where the man was, and from the looks of it, neither would

M'Adoc. And for the first time in centuries, Solin honestly felt sorry for someone other than himself.

"You can trust me, Arik."

"Thank you." He inclined his head to Solin before he faded out.

Taking a deep breath, Solin leaned back in his chair. His motto had always been to help no one because no one had ever helped him. He hated people.

He hated the gods most of all.

And he had no business getting involved in this. But how could he stand by and not do something? Megeara needed protection, and unlike him, she didn't have the powers to fight against them and win. They would tear through her in no time.

If he were smart, he'd contact ZT and let the Chthonian handle it.

"Nah," he said with a bitter smile. "I'd rather be vindictive than smart." And with that he flashed himself out of the safety of his home to search for a human.

It didn't take much to find Megeara. Her aura stood out even to the waking Dream-Hunter, especially since she was in such emotional turmoil.

But what gave him pause was the air of hopeless sadness that engulfed her. It'd been a long time since he'd seen its equal. "You okay?"

She jerked around at the sound of his voice to glare at him. "What are you doing here?"

"I have no idea, but I think it's to help."

She scoffed at him as she pulled down a book from her bookshelf. "That boat already sailed. You told us we were on our own."

"Yeah. But the amazing thing about boats is that they occasionally turn around and come back."

"Or they blow up while hosting your air supply," Kat added meaningfully.

He turned his head to see her entering the room from his left. "True, but not this one. Arik asked me to guard Megeara from the others."

Megeara gave him a suspicious look. "Why would he do that?"

"Because he's not able to."

Still suspicion was heavy in her eyes. She didn't trust Solin, and honestly he couldn't blame her for it. "And why would you do that when you've already made your position clear?"

He shrugged. "I'm basically doing it to piss off the powers-that-be."

"And?" Kat prompted.

"And what?"

"I don't know, there just seemed to be an *and* attached to the way you said that."

And . . . for some reason he didn't want to think about, he'd come to like and respect Arik. But that he'd never admit to. "There's no *and*."

"All right then," Kat said, clapping her hands together. "We're trying to save Arik. You said he came to you. Where is he?"

Solin hesitated. He'd assumed they knew already, but apparently the women had no clue what'd happened to Arik. "He came to me as a Shade, Kat. M'Adoc killed him."

Geary dropped the book in her hand at the unexpected news. If Kat hadn't reached out to steady her, she would have probably fallen.

Arik was dead.

It couldn't be—and yet she could tell by the look on Solin's face that he wasn't joking.

"I can't breathe," she whispered as her tears gathered in her throat to choke her. "He can't be gone."

"Sh," Kat said as she pulled Geary against her. "It's okay, Geary."

But it wasn't okay. Arik was dead and it was her fault. She hadn't even fought for him. M'Adoc had come and she'd all but shoved Arik into the hands of the man who'd killed him.

She sobbed as her heart shattered. How could she have done such a thing, even in anger?

"Uh, ladies. I hate to say it, but I'm not through being a harbinger here. Arik came to me because M'Adoc is hell-bent on cleaning this situation up."

Kat stepped away from her. "Cleaning it up how?"

He looked meaningfully at Geary. "Humans aren't supposed to know we exist."

That shocked Geary's tears away as a chill went down her spine. "He's coming to kill me, too."

"Yes."

Anger consumed her as she wiped away her tears. "What about Tory and Thia?"

"They don't know anything, so they're safe. But you, my dearest, are another matter entirely."

Well, she could handle that. Her life was one thing, theirs was another. So long as they were safe, she could deal with whatever came her way.

She bent to retrieve her book of mythology from the floor. "I can't believe this."

Solin nodded. "It's really quite pathetic, isn't it? Arik gives himself up because M'Adoc swears he won't hurt you, and then the lying bastard decides you need to die anyway."

Geary froze at his words as dread consumed her. "Arik did what?"

Solin looked ill. "Oh, don't tell me you didn't know that, either?"

"*No,*" Kat said, stressing the word. "She didn't."

Solin wiped his hand over his face. "Okay, I'm just going to stand here and be quiet."

"It's too late, Solin," Kat said from between clenched teeth. "You've already done your damage."

"Wait," Geary said as her mind whirled with thoughts. She looked down at the leather-bound book in her hands. "We can save Arik."

They exchanged a frown before Kat shook her head. "I don't see how."

"Oh c'mon, you're both *in* the pantheon. Shades have been brought back before." She held the book out to them. "Look at Orpheus and Eurydice. Hades allowed her to leave."

Solin snorted. "That's one example out of thousands Hades has denied, and laughed at while he did so."

Geary glared at him. "I thought you were going to be quiet."

"Sorry."

"As much as I hate to admit it, he's right," Kat said with a sigh. "Not to mention Eurydice never made it out. Orpheus looked back before he reached the surface, and she was snatched right back into the Underworld. Hades is a selfish bastard that way. He never willingly lets go of a soul."

Apollymi cleared her throat in Geary's mind. "*Were you not listening to me earlier? Why do I even bother? Just call me Circe or Cassandra for all the attention I'm paid. Why do I have to resort to them anyway? Ferandia would be a better example, but since she's Atlantean no one knows that story, do they? No. So I have to resort to those insipid Greek tales, half of which were stolen from us. But that's another matter. Point is, no one ever listens to a trapped goddess. . . ."*

Laughing in spite of everything, Geary realized Apollymi was right, and she was going to take the goddess's earlier advice. She looked up at Solin. "Oh, Mr. Dream Master, where's Persephone?"

"Good girl."

Solin narrowed his eyes. "You're not thinking what I think you're thinking, are you?"

Kat grinned. "You want to move the mountain, you give it something it can't resist. Geary and Apollymi are right. Hades won't even look at us. But he listens to his wife. We need her."

Solin was still shaking his head. "And if she won't help?"

"I'm not going to think about that," Geary said sternly. "I can't afford to."

Solin looked reluctant, but in the end, he agreed with them. "All right then, let's go."

"None of you are going anywhere."

Geary froze as M'Adoc appeared in the doorway before them.

And he wasn't alone.

CHAPTER 19

GEARY TOOK A STEP BACK AT THE SIGHT OF M'ADOC AND the Dolophoni . . . at least that's who she assumed they were. There were three of them, but she'd never seen them before. Unlike the first group, these were all women. Dressed in black leather, with black hair, nails, and lipstick, they looked mean and nasty. They were also fanged, with eyes so dark, she couldn't even see where the pupils ended and the irises began. All they needed was snakes in their hair to be even . . .

Oh wait, one of them had that. Black snakes slithered out of her ponytail to curl around her neck and hiss at them. Lovely. Just lovely.

Solin moved to stand in front of Geary and Kat. "This is over, M'Adoc."

"No, it isn't. Not until she's"—he indicated Geary with a jerk of his chin—"dead. Now either you and Katra can hand her over and leave or you two can bleed."

Solin let out an exaggerated breath. "Looks like I'm

bleeding then. Unlike some people I know"—he duplicated M'Adoc's action, indicating him with his chin—"*I* keep my word."

M'Adoc narrowed his eyes before he turned his head to address the women over his shoulder. "Kill them."

Geary tensed for the coming fight. Before she could even blink, Kat turned to her and grabbed her. Kat whispered something in Atlantean and then she kissed Geary fast on the lips.

Stunned beyond belief, Geary closed her eyes as she felt something hot and powerful spreading through her body, and Kat stepped away to confront the others. For a full ten seconds Geary couldn't move as indescribable power filled her. It was comparable to when she'd held Apollymi's medallion in her mouth, only this felt stronger, deadlier. And this time *she* was definitely in charge and not someone else. The power was incredible. It was as if her brain was alive and growing.

And when she opened her eyes, she no longer saw in the same colors. Everything was more vibrant now. More vivid.

The snake-haired woman seized her. Without thought, Geary dodged the punch and returned the blow with one so fierce, it knocked the woman off her feet and sent her flying. Literally. She cleared the ground by a good five feet before she slammed into the wall and fell to the floor. The snakes hissed and strained in anger.

Kat dispelled her attacker every bit as easily. But Solin appeared to be reticent to strike his. However, when the woman backhanded him and laid open his cheek, he changed his mind. Head-butting her, he knocked her to the ground, then turned to face M'Adoc.

The three women came to their feet to renew the fight. They took a step forward in unison.

"Enough!"

Geary was expecting it to be Zebulon, but it wasn't. Instead, there was another Dream-Hunter who was leaner than M'Adoc and Solin. He appeared between them and held his hand up for the women who strangely obeyed him. His ebony hair was long and braided down his back. He was dressed all in black and held a look that said "I'm in the mood to kill anyone who pisses me off." But more than that, there was an aura of power around him so strong that it actually made the hair on the back of her neck stand up.

"Whose side are you on, D'Alerian?" Solin asked as he wiped the blood away from his face with the back of his hand.

"Ours," another man answered as he appeared beside D'Alerian. Equal in height to D'Alerian, he wore his black hair cropped short and had on a pair of jeans and a button-down shirt. His eyes seemed to be a blue so pale, they looked colorless. Those eyes were eerie and deadly as they settled on Geary with purpose.

M'Adoc smiled in approval. "So you finally see my way of things."

It was D'Alerian who answered. "No. We can't let you kill the human. It's wrong and this isn't who and what we are. We protect, we don't assassinate."

Kat and Solin exchanged a puzzled frown.

"What's going on here, M'Ordant?" Solin asked the newcomer.

"We're taking M'Adoc into custody."

M'Adoc cursed. "Are you insane? You can't do this."

D'Alerian turned to face him. "Yes, we can, and yes, we are."

The women looked confused but didn't interfere as D'Alerian covered M'Adoc with some sort of shimmery web. M'Adoc tried to fight, but it held him tight and constricted more with every movement. Finally, it was so tight that all he could do was curse them.

"It's called a *diktyon*," Kat answered Geary's unasked question. "It's something Artemis uses to capture animals and not hurt them. Although how they"—she indicated the Dream-Hunters—"ended up with one of them, I don't know."

D'Alerian looked at the women. "Your services are no longer required. Furies, return."

They vanished instantly while M'Adoc continued to curse the others. "Do you understand what you're doing? What the gods will do to us?"

D'Alerian's eyes were sad and dark. "Sometimes our worst enemies are ourselves, M'Adoc. You are becoming the very thing they fear us to be, and that we can't allow." He met Geary's gaze. "You understand that you can never speak a word of us to anyone?"

Like this was something she'd be bantering about? Yeah, right. "Who would ever believe me?" she asked seriously.

D'Alerian nodded in approval. He took a small ring from his pinkie and placed it in Geary's palm. "I know what you plan and I wish you luck with it. Give this to Persephone and tell her that Neco supports you, that you're calling in the favor she owes him."

Geary was baffled by his actions and his words. "What?"

He closed her hand over the ring. "Don't question it, Megeara. Just do it."

Grateful and amused by his commanding tone, she couldn't help teasing him. "You're a bossy bunch, aren't you?"

One corner of M'Ordant's lips twisted. "You've no idea." An instant later, he vanished with M'Adoc in tow.

D'Alerian offered her a kind smile before he released her.

"What's really going on?" Solin asked D'Alerian as he turned to leave.

The humor fled from his face and he returned to being stoic again as he addressed Solin over his shoulder. "Nothing that concerns you, Skotos. Just know that we'll keep M'Adoc away from you."

She saw the suspicion on Solin's face. "Given our history, why would you do that?"

There was true regret in D'Alerian's eyes and in his stance as he turned to face Solin. The sincerity on D'Alerian's face was heart-wrenching. "I was wrong for what I did to you, Solin. I'm sorry."

Solin scoffed in derision. "Rote words to you, Oneroi."

"No, it's heartfelt, I assure you." He hesitated as if considering the repercussions before he spoke again. "Things change, Solin, and so do people. Even gods."

Solin froze as he finally understood what D'Alerian was telling him. "After all this time, you trust me?"

D'Alerian nodded. "Arik did, and you proved yourself by protecting Megeara even when it could have cost you your life. You had nothing to gain and everything to lose. I think that makes you trustworthy." Then he did the most unexpected thing of all. He offered his hand to Solin. "Brothers."

"Brothers," Solin said, taking D'Alerian's hand and shaking it. "Thank you."

He inclined his head to them before he vanished.

Kat cocked her head as she frowned over their exchange. "What did I just miss?"

"Nothing," Solin said quickly. "It's just Oneroi weirdness." He let out a deep breath as he faced them. He smiled at Geary. "Last I heard, Persephone was on Olympus with her mother. I can't go there, but Kat can and she can take you with her."

Geary didn't understand that. He was a god and should be as welcomed on Olympus as any other god. "Why can't you go there?"

"Solin is under a death warrant," Kat explained. "There are too many gods who would kill him on sight if he were ever dumb enough to pop into their backyard."

"Oh," Geary said in understanding. How awful for him. No wonder he'd been so angry over them in the past. It sounded like he was fully entitled to it.

Geary stepped forward and kissed him on his cheek. "Thank you for your help, Solin. I really appreciate it and I'm sure Arik does, too."

Solin nodded. "Just make me one promise."

"And that is?"

His gaze burned into hers. "If you get Arik back, you won't be stupid again. Love is a rare thing, Megeara. Hold on to it with both hands."

Tears gathered in her eyes as she realized he was speaking from his heart and from a past he had no intention of sharing with her. But his words were too genuine to be an arbitrary recitation. "I fully intend to."

"Then it's worth it."

That confused her. "What is?"

Solin chucked her gently on the chin. "Whatever they throw at me." He inclined his head to Kat. "You two kids have fun, and good luck." Then he vanished, too.

Geary frowned at Kat. "Is it just me or was that the oddest exchange?"

"No," she breathed, "it wasn't. You're just missing part of the story. Remember, at one time the Oneroi had feelings. Some of them were in love and even had families at the time they were rounded up and punished."

A bad feeling went through Geary as she noted the ominous tone of Kat's voice. "What happened to their families?"

"Let's just say Zeus was *really* angry."

It didn't take a genius to ascertain what that would have led to. "He killed them."

She nodded grimly.

Even though Geary had guessed it, she was still aghast that he'd be so callous to his own family members. "*All* of them?"

Kat nodded again.

Tears gathered in Geary's eyes as the magnitude of their punishment truly hit her. She couldn't imagine the horror that they must have been put through. No wonder M'Adoc was psycho. "Did Solin—"

"No," Kat said quickly, cutting her off. "He *was* the family they tried to destroy and he survived by the skin of his nose."

"Arik told me that, too. God, I feel so bad for them."

"All of us with any decency do, but there's nothing to be done for them as a group. Not unless you go up against Zeus, and that takes more god power than what we have." She offered Geary a smile. "But right now we have one god in particular we might be able to help."

She was right. Before they plotted a war, they needed to win a battle, and Geary was ready to take on all of Olympus for Arik. "Let's get on it."

GEARY DIDN'T REALLY KNOW WHAT TO EXPECT FROM Olympus and the gods. True, she'd spent the whole of her life listening to her father and grandfather tell stories about them. But that had only been speculation on everyone's part.

Now she was actually here.

And it was scary and invigorating to know that those legends were real. That things she'd taken for granted as fiction weren't. Wow.

Just like the stories told, Olympus was breathtaking. The weather was perfect. Not too hot. Not too cold. It was like a mid-spring day. The sky was so blue as to be unreal in its celestial hue, and the mountains around her were lush and green. The air was fresh and laced with a sweet scent. She'd never experienced anything like this.

Dreamy was the only word for it.

But what fascinated her most was that she could look down and see the world below in all its glory through the misty clouds that kept the gods isolated from the world.

"This is incredible."

Kat smiled. "Yeah, I know." She looked around with pride. "I was raised here."

Geary couldn't imagine having a childhood like that. "Really?"

"Yes." Kat pointed to a large circular gold building at the end of the golden cobblestoned street. "That is Artemis's temple. When I was a little girl, I used to sneak out of it and run to there"—she pointed to another temple at the opposite end—"to Athena's temple, and play with her owls." She laughed at the memory. "It used to make Artemis crazy."

"Why?"

"They have a long-standing feud with each other over some nonsense that happened aeons ago. And Artemis wanted me to stay as far away from Athena as I could."

"But you couldn't resist, huh?"

Her smile widened. "Not really. According to Artemis, I've made a lifetime study of irritating her."

Geary laughed as she looked around and saw three fawns sprinting across the walk ahead of them. The deer vanished into the woods, where she swore she glimpsed a centaur running. "I can't believe this is real."

"Oh, believe it. Scary as it can be." Kat pointed to a huge hall made of gold and ivory that was on a hilltop above them. "And that is where Zeus resides with Hera. It's the great hall where everyone gathers to mostly bicker and complain."

It was as magnificent as the rest of the area. Truly, it was like walking in a dream. "Is that where we're going?"

"No. Persephone doesn't play politics. Even though Zeus is her father, she only goes there when she's summoned, especially since Hera can't stand her because she's one of Zeus's bastards. She tries her best to stay out of their business." Kat pointed to another of the buildings down the street. "She'll most likely be hanging out at her mother's temple."

Geary followed Kat as she crossed the street and they were almost run over by a blur.

"Hermes!" Kat shouted. "Watch where you're going!"

"No time . . ." A faint voice drifted back to them as he vanished out of sight. It strangely reminded Geary of the Road Runner cartoon, as nothing but dust was left in his wake.

"That happen a lot?" she asked Kat.

"Yeah, he's always in a hurry. You have to be really careful or he'll run you down. It's like being hit by a Mack truck, too. Bloody bastard."

Okay . . . no hostility there.

But luckily no one else tried to mow them down as they walked the short distance to the smaller domed building. Geary paused outside to look up. It was only about half as tall as everything around it and not very large. Though it was still beautiful and bigger than any home Geary's family had ever owned, it lacked much of the awe factor that the rest of the buildings around it had. "Why is this so small compared to the others?"

Kat shrugged as she looked up at it. "Demeter isn't one for pretense. She's very simple compared to the others."

Moving forward, Kat opened the door to a massive foyer that was made of marble so white, it hurt her eyes to look at it. The entire room was surrounded by columns that were carved to look like people. And as Kat and Geary entered, one of the male statues on her right opened its eyes to stare at them.

"What brings you here, Katra?" the statue asked in ancient Greek.

Kat was completely unfazed by the fact that a living statue was addressing her, while Geary gaped at it. "I want a word with Persephone."

"She is in the garden," a female statue answered before she pointed to the opposite set of doors. "But she is not in a happy mood, so be warned."

"Thanks, Chloe."

Befuddled, Geary trailed along through the doors that opened of their own volition into a massive garden atrium. The wind was gentle as it stirred the scent of hyacinth and lilac. "Ooo, nice."

At least that was what she thought until they heard someone cursing. Repeatedly and with relish.

"Gardening is crap, Mom," the light, cadent voice whined from the bushes in front of them. "I hate it! Look at that. My manicure's going to be completely wrecked and for what? Dig the earth, plant some crap, do this, do that. Blah!"

"Seph?"

The bushes rustled before a small woman wiggled out from between them. Geary hid her smile as a very petite and extremely beautiful blond woman stood up. Dressed in dark green overalls and a white T-shirt, she had dirt smeared across one cheek and on the tip of her nose. Her hands were covered by large gardening gloves while green and brown leaves were stuck in her upswept hair, that still managed to be breathtaking on her. She slung her hands out and sent the gloves flying to the ground.

"Hi, Kat," she said as if completely unperturbed by the fact that they'd overheard her complaints. "What's up?"

"I wanted . . ." Kat's voice trailed off as a small set of flowers started to move toward the woods.

Persephone blasted them with some kind of energy from her hands. She laughed, then sent her gloves to go pull up more flowers.

"What are you doing?" Kat asked with a frown.

"Revenge," Persephone said proudly. "It's a small revenge, granted, but it's these little things in life that mean so much."

Kat cocked a brow and looked at Geary before she asked for clarification. "Revenge on who and for what?"

"My mother, who else?" Persephone gestured around the lush garden. "Sticks me in this godforsaken place nine months out of the year and thinks I ought to be grateful for it. Meanwhile all I want is to be with my husband. . . ." She gave them a meaningful look. "Have you any idea how hard it is to go nine months out of the year with no sex when you're married to such a fine piece of male anatomy that he should have been the god of fertility instead of the god of death?" She paused in her tirade as she finally saw Geary over Kat's shoulder. "And you are?"

"She's a friend. Megeara, meet Persephone."

Persephone frowned sternly as she raked a gaze over Geary's body. "You're not the Fury Megeara, are you?"

"No, but I was named after her."

"Ah." Persephone extended her hand as her features softened. "Nice to meet you then."

"You, too."

"So," Persephone said, looking back at Kat. "What brings you two here?"

"We"—Kat indicated the two of them with a wave of her hand—"are in need of some serious help."

Persephone scoffed. "*I'm* in need of some serious help." She sighed as she gave Geary a hopeless smile. "I know we just met, Megeara, but bear with me. I'm so horny I could die and my mother's answer to my complaints . . . weed her prized garden. Weed! What is she, insane?"

This was definitely more than Geary wanted to know about the goddess.

"Yeah, and on that happy note," Kat said with a hint of laughter in her voice, "it's your husband who brings us here."

"Oh, what'd he do now?"

"Made a pact with a Dream-Hunter who wanted to be human. Now the Dream-Hunter has been killed and we'd like to get him back from Hades."

Interesting summation Kat had come up with. Geary would have never been so succinct.

Persephone screwed her face up. "That's a bummer. You know Hades doesn't like to let anyone leave. Ever. He's kind of attached to those souls."

"I love Arik," Geary said, her voice cracking. "I'll do anything to get him back."

Both of the women cringed at Geary's words.

Persephone motioned for her to lower her voice. "Don't say that too loudly around here. There are a lot of folks who would take you up on it, and bargaining with a god is what got you guys into this mess in the first place."

"I'm sorry," Geary said quickly. "But I do love him, with all my heart."

Kat sighed. "The gods have really screwed her over. They've taken almost all of her family, and given that, I was thinking that we might be able to help her just this once."

Persephone shook her head. "You know the rules, Kat."

Geary frowned. "What rules?"

"Quid pro quo," Kat said irritably. "You have to give something in order to get a favor from a god."

Oh, that was just wonderful. But it still didn't stop Geary. She had to get Arik freed. "Tell me what I have to do."

Persephone looked surprised by Geary's response. "She's an eager little bunny, isn't she?"

"She's desperate, Seph. Of all people, I think you can relate to what it's like to be taken away from the one you love."

Persephone nodded. "Yeah, and you picked the right moment to approach me on this. I'm really missing my Hades."

Suddenly Geary remembered the ring D'Alerian had given her. "Wait!" She pulled it out of her pocket. "One of the Oneroi gave me this. He said to give it to you and to tell you that Neco wanted to call in his favor."

She saw the pain in Persephone's eyes as she took the ring from Geary's hand. Persephone's eyes shimmered from tears as she traced the scrollwork on it with her fingertip. "How was he doing?"

Kat gave her a sad smile before she answered. "Well."

Persephone placed the ring on her thumb before she nodded. "Well, there you have it. Neco is trading in his favor for this, so it's Neco you owe."

Who is Neco? Geary mouthed the words at Kat, wanting to understand exactly what was going on. And who she owed for this favor.

"Neco is D'Alerian."

Geary was floored by the news. "Why would he trade his favor in for me?"

Persephone brushed away her tears. "Because my brother is a gentle man. He doesn't like to see anyone suffer and he hates injustice. I imagine this is his way of making amends for something he feels they've taken from you."

Still, Geary didn't understand. "Isn't that hard to do for someone who doesn't have any feelings?"

Persephone didn't respond.

Kat, on the other hand, scowled at the much shorter goddess. "The curse on them is weakening, isn't it?"

Persephone gave a subtle nod. "But you can't tell anyone, Kat. No one. I won't have Neco punished again. Father was more harsh on him than the others because he was his son. If he ever learns this . . ."

"Don't worry," Kat assured her, "I won't tell anyone. Keeping secrets is what I'm best at."

"Good," Persephone breathed. "They've all been through enough."

Geary shook her head. "But I don't understand. I thought the Oneroi were the sons of Hypnos and Morpheus?"

"Some of the Oneroi are," Persephone said quietly. "Neco is my half brother. He was born of Zeus and D'Aria, one of the original Oneroi. So long as one of their parents is an Oneroi, then they inherit those powers and are given those duties."

Geary rubbed her brow as she tried to make sense of it and fit it into her mind. "You guys have the most convoluted family trees."

Kat laughed. "Believe me, we know."

"Yeah, and you don't ever want to try and figure out Kat's. It's scary." Persephone craned her neck to look around the yard. "Come on, guys, we have to hurry. If my mother returns and finds me gone, she'll launch a tornado or something."

One second they were in the sun-filled garden, in the next they were in a dark, stinking cavern. Geary held her hand to her nose in an effort to squelch the awful smell. "What is that stench?"

Screwing her features up in distaste, Persephone waved her hand in front of her face. "Cerberus's dinner. We picked a bad time to come."

She led them down a narrow corridor and through a door that opened into a large throne room.

Geary paused in the doorway as she saw the glistening ebony walls. But what held her enthralled was the gorgeous man sitting on a black throne that was made of what appeared to be bones. With shoulder-length black wavy hair, he was absolutely stunning.

And ripped.

Dressed in black leather armor, Hades had a presence that truly suited a god of death. It sent a ripple of fear over her, but even so, she understood why Persephone had been attracted to him.

He was compelling.

And as Persephone neared him and he saw her, the look of joy on his face actually made Geary's heart ache. He rose slowly to his feet.

"Seph," he breathed as if he were dreaming.

Persephone ran to him.

Laughing, he scooped her up in his arms and twirled around with her. "Oh, my precious Seph." He laughed again before he kissed her soundly.

Kat cleared her throat. Loudly. "Sorry for the interruption, but before clothing starts to fly or disintegrate, I wanted to remind you two that you're not alone."

Persephone blushed at the same time Hades growled at them. He took a step toward Kat, but his wife stopped him. "She's right, Hades. We have to be quick before my mother finds me gone and thinks that you've kidnapped me again. The last thing we need is for her to call out my father."

Hades cursed under his breath. "Like I fear that bastard."

"Hades," Persephone chided.

He relented, but by his face Geary could tell he did so reluctantly. "So why are they here?"

"They come seeking a soul."

He scowled at his wife. "Whose?"

"Arikos's," Kat said.

Hades looked even more confounded. "The Skotos?"

Geary nodded.

"He's not here."

"What?" Geary asked in disbelief, her heart sinking.

"Arikos hasn't made his way here," Hades repeated. "If he had, I would know it. I have a bone to pick with that bastard, too."

Kat ignored Hades' heated tone. "We were told he's on the other side of the river Styx and isn't able to cross. M'Adoc killed him and didn't bury him. Arik has no money to pay Charon for the crossing."

"Why would M'Adoc do that?" But before they could answer, Hades shook his head. "That little bugger. Trying to pull one on me. He doesn't want me to know Arikos is here. Bloody, freaking bastard. And you." He looked at Megeara. "You're the human Arikos bartered for. You're supposed to be here in his stead. So have you come to exchange places with him?"

Geary couldn't speak as fear took root in her.

But before she could think of something to say, Persephone slapped Hades on the arm. "Don't you even start that."

Rubbing the spot she'd hit, he scowled at her. "Start what? Arikos and I had a bargain."

"So what?" Persephone asked in an irritated tone. "Do you mean to tell me that you are going to stand there and make her die to save him? How could you?"

"It was a bargain," he said defensively.

"Yes, and my parents made a bargain, too, and look how that's turned out. I can't believe you would do this to someone else. I thought you were different."

His features turned placating. "Baby, I am."

"No, you're not. You're just like *them*. You intend to break up two lovers and for what? A stupid, meaningless bargain. You who know how much it hurts to be away from the one you love, and yet you would do something so cold and mean. Oh, that's it. I'm going home to my mother's and I'm not coming back."

His dark eyes snapped fire. "You have to come back. You have no choice."

She narrowed her gaze on him. "You're right. I have no choice about coming here, but I have a choice about where I sleep once I'm home."

His face went pale as he realized he was on losing ground. "You wouldn't dare."

Persephone put her hands on her hips as she stared down the man who was practically twice her size. It would have been comical if Geary's future with Arik didn't hinge on the outcome. "You break these two up and it'll be a cold day in Hephaestus's forge before you enter my bedroom. In fact, I'll get Eros to make you impotent. Yeah. Forever. That'll teach you."

His face completely ashen, Hades looked at Geary. "Take him. Get his ass out of here and don't look back."

"Are you serious?"

"Yes."

Persephone winked at Geary before she pulled her husband into a tight hug. "Now was that so hard?"

He answered her question with one of his own. "How long until your mother returns?"

Persephone turned to them. "You two better hurry along and claim him. Arik will be a Shade until you return to the sunlight in the human realm. Kat, you know the way. Once he's back in the world, he'll be human and flesh. But remember, Megeara, that you have to lead him out of here yourself, and you can't look back. If you do, you'll lose him forever."

Before Geary could even say "thank you," the two of them vanished.

Kat turned toward her with a laugh. "Fun, huh?"

"Yeah," Geary said lightly. "I think I'm a bit shell-shocked. I can't believe we have no test or anything to fulfill."

"We don't have him out of here yet. Remember, when they say don't look back, don't."

Geary nodded as she remembered that from her studies. They weren't out of the woods yet. And if they didn't find him soon, it would be too late.

ARIK WATCHED AS CHARON PASSED BY HIM ON THE RIVER. The old man was a sulking bearded figure, dressed in dark brown. His pitiless gaze scanned those who were gathered on the banks of the river. Charon would only take those who had an *obulos,* a Greek coin, or a Persian *danace* to pay the ferryman's fee. Only those with the coin could go to the other side, where they were divided up—those who'd done good deeds in their lives were taken to the Elysian Fields for a divine rest, and those who'd committed evil deeds were destined for Tartarus to be tortured.

But only a fool would give Charon the coin before he delivered them to the opposite bank. It was custom to show the coin to Charon, then wait and hand it over once the journey was complete.

If you couldn't show him the coin, then you were doomed to wait on the bank for a hundred years before you could cross. And if you paid Charon before he delivered you to your destination, he'd dump your soul in the river, where you'd suffer in eternal misery.

Personally, Arik knew where he was headed once he crossed the river and he could easily wait a hundred years before his torture began. Then again, he didn't have to. He was already aching from the loss of Megeara.

He felt her absence with every part of him. The despair weighed like a stack of anvils on his soul. All he wanted was to see her face one last time. To touch her cheek or to feel her hair on his flesh. Those memories seared him as he prayed for her safety.

"I hate that miserable old bastard."

Arik looked to his left as the Shade of a middle-aged man joined him.

The man was glaring at Charon, who no longer paid them any heed as he cut his way through the black water. "I wish that boat would turn over and drown him in the river Acheron. Would serve him right if it did."

Perhaps. Acheron was the river of woe and it was here

that all the troubles of the world were gathered. It was said that if any part of your body were to touch it, those woes would seep into you and tear your body and soul asunder with grief.

All the dead must cross it to reach their final destination. It was supposed to be a symbolic journey where the dead left such concerns behind.

The man looked up at Arik. "You didn't have a coin, either, huh?"

"No."

He spat on the ground by Arik's feet. "That's for both our families then. Leaving us stranded like this. A pox to them. May they all fall into the river Acheron and drown in their stinking misery."

Arik lifted a brow at the man's rancor. He sounded like he'd been bathing in the river Styx, where hatred flowed freely.

The man eyed him carefully. "So what brought you here?"

Arik answered without thought. "Love."

"Killed yourself, did you?"

"No. I traded my life to keep the one I love safe."

The man was aghast. "Why would you do something so stupid?"

"It's not stupid."

"Sure it is. Do you think she'd have done the same for you?"

Again, Arik answered without reservation. "Yes."

"You're a complete jackass if you think that." He made a rude noise before he wandered off.

"He's right, you know."

Arik froze as he heard the last voice he expected to hear. It was Wink, no doubt come to gloat. "What are you doing here?"

Wink shrugged. "I hang with the dead sometimes. They can be extremely entertaining, especially the whiny ones." He paused and smelled the air around Arik. Wink's actions reminded him of a hound on the scent of a skunk. Finally Wink pulled back and gave Arik a gimlet stare. "Where are your powers?"

"Don't worry about it." Arik tried to move away, but Wink followed him down the bank of the river even while he was weaving between other Shades.

"What gives, Arikos?"

Arik had no idea why he didn't rat out the others and tell Wink that all of them were regaining their emotions. He should. It was what they all deserved, but some misplaced sense of loyalty kept him from it. Wink would run with whatever Arik told him straight to Zeus and start trouble.

Arik had too much humanity in him now to do such a thing, and in the back of his mind he knew that Megeara would be disappointed in him.

Even though she hated him, Arik didn't want to disappoint her.

And still the god trailed after him. "Arikos?"

"Go away, Wink," he snapped. "I'm dead and I just want to be left alone."

Wink took Arik's arm, then hissed and recoiled. "You and your human?" he said, his tone accusing. No doubt that one touch had told the god everything about how Arik had ended up here—everything that had to do with Megeara anyway. "Have you lost your mind? Why would you give up your immortality for her?"

Arik couldn't explain it. It was stupid and he knew it. But it still seemed right. His life for her happiness. It strangely worked for him even though it shouldn't.

He was definitely a mental case.

Still Wink wouldn't relent and leave him in peace.

"You gave up immortality for her," Wink repeated. "Haven't you learned yet that humans aren't worth it? She was one of millions who are out there."

"No, Wink, you're wrong. She's one in a million. She's unique."

He snorted in response. "So unique that she let you die for her? Believe me, there are millions of women who are that selfish."

"Yeah, but there's only one willing to walk through hell to get him back."

Arik came instantly to a stop as he saw Kat in the darkness. But that wasn't what stunned him most. It was the sight of Megeara moving to stand by her side.

He wanted to run to Megeara and scoop her up in his arms, but he couldn't. For one thing, he was no longer corporeal. For another, he wasn't sure she'd let him.

But she was here. . . .

Geary covered her mouth with her hand to stifle her cry as she saw what was left of Arik. His translucent skin was ashen gray. His eyes were no longer blue but rather dark and sunken. And he bore a hole in his middle that looked like someone had stabbed him.

"Arik?" she asked hesitantly.

He appeared to be speaking, but she couldn't hear him. Terrified, she looked at Kat.

"He's a Shade now, Geary. Only the gods can hear him."

"What's he saying?"

"He wants you to leave before it's too late for you."

That succeeded in making her tears flow down her cheeks. "Can he hear me?"

"Yes."

She turned to him. "I'm here to get you, Arik. I won't leave unless you're with me."

The disbelief on his face tore through her. Even so, he held a hand out toward her. She tried to take it, but her hand went straight through his.

The Oneroi beside him snarled at her. "You don't belong here, human. Leave."

Kat stepped between her and the man who looked as if he wanted to kill her. "Leave her alone, Wink."

He turned his hostile glare to Arik. "Don't be stupid, Arikos. She won't be able to take you out of here. No human has ever been able to resist Hades' test. And he'll make you pay double for trying to leave."

Arik hesitated. Wink was right. Until Kat and Megeara had notified him, Hades hadn't even known he was here. Now the god did. If Megeara didn't safely lead him out of here, Hades would take pleasure in torturing him forever.

No, he was already damned and tortured here without her. There was nothing Hades could do to him that was worse than the thought of her with someone else.

Arik needed her more than he needed anything else. He had no choice but to follow her.

I love you, Megeara.

Geary sobbed as she read his lips. "I love you, too, Arik, and I'm taking you out of here. I promise."

He gave her a wan smile before he nodded.

Wink curled his lip at them. "It's not that easy, little human. Just—"

Kat cut his words off by clenching his throat in her fist. "Lay off, Wink. We're not in the mood."

"You can't help her," he choked out from his constricted windpipe. "She's going to die, too."

"Then you should be happy. Now go your own way or the world will be in need of a new Sandman." She let go of him so quickly that he stumbled through Arik.

"I'm going. But I plan on enjoying the sight of your failure."

Kat reached for Wink again, but before she could grab him again he dissolved.

Geary wiped her tears away. "What was he going on about, Kat?"

She let out a deep breath before she responded. "Getting here was easy. Getting out won't be. You know the old Eagles song 'Hotel California'?"

"Yeah."

"Yeah. That's our situation. And once we start out of here, if you look back or try to help Arik in any way, he's a goner and, since you're not born of a god's blood, so are you."

A cold feeling of dread settled as a knot in the pit of her stomach. "Nice. Could have told me this before we got here."

"Would that have changed your mind?"

Geary looked at Arik and felt the love inside her swell past the unsettling lump. "No."

"Good, then I didn't waste my breath."

Geary shook her head at Kat before she turned back to Arik. She wanted to touch him so badly that she ached from it. But that would be impossible until they freed him. "Lead on, MacDuff."

"I'm leading, but I can't look back, either. So stick tight and remember, stay on the trail. Don't worry about anything that comes at us. Just pretend we're in a haunted house and don't get distracted."

"Ooooo, scary." But even though she was making light of this, she knew just how serious it was. One misstep and all three of them would pay dearly for it.

Kat led her off into the bitter darkness that was so oppressive it made her eyes ache. The only way she could tell that Kat was still in front of her was that she could hear her breathing. At least she hoped that was Kat. In the dark, Geary's imagination was playing havoc. For all she knew, it was some creepy beast bent on eating her.

"Kat?"

"I'm right here. Keep your eyes forward."

"I am."

Something slithered beside her. Geary squeaked in dismay and had to force herself not to jump away from it. *C'mon, girl, you've been on dives with sharks and eels swimming around you. You can handle this. This is nothing. Stay your course. . . .*

But in the water, she wasn't this blind.

"Don't look back," Kat warned again. "They're trying to get you to glance behind you and see Arik. If you do, it's over."

That was easier said than done, especially since something seemed to be glowing in her right peripheral before it drifted back, away from her. And she was desperate to know if Arik was still there. There was no sound or sign of him.

Nothing. For all she knew, they'd grabbed him and pulled him away from her.

And to think she'd always thought Orpheus was an idiot for checking to see if Eurydice was behind him. Now it all made sense. No wonder the demigod had been so paranoid. No doubt they'd been tormenting him every step of the way, too.

What if Arik became distracted? What if he'd fallen and needed help?

Suddenly a light flashed before them. It was followed by a shriek and a green face so horrendous that Geary actually screamed out loud. Instinctively she started to turn to Arik, but she caught herself as the loud shrieking continued. "What was that?"

"Gorgon," Kat shouted. "Stay to the course and ignore them. They guard the barrier between the Underworld and the Outerworld. Their job is to keep us in here. Don't let them."

"I'm trying."

"Don't try, Geary, succeed."

She intended to.

And as they walked, more and more gorgons appeared. They marched alongside the trio, shrieking and lashing out. Feinting toward them. But the gorgons never touched them. They only did it to make them flinch.

The gorgons were every bit as hideous as the stories had foretold. Their green skin was scaly like a snake's and they had red eyes that glowed in the darkness. There was a shuffling, slithering noise that followed them through the cavern.

But the worst was their breath that would make toxic waste proud.

"He's not there, human," the gorgon to Geary's right said evilly. "You've lost him already."

"Shut up, Euryale," Kat snapped. "Leave her alone."

She hissed at Kat.

Geary did her best to distract herself from them. "I thought people turned to stone if they looked at a gorgon."

"Only men do."

A new fear went through her at Kat's words. "Arik?"

"I said *men,* Geary. Not gods or Shades. He's safe. Just keep moving forward and don't try to check on him."

That was so much easier said than done, especially when her mind was going wild with what-ifs. "Are you sure?"

"Well, are you stone?"

Not yet, she wasn't, but if Kat didn't take the condescension from her tone, Geary might "stone" her. "I don't mean me. I meant Arik."

"If you turn around to see, Geary, you will lose him."

"I know." But the compulsion was so strong. It was unnatural.

"She's lying to you, human. You've lost him in the caverns. He's weeping for you, wanting you to help him."

Geary shook her head to dispel the image in her mind of Arik doing exactly what the gorgon said. "You're the one who's lying to me."

The gorgon bared her fangs before she moved to walk directly beside Geary.

"Megeara, help me." It was Arik's voice coming from behind her.

It's a trick, it's a trick.

"Please, Megeara. I need you. Don't let me suffer here. . . ."

"Stop it!" Geary said from between clenched teeth. "He's a Shade. I know I can't hear him and Arik would *never* beg like that. You're just trying to piss me off."

One of the gorgons behind Geary clucked her tongue. "Poor Arik. See, she doesn't love you at all. She'd let you suffer rather than endanger herself."

Then she heard the muffled sound of a masculine cry that sounded like it could be Arik.

She clenched her fists, struggling not to turn around and check on him. She had to know he was okay. . . . "Kat," she whimpered. "Help me."

"Don't listen, Geary. Sing a song and drown them out."

"Sing what?" she asked in frustration.

"What's your favorite song?"

Geary plugged her ears with her fingers and started singing Gloria Gaynor's "I Will Survive."

Now it was the gorgons' turn to scream out in pain as they shrank away from Geary. Realizing that they couldn't stand her off-key harmony, Geary sang even louder.

"Stop! Stop!" they begged.

But Geary refused. It was time someone returned the favor to them and let them exist in torment for a while.

After she finished Gloria's song, she broke out to Wild Cherry's "Play That Funky Music" and then Lipps, Inc.'s "Funky-town."

To her misplaced delight, the gorgons continued to writhe and moan in agony, which caused Kat to help her serenade them with more disco tunes.

Geary was just finishing the Bee Gees' "Stayin' Alive" when she finally saw light ahead. Her heart pounded as raw excitement filled her. They were almost done.

A few more steps . . .

Her singing faltered as she struggled to hear some sign of Arik behind her. There was nothing.

Nothing.

"Down!" Kat shouted an instant before a blast of fire darted over their heads.

Geary squeezed her eyes shut and prayed with everything she had. She wanted desperately to touch Arik.

He's there.

He had to be. Trusting in Kat and in Arik, she opened her eyes and saw that Kat was already moving forward again.

It took some doing to make it up the sharp rocks that led to the small opening above them.

"I can't help you up, Geary," Kat said from in front of her. "Like you, I can't turn around, and you can't turn to help Arik up, either, understand?"

"Yes."

"Okay. Remember, we have to get clear and you have to wait right beside me, facing the east. Got it?"

"Got it."

As she neared the opening, Geary's foot slipped. She slid back and cursed as the rocks cut into her hands and knees. Before she could stop herself, her head turned, but she again slammed her eyes shut.

Would the gods count that?

Surely not. But if she opened her eyes to double-check, it would be over.

Counting to ten, she straightened her head and looked forward. "Don't let me down, Arik. Do you hear me? You better still be there."

With a deep breath, she started climbing again even though her cuts stung and her body ached from the fall.

It seemed to take forever before she was clear of the cavern. Kat was outside, waiting by a small clearing that overlooked the sea.

Geary joined her. "What now?"

Kat turned her head slightly to look at Geary with a frown. "What the hell happened to you?"

"I fell."

Kat screwed her face up in distaste and pity. "Sorry."

So was Geary, especially given how ferocious the pounding pain was.

But Geary stood there, silently waiting. After a few minutes, her panic set in. "Where's Arik?"

"Don't look for him."

"I'm getting sick of that warning, Kat. He's not here. . . ."

"Be patient, Geary." Her tone was placating and calm, and it was pissing Geary off more and more.

"We're in daylight. We're clear. Why isn't he here with us?"

"What if he's right behind you now, and you turn to look? You'll send him right back into hell."

Geary pressed her hands to her eyes, as she wanted to weep in frustration. This was cruel and mean and it made her hate the gods for it. "Don't die, Arik, please."

And then she felt it. It was a cold touch against her cheek. Light and gentle. She'd know that touch anywhere. Lowering her hands, she saw Arik next to her, but he was still pale and gaunt.

Even so, he was the best-looking thing she'd ever beheld. Before she could stop herself, she pulled him to her and kissed him senseless.

Arik growled as he tasted Megeara again. And the longer she kissed him, the warmer he grew. He held her tight against him, reveling in the feel of her warm body next to his. In all his life he'd never felt anything like this.

He could swear he could fly without wings right now. Never once had he even dreamed she'd come back for him, and the fact that she'd saved him . . .

Unbelievable.

Megeara pulled back to look at him, then laughed. "You're back!" She rained kisses all over his face.

His own joy filled him as he savored every touch of her lips on his flesh. "I can't believe you came for me."

"Are you kidding? I would always come for you."

And that was why he loved her so dearly.

"Uh, guys," Kat said, clearing her throat, "no offense, but this is getting awkward for me. You two take care and I'll see you around."

Before either could speak, she vanished.

Arik laughed as he picked Geary up and twirled around with her. "I can't believe you're really here and this isn't a dream."

"Me? Look at you. . . ." Geary frowned as a weird thought went through her. It was a question she hadn't even thought to answer before. "What are you now?"

"He's human."

Arik paused at the sound of D'Alerian's voice. He set Megeara down, expecting a fight. "What do you want?"

D'Alerian held his hands up in surrender. "I just wanted to make sure Megeara made it out alive. Now that you're together, I thought I'd take you both back to her home to celebrate."

"And we're supposed to trust you why?"

Geary put her hand on his arm to calm him down. "Don't, Arik. We owe him everything. He's the one who called in a favor from Persephone so that I could free you."

He gave her a confounded look, then turned it toward D'Alerian, whose face was completely stoic. "Why would you do that?"

"Because I lost what I loved, Arik, and I don't want anyone to know that pain. You two have earned the right to live in peace."

Arik scoffed at his good wishes. "M'Adoc will never allow that."

"Yes, he will. We'll make sure of it."

Geary didn't miss the ominous note in D'Alerian's voice. "What are you going to do to him?"

"Don't worry. We won't hurt him. We're taking him someplace where he can learn compassion. It's a simple emotion, but it escapes so many. He needs to relearn it."

Then D'Alerian held out his hand and a bright flash of light encompassed them. One moment they were outside the Underworld, and in the next they were in her flat.

Geary glanced around in disbelief. It seemed like a lifetime had passed since she'd last been here.

D'Alerian gave them a gentle smile. "Treasure each other."

Geary nodded. "Don't worry. We will."

He inclined his head to them, then dissolved.

As soon as they were alone, Arik leaned his head down and nuzzled her neck with his warm lips. "I love you, Geary."

She smiled as he used her nickname without her forcing him to. "I love you, too, babe." She reached to take his hand into hers and pull him toward her room.

"What are you doing?"

She glared menacingly at him. "I'm going to make you suffer like no man has ever suffered for the lies you've told and for putting me through so much."

His mouth opened and closed as he looked a bit shell-shocked. Finally, he clenched his teeth and narrowed his eyes on her before his features settled down to resignation. "And what do you plan to do to me?"

A slow grin spread across her face. "First I'm going to strip you naked and then I'm going to bend you like a pretzel and lick your body until you beg me to stop. I'll have you begging me for mercy in no time."

"Hmmm," he breathed. "That sounds positively awful."

"You've no idea. . . . My tongue has been known to let blood on four continents."

He laughed deep in his throat as she pulled him into the bedroom. "Well, in that case, let the torture begin."

CHAPTER 20

D'ALERIAN PAUSED INSIDE THE HALL WHERE M'ORDANT was waiting for him. M'Adoc was there as well, still bound by the *diktyon*.

"Are they safe?" M'Ordant asked.

D'Alerian nodded before he moved toward M'Adoc, who glared his hatred at them. "I can't believe you two have betrayed me."

The hostility saddened him. "We're not betraying you, Adarian. We're going to help you."

"What are you planning exactly?" M'Ordant asked.

"I'm taking him to Acheron. There's a Dark-Hunter who needs someone strong to help him with his nightmares." He looked at M'Adoc. "A few months with Zarek in Alaska and I think you'll see why it's so important to let go of your hatred."

"Bullshit. You can't send me away."

M'Ordant frowned. "Why send him to Alaska? He can tend the Dark-Hunter from here."

"No, he can't. Here he poses a threat to us. His emotions are out of control. If any of the other gods see the way he's been behaving, we're screwed. We can deal with Wink and Hades knowing. But Zeus learning . . . In Alaska, no one will know." D'Alerian looked back at M'Adoc. "You can stay there a short time, and once you have a better handle on yourself, I'll come get you."

"I won't stay there."

"Are you going Skoti then?"

"Never."

"Then that's your assignment. Take it or leave us."

M'Adoc's jaw twitched with his fury, but ultimately he conceded. "Fine. I'll go. But only for a short time."

D'Alerian nodded before he removed the *diktyon*. Then he flashed the two of them out of the chambers and into the human realm. They materialized in the living room of a Dark-Hunter's home in New Orleans.

Kyrian Hunter. A former ancient Greek general, he was now one of the Dark-Hunters who helped to guard mankind from the Daimons, or vampires as they were better known, who preyed on humanity. D'Alerian had been assigned to the general since the day Kyrian had sold his soul to Artemis for vengeance on the man who'd killed him. Nightmares had plagued him ever since.

But D'Alerian could at least mitigate them most of the time.

It took D'Alerian a moment to get his bearings in Kyrian's home as Acheron entered the room and came to a stop. At six eight, with long green hair and dressed in black leather pants and a shredded Sex Pistols T-shirt, Acheron was a hard man to miss.

"Greetings, gentlemen," he said, his voice thick with its Atlantean accent.

Before D'Alerian could speak, a young man on a skateboard came rolling through the room and almost collided with them. He skidded to a stop not far from Acheron, then cursed at the long black mark his wheels had left on the floor.

"I'm so friggin' dead," Nick Gautier whispered loudly before he kicked the skateboard up and grabbed it in a tight fist.

Acheron snorted. "Relax, Nicky, you're not as dead as I am."

"That's what you think. Kyrian's gonna stroke when he sees that." Trying to scrape the mark up with the toe of his tennis shoe, he met D'Alerian's gaze. "So what brings you here? Kyrian's not hurt, is he?"

"No."

Acheron offered the eighteen-year-old a kind smile. "They're here for me. Why don't you go see what Rosa's baking and give us a minute?"

Nick frowned at him. "You hurt?"

"No."

"Then why—"

"Nick, space. Now."

Nick made a face at Acheron. "Go, Nick, fetch. Here, boy, here," he groused. "You should let me borrow one of those leather collars you wear and give me a tag with Kyrian's number on it. 'In case of loss, call my owner.' "

Acheron snorted. "Trust me, Nicky, we're not lucky enough for you to get lost."

"Yeah, yeah."

D'Alerian frowned as Nick left them alone. "That boy has issues."

"You have *no* idea." Acheron closed the distance between him and M'Adoc. "You really want to go to Alaska to help Zarek?"

M'Adoc looked askance at D'Alerian. "I'm told I have no choice."

Acheron nodded as if he understood. "Well, I appreciate it anyway. The gods know he could use it. I'll take you to him tonight."

"Thank you, Acheron," D'Alerian said before he flashed himself back home.

"Ah jeez. Nick!"

Ash turned at Kyrian's irate shout to find the general standing in the doorway near the black mark Nick had left on the floor. A few inches shorter than Ash, Kyrian had short blond hair and was dressed in black. "I'm going to kick your ass, boy! How many times have I told you no skateboards in the house?"

Nick came up behind Kyrian with a face as white as chalk. Ash had seen condemned men look less panicked.

"It's not Nick's fault," Ash said quickly as Nick stopped behind Kyrian's back with his eyes wide. "It's these new biker boots. Sorry. I was so stunned when M'Adoc showed up that I skidded on the floor."

Kyrian gave him a suspicious glare, but since he couldn't prove Ash was lying, he let it go. "Well then, could you fix it?"

The mark vanished instantly.

"Thanks."

You're the friggin' best ever, Nick mouthed at Ash from behind Kyrian's back. He held his hands up in a silent gesture that said Ash rocked. *I love you, man.*

Kyrian turned sharply to glare at Nick, who immediately acted as if he were just scratching his head. "You called me, boss?"

"No. I've called you a lot of things, but boss has never been one of them. And it never will be, either."

Nick raked his hand through his long brown hair. "Dang, he's in a bad mood tonight. You need to get laid, boss."

"Shut up, Nick."

Deciding silence on this issue was the better part of not getting his ass kicked, Nick cleared his throat. "Well, if you guys are through ordering Fido around, he needs to go walk his mom home from work. I don't want nothing happening to her, you know?"

Kyrian scoffed. "I don't know why you bother, Nicky. You're the one who's going to be the death of her one day."

It was Ash's turn to scoff at that. "Not bloody likely. I'd be the death of her before Nick would. That kid lives, breathes, and dies for that woman." He smiled at Nick. "Give Cherise my best."

"Will do. Night, all."

Kyrian let out a heavy sigh before he grabbed his long coat from the couch and shrugged it on. "I'm out to patrol, too. I heard there's been a lot of Daimon activity on Bourbon Street lately, so Talon and I are going to do some extra rounds. I'll see you guys later."

Ash turned to M'Adoc, who was eyeing him strangely.

"Why don't you tell your Dark-Hunters about the Spathis? This one in particular needs to know."

Ash hesitated. Maybe M'Adoc was right. For centuries Ash had kept silent about the group of Daimons who lived a lot longer than any of the Dark-Hunters suspected. Daimons who served his mother, Apollymi, and who came out to prey on Apollymi's enemies. But the Spathis had been virtually dormant for centuries now and he hoped they would remain so.

"We all have our secrets we don't want out, don't we, Adarian?"

M'Adoc's gaze narrowed as he caught Ash's meaning. "You know what's happening to us, don't you?"

"I know, but don't worry. The Greek gods aren't exactly my drinking buddies. I couldn't give two shits about them or their curses. I owe the Oneroi too much for helping me with my Dark-Hunters to ever question you."

M'Adoc cocked his head as if he couldn't fathom Ash's reasoning. "With this information, you could own us."

Ash flinched as bitter, painful memories surged through him, but he banished them. "Contrary to Nick's opinion, I don't ever want to own anyone. It's wrong to take away someone's independence." And on that he sought to change the subject. "D'Alerian says that you and Zarek can help each other. I hope so. Z's too decent a man to keep suffering. If you can take any of it off him, then I'll owe *you*."

M'Adoc frowned at him. "I wouldn't say that if I were you. Being indebted to a god isn't the way to maintain independence."

"Yeah, believe me, I know. But it's all right, M'Adoc. I can see the future. You're going to be fine."

M'Adoc glanced to the door where Kyrian and Nick had vanished. "You can see my future so clearly. It's a pity you can't see your own."

"What's that supposed to mean?"

M'Adoc cleared his throat. "It's not my place to say. I'm a dream god. Not one of fate. Take me to this Zarek and let me see what I can do for him."

Ash obliged, but even as he did so he couldn't shake the

feeling that something had transpired this night that he should have picked up on. As a god of fate, he knew that somehow he'd just set something into motion and, knowing his luck, it was most likely something he shouldn't have.

EPILOGUE

ONE MONTH LATER

GEARY STOOD ON THE DECK OF HER NEW BOAT AS THE WAter lapped gently against it. While she stared out over the crystal blue sea that was as timeless as her quest, she could hear Cynthia below playing an old Andy Gibb album. They were right above the spot where Atlantis rested. Where Geary had held the old box and had touched a tiny portion of that lost, mythical city.

Two weeks ago, she, Arik, and Kat had retrieved everything that had marked this area, and they'd destroyed every piece of evidence that Geary and her father had collected.

No one would ever know what they'd found.

Arik came up behind her, wrapped his arms around her waist, and kissed her on her shoulder that was left bare from her sagging tank top strap. "Are you having second thoughts?" he asked warmly in her ear.

She shook her head as she felt her love for him swell through her. "How could I?" She smiled.

He leaned his cheek against the top of her head as he rocked her gently in his arms. "All you wanted was to save your father's reputation."

"And so I have. I don't care what the rest of the world thinks. *I* know the truth. That's enough for me."

"Are you sure?"

She nodded. Even Tory had taken it better than Geary had expected. True, the girl hadn't been pleased, but she hadn't argued, either.

Sitting on the couch at Teddy's house, Tory had stared at Geary in disbelief. "What do you mean we're through?"

Geary had flinched at Tory's irate voice. "It's over, Tor. We now know our fathers weren't crazy and that they didn't die in vain. It's enough. Atlantis wasn't meant to be discovered by us. She needs to stay on the bottom of the sea forever."

Geary had expected Tory to shout. Instead the girl merely got up calmly and gathered her books. "I see. So are you shipping me back home to New York?"

"Not right away. I thought we could enjoy the rest of the summer together. . . . Are you sure you're okay?"

Tory had shrugged. "I'm fine. The boat's gone. The research is gone, and you're giving up. How can I change any of that?"

Even so, Geary had expected more of a fight from her cousin. "You're taking this a lot better than I thought you would."

Cradling her books to her chest, Tory had merely sighed. "I'm a sane, rational person, Geary. I know when I can't change something. If I thought throwing a fit would sway you, I'd do so. But I know you better than that. If you say it's over, then it's done. All I can do is hope you'll change your mind one day."

Tory had then laid down her book of Plato and headed

for the door. "I'm gonna go make Thia's day by telling her the news. You two have fun."

And so their zealous quest had ended with nothing more than a whisper. What had seemed so important at the time had turned out to be nothing more than a fool's errand when put in perspective. Yes, finding the island was important, but not nearly as much as enjoying the lives of the people who really mattered.

Atlantis would always be there. But Tory, Thia, Scott, and the others wouldn't. At last Geary had come to understand the secret of Atlantis. It wasn't the power or the history. It was to value those around you—to treasure family. To love unconditionally in spite of faults and suspicions.

And as Tory had predicted, Thia had been ecstatic over the news that they were through seeking it.

But for Tory and Geary it was bittersweet.

Arik moved away from her, bringing her thoughts back to the present. "Close your eyes."

Frowning at him, Geary obeyed. She felt his hands at her neck an instant before something cold slid between her breasts. She opened her eyes and found a beautiful necklace there. It was a gold sun, the rays of which were outlined by diamonds. "It's beautiful."

He smiled. "Kat sent it to you. She said in her note that it was a gift from Apollymi to let you know there were no hard feelings for not releasing her."

"Really?"

He nodded. "Apollymi had said, 'Victory to the spider.' She's waited this long to be free, what's a few more centuries?"

Geary shook her head, grateful the goddess wasn't holding a grudge against them. "I miss Kat." She'd left them a week ago to head off to a new assignment for

Artemis. Apparently there was some woman in Greece being pursued by Daimons whom Kat was supposed to watch over.

"Yeah. She was a lot of fun. But I have a feeling we'll be seeing her again."

"I hope so." Geary turned around and took Arik's hands into hers. It was so strange to have him here with her. To know so much about him and the other world, but to not be able to share it with anyone, not even Tory or Thia.

But that was okay with Geary. She could definitely live with this secret.

Arik lifted her hand in his and kissed the back of her knuckles. "So when are you going to tell me your news?"

"And what news is that?"

He arched a brow at her and looked down meaningfully at her stomach.

Geary gaped as she caught his meaning. "How did you know about that?"

He gave her a wicked grin. "I still have a lot of my powers, baby. You know that."

She sighed heavily. "I wanted it to be a surprise." She pouted playfully until a thought occurred to her. "Do you think the baby will inherit your powers?"

"I don't know. Possibly."

Oh, that could be fun. She suddenly had images of Tabitha from *Bewitched* in her mind. Yeah. Just what she needed. A baby who held the powers of a god. But that didn't really matter. She would love her child no matter what. "Lucy, we'll have a lot of explaining to do."

"Yes, we will, but first, Ricky has to make an honest woman of his Lucy."

Warmth spread through her at his words. "I was wondering when you were going to get around to that."

"It's a yes then?"

She gave him a droll stare. "No. I thought I'd walk through hell to reclaim you and carry your baby just for the heck of it. Who needs marriage?"

"I do."

She smiled. "Good. I can let you live another day."

Laughing, he pulled her into his arms and held her close. "Thank you, Geary."

"For what?"

"For giving me a life that is the best dream I've ever had."